# HOLD CIRCULATION

## TRIAL AND REDEMPTION

## SYNTELL SMITH

ISBN: 1-952-50695-6

ISBN-13: 978-1-952-50695-6

Copyright © 2023 Syntell Smith Publishing Published By Syntell Smith

To obtain permission to excerpt portions of the text, please contact the author at syntellsmith@gmail.com

Chapter graphic courtesy of the Boston Public Library Foundation, used with permission.

Library of Congress Cataloging-in-Publication Number for paperback: 2022914439

Cover design by Andrew Rainnie

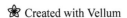 Created with Vellum

*For Krista, and Krista only.*
*(There, happy?)*

# ACKNOWLEDGMENTS

# CHARACTER INDEX

*The staff of the 58th Street Branch Library*

Robin Walker – Idealistic, intelligent, opinionated, full-time college student and part-time library clerk. Transfers to 58th Street from his neighborhood branch, Fort Washington, in upper Manhattan. Under the mentorship of Barbara Schemanske, Robin has been trained to take his position extremely seriously, and he follows the Procedures of Conduct to the letter.

Sonyai Yi – Branch Senior Clerk in charge of supervising and mentoring the library clerks and pages. Traditional and just, respectful to her clerks and overprotective of the three remaining female library pages, Sonyai values the integrity of the branch above everything and is constantly at odds with Augustus Chavez over policies to serve the public. Although, the two have recently declared a temporary truce.

Augustus Chavez – Head Librarian, determined to bring the branch to its fullest potential and to serve the public by any means necessary. Favoring those who privately contribute charitable donations, Augustus's politician-like mentality brings him close to breaking the rules and putting the library at extreme risk.

Zelda Clein – Branch Librarian and Augustus Chavez's assistant, long-time friend, mentor, and confidant. She does whatever it takes to protect all staff members of the branch, playing the dangerous game of keeping the balance when it comes to all the existing conflicts within its hostile work environment.

Heywood Learner – Information Assistant and Librarian-in-training. With a conservative outlook and an inclination for clean and wholesome family values, Heywood challenges Augustus's liberal agenda as the two constantly argue over the smallest aspects of branch politics.

Angie Trueblood – Information Assistant who is attending evening classes at Queens College to earn her Master's Degree in Library Science. Isolated and neutral in terms of the workplace conflicts that plague the branch, Angie strives hard to prove her worth and be a credit to her native indigenous people.

Tommy Carmichael – Library clerk with light experience who is learning everything he can from Sonyai Yi as her protégé. Once challenging newcomer Robin Walker, the two have now become friends. He and his wife of five years have welcomed the birth of their first child, but Tommy deals with the secret consequences of a choice that was brought to him.

Gerry Coltraine – Library clerk with enough experience, he believes he should be 58th Street's Senior Clerk instead of Sonyai Yi and makes that point loud and clear by questioning, challenging, and undermining her authority every chance he can. Ill-tempered, Gerry tends to engage in heated exchanges with patrons which are triggered sometimes due to racial tensions.

Ethel Jenkins – Experienced Library clerk who views 58th Street as her final stop in a long, illustrious career. With retirement within her sights, she wants no part in any of the drama in the workplace and the rest of the staff have obliged her out of respect… and fear.

Janelle Simms – Recent high school graduate and former page of 58th Street. After her hidden pregnancy was discovered, she was promoted to a full-time clerical position at the Van Nest Branch in The

Bronx. She was next in line for the part-time position at 58th Street that Robin Walker filled and holds a grudge against him for her being sent away from Sonyai and the pages.

Alex Stevens – Library page who becomes a strong opponent against Robin Walker's arrival because of her close friendship with fellow page, Janelle Simms. She has vowed vengeance against Robin, looking into his past for anything or anyone who could help her destroy the clerk's career at 58th Street.

Tanya Brown – Library page who is impartial to Robin Walker working at the branch when he arrives, staying out of the intense drama that unfolds. She had a previous relationship with Andrew Friedman, Sonyai's previous protégé and current Senior Clerk of the Webster Branch.

Lakeshia Seabrooke – The youngest Library page, very meek and naïve. Robin Walker's arrival has triggered emotional feelings she has never felt before. Which possibly has taken a toll on her physically.

*Supporting Characters*

Eugene Iscaro – Branch security guard re-hired from a brief hiatus to keep the peace after several tense incidents occur upon Robin Walker's arrival. Has a history with the S.I.U., a department that deals with library investigations of everything from book theft to accusations of corruption.

Franklin – Robin Walker's best friend, a former Library page himself, who worked at Fort Washington. Not taking his library career too seriously, he left and is still finding himself after recently getting fired from a boutique.

Barbara Schemanske – Head librarian of the Fort Washington Branch Library and mentor to Robin Walker. With a formidable reputation known throughout the New York Public Library, she is all-knowing, all-seeing, and a force to be reckoned with.

Sarah Carmichael – Tommy's wife, who recently gave birth to their first child. As she deals with motherhood, she also seeks answers to a question of her faith due to complications she experienced during childbirth.

Cervantes – Immigrant taxi driver who is indebted to Robin Walker for saving his life during an attempted carjacking. While serving as an occasional provider of sage advice, Cervantes also offers Robin free rides around the city.

# LIBRARY TERMINOLOGY GLOSSARY

Call Number – Combination of letters and numbers used to classify the specific location of library items by subject. Alternatively known as Dewey Decimal Numbers.

The System – A term known among dedicated library employees for the New York Public Library network of branches among the three boroughs of The Bronx, Manhattan, and Staten Island.

Procedures of Conduct (or P.o.C.) – Rules and guidelines on how library employees carry themselves. Proper etiquette on introducing themselves (identifying the previous branches worked), how to address others, how to present themselves to the public, and how to behave when working in a branch.

Patron – Men, women, and children of the public who frequently visit libraries for the use of their services.

IA – Abbreviated term for Information Assistant, the title for library employees acquiring or recently acquired college accreditation from American Library Association mandated schools.

Page – Entry-level part-time library position for adolescents attending high school. Duties include shelving returned books among other shelf maintenance tasks. Pages are expected to become clerks upon graduation from school.

Collapsible Security Periodical Baton (or CPB) – Adjustable plastic sticks in which newspapers and periodicals are kept in for public access by patrons. These replaced the extended wooden sticks used previously by libraries.

Shelving Cart (or Truck) – Used by pages to place returned items in their proper locations among the shelves.

Clustering – Temporary relocation or exchange of branch clerks between libraries, usually done on Saturdays or emergencies in which a location is short-staffed.

Weeding – The process of bookshelf maintenance that requires staff to review items and check their statistics. Those that have low circulation numbers are removed to make space for new books in the future.

# PREVIOUSLY ON CALL NUMBERS

After Robin Walker finds his grandfather collapsed on the floor at his apartment, he frantically calls 911 and the paramedics arrive to take him to the nearest hospital. Robin is relieved that Jon was able to recover, but doctors warn him that the elder guardian is in the final stages of his life. Meanwhile, Sonyai Yi and Angie Trueblood work together to find the box of office supplies that prove Augustus Chavez is manufacturing office memorandums to manipulate branch policies to his advantage. The box in question, however, is removed from the spot where Angie left it, after accidentally discovering it previously.

After learning of her infatuation with Robin, Tanya Brown attempts to help Lakeshia Seabrooke learn about human sexuality by checking out The Joy of Sex on her behalf. The book is discovered by her parents. They confront Tanya's mother, and learn that Lakeshia's family are conservative Jehovah's Witnesses. Lakeshia is mortified by the embarrassing revelation and both families instruct their daughters not to interact with each other. After several days, Alex Stevens helps the two girls make up and they all agree to stay friends with Lakeshia sharing her family secret with Alex.

Gerry Coltraine invites Robin to celebrate his birthday with him, his twin sister, Denise, and several of their friends. Robin brings along his friend Franklin to a bowling alley and they experience some friction between the rest of the friends due to their age difference. Franklin, however, makes an impression with Denise and leaves his phone number with the woman. Tommy Carmichael hangs out with Heywood Learner, security guard Eugene Iscaro, and Gerry, in a Mexican restaurant to celebrate Cinco de Mayo, but they end up in jail after a fight breaks out. Tommy's pregnant wife Sarah bails them out after a heated verbal tirade.

Meanwhile, Sonyai is still scrambling to find a full-time clerical position for Janelle Simms, before her secret pregnancy is discovered. The senior clerk is also using her medical insurance to provide prenatal care for the teenage mother-to-be, but time is running out. Jon is released from the hospital, but his recovery is short-lived, and he returns to the hospital again, under hospice care. Robin reaches out to other family members, including his estranged mother and aunt, but none come to Jon's side in his final hours. Franklin meets the library pages during a visit and secretly starts a brief fling with Tanya after she learns that her ex-boyfriend, Andrew Friedman, the senior clerk of the Webster Branch is involved with an information assistant.

Ethel Jenkins is approached by her sisters, Ernabelle and Elisse, about going in on a real estate deal that will restore a house in Georgia. She's skeptical at first, and requests more time before making a decision. Heywood Learner has invited his girlfriend, Jackie Daisy, to live with him temporarily as she figures out her next move after losing her nightclub job. She auditions at several other nightclubs but is unable to find stable work. As her frustration rises, a scout gives her the card of a mysterious benefactor who might help her get back to performing. Back at Jon's deathbed, Robin comes to terms with the fact that none of his family are coming, as his grandfather shares some final words of advice to his grandson. Jon then succumbs to his illness and passes away. Robin is devastated and the staff offer their condolences, but he refuses to show any emotion as he prepares for Jon's funeral.

After all the arrangements are made, the service for Jon is brief and Robin makes a controversial decision to commit suicide. After wandering aimlessly throughout the subway system, moments from

ending his life, divine intervention happens when a woman appears from the shadows to stop him. She is Shinju Hasagawa, the elusive Asian woman he met in passing months earlier. Robin and Shinju start a relationship and Robin once again has a refreshed outlook on life. He returns home to find someone waiting for him, a mysterious stranger known as "Synclair with a Y." Jon had instructed Synclair to escort Robin to meet Carmen Hernandez, the probate lawyer in charge of his estate and executor of his will. She informs Robin that he is the sole recipient of an inheritance, of an undisclosed amount to be determined later.

58th Street's assistant librarian Zelda Clein warns Augustus that the regional librarian, Cleopheous Baker of the 96th Street Branch, is close on his trail, looking for proof that Augustus manipulated the results of a media experiment. He scoffs at the accusation, since he is positive that the proof doesn't exist. Tanya and Franklin's relationship continues to heat up, and he arranges for Tanya to be pulled out of school for a day so they can take a limousine to City Island, where the two get to know each other better. Robin's relationship with Shinju also blossoms, but it attracts criticism from opposite sides in two separate incidents by African Americans and Asians who both object. Shinju is also showing some apprehension, leading Robin to believe she's hiding a secret.

Heywood invites Angie and Eugene to attend a concert featuring Jackie and other performers. Upon witnessing Jackie's act, Angie is enraged when the singer starts dancing sacred Native-American ceremonial dances and storms off. June arrives and Janelle attends her high school graduation wearing a tight-fitting gown. Her parents reluctantly celebrate the accomplishment, but Janelle's father leaves right after the ceremony. Alex prepares to attend a college party with her newly acquired fake ID and meets with a "Talent Scout" who is really a fraternity pledge looking to score points by gathering girls for his frat leader's sexual conquests. She is led to an isolated room under the ruse of auditioning for a music video role and rendered unconscious after her drink is laced.

Lakeshia and Tanya learn from Janelle that Alex didn't meet her after graduation, like she said she would, and the pair are afraid Alex might be in trouble. Robin overhears, and deduces that she might get sexually assaulted, if indeed she went to the college party. It is something he takes a sick pleasure in, possibly due to their feud. The two girls plead for his help, but he refuses, so they leave on their own after work, determined to help. When they arrive at the party, Tanya and Lakeshia are spotted immediately for being too young, but wearing a disguise, Robin appears and helps the girls, having had a change of heart. They search the party and knock out the fraternity leader moments before he would have had his way with Alex. With Robin's taxi-driving friend, Cervantes, they sneak her out of the party, but Robin loses his college ID.

Robin and the girls drive out to Janelle's house, where they take Alex so she can sleep off the effects of the laced drink. Robin takes off into the night with a bag full of drinks he stole. After a night of drinking with his friends he returns to Baruch College in the early hours of the morning and is followed by the fraternity leader, who stalks him for revenge. He turns the tables by capturing his stalker and takes him to an underground garage where he learns his name, and his alleged history of sexual assaults. Robin decides to extract some street justice by humiliating the deviant with a fitting punishment. Alex learns what happened and she is secretly thankful for his intervention.

This dark side of Robin scares even himself and he retreats to his grandfather's gravesite with an emotional breakdown. Shinju finds him and consoles him, then they engage in an intimate moment at his apartment. Over the next few days, she asks Robin if he would leave the country with her. He's taken aback by the sudden request but doesn't give an answer, instead asks for more time to consider the request. He promises to give his answer after he receives his full inheritance from Carmen. After snooping around the branch for days, Angie finally finds the box of office supplies she found before and shows it to Sonyai. The two collaborate with Annabelle Doyle and the senior clerk from Yorkville discovers the proof they need to confront Augustus.

Robin visits Shinju at her place and is surprised by a visiting family member. She panics and hides him in a closet while speaking to her

"Obasan." When the visitor sounds familiar to Robin, he slips out and discovers that Shinju is related to Sonyai! Obasan is Japanese for Aunt. Once Sonyai discovers Robin is dating her niece, Shinju disappears from the city, within 24 hours without a trace. Robin confronts Sonyai, demanding to know Shinju's whereabouts, but she refuses to tell him. He then breaks down in a hysterical display of emotion, on the verge of tears, begging to know where she is. When Sonyai rejects him again, he becomes enraged and threatens her with dire consequences and a declaration of war.

Augustus returns to his office one day to find Sonyai waiting for him, holding the box. She gives him 48 hours to resign, or she'll go public with her findings. Augustus is flabbergasted. Robin and Franklin shadow Sonyai and Janelle to a pharmacy, and learns that Janelle is pregnant, while finally figuring everything out. The animosity, the conspiracy against him. From day one the branch has been against him, all because they wanted Janelle to have his position.

With Augustus against the wall and out of options, he fears the worst. Meanwhile, Robin tips his hand in a conversation in the staff room with pages. Alluding to his findings with a taunting monologue leading up to a violent confrontation! Robin knocks out Tanya, but Alex smashes a coffee pot across his face. Robin grabs her by the throat and slams her through the kitchen table, shattering it to pieces. The noise attracts Sonyai's attention, and she rushes with Eugene upstairs to investigate. Robin slips away and makes it downstairs to Augustus's office, just in time to reveal Sonyai's deception. After tending to the pages, Sonyai rushes back downstairs and finds Augustus smiling back at her. Robin whispers to Sonyai that now they're even for Shinju and leaves her at the mercy of the head librarian.

As the staff await the aftermath, Gerry warns Robin to expect Sonyai's wrath. The two supervisors emerge from the office and announce that a deal has been made. Sonyai will keep Augustus's secret, and in exchange, Janelle will be sent to the Van Nest Branch in The Bronx to a full-time position. The girls are shocked, and Janelle is disappointed, but accepts her fate. Sonyai congratulates Robin in getting his revenge but swears she will have the last laugh.

Heywood and Jackie finally meet their mysterious musician-seeking client and it's none other than The Artist Formerly Known as Prince! The two are star struck about meeting him, as he gives Jackie the opportunity of a lifetime to be on his world tour. Jackie hesitates, but Heywood understands and encourages her to go. She thanks him and promises to come back one day. He smiles, and after a tearful goodbye, she leaves. Heywood is heartbroken. Robin braces for his possible termination after Sonyai sees Janelle off on her last day. Franklin asks if it was worth it, as he secretly decides to break things off with Tanya. Robin ponders the question.

The remaining three pages wish Janelle the best and Sonyai tells her to remember everything she learned at 58th Street. Janelle promises to make Sonyai proud and leaves the branch, preparing for her next adventure. Sonyai returns to the clerical office to confront Robin. She tells him that he's not fired, but that when she's done, he'll wish he was. He challenges her to do her worst. Alex approaches Robin, swearing vengeance, despite what he did to save her. He immediately regrets his actions as they become bitter enemies once again.

As soon as Franklin breaks things off with Tanya, Gerry's sister Denise finally calls him, and they agree to go on a date. The following Monday, a desk in the clerical office is set aside. Gerry comes in and asks why his belongings have been moved. Sonyai informs him to share a desk with either Ethel or Tommy. Robin arrives and learns he's been stripped of all his clerical duties, no longer doing any time at the circulation desk. Instead, he is given a seat at his own desk and forced to stamp date due cards indefinitely. Robin accepts his punishment, to Sonyai's delight, with no complaints. Tommy and Sarah are finally ready to welcome their child into the world when Sarah's water breaks and the couple rushes to the hospital. After several inconveniences, the doctors learn of complications with the labor and prepare for an emergency C-section.

The branch becomes short-handed in Tommy's absence, and when Sonyai refuses to bring Robin in for help, Ethel and Gerry accuse her of having a racial bias. An argument breaks out with Robin stepping forward to calm things down and defend Sonyai from the accusations, he then returns to stamp cards while Sonyai taps Alex to help in a rare opportunity to learn new duties. Ethel comes to a decision and decides to join her sisters, leaving a deposit down to restore the house, but will need additional funds. Sarah's parents, Acindina and Lorenzo, arrive at the hospital to support their daughter, but Tommy is approached by the doctor in charge and presents him with a difficult choice. The procedure can go both ways and he must choose who to save in the event that something goes wrong. Tommy chooses Sarah, but miraculously, both are saved.

Alex contacts a page from the 67th Street Branch for some background information on Robin. She learns of his flirtatious relationship with a page named Rosana Comanos and that a clerk named Trevor Guzman tormented Robin when he was a page. She plans to use this information to make Robin pay for what happened to Janelle. Gerry visits his sister, finds Franklin in a compromising position with Denise, and while Franklin manages to escape her place, Gerry finds out where he works and tracks him down. Robin is called by Franklin's co-workers and alerted to a fight breaking out between the two, leading him to rush to his best friend's aid. He arrives and deescalates the situation, but the damage has been done. Franklin is fired from his job after the altercation.

Robin returns to Jon's gravesite, uncertain of his situation. His mentor, Barbara Schemanske, arrives and offers an opportunity to start over by transferring to a new branch closer to Baruch College. He declines the offer, determined to serve his punishment for as long as it takes to earn back Sonyai's respect. The staff celebrates the birth of Tommy's daughter, along with the temporary truce between Sonyai and Augustus. Ethel shocks Zelda with an unusual request for a loan, while Robin remains in exile, stamping date due cards.

# PROLOGUE

Jon Walker was watching the horse races from the aqueduct on a television screen in the Off-Track Betting parlor. A racing form was in his hand as it shook with an infrequent tremor. He had one of his episodes that morning, but had hidden it from his grandson, Robin. The youth had enough things to worry about, both juggling his college studies and his new part-time position working as a library clerk.

Transferring from their neighborhood library in Washington Heights to a compact and unique branch on the east side of midtown Manhattan, in the past three months Robin found the transition difficult, but he was determined to prove himself.

They were halfway through the thoroughbred races when something caught Jon's attention.

"Hey, hey is the name of that horse right!?" he called out in a monotone voice.

Sensing his deaf friend's excitement, Arthur Finkleberg turned around to see the list of horses cued to start the fifth race. He scanned the list on the screen and turned to face Jon so he could read his lips, "Yeah, doing the Archie Comics bit, I guess... pays 500 to 1." He shrugged. "Stranger things have happened."

Jon stood transfixed on the screen. He couldn't believe the coincidence. "Put a cent on her," he said with a nod.

Arthur frowned. "I know you're good for it, Jon, but you sure? Ain't played a horse in years."

Jon nodded, looked down at his racing form, then up at the row of monitors. "Fate's been talking to me, Artie... fate's been talking..."

Later that evening at home, Jon was speaking to someone through his TTY phone. "Is it all set up? Very good, I want you to check up on him for a while, this was something I wasn't expecting, and it could take care of him for several years... or several months if he's reckless. Alright, thank you." He hung up the device.

It was almost seven. Robin was due to return from a basketball game he was attending with some friends. Jon was thinking about his grandson, being overdressed, borrowing his clothes, and wondered if he was possibly with a girl...

As he approached his recliner in the living room, he suddenly felt a shortness of breath and a gasp for air escaped him. "NO!" he cried out, *not now, not now... Robin, I'm sorry...* his last thought ran through his mind as Jon Walker fell to his knees and collapsed on the floor.

# CHAPTER ONE

IT WAS A WEDNESDAY MORNING IN OCTOBER WHEN ROBIN WALKER and his best friend, Franklin, were playing Twenty-One on an outdoor basketball court at P.S. 187. The pair were in fierce competition and evenly matched. Where Franklin excelled at perimeter shooting, Robin dominated the key by playing defense, blocking nearly every attempt at a layup.

"So… you still at that branch stamping cards?" Franklin asked as he moved around the court.

"Yep, I go there, stamp cards then leave, it's the easiest nine bucks an hour I've earned in my entire life!"

Robin blocked a shot and wrestled for the ball, then took it past the arc and started to sidestep his way to the basket. Franklin played defense, bracing Robin, trying to steal the ball. Robin spun by him and made an easy layup.

"That's 14," the stocky teenager said, as he took the ball back to the free-throw line.

"I still got 15," Franklin replied, as the blond-haired athletic opponent waited for the ball to be checked to him.

Robin checked the ball and played defense.

"It's been three months, man… why are you staying there?"

Franklin asked. "All the shit you've been through? It's not worth the aggravation!"

"I can't give them the satisfaction of running me off."

Franklin took a shot from behind the three-point line, and it went through the basket.

"That's 18."

"Remember, you gotta score 21 on the dot, which means another three," Robin said, waiting for the check.

Franklin checked the ball and moved in real close, hacking and swiping. Robin grunted, "You keep hand-checking me, I'm gonna go Charles Oakley on your ass."

Robin jumped, took a shot, and was fouled. The ball bounced off the backboard through the basket.

"My ball!" he yelled.

"I didn't touch you!" Franklin yelled back.

"That's a free-throw, you damn hack!" Robin walked to the free-throw line. He missed his foul shot on purpose, got the rebound, went back to the key, and made a jump shot.

"Okay, we're tied at 18." He checked Franklin the ball and followed him behind the arc as he attempted a quick three-pointer. Robin swatted the ball down and the pair dove to recover it. Franklin gained control and posed to shoot a regular shot. Robin jumped across, flailing his arms, and missed the block as Franklin double pumped and held the ball.

"Psyche!" Franklin yelled, then dribbled back behind the arc and took another long shot. The ball dropped through with a swish and the game was over.

"Damn!" Robin cursed in defeat.

"Ah, don't get all sore. It was a good game, had me scared there for a sec."

"Oh bullshit!" Robin spat. "You condescending sonofabitch!"

The two shared a laugh as they both grabbed towels to wipe the sweat off their faces. The weather was unseasonably warm indicating an Indian summer. Robin was wearing sweatpants and a generic green

Nike mesh tee-shirt. Franklin was wearing blue basketball shorts and a matching blue sleeveless jersey.

"By the way, happy belated birthday, man. You're getting closer to 21, two more years then we're gonna celebrate!"

"It's no big thing. This was the first birthday without granddaddy, so I really wanted to keep things to myself."

Robin had just turned 19 last Tuesday, on September 26th.

"Kids are gonna be coming out soon for recess, we better split." Robin said, checking his watch.

"It's still early, wanna swing by? Play some NBA JAM?" Franklin asked.

"Sure."

After grabbing their ball, they moved to leave the court and noticed five Hispanic teenagers approaching. They looked too old to be elementary school students.

"The court free?" one of them asked.

Robin exchanged glances with Franklin as they put their guards up. "Uh, yeah. All yours, guys."

Another pointed at the ball in Franklin's hands. "Can we use your ball? We don't have one."

Franklin laughed. "Who comes to a court to play with no ball?"

"You better walk on over to Hobby Land. We're leaving with ours," Robin finished.

They moved to walk past them, but the group didn't give way. The five made a semi-circle blocking their path.

"I think you need to let us have the ball, or you're gonna find out the real reason why white men can't jump, cabrón," The leader threatened.

Franklin smiled at the joke. "Hey man, it ain't that serious." He bounced the ball and held it out in front of himself. "You want the ball? Here ya go."

The leader of the group stepped forward and reached, but Franklin tossed the ball over to Robin quickly. He caught it, and flung the ball hard, square in the teenager's face. The leader fell back as blood squirted out of his broken nose. Robin and Franklin then proceeded to take out the others within minutes.

"You boys need to stick to baseball," Robin taunted.

"Yeah, there aren't any oyas in the NBA!" Franklin finished.

The heavy door creaked open slowly, echoing throughout the house. It was dusk, so there was no sunlight to fill the room, but a flashlight made a path for Ethel Jenkins and her two sisters, Elisse and Ernabelle to walk in. The three women looked around what appeared to be the foyer, trying to make sense of their surroundings.

"Is the power on? Anyone see a light switch?" Elisse, the youngest of the sisters, asked.

Ethel shined her flashlight in every direction, saying nothing.

"We just turned it on yesterday," Ernabelle announced, as she closed the door behind them, then pushed a switch across in the fuse box on the wall. Several dim lights came on, revealing several hall-ways and staircases leading to the rest of the house.

"What a shithole," Ethel sighed, as she turned off her flashlight.

"Okay, so we have a long way to go," Ernabelle began. "But if we stay on schedule..."

"We're *behind* schedule already!" Ethel interrupted. "And this dump is going to need more money put into it before it's livable, Ernie!"

Elisse flashed a look of concern as she saw the oldest of the sisters stomp her way to stare down Ethel. "We'll make it work, okay? Calm your tits and have a look around."

"I've seen all I need to see. my flight back to New York leaves at 8 am tomorrow morning." She turned and walked toward the door.

"Ethel, please. Give the place a fair look," Elisse pleaded. "I'd hate for you to miss something and resent us for picking out the best spots in the place once it's done."

Ethel stopped before the door and took a moment. She then turned around and started walking toward a hallway on the left side of the room.

Everything hurt when Janelle Simms woke up. Starting with her bladder's urgency at six in the morning. Then her swollen ankles, aching with every step she took to the bathroom. The full-time library clerk was nine months pregnant, and this was her last week before going on leave, after transferring to the Van Nest Public Library three months ago.

After getting dressed, she emerged from her bedroom to see that both her parents were gone. It was normal for her father to be out of the house at seven in the morning, but her mother would usually be preparing breakfast for them before she would leave for work.

"Mom?"

She found a note held up by a magnet on the refrigerator door and read it aloud, *"Aunt Jean fell down the steps last night. Went to Bensonhurst to see if she's okay."*

Janelle rolled her eyes and grabbed a box of Cheerios from the cupboards, then proceeded to pour herself a bowl. Twenty minutes after eating, she grabbed her purse, put on her Yankee's jacket, and left her apartment.

Taking two buses from her neighborhood in Kingsbridge to Pelham Parkway, Janelle arrived at Van Nest a few minutes before nine o'clock. Senior clerk Reginald Brantley was turning on the computer terminals behind the circulation desk and greeted her with a wave. The tall German had dark hair and a full, apple round face with pronounced cheekbones.

"Good morning, Simms. Feeling alright today?"

"Yes, Mister Brantley, sir."

"That's good. With this being your last week, I'm going to take it easy on you, scheduling only two hours on the desk each day."

She smiled. "You really don't need to do that, sir... the other clerks—"

"Are none of your concern," the senior clerk interrupted. "There's some New Books that just arrived on your desk in the back," Reginald said, with a nod. "Find the red triangle stickers that say, "One Week Loan" and apply them on their spines, please."

"Yes, sir," Janelle replied.

She walked past the desk schedule that was posted next to the cash register on the returns side of the desk and saw that she was working circulations at noon and four.

*Light hours, great.*

Since arriving at Van Nest back in July, Janelle has earned a reputation from her fellow clerks for being a *teacher's pet*. Receiving extra attention due to her condition. That also came with a certain resentment from them. She couldn't help noticing the irony of her situation. Being treated with animosity, exactly as Robin was when he arrived at 58th Street. A flash of anger came over her face as she thought of the one who was responsible for her transfer.

Janelle made it inside the clerical office and plopped in her chair with a huff. "Walker," she hissed, with a scowl.

"I. Brought. Muffins!" Augustus Chavez exclaimed, as he walked into the staff room.

"Wonderful!" Sonyai Yi replied, putting on a fake smile at the sight of the head librarian holding up a basket of muffins.

It was one o'clock in the afternoon and the two supervisors of the 58th Street Branch Library were having a meeting. Tensions between the two have been at an all-time low since putting their differences aside after a scandal nearly put both of their careers in jeopardy. Exchanging false pleasantries from summer into the fall was beginning to take a toll, but neither one of them was showing signs of backing down.

Augustus placed the basket in the center of the kitchen table and took a seat.

"We have the joint meeting of senior clerks and head librarians from the region coming up at 96th Street," Augustus began, getting right to the point. "Would you like to share a ride up there, or meet me out front before going in?"

"Thank you for the offer." Sonyai took a blueberry muffin from the basket. "But I can get there and back to 58th Street myself... I'll meet you at the entrance."

He nodded. "Very well. I have that Saturday off, so I'll be going home afterward anyway. I believe they will be discussing plans for the centennial celebrations next year. I hear there'll be a grand ball at The Main Branch."

Their meeting covered several other topics regarding library operations and led to no arguments or difference in opinions... until now.

"Before we adjourn, I'd like to bring up a... *sensitive* subject."

Sonyai fought the urge to raise her eyebrow, instead, the corner of her mouth twitched. "Oh?"

"It's about Mister Walker."

The senior clerk saw this coming. "There is nothing to discuss," she replied coldly.

"I respect that, and it's not my place to say anything in the matter of the clerks, but... it's been three months. Hasn't that been long enough?"

The part-time clerk's punishment for revealing Sonyai's secret support of her former page Janelle Simms, which included defrauding her employee health insurance to provide the teen's care, had been swift and absolute. She was determined to break Robin, discouraging him to the point of resigning.

"I will not be questioned by you about this. We have the coverage, even if it's help from clustering branches at times, so he will not resume normal clerical duties until I see fit."

She rose from the table to leave. Augustus didn't move and said, "We're not finished here."

"Yes, we are," she replied, and walked through the door.

"Man, I'm getting tired of these two-hour afternoon blocks," Tommy Carmichael sighed.

To his right, on the returns side, Gerry Coltraine shrugged his shoulders. "Yeah, they're rough."

The two library clerks were behind the circulation desk at the corner near the entrance of 58th Street's first floor. It was two-thirty in the afternoon, and Tommy was due for his break at three.

"It's a shame we don't have a part-time clerk available to relieve us of this heavy workload," Gerry remarked sarcastically, as he glanced inside the clerical office behind them.

Tommy rolled his eyes and snuck a glance at Robin stamping date due cards at an isolated desk in the back of the office. "You think she's ever going to forgive him?" he asked, turning back to Gerry.

"I've given up thinking about it. I honestly thought she'd bring him back around September."

"With just the four of us, we're barely getting it done, even with help from the other branches." Tommy groaned and rubbed his eyes.

Gerry noticed his fatigue. "I take it the baby's been keeping you up at night?"

Tommy and his wife, Sarah, had welcomed a baby girl to their family the previous summer, the couple's first child. "Little Carrie cries like clockwork just after midnight." He shook his head. "It's either a diaper change or she's hungry... then she needs to be rocked back to sleep."

A patron walked up to check out several books. Afterward, Tommy looked up behind him at the clock, impatiently waiting for the top of the hour.

"Hey," Gerry said, getting his attention. "I got the points off my license finally, so I'm getting a new car!"

"Yeah? That's cool. There's nothing like driving, man. The trains are brutal, when I go out to Long Island to see my folks, that L-I-double-R be full of weirdos."

"Excuse me gentlemen. I have a question and wonder if you can help me," an elderly patron said, appearing at the circulation desk out of nowhere.

Tommy stepped forward. "If it's something we can answer, sir, we will."

"Thank you." The man pointed to his left, at the library's water fountain, between the two doors on the wall. One door led up to the staff room, while the other was the public restroom. "Is the water from that fountain New York City reservoir water?"

Gerry froze in place as Tommy turned to exchange glances with him. The pair were puzzled by the question and how to answer it.

"I... honestly, don't know, sir," Tommy finally replied. "Is there a particular reason why it would need to be?"

"Well, I have a sensitive stomach, and require water of a certain filtration that only the reservoirs can provide. Any other kind of water that could have been exposed to chemicals or impurities could be very harmful... to my digestive system."

Tommy nodded. "Ah, well, to our knowledge, sir, the water coming out of that water fountain can be from a combination of aqueducts, tunnels as well as reservoirs in the surrounding tri-state area. The specific location, however, is unknown to us."

The man looked over to the water fountain, then back at the clerks. "Well... I think it'd be wise not to take a chance then, huh?"

"Uh, yeah, I guess," Tommy said, noticing Gerry holding in a giggle behind him.

The patron then walked through the security threshold and exited the branch.

It was three o'clock, finally, as Sonyai came down from the staff room to relieve Tommy. Gerry asked Tommy before the senior clerk approached him. "Think that guy's taking the railroad out to Long Island?"

Tommy grinned back at him. "Definitely."

Several minutes after four, Robin stepped out of the clerical office to take his break. He walked to the exit without saying a word to anyone. Among the shelves, library page Lakeshia Seabrooke stole a glance, watching him leave with some concern. She was so distracted she never saw the punch land on her left shoulder.

"Owww!" she whispered, with a hiss.

"Punch Buggy!" Tanya Brown let out in a hushed tone. "Caught you staring again," Lakeshia's co-worker exclaimed.

"Punch Buggy's for cars, Tee… and I wasn't staring," she insisted, as she started walking toward the back of the branch. Tanya kept in step behind her and whispered, "Sure you weren't, just like you weren't staring Friday last week, and the day before that, the day before that…"

Lakeshia stopped and looked back at her with a sneer. Ever since Tanya discovered that Lakeshia had feelings for the part-time clerk, who was four years older than her, the page went out of her way to taunt her about her forbidden love.

"Still feeling sorry for what Miss Yi's done to him? Even after he got Nellie shipped out to The Bronx?" Tanya asked.

"I'm not gonna lie and say he didn't deserve something for what he did, but Janelle is gone and she's not coming back," Lakeshia sighed. "Robin should get a second chance."

"No way in hell that's happening," someone said from behind them.

The pair turned to see Alex Stevens pushing a shelving cart their way. The dark-skinned teenager was the last of 58th Street's library pages and a close friend to Janelle Simms before her departure.

"That fat bastard can stay benched, stamping cards until Christmas for all I care."

As a contrast to Lakeshia's secret affections, Alex had a public, outspoken hatred for Robin, which he, in turn, matched just as intensely. Since Robin's arrival, the two have had several physical altercations which is why they have been instructed to stay away from each other at all times.

Lakeshia ignored Alex as Tanya asked, "You still hatin'? Even after he risked his neck to save you?"

Alex squinted at the reminder that despite their animosity, Robin had saved Alex from being sexually assaulted at a college fraternity party. Tanya stared back at Alex's icy gaze quietly, then the spiteful page resumed pushing her shelving cart past the pair of co-workers without another word.

"The muffins didn't work," Augustus said, as he took a seat behind his desk. His office was dark and quiet, with only a desk lamp providing a sliver of illumination to the ceiling. To his right, at a corner desk, Zelda Clein, 58th Street's assistant librarian and Augustus's closest confidant, sat quietly drinking a cup of herbal tea.

"I didn't think they would, but it was worth a try." Zelda tapped her spoon on the brim of the cup and placed it on a napkin that the cup was resting on. "You need to stay focused on this meeting coming up," she told him. "The centennial is an opportunity to befriend the right people." She adjusted her glasses and stated, "I hear there's a new branch they're announcing the plans for."

That got Augustus's attention. "A new branch?"

"Bigger than Donelle, and Mid-Manhattan… a huge faculty, dedicated to the future."

"Where would they build it?" he asked.

"Several locations are being considered, the land near the Jacob Center."

"The yards?"

Zelda nodded. "Among other locations."

"Interesting." The head librarian grabbed his chin. "Find me everything you can about this."

"Of course," Zelda replied, with another sip of her tea.

"I'm sorry ma'am, but we are unable to place any holds for *The Bridges of Madison County*," Angie Trueblood explained into the phone receiver. The information assistant was sitting at the information desk, located at the center of the branch. It was the final hour of the day, before closing at six. "Once a book makes it on the New York Times Best Seller list, we stop accepting holds for it."

The caller responded with a plea and complained with an observation.

"Yes, we are aware that it's been on the list for over 100 weeks in a row, ma'am, you'll just have to find a One Week Loan copy or be lucky to come across a copy on the shelves that someone else has returned… for what it's worth, I hear they're making a movie version due out next summer."

There was another response from the caller.

Angie adjusted her wire glasses and sighed. "Yes, I know the book is always better than the movie. Happy hunting, ma'am." She hung up the phone and glanced over to the right, at the pillar next to the desk. On the wall hung the current list from the New York Times Book Review. Ranked at number eight and holding strong, was the popular book in question.

"Ugh," the information assistant let out a frustrated grunt. She couldn't wait until her vacation weekend at the end of the month, she needed a well-deserved break from phone calls regarding patron requests.

The door leading to the second floor opened, and Heywood Learner stepped out with his jacket on, heading toward the exit. As he passed the desk Angie waved her hand up to get his attention, "Heywood!"

He stopped for a second, "Uh, yeah?"

"I never got your answer about my proposal for the Native-American presentation I wanted you to run by…"

"Oh, right, sorry, I forgot, I'll mention it next time… have a nice night." he turned quickly and left the branch.

Angie was hurt by the sharp dismissal, looking down for a moment. She didn't notice Eugene Iscaro taking a seat next to her on the usually vacant chair to the left of the desk.

"Felt that cold shoulder from my post across the floor," the branch security guard began.

Angie turned to give Eugene a pout, "Funny."

He shrugged, "I can't help to notice Heywood's been moping

around keeping things all business since the end of July, after his break-up with that rocker girlfriend *you* had a problem with."

The previous spring, Heywood began a relationship with a female nightclub performer who went by the name "Stormin' Jackie Daze". The couple turned heads as the conservative information assistant walked the streets with the wild rocker. After an emotional performance resulted in her losing her stable club residency, the singer moved in with Heywood for several weeks. Sadly, an opportunity of a lifetime was offered, and with Heywood's blessings, Jackie left New York to tour overseas.

"I may have had a problem with his girlfriend stealing Native American mannerisms, but I still say she had a positive effect on him. He was happy, driven, focused."

"Now he's just driven and focused." Eugene replied. "He's getting back on Chavez's good side again, instead of sneaking around with hidden agendas." the guard started tapping his thumbs together, "It could be why he's been shooting you down, too."

A patron approached the desk, asking where the books on architecture were. She referred them to the 720's section, then looked back at Eugene.

"I don't think he's mad at me, but there's got to be another reason why I'm being given the brush off."

"Well, I wouldn't push things. He'll come around... sooner or later." Eugene stood up and made his rounds throughout the open floor.

Robin stepped off the 1-train station at 181st Street, walking several blocks south to 179th Street. At the corner of 1365 Saint Nicholas Avenue, on the second of the four high-rise apartment complexes known as the bridge apartments, was a deli that sold limited groceries and hot sandwiches.

He walked in and grabbed some potato chips and conspicuously went in the back to get a six-pack of beer, then headed to the counter.

"Got ID for that beer?"

Robin gave the cashier a look.

"$7.99."

He narrowed his eyes, knowing the six-pack would be no more than five dollars and change if he was over twenty-one. After fishing out a five-dollar bill and three singles, Robin hissed, "I want my penny." and left the store.

Several hours after arriving at his apartment, Robin sat in the living room quietly. The television was off, with light coming from a single lamp near his computer desk. He missed his grandfather. His thoughts went back to the hospital that night in May, when he stepped out to go to the bathroom and missed his grandfather's final moments.

Three beers later, Robin staggered to his bedroom. The door to his balcony was closed and covered by a curtain on the opposite side of his bed. Among the posters of Bolo Yeuen, Sammo Hung, and other martial artists was a scarf held on two hooks on the wall on his left side.

After losing his grandfather, he had been moments away from taking his own life. By divine intervention, an Asian woman named Shinju Hasagawa had stopped him. She had been elusive to Robin since the two missed each other during their first encounter on a train in February. After finally meeting each other, they started a relationship.

In a cruel twist of fate, as quickly as she entered his life, she was gone. The couple discovered that Shinju's aunt was none other than Sonyai Yi herself. Within the blink of an eye, the senior clerk had her sent to parts unknown, leaving Robin devastated. He then exacted his revenge and accepted his exile, but once again he was alone.

He looked up at the scarf, remembering his conversation with Shinju in his bedroom.

*We say Koishiteru... it's how we say 'I love you.'*

*Koishiteru...*

*Koishiteru...*

"Everybody's gone," he mumbled to himself. "Gone... gone... gone."

He wasn't in school and he still hadn't heard from his mother or any close relatives who didn't attend his grandfather's funeral. All he had was stamping cards for three to four hours a day, then coming home and drinking.

He couldn't even bring himself to cry.

With his clothes still on, Robin closed his eyes and slept sitting up against the wall on his bed. The beer can slipped out of his hand, leaving a small wet spot on the corner of his mattress.

# CHAPTER TWO

Tommy didn't have to open his eyes when he heard the ear-piercing wail of a crying infant to know it was midnight. He was adjusting to the nocturnal disruption to the point of tuning it out and continuing to sleep, but it was the nudge from his wife that finally woke him up.

"Baby, Carrie's crying," Sarah Carmichael moaned as she turned to face the opposite side of the bed.

"Honey, can you feed her this time, please? I really need some sleep. I've been nodding off at work lately."

"I fed her the night before, it's your turn."

The baby continued crying when neither parent moved.

"Don't make me ask you *twice*," she threatened.

Tommy sprang up from the bed as if a fire alarm went off.

In her crib, baby Carrie was still crying and fussing as Tommy approached with a warm bottle of milk. After checking her diaper, he put the infant in his arms like Sarah had shown him and placed the bottle nipple close to the baby's mouth. Watching his daughter suck her milk made him reflect. The life-altering decision he had made three months ago.

Carrie's birth was not routine for the couple. There were serious complications that resulted in the life of his daughter and his wife being held in the balance. He had to make a decision on whose life was more important, in the event that only one could survive. Tommy's choice was irrelevant, thankfully, and both were saved by the efforts of the doctors and nurses of the hospital, but guilt has still been taking a heavy toll on his heart.

He was advised to never tell his wife of the choice he made, but the secret seemed too hard for him to keep.

Robin woke up at four in the morning. Staring around in the dark room, he felt as if he just had a nightmare he couldn't remember. The disadvantage of drinking yourself to sleep as soon as you get home is waking up early at all hours of the night.

"Fuck," He whispered, wiping his eyes.

*No point in going back to sleep,* he thought.

He stepped off his bed and picked up the can off the floor. Without looking, Robin flipped the can over his left shoulder, and it landed in his garbage basket across the room. After a shower, he started a regimen of exercises in the living room. Despite his stocky physique, Robin was very physically active. He started with a series of push-ups, sit-ups, and some shadowboxing.

It was six when he left the building on a neighborhood run. As he ran, he listened to *Project: Funk da World* by Craig Mack on his Walkman. He wasn't too impressed with this new Biggie Smalls rapper from Bad Boy Records, but Craig Mack was taking his attention away from his usual favorites like A Tribe Called Quest and the Wu-Tang Clan.

He was listening to the track "Get Down" when he stopped by Twin Donut on Broadway and bought a cup of coffee and four jelly donuts. He took the order around the corner to 181st Street and entered an office building, walking up to the second floor. The sun was coming in the windows of the suite and Robin was surprised to see that Carmen Hernandez was so energetic this early in the morning.

"Robin! You remembered my coffee! Thank you so much, cariño."

He handed her the cup and two donuts, while he reached in the bag and started on a donut himself.

Carmen was the executor of Jon's estate. Robin's grandfather left all his possessions to him with an undetermined sum of money that he was still waiting to hear about. He had been checking in with Carmen, who had been showing some concern about his quality of life, since he lived alone in a two-bedroom apartment, with a part-time job and not attending college.

"How ya doin', hon?" she asked.

"I'm doing alright," he lied. He didn't share his current situation at the library but did reveal he took a break from school.

After taking a bite he said, "I'm... I'm ready to go back..."

"Don't talk with your mouth full," Carmen chastised.

He chewed for a few seconds and swallowed, then started again. "I'm ready to go back to Baruch. They have late-registration of six-week classes instead of the regular eight-week ones. I want to catch up by taking a couple. Get my status back up from being a part-time student."

Before Jon's death, Robin had been attending Baruch College, earning his bachelor's degree in Computer Information Systems. He was very eager to get back to his studies and one day be a software engineer for Microsoft.

"Well, that's good," Carmen said with an affirmative nod. "But don't be afraid to give yourself time to grieve. What are you doing with the apartment? Did you speak to the landlord about moving to a single bedroom unit?"

"I'm staying put. I haven't cleaned out granddaddy's bedroom yet, but I will."

"But a one-bedroom might be cheaper with the rent and would extend the money left to you. You're not allowed to sublet to anyone so it would be a waste—"

"There's also a waiting list," Robin interrupted. "Only one-bedrooms are in 260 Audubon, the shitty building... I don't want to move there."

Carmen finished her coffee and placed the empty cup on her desk. "Alright, fine. The rest of your inheritance should be coming soon. I just want you to stay..."

"...fiscally responsible..." he said with her. "Yes, yes, yes, I know, I know... you realize Baruch is a business and accounting college, right? I took money management my freshman year."

She smiled. "Talk to me when you graduate from Columbia Business School, sweetheart."

He flinched as she pushed a framed copy of her Graduate Degree in Business Administration in front of him.

"Showoff," he mumbled, then got up and called out over his shoulder, "I'll see you around," while turning to leave.

"Be good, Robin..." Carmen said back.

Ethel was due in at noon, so she spent the morning rearranging the furniture in her apartment. Her intercom buzzed, and she walked over to answer it. "Yeah?"

"It's Deacon, Aunt."

"Okay!" She pressed the DOOR button to let her nephew in and cracked her door, then walked to a box on her coffee table.

Deacon Patterson stepped in and closed the door behind him. "Hey, Aunt, you got the place cleaned up, huh? Mom told me you had some stuff you were throwing away."

The man-child dwarfed his aunt, standing six foot, three inches. Deacon had taken over his mother's two-bedroom apartment and was sharing it with a roommate, while his younger brother prepared for college.

"It's all over there." Ethel waved to the coffee table. "What's Elisse doing with all her stuff, since she's staying at a hotel down in Edgewood?"

"It's all in storage. Someplace near Downtown Atlanta. They took the last of her belongings last week." Deacon replied. "She's really excited about the house. What did you think of it when you went down to see it?"

"It was a shithole," Ethel said flatly, repeating herself. "That place ain't gonna be done no time soon."

Deacon stared back blankly, as Ethel walked to the kitchen to open a can of Diet Sprite from her refrigerator. "If I have to stay here till the spring next year, those two idiot sisters of mine will need another person to live with them!" She pointed to her nephew. "And best believe I'll get back the money I poured into that dump!"

"Don't worry, they gon' get the house ready. You got any other things you don't want?" He nodded to her entertainment center. "How much you want for that TV?"

Ethel looked at her television and looked back at him. "Boy, you outta your mind? That is a 40-inch Zenith! That sucker will be buried with me when I die!"

The young man laughed. "Alright, I had to ask."

Ethel nodded and asked with a squint, "You and your *roommate* getting along?" putting some emphasis on the label. He didn't admit it yet, but Deacon's female friend who moved into his apartment made Ethel wonder if they were in a relationship.

"We're doing fine. Keeping it just friends and dividing the bills equally."

"Uh-huh," Ethel grunted.

Deacon looked back and smiled.

*You ain't fooling me, boy!* "Well, if that's all you can take, I gotta get going."

He lifted the box. "Thanks, Aunt. Could you get the door?"

"Sure, sure." She walked around him and opened the door, letting him out.

Once the door was closed, she wiped her brow and sighed. Her concerns were still strong about this move, but with most of her furniture gone, she was at the point of no return.

Tommy woke up and felt like he had only three hours of sleep. Sarah had Carrie in her highchair at the kitchen table, dangling a plastic ring of toy keys in front of her. In a fresh pair of jeans and a black turtleneck, Tommy walked into the kitchen and gave each of them a kiss.

"Good morning, my special girls!"

He took a seat at the head of the kitchen table, as Sarah stood up and came back with a plate of scrambled eggs and bacon strips with two pieces of toast, and placed it in front of him.

"Thank you, honey." Tommy said, beginning to eat.

Sarah sat down and played with Carrie again in her highchair.

"Baby, I'm taking Carrie to the city to see mom and dad, so I'll need my Buick today, okay?" Sarah asked.

They each owned vehicles, but Tommy's truck required a new transmission, and had been in their garage for months, so he usually drove Sarah's Buick Grand National.

"It's just as well. I didn't get that much sleep last night. I shouldn't be driving."

The two exchanged sarcastic looks, then Tommy asked, "Can you swing by and pick me up around six on the way home?"

"Ay, you know midtown traffic is crazy…"

Tommy tilted his head, staring blankly at her.

Sarah blew out a breath. "Fine, but we're bringing in something for dinner. I'm not coming home all late just to turn on the oven."

"That's cool."

A few minutes went by, before Sarah took Carrie to her playpen in the living room. Tommy was finishing his meal when she came back in.

"I… um, I want to apologize for keeping you up at night with Carrie. I'll take the next few nights 'till the weekend."

He was shocked by the apology and smiled. "Thank you, I appreciate that, hon'."

Sarah sat back down at the table and reached over for his hand.

This alarmed him, and he sensed a serious conversation was about to start.

"It's been a while since we talked about what happened," she began.

*Uh-oh, I knew it.* He thought.

"I know you still don't believe me, but I really want to speak to someone about... about what I saw."

During her labor, Sarah lost a lot of blood and temporarily lost consciousness. For a brief moment, she felt like she had an out-of-body experience, in which a mysterious figure appeared before her. She was convinced that the person she saw... was God.

"I believe you," Tommy told his wife. "But I don't see the point of... making a big deal of it."

"It must have happened for a reason. Maybe he gave me a message, or maybe I'm supposed to do something."

"Like what?"

"I don't know! I really need to speak to someone about it, seek guidance."

Tommy chose his words carefully. "Sarah, I'd be careful who you talk to about this... you don't want to have people thinking you're um... um..."

"What!? *Crazy?*"

He held his palms up. "I didn't say that! You said 'Crazy,' I didn't say..."

"But that's what you think I am, isn't it?!"

"No, no, no..."

"Well, you go ahead and think that! I know what I saw, and if you don't believe me, I'll find someone who does!"

She stood up to leave as Tommy called out behind her, "Sarah! Sarah, wait!"

When she didn't reply he asked, "Are you still picking me up?!"

"I don't know why you care what these bitches think about you, just ignore them!" Marcus Shirkey said.

It was ten o'clock in the morning at Van Nest and Janelle was working the circulation desk. Since the branch just opened, she was in charge of both checkouts and returns. Sitting next to her on a shelving cart, was Janelle's only friend in the branch, Marcus Shirkey.

The outspoken full-time clerk had the most experience at Van Nest, having worked seven years and counting, reminding Janelle of Ethel Jenkins. She saw a lot of similarities between 58th Street and Van Nest. Both were small, quaint, intimate settings. Van Nest had a staff of six full-time clerks and two part-time clerks. There were four librarians and one information assistant, with three pages working the shelves.

While 58th Street had the two ground floors inside an office build-ing, Van Nest was a one-level facility, the size of a parking lot, located between a grocery deli and an apartment complex.

Marcus had been Janelle's confidant since she arrived. While the rest of the staff shunned her as the "single-teenage-mother-welfare-case," Marcus was able to relate to her, after receiving the same treat-ment about his homosexual lifestyle. Born to Cuban and Irish parents, the clerk grew up in Miami, before being drawn to New York City by the "Club Kids" nightlife party scene during the 1980's.

Janelle chuckled at Marcus's remark. "Marc! How can you call everyone that?"

"Ay, it's a term of endearment by my people. But not in this case."

She moved to receive some returns from a patron and then moved back to the middle of the circulation desk, standing next to the shelving cart. "Maybe… maybe I should just transfer, when I come back from maternity leave," she said, with a sigh.

"Don't give them the satisfaction," Marcus replied. "You have to be tough, or society will walk all over you… and your child."

She looked at him and nodded. The support he provided was so inspiring. She almost wanted to name him the godfather of her child.

*If only he wasn't…* she thought.

Marcus entrusted Janelle with a secret he shared with no one else. Three years ago, he learned he was HIV-positive.

"Speaking of which," he began. "When is your next appointment?"

"Thursday. I was thinking of going earlier and taking a half-day, but my doctor had no cancelations, so I'll be going there at six in the evening."

"And then Friday's your last day, right?"

"Yep. I'm almost due. I wanted to make sure I wouldn't have the baby here in the 600's under gynecology."

"Dewey decimal 618... yuck!"

The two shared a laugh.

"Oh, I'm going to miss you," Marcus said. "You've been my own personal 'Carla' from *Cheers*."

"I'll be back in time for Thanksgiving. They're only giving me five weeks off."

A patron approached the desk, but had no books, CDs, or VHS tapes in her hand.

"Good morning, may I help you?" Janelle greeted, approaching the checkout terminal.

"I couldn't help overhearing your conversation. May I ask you a personal question, young lady?" the woman asked. She was a tall brunette wearing a business suit.

"That depends," the clerk replied, tensing up.

"Have you considered giving up your baby for adoption when it's born? I can make you a lot of money and assure you the child will be raised in a good home."

Marcus stood up from the book cart. "What the...?" he hissed.

Janelle's mouth dropped open, as she stepped back.

"Don't give me that look. You obviously don't have the means to provide for the child by yourself, and you should be thankful I'm offering a chance..."

"It is none of your business whether I have the means to raise my child!" she gasped. "Now, unless you have any questions regarding our library items, I suggest you leave. Immediately, you *ghoul!*"

The outburst caught the attention of the librarian working the information desk, some patrons, and several clerks from the office across the room.

The woman stared back and said, "Fine, do things the hard way. Your people always do." She walked past the desk and left the branch.

Janelle's body shook in anger. She tried her best to keep her composure for the rest of the hour. Once she was relieved, she rushed to the employee bathroom and burst into tears.

Tanya had the day off, so she could work the upcoming Saturday. After leaving Park West High School, she took the train up to 184th Street and Grand Concourse in Fordham Heights. When she approached her apartment building, she gasped when she saw that someone was waiting for her.

"Andy?"

Tanya's ex-boyfriend and senior clerk of the Webster Branch Library, Andrew Friedman turned to reveal a bouquet of roses in his hand. He adjusted his glasses and flashed a big smile at the sight of the young page.

"Hey, Brownie. How you doin'?"

She nearly faltered at hearing the special nickname he gave her. They engaged in a secret relationship when Andrew worked at 58th Street, training under Sonyai. The pair parted ways when he took a promotion, and later, Tanya learned that he was dating a co-worker at Webster, which broke her heart.

She gathered herself and put on a stoic face. "I'm doing fine... nice flowers," she said nonchalantly.

"They're for you," he said, extending his arm as she approached him slowly.

"Why don't you give them to your IA girlfriend?" she scoffed, as she began to walk past him.

"Yeah, I kinda figured you'd mention her." He caught up and stepped back in front of her. "Look... she was just a summer fling, okay? She was using me to get back at her waspy parents. We went to Cape Cod on Labor Day weekend, and I knew it was a setup the minute we arrived."

"So now you know how it feels. Have a nice life," she said, and resumed walking past him.

Andrew squeezed the stems of the flowers in anger and felt the sting of the thorns. "You know, you're all mad at me, but you seemed to have moved on yourself, going out with that blond-haired Calvin Klein model!" he said to her back.

Robin had Franklin visit the branch for the first time, months ago, and upon meeting his friend, Tanya went on several dates with Franklin, in an attempt to make Andrew jealous. They succeeded, but then stopped seeing each other once the thrill was gone.

She turned around to look back at him. "What difference does it make? We've outgrown each other, and there's nothing else to say about it! Now if you'll excuse me…"

She turned, making her way to the entrance.

"Look, I made a mistake, okay? I wanted to call you when I was settled at Webster, but I couldn't pick up the phone. I never forgot about you, Tanya… I was just… scared."

She stopped in mid-stride and turned around again. "Scared of what?"

"You know? Our age difference."

Tanya turned 17 this past May. Andrew will be 24 in January next year.

"I'm 17 now, so there's nothing to worry about, and for someone so scared, you taking a big risk showing up here. What if my mom was home?"

"That's why I wanted to plead my case. I think we both miss each other and can make this work."

He extended the bouquet again. "Just one date, two weeks from now…"

She just looked back at him, ignoring the flowers.

"Please?" he pleaded.

She reached out, plucked one rose, and held it under her nose for a smell. "Less is more," Tanya replied, after opening her eyes.

He nodded and smiled.

"Friday, the 21st," she said, then held up a finger. "Just, dinner. No movie, and definitely *no. fucking.*"

"Someplace nice. You got it."

"And you paying!"

"Of course, Brownie…" He put on a sly grin and took a step toward her. "…you remember why I call you 'Brownie' don't you?"

Standing over her, he brushed his fingers down her right cheek. Tanya's thighs quivered, remembering she asked him the same question months earlier. She wanted him, and he knew it. After gathering her composure, she cleared her throat. "Ahem, call me this weekend… you know the times when mom is working. Don't forget."

She turned around quickly and went inside.

"I won't," he replied.

Sarah Carmichael was sitting in the living room of her parent's apartment. Her mother Acindina was playing with Carrie on her lap.

"She is such a cute baby, qué linda! Hey, maybe we should try to get her in commercials… like that Gerber Baby?"

"Mama, all babies are beautiful," Sarah dismissed with a laugh.

Acindina placed the infant on a blanket that was laid out on top of their carpeted floor.

"So, what did you want to talk about?" she asked Sarah.

"Mama, do you believe in visions?"

The question gave the elder pause, she narrowed her gaze and whispered, "What do you mean, *visions*?"

Sarah chose her words carefully and started playing with her hands, a tic she always did when she was nervous. "You think you can get me a sit-down with Titi Ada?"

A sneer of contempt came across Acindina's face at the mention of her older sister. "I haven't spoken to that bruja since you were 18-years-old." She hissed. "I rather hold a burning piece of coal in my hand than *look* in her direction."

"I know you and Adamari are not on good terms, but she's the only one who can help me." *And believe me,* she quietly added.

"Help you with what, mija?"

Sarah sighed, debating whether she should tell her, wondering how she would react.

"Ay, tell me already! Spit it out!" her mother yelled.

"When I gave birth to Carrie, my spirit left my body temporarily and I saw God," Sarah exhaled in a single breath.

Acindina looked at her daughter quietly once again. Sarah looked back at her.

"Well… what did God look like?" Acindina asked.

Sarah opened her mouth to answer when the door to the apartment opened and Lorenzo Gonzales walked in.

"Cindi! The damn health inspector's been getting on my ass, calling the damn restaurant! I gotta get those papers real quick and head back down." He rushed to their bedroom without noticing Sarah or the baby.

Her father's restaurant was several blocks away, so he was able to take his lunch break to come back to the apartment. Loud crashes were coming from the bedroom as Lorenzo searched furiously.

The two women sighed as Acindina stood up. "Let me help you find whatever you're looking for. Don't tear this place up!" She then looked at Sarah. "Before we contact Ada, we'll talk about this further. In the meantime, talk to Tommy about Thanksgiving and Christmas… we'll go out to Long Island for Thanksgiving, but we wanna do something special for Carrie's first Christmas."

Sarah gave a concerned look as her mother headed to the bedroom. "Special? Do what special?" she called back to Acindina.

"And when are you gonna get the baby christened?" Acindina yelled back, disappearing into the next room.

"Baby? What baby are you talking about?" Lorenzo asked.

Gerry was in the staff room, laying on the couch and writing in his notebook. The direct line telephone on the wall rang and he sat up to answer it.

"Hello?"

"You got a phone call on the main line, Coltraine," Augustus said coldly. "Keep it brief."

Gerry rolled his eyes. "Yes sir." He then pressed the switchboard button for the main line.

"Yeah, this is Gerry."

"What's up, man, it's Blue."

"Oh. Shit man, wha'cha want?"

"Remember when you told me you were looking for a car? Well, it just so happened, someone unloaded me some wheels that I'm looking to move."

Gerry's left eyebrow jumped with skepticism. "How much?"

"A few grand," Blue answered.

"Man, what kind of lemon you trying to gyp me with?"

"She's a steal. Come over and check it out, take a test drive."

Gerry thought about it for a moment as the direct line rang again. It was probably Augustus warning him to finish the call.

"All right, man, let's meet out at that mall in Staten Island. You better be straight with me."

"Straight as an arrow, man. Peace." The phone clicked off.

Gerry put the receiver back on the wall. When it came to Blue, an arrow was as straight as a bobby pin.

Tommy and Sonyai were working with patrons at their designated terminals during the four o'clock rush.

When they had a break to themselves Tommy whispered, "Times are getting hard, ma'am. We could really use some help," he turned to look inside the clerical office.

Sonyai resented being called ma'am even though it was a sign of respect. "I don't want to hear it, Thomas."

"If I was able to get some sleep at night, I wouldn't mind, but I'm barely able to keep my eyes open." He pointed to the bags under his eyes. "It's time."

She looked up at her tall protégé. "But won't I appear weak?"

He shook his head. "You could never look weak... he's learned his lesson."

The senior clerk took a moment, then walked inside the clerical office.

Robin was at his desk, and didn't look up when Sonyai walked in, closing the door behind her. She noticed that his left hand was marking the cards with a red smudge due to his disfigurement. There was a handkerchief next to the piles that he used to blot the occasional bleeding from his scarred hand. He once wore a glove to hide the mysterious injury, but Sonyai prevented him from violating their dress code.

"You're bleeding a little on the cards there, Walker," she noted.

He stopped and took a moment to wipe his hand, then resumed stamping without saying a word.

She cleared her throat. "It's been three months. You've come in every scheduled day, even Saturdays... and have been stamping cards while doing no other clerical duties. This was intended to break you, make you quit."

Robin listened and said nothing, continuing to stamp.

"So why haven't you?" Sonyai asked.

The question made him stop for a moment, he looked up and stared out in front of him. "My grandfather once told me... *'Never walk away from a fight... unless you did something wrong.'*" He finally turned to look up at her. "You broke the law, committed insurance fraud..."

"Society views unwed mothers with a scarlet letter!" she interrupted. "Like they're an embarrassment, to be shamed and crucified! It's not fair! You are not a woman, you wouldn't understand!"

"I have nothing else to say," Robin replied. "You want to punish me for what I did? Just remember why I did it! Because you sent Shinju away! I accomplished my goal, and have no intent to retaliate further." He resumed stamping. "…but I'm not quitting for something I didn't deserve to be punished for!"

The clerk looked back down and resumed stamping date due cards.

The senior clerk watched as he stamped card after card. A minute went by as Sonyai clenched her jaw and her fist.

Without warning, she swept her arm across the piles of cards, sending them flying in all directions, then slammed her fist down on the desk. Robin didn't flinch, holding his date stamp in mid-air.

"I'm not picking them up," he said coldly.

Sonyai, normally the epitome of calm, had finally given in, with a rare display of emotion.

"I had my reasons!" she barked. "I sent her away for YOUR safety as well as hers!"

"You sent her away…" Robin turned to her. "Because you couldn't accept her being with a BLACK MAN!"

"NO! That had nothing to do with it!"

"LIAR!" he screamed. "No matter how many times you say it, no matter how you try to justify yourself with this feminist bullshit, YOU… ARE… WRONG!"

They stared at each other, neither one turning away. Sonyai then bent down and placed several loose date due cards on Robin's desk. He waited a few minutes until she picked up enough to make a sizable stack and then resumed stamping as if the last ten minutes didn't happen.

Angie was upstairs, studying in the staff room. Next to her notebooks were several old magazines of *Family Computing*. The door opened and a rush of excitement came over her as she expected Heywood to walk in. She was disappointed when Zelda walked in, carrying a paper bag of unknown contents for her lunch.

"Oh, I thought you were Heywood," she sighed.

"Ah yes, I hear he's been keeping to himself lately," Zelda replied, taking a seat. She glanced at the magazines and frowned. "My goodness, are you traveling back in time ten years to relive the birth of the Macintosh?"

"My personal computer is giving me problems. I was looking up some troubleshooting advice."

"Hmm. Robin goes to Baruch College. He might know his way around a disk drive."

Angie shrugged as Zelda pulled out a Lox and Bagel sandwich. After several bites, Zelda said, "if you ask me... Heywood is distancing himself from you because subconsciously you remind him of his failed relationship with that singer."

The information assistant looked up with a frown. "What?"

"Look at her appearance," Zelda concluded. "You yourself accused her of adopting Native-American aspects... don't you think it's possible he thinks of her when he sees you?"

"We've been friends for over a year, and he only knew her three *months*, barely."

"He's still hurt, putting on a brave face, but believe me... he's crying himself to sleep at night."

"So, what should I do, then?" Angie asked.

"Wait it out, give him space..." Zelda took another bite, then wiped her mouth. "He'll come around."

Angie thought about the advice. "Okay, I'll concentrate on more of my business and see what happens. Thank you, Zelda."

The elder nodded with a smile. Several minutes later, Angie gathered her books in her book bag and left. Before Zelda could enjoy the silence, Ethel entered the room, winded from taking the steps to the second floor.

"I heard you were up here," she said, wiping her brow.

"I know you recently found out you're a diabetic, Ethel, but if climbing a flight of steps..."

"Save your breath and let me catch mine for a second," Ethel interrupted. She sat at the table and took three deep breaths to steady herself.

"I thought these pills and changing my eating habits would work," she continued. "And Yi sitting the kid behind a desk hasn't been helping the situation!"

The two sages of the library looked at each other. Between them, over 50 years of service, in over 12 different branches from Manhattan to The Bronx. Surviving four governors and five mayors, while seeing the worst in New York City residents and the best. For one, it was enough.

"I'm retiring at the end of the year," Ethel finally said, with a sigh.

It felt great to hear it from her mouth, aloud. Coming to terms with the decision she had already made up in her mind months ago.

"You're the first person I've said this to," she admitted. "I've dropped hints to Yi, but she refuses to accept it. It's going to be a serious blow. She's going to need someone else to be the voice of reason."

"And she'll find it," Zelda replied. "Maybe not at first, but someone will rise to the occasion." She let out a weary sigh herself. "Someone always does."

"She'll need another woman," Ethel noted. "They can't have her in charge of this boy's club, you know that right?"

"You speak as if *I* have anything to do with…"

"Don't insult my intelligence, Clein. We both know you had a hand in the boy coming here, after Yi fought to keep that vacancy for as long as she did."

Zelda said nothing to the sharp, interrupting remark. She decided to change the subject. "I take it you'll be settling up your debt before your departure?"

Ethel nodded. In the midst of her real estate investment dwindling her savings, she turned to Zelda for a one-time loan of a thousand dollars to cover her commitment, with the intention of paying her back in six months.

"Rest assured, you will be paid in full, every penny before I'm gone. In fact, I swung down to see the place for myself this past weekend."

"Oh?"

"Yeah, not too shabby," Ethel lied. "It'd be nice to leave the cold of the city in the middle of winter… what is it they call it?"

"Snowbirding," Zelda answered.

"Yeah, only permanently." She looked at Zelda with a straight gaze and nodded. "You gonna keep this to yourself?"

"We go back a long way, Ethel," she said with an endearing tone, being one of the few to address her by her first name. "You would be the only person I would share such information with."

They smiled at each other at the show of mutual respect.

# CHAPTER THREE

TOMMY STEPPED OUT OF THE BRANCH AND FOUND SARAH WAITING FOR him in their car. He entered the passenger side then looked back to check on Carrie in the car seat.

"Thanks Honey. It's been a long day."

She pulled out, heading east toward the Queensboro Bridge. Tommy could sense she was still upset so he decided to start a conversation. "Uh, how'd it go at your parent's house?"

"Fine. Mama keeps asking when are we christening Carrie *and* where are we spending the holidays this year?"

In five years of marriage, the couple had alternated between spending Christmas with Tommy's parents and Thanksgiving with Sarah's. This first year with the baby, the pressure was on from both sides.

"What do you want to do?" he asked.

"I really don't want to think about it now, what do you want for dinner? I just want to stop by a drive thru. Wendy's or Mickey D's?"

Tommy didn't answer.

"Baby?" Sarah called out, "Ba... baby?"

She stopped at a red light on Queens Plaza then looked to find Tommy asleep and leaning against the window.

"Damn," she whispered. "Looks like we're going to McDonald's, Carrie!"

Carrie cooed and clapped at the good news.

Heywood walked into the Pig 'N' Whistle at five forty-five. The Irish bar was blocks away from 58th Street, on 3rd Avenue, and a frequent hangout for the staff. He flipped his long, brown, unkempt hair over a shoulder and plopped on an empty barstool with a sigh.

After a half-hour and three bottles of Michelob, the information assistant saw a familiar face approach him and take a seat to his right.

"I'm not really in the mood for company."

"Then you came to the wrong place," Eugene replied, and held his hand up for an order from the bartender.

They continued drinking in silence, when Eugene said, "So Angie thinks you've been ignoring her lately…"

"I told her to go! It's all my fault!" Heywood suddenly exclaimed.

Eugene blinked hard, wondering if he was even heard, then continued to listen.

"I keep replaying that night in my mind… thinking of what I could have said to make her stay."

"I…" Eugene began.

"Who was I to say anything, huh? Just some guy that gave her a place to stay… I mean, I thought we were in love, man!"

Eugene shrugged and started to say something.

"She could have found some other gig in the city, she didn't *have* to go, right?"

Heywood turned to see Eugene staring back at him."I'm waiting to see if I can talk, now."

"You can talk now," he replied with a nod.

"Thank you. First off… it's not your fault, okay? You couldn't help the way things turned out. She was a performer, made for the stage. She would have been miserable if she passed up that opportunity.

Blaming you for ruining her life? You would have been at each other's throats."

Heywood listened and nodded to himself. "Yeah, you're right. I just need to move on."

"Okay, now can we talk about why you're taking it out on Angie?" Eugene asked.

"I'm not blaming her," he replied, sucking his teeth. "I'm just focused on getting back on Chavez's good side. After overstepping with that film deception months ago, I think he's ready to trust me again."

Back in March, Heywood organized a film presentation of his own choices behind the head librarian's back, even going the extra mile by impersonating Augustus in a phone call to the Donelle video library, where most media requests were fulfilled.

"Maybe you could talk to her, then? Just let her know."

"I'll see..." Heywood said dismissively, then took a swig of his beer.

Sonyai had always loved walking through gardens. It's not known to her staff, but she actually had experience in botany a lifetime ago. However, since moving to New York City, and living in an apartment, the senior clerk didn't have the resources to keep up with the hobby.

She was still nursing her injured hand after the explosive confrontation with Robin hours ago. So, to clear her head, Sonyai traveled to the conservatory garden between 104th and 106th Street in the northeast corner of Central Park.

After taking a seat on a bench, she took a deep breath and let out a long, noticeable sigh.

"I heard that all the way from here," a voice said to her right.

Sonyai turned and greeted Jessica Coons with a thin smile. The senior clerk of the 96th Street Branch Library was wearing a red three-quarter-long trench coat with an oversized fedora.

"You look like Carmen Sandiego," Sonyai said.

"Is that an invitation to travel the world and let children guess where we are?"

"No."

"Well, don't blame me for having a sense of style. You look like someone looking for furniture in an IKEA store."

Sonyai chuckled at the jab and started to feel better in the presence of her long-time friend.

"What happened to your hand?" Jessica asked.

"A slight lapse in judgment… you—"

"Ah, ah, ah… don't change the subject, what happened?"

Sonyai pressed her lips together and squinted but remained silent.

"It's about that boy, isn't it? He's the only one that gets underneath your skin, besides Chavez."

A smile came across Jessica's face, seeing Sonyai so uncomfortable was a rare occasion she reveled in.

"He's not quitting, and everyone else is getting restless."

Jessica nodded. "Well, it's been long enough, I'm sure he's learned his lesson."

"I… I just don't want to seem weak."

"Aaaah, nobody's thinking you're weak," she scoffed.

Sonyai raised an eyebrow. "Then what *do* they think of me?"

"Does it matter?"

Sonyai thought about it.

"Exactly… it doesn't."

Sonyai turned to her. "Is this cavalier attitude how you look at things running the entire region of branches in our cluster?"

Jessica smiled. "Of course, how'd you think I got here?"

Sonyai let out another sigh. "Maybe you're right." She rose to leave. "See you at the meeting, Saturday?"

Jessica pulled up her collar with a flourish. "I'll be there."

The pair walked their way past the fountain to the nearest exit.

Franklin was in his apartment watching television when the phone rang. He reached over and picked up the receiver. "Hello?"

"Franklin?" A voice asked.

"Hey Benny, how's it going, man?"

"I'm good, I'm good, man. Um, you remember asking me to look into that thing you asked me to around six months ago?"

Franklin stood up. "You found her?"

The line was quiet for a second as the caller felt apprehension. "I have a good idea where she might be, but um, what exactly do you plan on doing?"

Franklin scrunched his face. "What do you mean?"

"I don't wanna be an accessory to anything man..."

"Damnit, Beinvenido. I'm not going to kill her or anything. I just wanna talk and tell her how I feel!"

"Didn't you do that already?" the caller asked.

"Look, if you felt this way, why did you ask around?"

"Well, I *did* owe you."

Franklin nodded. "Right, and you still do. You were there when The Game started, and Trevor could have made you his bitch, but I stood up for you."

The caller said nothing as Franklin continued.

"And it's not over. If the truce is broken, you'll have a bullseye on your back, you still need me. I'm the only one who can protect you from Trevor *and* Robin. It's only a matter of time before they go at it again."

Beinvenido sighed. "Alright... from what I heard, she's currently at the end of a six-month stint at the Lincoln Center Branch, down at—"

"I know where it is," Franklin interrupted.

"She's only there until the end of the year, then she'll be on the move again."

"Thanks, Benny."

"Yeah, yeah... after this we're even. I pray the truce is never broken," he said, as he hung up the phone.

Franklin hung up as well. After all this time... he finally found her again.

"She's got 45,000 miles on her, power steering, folding mirrors, and front clear corner lights."

"So, what does all that mean?" Denise Coltraine asked.

"Let me handle this, Sis." Gerry dismissed his twin sister.

The two siblings were in the parking lot of the Staten Island Mall, examining a silver 1990 Toyota Celica, Thursday morning. Gerry's friend, only known as 'Blue' was showing them the car on Gerry's day off, hoping to sell it.

"I'm telling you, man… you're getting a steal here," Blue said. "I could get five, six grand for this car, but I'm willing to let it go to y'all for only three."

"Why you selling it? How'd you get it?" Gerry asked.

Blue raised his eyebrows. "You askin' a lot of questions and you ain't even step a foot inside, Bro."

Gerry stared back. "I don't want my fingerprints on this car until I hear where it came from!"

Even though they were friends, Blue had a reputation. He never held a real job but still had enough money to live a lavish lifestyle. Rumors surrounded him related to activities of loansharking, pimping, gambling, and even extortion. The less Gerry knew, the better off he would be in case the police came asking questions later.

Blue pulled out a piece of paper from his suit jacket pocket. "Here's the title. The car was signed over to me as a form of payment. Free and clear. It's all legit."

Gerry reached for the document when Blue pulled it back. "You read with your hands, now?"

Denise was tired of the runaround. "Gerry, let's go. Y'all can't trust each other, and I got better things to do!"

"Hold on, Dee, we're just chewin' the fat. Put on those gloves I gave you and get in the passenger seat."

He watched her roll her eyes, blow a breath, then walk over to the car. After looking back at Blue, Gerry pulled out a pair of leather gloves and held up a finger. "You better be straight with me. This car stolen or got drugs in it, I'm gonna mess you up."

Blue just smiled. "Would I do that to you?"

Gerry joined his sister in the car. The keys were in the ignition, as he felt around the dashboard and checked the glove compartment.

"I already checked," Denise said. "This car feels nice, but I trust Blue as far as I can throw him."

"I know, I know... but $3,000.00? The miles? That's crackhead price, Dee."

"Uh-huh, and Blue ain't no crackhead, so turn the damn thing on and make sure it runs... if you remember."

"It ain't been that long!" Gerry huffed and turned the key.

The engine turned over and he proceeded to drive the car around the parking lot, doing several laps and turns while avoiding other vehicles arriving at the mall. They then switched seats and Denise drove around for fifteen minutes before pulling up in front of Blue.

"Well? Do we have a deal?"

"I wanna take it to a mechanic," Denise said, as she stepped out. "My neighbor Julio has a garage on Atlantic Avenue."

"Hey, no problem, let's go right now," Blue replied.

"Give me two days," Gerry said flatly.

Blue's smile disappeared from his face. "What?" He spat.

"We'll bring the money, drive it over the bridge to Brooklyn..."

"Nah, nah, nah, man, it's $3,000.00 right now, in my hand *today*. The car's priced to move. Every damn day I have it costs me money. I gotta pay to park it in a secure lot, keep filling it with gas..."

"Two days won't kill you, man."

"If you're wasting my time, I can sell it to someone else. My time is valuable and I'm giving you first dibs."

Denise was already walking toward the mall entrance. "I'm going to Macy's!" she called out, giving the two men a dismissive wave. Gerry tilted his head. "Two days."

"I ain't making no guarantees, Gerry. If I still got it, I got it."

Gerry nodded and then took off to catch up with his sister.

It was a long and hectic day at 58th Street. Despite a clerk coming to help from the Webster Branch, Tommy, Ethel, and Sonyai were pushed to their limits since opening at ten o'clock. After the lunch hour rush, there was a slowdown period, which gave Sonyai a moment to step inside her office.

She had been regretting this moment all day, looking over at Robin stamping cards quietly at his desk. He didn't flinch as the senior clerk slowly walked across the office and stopped by his side. Sonyai cleared her throat and took a breath.

"I... I'm not going to ever admit to any wrongdoing when it comes to this matter," she began. "But I will admit this... you were right."

Robin stopped in mid-stamp after hearing the admission.

"The odds were stacked against you before you even walked through the door." She let out a sigh and continued. "We had a situation and you had to go, no matter what. It was just that simple. We needed to protect our own."

Robin put down the stamp and looked up at her.

"What I didn't know, is that *you* are one of our own as well, and I accept that now." There was hesitation in her voice. This was obviously difficult to say. "I have no regrets over sending Shinju back home. It had nothing to do with you personally, it was what *she* chose to do herself rather than the alternative."

Robin's jaw clenched, as if he refused to believe that last statement.

"But I see now how it affected you... and I forgive you for what you did to make me feel the same."

She waited for an emotional response to the apology, but when Robin looked back at her undaunted, she gritted her teeth and nodded. "Tomorrow, you will resume your regular duties as a part-time clerk in this branch."

She then reached in her pocket and pulled out a glove, then set it down next to the stack of date due cards.

Robin looked at the glove, understanding the gesture. "Thank you," he said quietly, with a nod.

Sonyai nodded back and turned to leave.

Robin smiled to himself. He picked up and looked at the glove Sonyai left, then put it on and started stamping again.

"So, what do you think about the car?" Gerry asked.

He and Denise were eating Chinese take-out they picked up on their way back to her place. They spent most of the afternoon shopping and making arrangements to have the Celica checked out.

"If it was anyone other than Blue, we'd be driving it home, but him? I just don't know."

"Yeah, I'm sure he had to break some legs to get it as a form of payment."

She nodded. "You gonna have your half of the money?"

"Sure, even some extra, just in case."

"And your record is clean?"

Gerry threw the carton of chicken on the table. "Damn it, Dee, why you gotta be like that?"

"You had your license suspended for a reason. I'm just looking out for you!"

"I'm fine! Okay? I got the points off, been taking the classes. I'm good, now drop it!"

They continued eating quietly for several minutes, then Gerry whispered, "sorry," with an apologetic look.

"It's okay," she replied.

After a few more moments, Gerry tried to change the subject. "So, been on any dates lately?"

Denise ignored the question and continued to eat her dumplings. After she finished, she said, "Do you mean have I had anymore half-naked 18-year-old white boys in my house *lately*?"

On their last birthday celebration, Gerry invited Robin and Franklin to attend. Franklin made a lasting impression on Denise and charmed his way into giving her his phone number. One night after a heated argument at the library, Gerry came to her house after drinking and found them in a compromising position.

"Well, since you brought it up..." Gerry began.

"It's none of your business, but no, I haven't seen no hide nor blond hair of that boy since you ran him off."

"Good," he spat. "Had no business messing with you—"

"Hush! We ain't talking about who I could do whatever the hell I want with, Gerrald!"

"All right, calm down, calm down. You were getting up in my ass about my record. You gonna have *your* half for the car? I ain't covering you if you come up short!"

"I got my money ready, let's go over who's gonna have the car when. You know damn well we don't share things well."

"I agree. We couldn't even share that Atari game system we saved up for when we were kids!"

The twins looked at each other, then started laughing.

"Yeah, because you wouldn't let me play Ms. Pac Man," Denise said.

"Whatever happened to that Atari, anyway?"

"I think dad threw it away, because it started so many fights."

Gerry grunted. "Well, he ain't doing that with this car!"

"That's right!" Denise agreed.

Robin was laying down on the couch upstairs in the staff room smiling to himself. Tomorrow, he would be back to his regular duties, and along with college registration coming up, things would finally start getting back to normal.

He was planning a celebration, with drinks, pizza, video games and planned to invite Franklin to come, when the door opened, and Alex stepped in. She couldn't ruin his mood if she tried, so he decided to ignore her.

"You're in a good mood," she said.

He wasn't taking the bait.

"Maybe you've finally accepted that no one wants you here and you're finally leaving, huh? C'mon, you can tell me, I'll keep it a secret."

She was really working his last nerve. It had never occurred to him when he arrived that Alex would be his biggest adversary. When he first arrived, he half-expected it to be Tommy, who reminded him so much of the bully who tormented him back at Fort Washington, Trevor Guzman. Alex was working her way past Trevor up his chain of enemies.

With Trevor, it was all a sadistic game of cat and mouse. With every action, there was an equal retaliation to their animosity. But Alex was all attack, attack, attack, with Robin holding back. But just because she was a girl, that shouldn't protect her from extracting some form of revenge.

"I'm not going anywhere," he finally told her. "Get used to it."

"I don't think so," Alex taunted. "One way or another... you're going down!"

That triggered an emotional response, as Robin thought back to Fort Washington with a painful memory. Those last words echoed in his head as he let out a growl.

"Alright, look! I want you to remember that night at that college party," Robin began, as he stood. "Those frat boys were going to rape you!" He pointed at his chest. "I didn't have to save you. I *didn't want* to save you... but I did it anyway."

Alex swallowed hard.

"I know Janelle was your friend, but she's gone. You need to let it go!"

He walked past her and stopped at the door. Without looking back at her, he clenched his fist. "Because if we keep doing this dance... I'll make what those boys *could* have done, look like a birthday party!"

He opened the door and slammed it behind him.

It was the last hour before closing. Tommy and Ethel were working the circulation desk, when Tanya parked an empty shelving cart at the wall next to the entrance to the clerical office. Tommy came over and took a seat on the cart.

"Thank you," he sighed. "I've been waiting for an opportunity to sit down."

Tanya folded her arms in front of her. "Tired, are we?"

He brought his finger to his lips. "Shhh… let me have this," then waved his hand. "Go away."

She leaned on the doorway to the clerical office and whispered to Tommy, "Miss Jenkins has been acting kind of weird lately."

"With Robin sidelined, *everyone's* been acting 'kind of weird,'" Tommy mumbled.

"Speaking of which… you think Miss Yi will bring him back anytime soon?"

"You'll have to ask *her*. Why are you still talking to me, can't you see I'm trying to—" Tommy sucked his teeth as he saw a patron walk up to return some books.

Tanya walked back out on the floor and started checking the rotating paperback shelves located in the front of the branch. She tried not to think about Andrew, but her thoughts kept coming back to him. Sooner or later, she needed to confide to Alex or Lakeshia about this.

Eugene sat in his chair at the entry threshold. "What's going on?" he asked.

"Just bored outta my mind and got nobody to talk to," Tanya replied.

Eugene chuckled. "Well, I'm here."

Tanya grinned and began to say something, but then a patron across the room pulled out a sandwich from a paper bag and began eating it.

"Hold on for a minute, duty calls," the security guard said, as he got up and walked across the room.

The man repulsed the other people around him as he started to munch very loudly into the sloppy sandwich.

Eugene approached and stopped in front of his table. "Excuse me, sir. There is no eating in the library. I'm afraid you'll have to take your meal outside."

The man turned and looked at the clock on the back wall above the copier machine. "Y'all closin' in five minutes, man," he replied.

"Exactly, so we don't need someone who's making a mess that will take *more* than five minutes to clean up."

"Well, I'll finish my sandwich and then leave... piss off!"

"Look, if I gotta mop up the floor with your face, you're not gonna like it and you won't be welcomed here again afterward, so save both of us some grief, okay?"

The man ignored Eugene and took another bite out of his sandwich.

Eugene squared up and cracked his knuckles. "Last chance."

He looked the security guard up and down and scoffed. "You ain't worth it." He put the remainder of his food back in the paper bag and stood up to leave.

Once he was past Eugene, the guard followed the man as he walked to the exit threshold.

"You don't need to follow me!"

"I know, but I'm doing it *anyway*. Keep moving." He gestured his hand in a scooting motion.

The patron left the branch without incident and the guard returned to his post.

Tanya came back and whispered to him, "You wanted to beat the shit outta him, didn't you?"

"Any aggressive behavior that ends peacefully is always the acceptable outcome," he replied. "But between you, me, and this chair... I was ready to throw down."

Augustus walked into his office after locking up the branch, a few minutes after six o'clock. After taking off his suit jacket, he loosened his tie and sat down behind his desk. Impatiently waiting a few moments, he answered a call to his direct line on the first ring. "Augustus Chavez speaking..."

"I hear you are interested in some real estate, sir," an unknown caller began.

"Yes, I was wondering if I could buy in on a deal your investment group is proposing."

"We're in several bidding wars over certain locations... which are you referring to?"

"33rd Street, Between Eleventh and Twelfth Avenue versus 34th Street and Madison." Augustus answered.

There was a long silence.

"Hello?"

"Who are you?" the caller hissed. "What do you know about our acquisition proposal?"

"I'm someone with information."

"Yeah, information that can get us in serious trouble with the Securities and Exchange Commission! We don't need that type of heat coming our way..."

"Precautions will be—"

"Take your money elsewhere. Don't call us again."

The phone clicked off and Augustus slammed the receiver down. "Damn!"

He massaged his temples for a moment, *Alright, we'll try this another way.*

The doorbell rang and Robin opened the door to see Franklin in the hallway.

"What the hell's so important I had to rush up here?" he asked impatiently.

Robin laughed loudly and handed him a bottle of Coors Artic Ice. "I'm back, baby! They finally caved!"

Franklin grabbed the bottle. "Oh, for real?"

"You damn right!" he replied, and took a swig. "Friday afternoon, Cotton comes BACK to Harlem! Shaft... goes BACK to Africa!" He saluted with his bottle. "Can you dig it!?"

Franklin walked in and waved his arms. "Okay, okay, calm down, Dolemite... you gonna get Charlotte and Liz downstairs to start banging on the ceiling."

Robin had his television on MTV and his radio blasting Hot97. He took a seat on the couch and put up his feet over the armrest, sitting sideways. "Man, I knew they wouldn't fire me... I did nothing wrong. That racist little tight-ass finally felt guilty for what she did! Well, now we're even... I'm gonna show her..."

He drained the bottle and aimed. With a flip of his wrist he threw the bottle across the living room where it landed in a plastic garbage container.

"Three-pointer!" he cheered.

"Dude, you go back tomorrow. You don't wanna go in all fucked up. Take it down a notch," Franklin warned.

"You right, you right, you right..." Robin nodded repeatedly. "That's why I called you, didn't want to celebrate alone... So! What's going on with you, then?" he waved his hand toward himself. "Why don't you come back, man... I can probably put in a good word and get you down there with me," he giggled.

"Nope, I've put the library behind me for a reason," Franklin dismissed.

Robin got up and went to the kitchen to get another bottle.

"I'm actually thinking of..." his friend started, with some hesitation.

"Yeah?" Robin pulled out a fresh new beer. "Thinking of..."

"Um, I've been thinking of... going to college."

Robin dropped the bottle in shock. It shattered on the floor. "Congratulations, you have just shocked me sober."

"Supa's given me till Christmas to make a decision. With my mom coming home for Thanksgiving, the pressure is on me to show them I'm doing something with my life, since getting fired from Bolton's. Everyone's going to be there. Lenny, LaSandra... I'm scared shitless, man."

Robin saw the fear in his eyes, something he rarely showed with his abundance of confidence. Usually.

"Okay I get it, and while I'm all in support of continuing your education, let me state the obvious... high school nearly kicked your ass."

"I know," Franklin sighed.

"You almost had to drop out and get your GED."

"Thank you!"

"Between the two of us, you know you only graduated because you finger-fucked your math teacher..." Robin began.

"Hey, Warner Wolf! I don't need you going to the videotape! I was there!"

"Sorry! Damn, touchy subject, I get it!"

Franklin stood up and looked out the window for a moment.

Robin was hesitant but couldn't resist asking, "So, where were you thinking of going?" *Please don't say Baruch, Please don't say Baruch, Please don't say Baruch...*

"I was thinking about... Bronx Community," he replied.

Robin exploded in a robust belly laugh. "Holy shit, really!?"

Franklin gave him a hard look. "C'moooon man!"

"Oh fuck! I think I just pissed myself!" He continued laughing hysterically.

Franklin started walking to the door. "You know what? Fuck you."

Robin ran in front of him and stopped laughing. "Okay, okay, okay, man, I'm sorry..."

"This ain't no joke man, this is my life..."

"I know..." Robin began.

"My LIFE, man! My father is not above shipping my ass to the marines or just kicking me out of the house, period. And you laughing ain't helping the situation!"

"I'm sorry, man... my bad. It was insensitive of me." *Bronx Community!?* he screamed in his head.

He led his friend back to the couch. "Okay, dare I ask what your major would be?"

"I haven't thought that far ahead. I gotta prepare my body for it, first," Franklin replied, with a sigh.

"Hey, you can find another job, man… It ain't the end of the world. You can do this."

"I hope so." He shook his head. "I really hope so."

Janelle walked into the Montefiore Medical Center building on 233rd Street and Carpenter Avenue. She approached the front desk and signed in, then took the elevators to the Obstetrics and Gynecology department on the third floor.

Once she was in the examination room wearing a hospital gown, her anxiety started getting the best of her. She was still unsure what her father was going to do when she had the baby. Her parents hadn't bought a crib or prepared their home for raising her child there. They only bought her a stroller.

*What if they really do kick me out? Where would I go?*

At that moment Doctor Heather Timmons walked in, a clipboard in her hand. The gynecologist had been seeing Janelle for the past several months, supporting her with valuable information.

"Ah, good evening, Miss Simms. How are you feeling?"

"The same, just a little nervous."

"Well, that's to be expected. I'll try to make this as painless as possible."

The first physician Janelle saw, at the beginning of her pregnancy, was a tough European woman who spoke Broken English. Doctor Timmons was more friendly, reminding her of a teacher from elementary school who probably smiled in her sleep. After some deep breath examinations and checking her pulse, she looked down at the report on her clipboard.

"Well, there are some alarming levels of protein in your urine, and you mentioned your feet swelling up. These may be early signs of preeclampsia."

A concerned look came over Janelle's face. "Huh?"

"Hmmm, your blood pressure is extremely high, young lady. Have you been doing any strenuous tasks lately? You've told me you work in a library. I can't see anything stressful in that type of environment."

*You don't know the half of it, doc,* she mused. "I uh…"

"This doesn't sit well with me. I'm afraid we're going to have you stay overnight to get your pressure down," The doctor announced cheerfully.

"What?"

"And if need be, we'll have to induce."

"But… but…" Janelle's eyes darted in all directions.

"Don't worry, you can call your parents once you're admitted. Let's find you a room."

*Oh my God, is this really happening?*

# CHAPTER FOUR

ANGIE WAS SITTING AT THE INFORMATION DESK FRIDAY MORNING, finishing up an essay for her philosophy class. The doorbell rang and Zelda unlocked the door to let Heywood in. After he went upstairs to hang up his coat, he came back down and walked over to the New Books section at the front of the branch to check the displays.

*...Give him space...* Angie remembered Zelda's advice.

She saw him approaching the desk and took that moment to pack up her schoolwork then stood to go upstairs to the staff room. Heywood raised his arm and called out, "Angie, wait up... I have something to tell you."

Angie tensed up and slowly side-stepped to give him access to the desk. "Yes?" She asked.

Heywood stroked his beard and sighed. "I've been acting like a dick lately... and I just wanna say I'm sorry."

"Okaaaaay."

"I've just been focused on the job because my personal life is... shit."

"I... I understand, with everything that happened with *her*. I get it. I just hope you're not taking what happened out on me."

Heywood frowned. "Wha... what would make you think that?"

*I knew Zelda was wrong!* "Um, never mind. I'm just glad we're okay."

"Good. Good, heh…"

They looked at each other awkwardly. Then Angie chucked her thumb. "I should go."

"Um, yeah, but um, before you go, you wanna tell me about that Native American exhibit pitch you mentioned?"

She smiled, happy that he remembered. "Sure." With a nod they both started walking to the reference corner.

"I think Jainy's gonna like this little surprise send away party we're throwing for her," Gertrude Trentini said, while blowing balloons.

She and two of Van Nest's full-time clerks were in the clerical office, hanging up decorations and placing paper plates around a cake centered on Reginald Brantley's desk.

Gertrude was an Italian mother of two, in her mid-forties, with dark hair and olive skin. Theo Pearson, a stout 25-year-old African-American, was hanging streamers with Marcus Shirkey.

"Yeah, been feeling kinda bad for not talking to her since she's been here."

"As well you should, Theo!" Marcus snapped.

"Hey, she's been moping around, keeping to herself," Gertrude said. "It ain't our fault she's a damn statistic! Acting like coming here from her snooty Manhattan branch was a prison sentence."

Marcus snapped his head toward her. *Bitch! I ought to scratch your eyes out!*

Reginald opened the door and walked in. All heads turned to him and noticed a disappointed look on the senior clerk's face. "You can stop with the decorations and just cut the cake," he began. "I got a call outside… Miss Simms won't be coming in for her last day."

There was a collective round of groans from the trio. "What?" Theo gasped.

"Why?" Marcus asked. "She wasn't due for another week."

"She's being held at the hospital for observation. They might induce labor over the weekend. I'll keep everyone informed if I hear anything else from her."

"We chipped in for the cake, a card, and some gifts…" Gertrude whined. "That's gratitude for you!"

"Hey! We'll give her the card and toys when she comes back from maternity leave, okay!?" Marcus said.

The clerks shrugged and nodded. "Hey, in the meantime, let's start on this cake!" Theo said, and opened the paper box, cutting himself a slice.

Robin arrived at 58th Street at two o'clock, wearing his original bike glove and red baseball cap. He entered the branch head held high and chest pressed out. *Napoleon has returned from Elba,* he thought.

From the information desk in the middle of the branch, Augustus registered actual shock at the clerk's entrance. Sensing Gerry and Tommy's reactions at the circulation desk, Sonyai stepped out of her office as Ethel peeked out from her vantage point at her desk.

Robin stopped and checked the desk schedule, which was hung on the wall, next to the door to the clerical office. He found his name under checkouts at the three o'clock hour, then turned to face Sonyai at the doorway. All eyes were on them from the clerks in various locations.

"Robin Walker," he began with a nod. "Reporting for duty."

Sonyai nodded in acknowledgment.

"I'd like to take this time, ma'am… to apologize for my actions several months ago."

From their terminals, Tommy and Gerry exchanged wide-eyed glances. Inside the office, Ethel tilted her head. Augustus continued to look on attentively.

"I let my emotions surpass my professionalism. It was a total display of disrespect to you and this branch, and as an employee of the NYPL I want to assure you, it will never happen again."

The senior clerk was very impressed by his humble apology. She realized it was for appearances only and wondered how sincere he was... but decided to oblige him.

"Thank you, Mister Walker, I most certainly hope so. I'll see you back here at 3 pm."

Robin turned and walked to the door leading upstairs to the second floor. Sonyai returned inside the clerical office. When they were alone again, the two clerks behind the circulation desk high-fived each other in a quiet celebration.

Tanya was outside the branch, pacing back and forth at two forty-three, when Lakeshia got dropped off by a cab. She stepped out and walked up, approaching Tanya with a questionable glance.

"Wha'cha out here waiting for, Tee?" Lakeshia asked.

"I wanted to catch you before coming in."

"Okay, but make it quick. My nose is frozen."

"I can see why, girl. You're looking more boney than usual. You trying ballet now instead of singing?"

"Shut up!" Lakeshia shouted, with a laugh.

"Nah, but seriously... I got a visit from Andy, he wants to... get together again."

"Oh Tanya, c'mooon..."

"I know, I know! I shouldn't give him the time of day."

"He broke your heart, Tee. You can't let him do it again. You're better than that."

"But... but, maybe he's changed. He brought me flowers..."

"Flowers?"

"I really think he deserves a second chance."

"He's playing you! It'll go good for a while, but then it'll only be a matter of time before you catch him with someone else."

Tanya sighed. "You think so?"

Lakeshia nodded.

"Well, maybe you're right."

"I know I am."

"You know, for someone not getting any action, you sure are smart about dating!"

She started walking toward the entrance.

"Um, Tanya...?" Lakeshia asked.

Tanya turned around. "Yeah?"

"What's it like? When you um, you know... do it? How does it, uh... feel?"

"What makes you think *I* know? I could be all talk, still be a virgin."

Lakeshia pouted her lips with a look.

Tanya grinned and rolled her eyes. "Alright... words can't express it. *But,* if I had to compare, hmmm... you know that feeling when your grandfather or grandmother gives you a birthday card with a 50-dollar-bill in it?"

"Yeah?"

"It's TEN TIMES that!" she exclaimed, with a big smile.

The girls giggled and entered the branch. As they walked past the circulation desk, they noticed that Gerry and Ethel seemed to be in higher spirits than usual.

Lakeshia noticed Gerry was bopping in place and humming a song, as if he had a spring in his step. Tanya squinted at the clerical schedule, posted next to the doorway to the back office.

"No way..." she whispered.

"What?" asked Lakeshia.

"I'll tell you upstairs!"

They made their way to the staircase leading up to the staff room.

Sonyai was speaking to Augustus, inside the head librarian's office, so Tommy took a moment while alone at his desk to make a phone call.

The phone rang and a raspy voice answered, "Hello?"

"Hey, Dad."

"Tommy! What a pleasant surprise! How's it going, Son?"

"Fine... is mom there?"

"What, you got no time to talk to your old man?" He chuckled. "Just kidding, she's right here... MAUREEEEEEEN!"

Tommy pulled the receiver off his ear and winced.

"Oh, give me the phone, already! You don't have to yell... Yes?" his mother greeted.

"Does dad think you're going deaf, or something?" Tommy asked.

"He just talks loud, to make up for his short stature," she dismissed. "What brings you to call us out of the blue?"

"I just wanted to see when's the next time you're coming to the city. I'd ask dad but..."

"Oh, yes, I know... He never does," she said, with a chuckle. "My friend's having a gallery opening in Long Island City this evening. You could use some exposure to some culture."

Tommy looked up at the ceiling with a pout. "Okay, sure... I'll see you there, bye."

He hung up the phone and ran his hand through his hair. "Hmph, culture."

"He loves me... he loves me not, he loves me..." Tanya plucked petals from the rose Andrew gave her while sitting at the kitchen table in the staff room. She had been daydreaming about him all day at school and the longer she waited... the more excited she got.

"He loves me... not?" she gasped, picking the last petal off. "Ohhh, what do you know!?" she yelled and tossed the remains in the garbage can.

Several minutes before three o'clock Alex walked in and saw the sour look on Tanya's face. "Hey Tee, what's bugging you?"

She snapped out of her funk and gave a dismissive wave. "Noth- ing... did you hear the news?"

"What news?"

"Robin's back working the desk, I saw his name on the schedule, everyone's happy they don't have to bust their butt anymore."

"No way!" Alex screamed and left the room, heading back downstairs.

She opened the door to the main floor and gasped in horror. Tanya was right. Robin walked out from the clerical office to the checkout terminal and relieved Gerry. He then caught her looking back at him. A wide smirk crept across his face.

"Sonofabitch," she hissed quietly.

He gave her a curt wave and proceeded to checkout a pair of books handed to him by a patron.

Lakeshia pushed a shelving cart across the floor and waved at Robin, who waved back. It was as if the last three months never happened. And Alex couldn't be more furious. A hand rested on her shoulder, she turned to see Sonyai staring back at her.

"It's not fair!" she hissed.

"It was time," Sonyai explained softly. "He got the message. He's learned his lesson."

"And what about Nelly? We just forget about her?" Alex snapped.

"Janelle will always be one of us, as is Robin, now. You can either accept it or *leave.*"

Her tone surprised Alex as she blinked hard. Sonyai stepped past the page and returned to the clerical office. Robin was still smiling from the circulation desk.

Janelle was getting impatient with the doctors taking her blood pressure every four hours. After calling Van Nest to inform Mister Brantley of her situation, she spent the rest of her day trying to relax as they proceeded to strip her membranes. It was five o'clock in the afternoon, and they were monitoring her cervix closely.

Calling her parents was the furthest thing from her mind, but she was thinking about calling Avery and Sonyai. The only thing that stopped her was the 48-hour wait before contractions would possibly start and she wanted to make sure before calling them.

Another hour passed by, and she realized that this was getting serious. Janelle picked up the phone and dialed Avery's number.

The phone rang several times and then the answering machine picked up with a recorded greeting. She rolled her eyes and waited for the beep. "Hello Avery? It's Janelle, I'm in Montefiore and the doctors are going to induce me. I know it's a week earlier than we planned but as soon as you get this, come to the hospital."

After hanging up the phone, she let out a sigh. "Okay, I think it's time to call my parents."

Janelle dialed the phone again that was provided by the hospital and her mother answered after several rings.

"Hello?"

"Mom, it's me, I'm at Montefiore, they're keeping me here for observation and decided to induce... I... I think it's time. Can you come to the hospital, please?"

There was nothing but dead air, Janelle almost thought the call was disconnected.

"Mom?"

"I'm on my way, baby," her mother whispered, then quickly hung up.

After two hours, she was convinced that her mother wasn't coming. Visiting hours ended at ten o'clock and her contractions still hadn't started.

Luanne finally came down the hallway and found her room.

"Mom! What took you so long?" Janelle asked.

"I didn't have money for a cab. I had to take the bus."

"Where's dad?"

Luanne simply shook her head.

She let out a sigh. "Okay."

"Where's the doctor? How are you feeling?" Luanne asked.

As if she were summoned, Doctor Timmons walked in and introduced herself. "You must be Janelle's mother. It's nice to finally meet you. Let me tell you where we are, because it's going to be a long weekend."

After leaving the branch, Tommy took the train to Astoria where his mother was supporting a friend having a gallery art show. He got off the N-train and walked downstairs from the elevated subway tracks at 30th Avenue and 31st Street. Astoria was always confusing to Tommy, because the neighborhood had a street, an avenue, a drive, and a road all with the same number. After walking down a few blocks he found the art studio his mother told him she would be at.

As soon as he walked in, Tommy immediately felt underdressed. On any other day, his slacks and turtleneck would have let him blend in, but on this occasion, he was the only man *not* wearing a suit. He thought about turning around and waiting outside when Maureen spotted him.

"Hey! I'm so glad you came! Come, come, let me introduce you…"

"Geez, mom… Why didn't you tell me this was a fancy-type event?" Tommy fidgeted.

"Obviously you've never attended a gallery opening before. Think nothing of it, they'll probably think you're some incredibly rich play-boy, staying low-key…" she scoffed.

They maneuvered through the crowd and stopped in front of a short, stout, elderly white woman with thin eyebrows.

"Judy, this is my son, Tommy," Maureen introduced. "Tommy, meet Judy Thorne."

She turned and looked up. "My, my, I see you share your mother's gargantuan statue…"

"Uh, yeah," he said.

"Well, your mother has an exquisite eye for taste. She helped me pick what to display and they're selling like hotcakes."

"Wow, great to hear that." Tommy looked around and thought each piece was more hideous than the last. "Um, will you excuse us?" He politely nudged his mother into an empty room to speak privately.

"So, what did you want to talk about?" Maureen asked.

"First off, all this art looks like a kindergarten student painted them."

"Art is relative, Tommy. Rich people pay insane amounts for it because they have nothing else to spend their money on. They buy these paintings then sell them in five or six years when the price goes up."

He shook his head. "Okay, second, where are you and dad on the holidays this year?"

"We did Thanksgiving last year, so I figured we had Christmas."

"Well, Sarah's leaning toward switching up. Nothing's set in stone yet, but I was wondering if you could soften the blow with dad and talk—"

Maureen held up her hand. "Say no more, whatever Sarah and her parents decide, we'll take the other holiday... You *will* give us one or the other, right? They're not taking both?"

"No, no, no... we'll definitely split it, don't worry. I just don't know which one she wants yet. She might be leaning toward Christmas."

"Well, that's fine. We just want to spoil our cute granddaughter rotten," Maureen said, with a smile.

Tommy relaxed. "Thanks for understanding, Mom. I think I'll duck out through the back. These yuppies make me nervous."

"Hey, there's nothing wrong with wanting to improve your social circles. You could learn a thing or two from these people."

He snorted, "not likely," and headed toward the exit.

Gerry drove the Celica to JBA Auto Repair in Brooklyn on Saturday morning. Blue was in the passenger seat, chewing on a toothpick, while Denise was sitting in the back.

As they pulled up, Blue said, "Y'all better not be jerking me around this time."

Gerry stopped the car and took the key out of the ignition. "If the car checks out, you'll get your money today."

They all stepped out and Denise yelled, "Is Julio here?!"

"Qué?" an old man sitting on a chair replied.

Gerry shook his head. "Dónde está Julio?" he said to the elder, and then turned to Denise. "How you gonna come here saying you know this guy and you don't speak Spanish?"

She raised her middle finger at him as a young Hispanic gentleman wearing coveralls stepped out to greet them.

"Yeah?"

"You Julio?" Gerry asked.

"Nah, I'm Miguel. Julio's my brother. What can I do for you?"

"I called for Julio to inspect this car we're buying," Denise explained.

"Well, I can do it for you, but it'll take a couple of hours... and cost you $50.00."

"Julio would do it for free," Denise said.

"Why?!" Gerry asked, suddenly interested.

She dismissed him with a wave.

Miguel chuckled. "Yeah, my brother has his special friends, but I *ain't* my brother."

She looked over to Gerry and he gasped. "Wha...? Ugh, fine, but you're paying me back!" and grunted as he pulled out his wallet.

While the mechanic worked over the vehicle, Gerry, Denise and Blue went across the street to a Burger King. Blue ordered a soda while Gerry settled for an order of french fries, and Denise had a Whopper meal.

"So, you wanna tell me how you know Julio and why he'd check the car for free?" Gerry asked.

"No, I don't. Mind yours," she replied.

Blue laughed at the answer as Gerry pressed on. "Fine, I just hope he's old enough to drink at the bar, unlike your other 'friends,'" he said, with air quotes.

"My friends are none of your business." She finished her meal and stood. "C'mon, I think he's done by now."

Julio was waiting for them with Miguel when the trio returned. "Denise! Sorry I wasn't here when you came, had an emergency call."

"It's okay. Anything wrong with the car?" She asked.

Blue took a handkerchief from his jacket pocket and wiped his brow.

"It's a quart low on oil, brake pads are kinda thin and the carburetor could use a cleaning," Julio explained.

The two siblings looked at Blue, who gave a weak smile.

"I got some free pads I can give you but depending on if I need to replace the carburetor or not, it'll cost you $100.00 to get 'er good as new."

"Alright then, Blue…" Gerry began. "I think $2,900.00 for the car and we got ourselves a deal."

"C'mooon, man! You gonna shave $100.00 on a decent car that's worth—"

"Take it or leave it, Blue!" Denise barked.

He stared at them for over a minute, then threw his hands up in the air. "Fine! Gimme the money and let me get out of here. I got places to be!"

Gerry counted the money from his wad and placed it in a yellow envelope, pocketing the rest. Blue accepted the envelope and handed Gerry the title after signing it over.

"We have any problems registering it at the DMV, I'll be looking for you," Gerry warned.

Blue sucked in a breath with a snarl. "You know where to find me." He turned to leave. "Like you really gonna do something…" he mumbled, while walking away.

Gerry turned around and smiled. "Here you go, Julio!" He handed over the remaining hundred dollars. Denise bounced up and down with excitement. "I'm driving it home!" she cheered.

"Not without paying me my $50.00 you ain't!" Gerry replied.

"With Yi and Chavez at their big pow-wow this morning, it's nice and quiet here," Ethel said.

She was sitting in the chair next to the information desk as Zelda read the latest NYPL staff newsletter, noticing several promotions and employee achievements.

"Yes, they're still trying to be civil to each other… which of course is driving them crazy."

"Oh, of course…" Ethel replied, sharing a private laugh.

A minute went by, then Zelda asked, "You're going to miss it, aren't you? It's going to be so boring for you down there among the magnolias and peaches."

"As long as I have a porch, with a rocking chair and cold glass of lemonade to sip on, I'll be fine," Ethel replied.

"Sure."

Ethel chuckled again at the skeptic reply. "I just read this book that supposedly gave me an idea on how they live down there. Didn't help one bit, though."

"What was the name?"

She thought for a moment. "Uh, it had a long title, 'Midnight…' something."

"*Midnight in the Garden of Good and Evil?*"

"Yeah, that's it. Crazy book." Ethel grunted. "I ain't gonna miss this at all." She suddenly smiled. "I'm ready for that porch and the lemonade."

There was another moment between them, then Ethel asked, "When do you plan on hanging it up? You really wanna be one of those who they just find dead on a reference desk one day? Surrounded by periodicals and microfiche… dust, cobwebs covering you?"

Zelda lowered the newsletter. "I'm fine where I am in life. After this, I got nothing waiting for me. A timeshare in Miami I never use, no family. I suppose I could write my memoirs, but who the hell would read it?"

"That's kind of bleak, ain't it?"

"I suppose some might see it that way, but then I think of my aunt Matya and several of my cousins who were in Auschwitz."

Ethel noticed the pain in Zelda's eyes as she recalled the painful memory.

"They were only in their twenties when they died, and Matya was only 47. After everything we've gone through, to live a long full life in the face of so many who didn't... almost out of spite... that alone is the reward."

After a moment of deep thought, Ethel said, "I see what you mean. I'm going to miss these conversations, Zelda..."

"Well, you don't have to, you'll have a phone down there with your lemonade. You give me a call whenever you wanna talk, you hear?"

Ethel smiled. "You know what? I think I will."

They nodded in agreement.

The 96th Street Branch Library opened at ten in the morning on Saturdays, so the regional meeting of senior clerks and head librarians was scheduled for eight-thirty in the morning. Employees from the six libraries that formed the east side cluster arrived one by one.

Jessica Coons greeted Sonyai with a smile, as she opened the door and locked it behind her. They walked inside where there was an assortment of breakfast food and refreshments on a table near the staircase to the second floor.

"Good morning," Jessica greeted. "You take care of that problem of yours we talked about?"

"Yes," Sonyai replied, reaching for a styrofoam cup of orange juice. "He was back to active duties as of yesterday."

"Good to hear... the region was starting to get a bit pissed off sending help your way. I received a few complaints."

"I'm sure you gave them a proper response."

"Oh yes, the typical three-word statement that started with 'kiss' and ended with 'ass.'"

They shared a private chuckle. Sonyai then saw Andrew Friedman across the room talking to Salimah Gray, the senior clerk of the 67th Street Branch. She excused herself and walked toward her former protégé. Andrew finished his conversation and greeted Sonyai with a nod.

"Andrew, how are things at Webster?"

"They are going well. I'm getting the hang of being a mentor to my staff. Have you heard from Janelle?"

Sonyai nodded. "Yes, she's settling in just fine at Van Nest. She should be due any week now."

"Hey, that's great!" he cheered.

Augustus walked inside, being led by regional head librarian, Cleopheous Baker. Andrew noticed Augustus and Sonyai exchanging glances and asked, "You two alright?"

"We've moved on from our differences of the past and are working together for better things in the future." She didn't believe the lie from the moment it left her lips, but appearances are key in the eyes of your fellow peers. It was time to change the subject. "I'd like to thank you for distancing yourself from Miss Brown. I take it you haven't heard from her since the summer?"

He didn't flinch at the question, still looking forward to their date in two weeks. "Haven't given her another thought," he lied. "I've moved on."

"Good," she replied with a nod.

Andrew excused himself and walked past her. Looking back at her former protégé, Sonyai wanted to believe him, but she knew better.

"So, things have been quiet between you and Yi, eh?" Cleopheous asked Augustus. "Took you long enough to come to your senses."

The short white man stacked his plate with pieces of toast, bagels, and a muffin. Augustus poured himself a cup of coffee and took a sip. "We're being cordial, but there's still a long way to go."

They mingled among others who were arriving on the main floor then Augustus asked, "What do you know about this new branch they're talking about?"

"It'll be discussed today. Just hold your horses."

"I need to know where they're building it."

"The hell you care?"

Augustus thought for a moment before revealing his plan, but he knew Cleopheous wasn't the adventurous type with his money. "I'm looking to get in on the land deal. Is it true they're looking at the train yards for the location?"

"That's what I'm hearing. They need the space. Looking to make this facility bigger than The White House."

Cleopheous bit into a blueberry bagel, then looked up and asked, "Has anyone talked to you about the race for governor?"

"Huh? No, why?"

"There's talk about someone approaching individual employees for an endorsement, look out for it."

"DC37 is backing Cuomo for the easy re-election. This George Pataki fellow doesn't have a chance."

"Of course, but be on the lookout. We don't need any independent support for the Republicans. It's bad enough we have a Republican mayor now. A Republican up in Albany would make things worse."

"I couldn't agree more. Looks like they're ready to start," Augustus said with a nod, as they moved to the staircase leading upstairs.

The twelve attendees sat around a huge, rectangular table, with two on the ends and four on each long side. While Jessica took the minutes, Cleopheous started the meeting by asking for formal introductions, after which he addressed everyone.

"As you are aware, the New York Public Library will celebrate a hundred years with a year-long exhibition of events. Kicking things off with a gala at the Stephen A. Schwarzman building, also known as The Main Branch. Staff are encouraged to attend. The event will be on Saturday, May 20th. It is expected to be formal attire with men wearing black tie suits and women in evening gowns.

To commemorate the celebration, staff will be required to wear pins starting in January with the new proposed logo on them. The final design will be revealed in November with the issue of new library cards, that have also been redesigned with a spiffy new look, to take us into the 21st Century. Please notify branch staff that anyone not wearing a pin will be subjected to a fine of $25.00 and a reprimand will be put on their employee record. We're taking this centennial seriously folks. There will be checks done at random times in all the NYPL facilities.

And finally, I know there's been talk of a new branch the city is building, and I'll tell you what I know. It is affectionately known as 'SIBL,' which stands for The Science, Industry and Business Library."

There was a murmur of excitement among the table as people exchanged affirmative nods.

"This facility will be the fifth Central Library joining Mid-Manhattan. Donelle, The Library for Performing Arts, and The Andrew Heiskell Library for The Blind. While the location is still unknown, it is slated to open in 1996 and promises to be a resource dedicated to the technology of the future."

There was collective applause, then Cleopheous opened the floor for new discussions.

After the meeting concluded, Augustus stayed and talked with several other librarians until the branch opened. He browsed the collection of New Books, comparing them to 58th Street's collection, and then walked out. The bus stop for the M96 crosstown bus was across the street. He despised taking public transportation, but since Sonyai declined his offer, using a car service felt like a waste of money.

Augustus lived across the park on the west side at 96th Street and Columbus Avenue. It would be a quick fifteen-minute ride once the bus arrived. He sighed and checked his watch, tapping his foot impatiently.

"Excuse me?" a voice behind him called out.

In his annoyance, he didn't notice a gentleman had walked up to the bus stop to join him. The stranger was nearly his height, wearing a green jacket, a black turtleneck, and matching slacks. His gray hair was cut in a military-style buzz cut.

"Hey! Sneaking up on people can get you punched in this city!" Augustus yelled.

"My apologies, Mister Chavez. I was just wondering if I could have a moment of your time."

"Who are you? How do you know my name?"

"My name is Kenneth Szabo. I work for the campaign manager of George Pataki."

*My God, it's like Cleo spoke them into existence!* Augustus thought. "Sir, before you begin, I must inform you that as a library employee, I'm an active union member of DC37."

"I'm aware of their endorsement of Governor Cuomo, but if you would oblige me... Pataki has recently received support from very influential people, and we want you to know that he's looking to help minorities such as yourself."

"Oh really? How so?"

"I'd love to tell you more! Perhaps we can take the bus together and we can talk further."

Behind him, the approaching M96 was waiting down the street behind a red light.

"I'm afraid that would be a waste of your time. I have no intention of supporting a Republican who plans to defund our libraries. Have a good day, sir."

The bus pulled up and Augustus climbed on, dropping a token in the farebox. Kenneth stayed behind on the sidewalk as the doors closed in his face and the bus started out into traffic. After taking a seat, the head librarian pondered how he was found by the mysterious individual. It was as if he were being watched.

# CHAPTER FIVE

ANGIE AND HEYWOOD WERE EATING LUNCH TOGETHER IN THE STAFF room when Eugene walked in.

"Heeeeey guys! Nice to see you two talking again."

The security guard took a seat on the sofa and grabbed a leftover copy of *The New York Post*.

At the table the two exchanged smiles. "I wasn't really shutting Angie out. I just needed some time... to myself." Heywood explained.

"Luckily, I was patient enough before presenting him with my idea for a branch exhibit."

"Oh yeah?" Eugene gasped.

"I'm preparing an official proposal, but my computer at home has been acting up lately."

"Hey, speaking of computers, have you been hearing about this new branch they've been talking about?" Heywood asked.

Eugene opened the newspaper to the sports section.

"They've been talking about a fancy new library filled with computers for over a year. It probably won't open until the year 2000," Angie replied.

Heywood snickered. "Yeah."

After a few minutes of silence, Angie tilted her head and said, "I know it's none of our concern, but it's nice to see all the clerks working together again, including Robin."

"Quite honestly, aside from Gerry and Tommy, I could care less about them... *especially* Walker."

Eugene grunted in agreement.

Angie frowned. "Why? What has he done to you?"

"Nothing, he just comes off as... a bit of a dick, that's all."

Eugene let out a chuckle this time.

Angie turned to look at Heywood. "What are you basing that on? He hasn't exactly been welcomed with open arms here. Whatever reason Yi had to exclude him months ago, they've moved on."

Angie noticed Eugene was quiet again, then turned to him. "You have something to add from the peanut gallery?"

He shrugged. "All I'm saying is, you didn't need a security guard here again until *he* showed up."

Angie didn't say it, but she had a strong feeling Eugene and Heywood wouldn't have a problem with Robin if he wasn't African-American. As a minority herself, she knew prejudice when she saw it.

After breaking her water, Janelle was finally dilating. Luanne sat at her bedside, squeezing her daughter's hand and trying to comfort her.

"Just keep breathing, baby!"

"Mom, I am breathing. It's not time for pushing or anything... why are *you* hyperventilating more than me?"

"I'm sorry, I'm just... it's just... you're my baby and you're having a baby!!"

Luanne started crying hysterically.

"I'm so terrified for you! Your father's not gonna let you stay in our house, and you'll be out in the street!"

"Mooooooooom, you're not helping!" Janelle cried out.

The mother wiped her face, trying to gather her composure.

"You think you could um, step out in the hallway for a minute? Maybe catch your breath and calm down?"

Luanne nodded. "Okay... okay, Baby." She turned to walk out of the room.

"This... this is not working... I'm sorry, mom." Janelle let out a sigh. "Pass me the phone, I need to make one last call."

Sonyai and Robin were working the circulation desk a few minutes after four o'clock when the direct line to the senior clerk's desk rang from inside the clerical office. Sonyai stepped to the public line phone and transferred the incoming call, then picked up the receiver. "Hello?"

Robin was taking it all in on his second day of being back doing returns and not stamping cards. He noticed Zelda was looking back at him from the information desk, noticing how happy he was. They exchanged nods as a patron walked up and handed Robin a set of books to check back in.

"That was Janelle!" Sonyai gasped after hanging up. "She's been in the hospital since Thursday, the doctors have been trying to induce... she's having the baby!"

The pages popped their heads up at different locations on the floor. "Really?!" Alex squeaked.

Zelda shushed everyone from the information desk as the trio approached the front of the branch. With Ethel and Tommy gone for the day, Sonyai started to panic, her hand shaking the receiver on the phone. "She... she needs me there... I... don't know what to do!"

Robin shrugged while standing near his terminal. "Well, what are you waiting for? Go!"

She turned to him. "You'll be able to handle it here?" she asked. "Closing alone?"

"I'm going too!" Alex yelled. "Let me get my coat!" She rushed to the door upstairs. Sonyai looked at Robin as he waved his hand, then went inside the clerical office for her purse and jacket. Alex was back downstairs as Sonyai stepped around the circulation desk to the security threshold.

"You sure about this?" Sonyai asked one last time before leaving.

"Sure, it's Saturday! I'll be fine," he assured her.

Alex was next to her, pushing the door open. Sonyai wanted to thank him, but he waved her off a second time. The pair left the branch and hurried down the sidewalk to the nearest train station. Alone behind the desk, Robin nodded his head. "Leelee?"

Lakeshia gave him a puzzled look as he said, "I could use a hand here on checkouts," a sly grin on his face.

She looked over to Tanya who shrugged and whispered, "It's for Nellie. I'll do all the shelves."

Lakeshia then quickly walked around to join Robin as he worked the returns side.

"And Leelee?"

She turned back to him.

"Let's keep this between *us*, this time?" he winked at her.

Lakeshia blushed, then nodded with a smile.

The last hour was slow, even during the last ten minutes.

There wasn't much of a rush, but Robin still helped Lakeshia with some of the checkouts and they made quick work of the line. The last few patrons left the library and Zelda locked the door.

"You're getting better, kiddo," Robin praised Lakeshia.

"Thanks! That was fun!"

"Hey, think I can give it a try next time?" Tanya asked.

"Sure, as long as Sonyai doesn't find out," Robin replied with a grin.

Zelda approached the trio. "Mister Walker, not sure I approve of you having the pages work the circulation desk... but, seeing this was an emergency, I'm willing to overlook what occurred this evening."

She gave Robin a quick wink and then walked to the librarian's office to put on her coat.

"Hey, I feel like celebrating my first days back from working the bench these past few months. Whaddya say I treat you girls to some pizza?"

"Sure!" Lakeshia cheered.

"I'm down..."

Tanya smiled when she saw Lakeshia's disappointed look at the fact that they were *both* invited. They proceeded to get their coats and then leave the branch.

Augustus arrived at his apartment complex after a day of window shopping, browsing, and a few occasional guilty purchases. It was six o'clock and he was looking forward to finishing off the salsa de chicatana he had earlier, by putting them in a quesadilla.

He approached his building as a silhouette appeared behind him.

"Excuse me, Mister Chavez," a female voice called out.

*Christ, not now!* The librarian thought. He started to turn, thinking... *Another campaign—*

He stopped in mid-thought as a fair-skinned woman caught his gaze. She had long brown hair with highlights. Wearing a Christian Dior tuxedo wrap jacket and matching black pleated pants. Her dark eyes had a piercing stare that melted him like butter.

"If I may have a moment of your time," she requested.

"Why certainly," he replied, with a huge welcoming smile.

You couldn't tell from his composure, but inside he was whooping and hollering like a schoolboy.

"My name is Dea Ximenes, I believe you have an interest in our investment group."

Augustus was taken aback. This wasn't about the governor's election.

"How did you—?" he gasped.

"Your phone call ruffled a lot of feathers, but I was able to deter any snap decisions and humor your request... out of curiosity. So, I tracked you down."

She took a moment to move a strand of hair from her face. He was drawn to the power she emanated with every word she spoke.

"Interesting," he replied.

She nodded. "I would like to know why you wish to invest in our bid for commercial property in the areas of 34th Street."

"Your investment firm's reputation precedes itself," he replied. "I'm looking to expand my portfolio."

The visitor wasn't convinced. "There are other firms out there, what makes *us* so special?"

"Your tenacity for one, followed by your leadership, from where I stand."

He waved his arm toward the building's entrance. "Why don't we take this conversation inside, where you can pick my brain in private?" *Among other things.*

"I don't think so. If you want in on our bid, I need to know what insider information you have."

"Before I tell you anything, how much would I need to invest in order to get in?"

"$2,500.00."

"Ridiculous. I know on good authority that the rest of your group put up $1,000.00 each."

She sighed. "I came here on a courtesy, but I see I've wasted my time."

"Alright! I'll tell you what I know."

She nodded.

"Once I meet the rest of the group," he finished.

"They're a hard sell. I'm only here because of a curiosity. Our investors are all rich powerful white men, who believe *we* should be emptying the trash and sweeping the floors."

"Well, how did you get in?"

"Working twice as hard to do half of what they're doing, then doing more. I am only the third Hispanic in our group and the *only* woman."

"Out of what? 25 members?"

"20," she corrected. "You need to be really convincing if you want to be lucky 21."

Augustus smiled. "I've charmed over 50 individuals in a room countless times. Put me in front of them and watch me work."

She thought about it for a moment. "The stories were true... you *are* confident."

Augustus chuckled. "Whatever you've heard doesn't begin to scratch the surface."

"Okay, you better not come off too overconfident. These guys can smell a bullshit salesman miles away." She handed him a card. "Monday, 11 am sharp. You better be ready."

After placing it in his hand, she turned and walked up the street.

Augustus watched her walk away until she turned the corner, then looked down at the card and brought it up to his nose for a deep whiff. He would not rest until he found out what perfume she was wearing.

Franklin emerged from the 1-train Lincoln Center station and climbed another set of steps to the Library for Performing Arts branch. It was a few minutes before six o'clock, when the branch would close, and he stared inside through the glass wall revealing the interior.

One particular staff member caught his eye, as he continued to stare from a distance.

She was of average height, no more than five-foot-nine, dark curly hair, and pale skin. Wearing black trousers that cut off at the calf, with a purple blouse. The mysterious library clerk made her way throughout the floor turning off both terminals and then heading toward the exit.

Franklin sensed that the woman was leaving and afraid of being seen lurking, he took off to a nearby pillar by the reflection pool. Hiding in the shadows, he wasn't seen as she left.

Rosanna Comanos left the branch as a librarian locked the door behind her. She looked around for a moment, feeling like someone was watching her for some strange reason. It had been fifteen months since she learned of Robin's death, and she had a feeling that his spirit was watching over her. As crazy as that sounded, she still had problems coping with his loss.

Even now, as she maneuvered through the system, from one branch to the next, she felt unfulfilled, unable to commit to just one single library. With no commitments, she felt obligated to not get involved personally with staff anymore. Which would be harder, especially with the upcoming holiday. It would just be too hard to lose someone again.

When she was certain there wasn't anyone around, she walked toward Broadway and caught a cab heading uptown.

Franklin came out of the shadows and cursed himself when he saw Rosanna quickly get away. He hoped she would take the train.

The Yorkville Library was one of the few branches that was open later on Saturdays, closing at seven o'clock. Ethel rarely clustered to other libraries in the area, but Yorkville was her preferred location, because it gave her the chance to sleep in and work the late shift.

Upstairs on the second floor was the children's section, which closed an hour before the main floor did. Several clerks came down the steps and Ethel's friend, Claude Robinson, walked over to greet her behind the circulation desk.

"Hey, Miss Lady, wha'cha thinking about?" Claude greeted.

Ethel sighed. "As I'm coming up on retiring, I'm looking back at my 20 plus years doing this job and I can't help wondering... if I made a difference?"

"What? We make a difference every day in people's lives. Someone here could be the next leader of the free world 20-30 years from now," Claude said.

"Yeah, we wanna believe that, but who knows the odds of running into someone—"

A woman brought her son down the steps and noticed Ethel behind the desk, then slowly approached the clerk.

"Excuse me? Um, did you work at the Mosholu Library around 12 years ago?"

Ethel was taken aback by the question and answered with a questionable, "Yes…"

A smile came across her face. "Oh my God, I remember you! I was 16 when you caught me stealing library CD's and threatened to call my mother!"

Ethel laughed. "Yeah!" She snapped her fingers. "Betty... something, you always wore your hair short back then, you little tomboy you. How have you been?"

"Marlowe... Betty Marlowe, but it's Betty Quirke, now. I'm fine, but I'll tell ya, you put the fear of God in me! After letting me go, I swore to never steal anything again. I was so scared that phone call was coming, you don't know! I wanna thank you for changing my life! Can I hug you?"

Ethel looked back at Claude who just shrugged. "Um, sure, let me come around."

Betty was taller now, and she brought her arms around the clerk.

"I know it's silly, but I owe you everything. I'm married, I have a son... this is Eli." She turned and waved to the child standing near a bookcase. "You're an inspiration. I always wanted to thank you if I saw you again."

"You... you're welcome," Ethel said with a nod.

Betty went back and picked up her son. As Ethel walked back behind the desk, the clerk heard her whisper to her son, "You see that nice lady over there? She caught mommy in a bad situation and found it in her heart to forgive her..."

Ethel smiled as Claude walked over to her. "Still think you didn't make a difference?" he asked.

Robin, Lakeshia, and Tanya walked in a narrow pizza restaurant, a few blocks from the library on 56th Street between Lexington and Park Avenue.

"How'd you find this hole in the wall?" Tanya asked, with her nose twisted up.

"Yeah, let's just go to McDonald's on 3rd Avenue," Lakeshia pleaded.

"I know it's not much, but the pizza's pretty decent here."

Looking around, Lakeshia did notice they were the only ones there. It gave her an idea to make a move on Robin by letting her hand slip.

They approached the high counter, which under a glass display had an assortment of specialty pizzas and other Italian delicacies.

"Let me get two to stay, not too hot, and a can of Sprite." Robin then turned to the girls and asked, "What y'all want?"

"I'll just have a Sicilian," Lakeshia replied.

"No soda?"

She shook her head. "Nah."

"Tanya?"

"I'll take a slice with pepperoni and a Jamaican Beef Patty, with a Pepsi."

Robin completed the order and pulled out a twenty from his wallet. "Keep the change!"

Lakeshia led Tanya to a booth in the corner while Robin stayed at the counter. They took opposite seats and waited.

"You could have *politely* declined, you know?" Lakeshia hissed.

"And miss out on the fun?" Tanya laughed. "You really think he would have only taken you? So, you could play *Kissy-Face?*" she mocked her by puckering and smacking her lips.

Lakeshia growled, then noticed Robin approaching with two plastic trays. When he got to the booth, he cleared his throat. "Leelee, switch over and sit next to Tanya."

She looked up at him, crestfallen.

Robin noticed and added, "Please."

She obliged him as he placed the trays on the table and took a seat opposite of the pair. A raised eyebrow appeared on his face at the shy girl's attempt to sit next to him.

Lakeshia nibbled on her rectangular thick-crust pizza, while Robin and Tanya folded and bit into their slices.

After a few minutes, Robin asked, "You think she's having a girl or a boy?"

"Who?" Lakeshia asked.

"Nelly!" Tanya exclaimed, rolling her eyes. "She wanted to be surprised, so we don't know."

"Well, I hope all goes alright. Despite what she thinks of me, I wish no ill-will toward her. Let her have the baby and live happily ever after."

"You mean that?" Tanya asked.

Robin shrugged. "Yeah. Look, I held out for a branch that was close to the college downtown. When I put in for a clerical position after graduating, they were trying to send me north to Inwood, Spuyten, Duyvil... working in Manhattan branches is a privilege, well, south of 110th Street, anyways. My point being, I didn't wake up one morning, throw a dart on a map to 58th Street and say *I'm gonna fuck up Janelle Simms' life by taking her clerical position, Muhahahahaaa!...* I should have had a fair chance to prove myself to y'all and that didn't happen."

The two girls looked at each other and felt a tinge of guilt.

"These past few months stamping cards, I almost thought about quitting. I didn't wanna go out like that. Now that I've been given a second chance and Janelle's moved on, I'm not trying to get in any more trouble."

They ate quietly after his speech, then Robin walked the girls back to the branch. Lakeshia's older brother, Derrick was waiting with his car to drive her home.

"Sorry for holding her up, I felt like celebrating."

"No problem, she called before leaving to give me the heads up."

After the siblings left, Robin turned to Tanya. "I'll walk you to the train station."

"I'll be alright."

"I insist."

Tanya sighed. "Fine."

They walked together up the street toward Lexington.

Sonyai and Alex arrived at Montefiore Hospital and found Leanne in the lobby, buying a Coke from the vending machine.

"Miss Simms, we came as soon as Janelle called. How is she?" Sonyai asked.

"She's been asking for you," Leanne began. "More than her own mother…" she shook her head in shame.

Sonyai put her hand on Leanne's shoulder. "She's scared. It doesn't mean she doesn't need you."

Leanne gave them Janelle's room number and the three of them walked to the nearest elevator.

When Alex walked in with Sonyai, she froze. Despite leaving 58th Street back in July, she met up with Janelle a few times over the summer. She wanted to organize a baby shower for her close friend, but Janelle was too busy adjusting to her new position at Van Nest.

The sight of the former page, her stomach twice the size than she remembered, eyes full of panic, with sweat pouring down her face… it gave Alex pause. Now, Janelle looked crazed, exhausted beyond comprehension, and in an insufferable amount of pain.

Sonyai rushed to the side of the bed as Janelle looked up, smiled, and extended her hand. "Miss Yi! I'm so glad you're here."

Tears fell down Janelle's cheeks as Sonyai grabbed her hand and attempted to calm her. "It's going to be okay," Sonyai whispered.

"I'm scared… I'm so scared, I can't…"

"I know, I know… nothing could prepare you for what you're feeling, you have to be strong."

Alex finally gathered the nerve to approach. "Nellie," was all she could get out.

Janelle was about to acknowledge Alex when suddenly she let out a moan that got louder. Sonyai clenched her jaw as she felt pressure on the hand that Janelle was squeezing, then joined her, letting out a loud wail from the pain.

The contraction passed and Janelle sighed. "Sorry… they've been coming every eight minutes."

Sonyai pulled her hand back and rubbed it thoroughly. "It… it's okay."

Despite visiting hours being over, the doctors let Leanne, Alex, and Sonyai stay overnight into Sunday. Alex helped pass the time talking about the latest episodes of *Beverly Hills 90210, Martin,* and a new show that recently premiered called *New York Undercover*. Sonyai attempted to keep Janelle calm and encouraged her.

They tried to contact Avery again and still heard nothing about his whereabouts. "Why can't men give birth to babies?" Janelle gasped. "I'd pay good money to see that asshole Robin push a big head through his balls!"

Alex couldn't resist a laugh. "Yeah, that would be funny as hell."

After a moment Janelle looked at her. "Alex…"

"Huh?"

"Whatever you do, and I can't stress this enough… Don't. Have. Sex." Janelle shook her head furiously. "It's not worth it, no matter what they say, no matter what they do… no matter how big their dick is, dammit don't do it before you're ready. Take it from me."

The intensity in Janelle's eyes scared her. Alex knew she was speaking from emotion but maybe she was right. Apprehension was taking a hold of her, and she wondered if she could contain her chastity.

Doctor Timmons came in. "Okay, you're at ten centimeters… it's time to push."

"Wait! Do we—"

"Ah, ah, ah… this is it, don't worry, it'll be over in no time."

Alex took a step back as Sonyai took Janelle's hand again. "I'm here, just breathe." she instructed.

"Okay, I need you to take one deep breath… and hold it."

Janelle sucked in a gasp of air.

"I want you to start pushing and I'm gonna count to five… Go."

She buckled down and started a long grunt. "Nnnngggghhhhh…"

"One… two… three… that's it, that's it… keep going… four… five… and stop! Take a breath."

Sonyai noticed Janelle didn't squeeze too hard this time.

"Okay, we're going to do this two more times… we should be able to see something soon."

"*TWO* more times?" Janelle gasped.

"I know it sounds like a lot…"

"It *IS!*"

"Just take another breath, you can do it, now... c'mon," Heather coached.

Janelle fought back tears and took a breath.

Two times led to two more, then another. For forty minutes, Janelle felt like she was pushing to her limits of sanity.

A certain stench overcame the room. Alex suddenly gagged as she held her nose while covering her mouth.

Sonyai turned her head and whispered, "Oh dear..."

Janelle felt uneasy. "Wha...?"

Heather quickly dismissed it. "That's just the unpleasantness, nothing to worry about." She began to apply some wet towels to clean her up.

A puzzled Janelle was wondering what the doctor meant, then screamed, "OH MY GOD!"

It was Sunday morning, around five o'clock. Nearly three days since her appointment and being under observation, then going through the induced labor. Janelle wasn't even sure if her mother was still in the hospital. The baby was finally crowning, and she was running on an empty gas tank.

*Just kill me now and get it over with!*

"Okay... One. Last. Push. This is it. You're doing great..." Timmons encouraged.

"How can you be so fucking cheerful at a time like this you bitch?!"

Sonyai gasped at the outburst, while Timmons nonchalantly replied, "I'm just going to *ignore* that last remark and chalk it up to your emotions... Now, I'm going to count, and you're going to push!"

Janelle balled up all her rage as she took a breath, she waved Sonyai's hand off and grabbed both sides of the hospital bed guards. Tapping into her last bit of strength, filled her lungs with a gasp of air and let out the primal scream of a lifetime.

"Two... three... that's it, THAT'S IT! Here it comes!"

"EWWWW!!!!" Alex screamed.

Heather cut the umbilical cord and cleaned the newborn as it let out a loud wail.

"It's a boy!" Sonyai cheered, the emotion dam finally breaking as tears streaked down her freckled cheeks.

Janelle collapsed in the bed, lying motionless and staring up to the ceiling. "A boy..." she whispered. Heather placed the baby on her chest. "There you go..." she cooed. "Welcome to the world, little boy... here's your mama."

Janelle looked down and embraced her infant for the first time. "Ohhhh... he's beautiful." She looked around the room. "Where's my mother?"

Alex ducked to the hallway, checking both directions. "She's not here," she replied, after stepping back in.

"It's late," Sonyai said. "She probably was tired and went back home."

Heather stepped forward. "Well, let's give the baby some time to warm up and get weighed, measured, start the paperwork... and give you time to rest!"

Janelle sighed. "Yes..." and began to close her eyes as Heather accepted the newborn.

"Do you want me to call the father?" Sonyai asked discreetly.

"Yes. Hopefully, he and mom can come tomorrow..."

"You mean, later today," she corrected.

"Oh, yeah..." she looked up at Sonyai with a weak smile. "I never could have done this without you. Thank you."

"You were strong. I'm so proud of you... rest now, we'll talk later."

Sonyai stepped away from the bed as Janelle nodded to sleep. She was taken back to a tragic memory...

*September 1984*

*The couple was driving frantically out of the city.*

*Hurricane Diana was forecasted days ago, but then a shift changed its direction and brought it in the path of Miami, and residents were forced to evacuate.*

*Sonyai was five months pregnant and her fiancé, Steven, drove the car as fast as he could while rain poured down. They were almost there, after driving north through Georgia, then South Carolina. They* were 50 miles outside Charlotte, North Carolina... when the car started to stall.

"No, no, no, no!" he yelled. "Don't give out on me, now!"

They were on I-77 with Fort Mill behind them, unable to turn around.

"Oh my God, what are we going to do, Steven?" Sonyai asked.

"Stay here, let me check the car, maybe I can get it running again. Don't worry, I'll take care of this."

Steven Gao stepped out of the car and lifted the hood. Sonyai tried to relax, but her anxiety was through the roof.

Twenty minutes went by, and the rain was getting worse. Steven tried to wave someone down for help, but the few cars that passed them wouldn't stop. Steven came to the passenger window next to Sonyai.

"The car's dead. We need to walk. We can find a hotel somewhere. They'll take us in."

His voice was trying to stay calm, but Sonyai could always sense when Steven was afraid, and this was one of those times. They took their luggage from the truck and started walking.

They passed the state line and were walking west off the road through fields of deserted land, when Steven spotted an isolated house on the horizon. "There!" he pointed. "We can make it!"

The winds were picking up and the rain was blowing in all directions. As they approached, the front door opened and a man appeared.

"What are y'all doing here?" he asked.

"Our car broke down. Can you please help us with shelter?" Sonyai pleaded.

The man waved them over before she finished the question. "C'mon!"

Sonyai and Steven made it inside and the man closed his door again.

"I was just about to nail these boards to the door when I saw you out the window," the man said, as he reinforced the door with several wooden planks.

"Thank you, sir," Steven said with a breath. "My fiancé and I were *heading to Charlotte when they said on the radio the storm was upgraded to a Category Four."*

*"Well, we should be safe here. Name's Hank Rainey, how are ya?" he extended his hand.*

*"I'm Steven Gao, this is Sonyai Yi." Steven shook his hand.*

*The man raised an eyebrow as he noticed Sonyai holding her stomach. "Am I to assume you are with child, young lady?"*

*She blushed while looking down. "I am, sir."*

*"But she's nowhere near due!" Steven assured the man with a smile.*

*The man smiled back. "Well alright, you can have a seat and your husband-to-be can help with the windows," he said with a nod.*

*Sonyai walked to the couch while Steven followed Hank.*

*Several hours went by. It became really dark, and the storm had become more intense. Every once in a while the house would shake.*

*"Um, you sure we'll be okay?" Steven asked.*

*"This house has been here withstanding hurricanes for forty years. We'll be fine."*

*Suddenly there was a loud crash, and the house shook.*

*They looked out the windows and saw a funnel cloud slowly forming and heading toward them.*

*"Whoa," Steven whispered.*

*Sonyai gasped and Hank yelled, "Head for the bathroom! Now!"*

*The house started to shake again. The couple moved to the back of the house down a hallway and found the bathroom.*

*"The bathtub! I heard that's where you're supposed to hide in the middle of a storm. Lie down and curl into a ball!" Steven yelled.*

*There was another crash followed by a scream. The roof had collapsed.*

*"What about you!?" Sonyai asked.*

*"I'll protect you, just get down, now!"*

*The house started to tear apart as the two huddled in the bathtub. Steven lay on top of Sonyai as they closed their eyes and braced for the worst. Within minutes the storm passed on and the house that withstood forty years of storms... was destroyed.*

*Sonyai opened her eyes finally. She was afraid to move. A trickle of water was in the tub as she shifted her weight to look up.*

*"Steven?" she called out.*

*He didn't move.*

*"Steven, get up. Steven please, I can't move."*

*The body rested on top of her, motionless.*

*"Steven...?"*

*She shook him and noticed his arm fell limp. Concerned, she sat up and shook him again. "Steven... Steven! Oh, dear God!"*

*Part of the house had come down on him. His neck had been broken. He died instantly. The corpse covered her for as long as it could, even after it cost him his life. The one isolated corner had been spared, but the rest of the house was a total loss. Sonyai slowly pushed Steven's body off her and noticed the water in the tub... wasn't water.*

*It was blood.*

*She heard a helicopter in the distance. The ear-piercing scream that followed was how they found her.*

Tears were coming down her face again, as Alex looked on with a puzzled glance.

"Miss Yi? Are you crying?"

"Oh!" she gasped, brought back to the present from the memory. Surprised by the attention, she wiped her face with her hand. "Um, just... some tears of joy, Alex, tears of joy." She gathered herself, and said, "We better get going... it's a good thing tomorrow's Columbus Day. Schools and libraries are closed."

"Yeah, you can say that again!" Alex agreed.

# CHAPTER SIX

BECAUSE OF THE FEDERAL HOLIDAY, MOST OF THE BANKS AND OFFICE buildings were closed, as Augustus made his way through the financial district. He had on his best cream three-piece suit and complemented it with a powder blue tie. With finishing touches to his pencil-thin mustache and a clean shaved head, the head librarian was ready to dominate the investment group that previously rejected him.

The address on the card was at 127 Williams Street near the South Street Seaport, Suite 913. He took a cab and arrived at ten-thirty. He had plenty of time to get ready. There was a deli next to the building, so he went in and bought a bottle of water. After refreshing his throat, Augustus entered the lobby and checked with the security desk. He was asked to sign in a logbook and then directed to the elevators.

On the ninth floor, Augustus walked down a hallway and found Suite 913. The office was very small. There weren't any seats in the reception area. Just another desk, where a young white man with glasses greeted him.

"May I help you, sir?"

"Yes, Augustus Chavez. I have an appointment for eleven o'clock."

The receptionist checked his book and then stood up. "Right this way, sir."

Augustus followed the gentleman down another hallway, where he saw Dea Ximenes waiting for him, outside the entrance to the conference room. They exchanged formalities and the receptionist returned to his desk.

"Everyone's inside. I hope you're ready."

He smiled and took a moment to admire her current outfit, another stunning business suit, and said, "They'll be putty in my hands." He wanted to add an invitation for her to lunch but held his tongue. *One thing at a time.*

They waited a few minutes, then at the top of the hour, she walked in first to introduce him. At the mention of his name, Augustus entered the room and closed the door behind him. Twenty sets of eyes focused on him.

"Good morning, ladies and gentlemen, and thank you for giving me the opportunity to speak at your distinguished investment group. I believe we have an opportunity to help each other and make a *lot* of money together."

In fifteen minutes, he presented his plan to buy land in the yards and sell it to the city, once the proposed plans to build The Science, Industry, and Business Library was in place. He assured them that the site was the place they would pick, and they could keep their anonymity with nothing tracing back to them after the sale was complete. The budget the city had set aside for the project meant they could charge three times what the land is worth now, resulting in a sizable profit on their part.

Augustus took several questions from the group, and he could tell they were impressed with him.

One man sat on the opposite side of the table. He wore a pinstripe suit, with gray hair that was balding. He stood up. "You have given us an excellent proposal, Mister Chavez. And despite our early objections, I think I speak for everyone when I say we would be honored to welcome you in our private group."

He smiled with a modest nod.

"For a buy-in price of $5,000.00."

His smile disappeared. "I beg your pardon?"

The man shrugged. "You can understand that we would need some extra assurance of your knowledge that the land deal will go the way you predicted, and we believe that double the initial buy-in each of us had to contribute would alleviate any doubts we might have. Surely you can afford it, right?"

He cleared his throat and looked in the direction of Dea, who didn't return his glance.

*These bastards are fleecing me!* he thought. *Alright, I'll up the ante.* "Of course. As a matter of fact, to show how serious I am in this deal and to dissipate any doubts you might still have, I will invest $10,000.00."

There were wide glances exchanged among the group. At the head of the table, the gray-haired man sat back down and leaned back. "Well, once the check clears, you will be the 21st member of The Langston Investment Group. Congratulations, Mister Chavez. We're very happy to have you on board."

Augustus adjusted the knot on his tie. "Indeed."

The meeting adjourned and he shook hands with everyone. When Dea came forward, she whispered something in his ear and then left the room. He pulled out his checkbook and wrote a check for ten thousand dollars. When the investment group left, only one man remained behind. Donald Langston looked into the head librarian's eyes with a stare that could cut through concrete.

"I hope you know what you're doing. I warned you on the phone, if the S.E.C. finds us out, I'll see to it you, and *only* you, do time."

Augustus matched his gaze. Upon a closer look at the man, his gray hair looked silver. He wondered if the man dyed his hair to appear older. His features were a bit confusing. "This isn't my first deal. I'll take the precautions."

Donald accepted the check and Augustus walked out of the room, leaving the mysterious individual alone with his ten thousand dollars.

When he walked out of the building downstairs, Augustus heard Dea say, "I wouldn't have done that."

He turned to find her leaning against the wall with her arms crossed. "We each put in at least a thousand dollars, and then you show us up by putting in ten times that much? They're still going to second guess every step you take."

"I know. It's all part of the plan. Are you free for lunch?"

"I might be." She gave him a coy look. "Depending on where you had in mind."

"I know people at Sweets Restaurant. They have broiled scallops to die for." He extended his hand.

She looked down at it then nodded with her chin, refusing his hand. "Lead the way."

He started walking and she followed, a few steps behind him.

Janelle opened her eyes after eight hours of undisturbed rest. She had several dreams of growing up with her son. Helping him take his first steps, walking with him on the first day of kindergarten. There were two people in her hospital room. She focused as the figures took shape and Avery looked back with a wide smile on his face. His mother, Evelyn was sitting in a chair, staring at her first grandchild on her lap.

"Hey, Beautiful," Avery greeted.

She smiled back and whispered, "Where the *fuck* were you?" The question rolled out of her mouth in a way that didn't sound angry, due to the fact that she was still out of it.

Avery gave a sheepish look. "Mom took me up to Binghamton University on a recruitment trip. We just got back this morning and headed over here after hearing your message."

"I'm *so* gonna kill you when I become conscious," she said softly, and fell back to sleep.

"I know, I know, I'm sorry." He couldn't stop smiling, then looked back at his mother, still holding the infant.

"Let her sleep, boy. She's been through a lot."

He came over and looked at his mother holding their child. "Who do you think he looks like?"

"I see a little bit of both of you. Her nose, your eyes. He definitely has your ears," Evelyn said, then looked up at her son. "You're going to take care of this child... you hear me?"

Avery nodded. "I am, mom. I swear."

"You love this girl? Is she the one you gonna marry?" Evelyn asked.

The boy remained silent, unable to answer those questions.

She saw the fear in his eyes and just shook her head. If he couldn't answer, then this child's life was going to be very complicated.

Alex walked inside the staff room Tuesday afternoon at two-thirty. She was shocked to see Tanya and Lakeshia waiting, eager to hear about Janelle's delivery.

"Whoa," she gasped.

"Did she have the baby? Was it a boy or a girl?" Lakeshia squeaked.

Alex gave a weak smile, still exhausted, and haunted, by the experience.

"She had a boy, uh, six pounds, two ounces, I think... 18 inches long. She was in labor until five in the morning Sunday!"

Alex plopped in the middle of the couch as the two girls sat down on opposite sides.

"Wow, was her mom there? With Miss Yi?" Tanya asked.

Alex shook her head. "She went back home. We were there all weekend. I kept nodding off. I was barely able to function at school today. Slept all day Monday, then woke up wide awake at like 2 am this morning."

She looked at each of them. "It was *crazy*."

"It was?" Lakeshia asked.

Alex whispered something in Tanya's ear. She flinched and grunted. "Gross!"

"What?!" Lakeshia yelled.

"She shit herself!"

All three let out a disgusted, "EWWWWW!"

"She told me never to have sex," Alex began. "Saying it's not worth it... I almost believe her."

"I don't!" Tanya barked. "Shiiiiit! As long as they wrap it up, I needs me some dick!"

Lakeshia shook her head, as Alex turned up her nose at her sex fiend co-worker.

Tanya looked back at them. "Don't worry, you'll find out! Don't be judging me!"

"When did you get back, Ernie?"

Ethel was sitting in a Chinese restaurant on 145th Street and Amsterdam Avenue, a few blocks from where she lived. Her older sister, Ernabelle, was sitting opposite from her in a booth. The sisters had just ordered and were waiting for their food.

"I've been here for a few days. I'm just signing a few more papers and updating my will. Making sure everyone's taken care of and the house goes to you next."

Ethel was unsettled at the idea of her sister passing before her, especially with her current health condition. "Is there something I don't know about? Since when are you worrying about the end?"

"I'm fine," Ernabelle replied. "I've just seen families tear each other apart from misinterpretations of final wishes."

"Okay... so why are we here, about to eat this slop that'll make us hungry an hour later?" Ethel asked.

"We caught a break. The water heater got fixed and the insulation got installed without a hitch. All the bathrooms are done. A new paint job and we're ready for the inspectors. We pass and get the paperwork done, the house will be ready on the first."

Ernabelle leaned back with a smirk.

"I better not hear a 'told you so'. That look on your face is enough."

"I ain't rubbin' it in. I'm just letting you know so you can pick the room farthest from me."

Ethel rolled her eyes. "Fine, I'll take the second bedroom facing the extension. You can have the room on the opposite side with the sunroof. You circled that room three times. I know you want it."

The elder sister nodded. "Elisse wanted that second bedroom, too."

"I know, but that first bedroom has a view of the backyard. She plants her garden and she'll get over it."

Their food arrived and they started eating.

"Ethel?"

"Mmm?"

"It's gonna work out, Sis... told you so," she said with a smile.

Janelle stepped out of the cab as it dropped her off on Saint Nicholas Avenue at one o'clock. She checked out of the hospital at ten o'clock that morning and couldn't help being happy that it was also her eighteenth birthday today. Avery and her mother insisted Simon would spend the first few nights out of the hospital at his place. Janelle had no objections to the request.

Evelyn opened the door and let Janelle inside.

"Thank you for this. My parents didn't visit me once in the hospital after the baby was born, so I'm not sure how they'll react."

"It's no trouble at all. Take all the time you need."

Janelle looked at Simon sitting in a swing chair then back at Evelyn. "Um... I couldn't help noticing you requested the hospital do a paternity test."

Evelyn blinked hard. "I said I would. I don't know why you're surprised."

"Well, maybe it was for your own assurance, but I can definitely swear that he's Avery's."

She shrugged. "I'm just dotting my I's and crossing my T's."

"Right... okay. I'll call tonight and be back in a few days."

They started back to the door and Evelyn said, "I hope you have a plan young lady because it's not going to get any easier from here on."

Janelle was frightened but put on a brave face. "I... I'll be alright."

Evelyn didn't believe her, but didn't say anything either, as she left the apartment.

The Celica turned the corner and came down the street. Gerry stopped at a car wash that morning and then pulled up to Denise's house. He honked the horn twice and waited. With the day off to work on Saturday, the siblings decided to take a drive out of the city. Denise was willing to pay for gas money to swing out and stop at a mall. He checked his watch, waited two minutes, and then honked again. The door opened and Denise stepped out, walking across the sidewalk to the car.

"About time!" he grunted.

She opened the door and slid into the backseat. Gerry turned and looked at her. "What are you doing?" he asked.

"What?"

"Sit up here in the front seat. I'm not driving you around like a chauffeur... do I *look* like Morgan Freeman?!"

"The only time I sit up front is when *I'm* driving!" Denise explained.

"Since when!?"

"Since always!"

"If you don't get your ass in this front seat," Gerry yelled, "we ain't going nowhere!"

"The only way I'm sitting up front is if *you* pay for gas your damn self!"

"We had a deal!" Gerry barked. "I'll kick you out and drive off without you!"

"I'd like to see you try!" Denise snarled back.

The two stared each other down. Gerry cursed under his breath, turned around, and put the car in drive. Denise gave a stern nod and pulled a twenty-dollar bill from her purse.

"We're going to Jersey. It's gonna be $25.00," Gerry said.

"I'll give you five on our way back."

Gerry mumbled something his sister didn't hear, then drove in silence.

They were two minutes out from the Holland Tunnel when the car started to sputter.

"Uh oh," Gerry whispered.

"What's that noise?" Denise asked.

"I don't know... I wanted to head over to downtown Jersey City, but we better stop at Newport instead. There I can see what's wrong."

"Good, there's a mall there. It's right up ahead."

*You and your damn malls,* Gerry thought. *Probably knows the location of every shopping mall in the tri-state area... can sense them like radar!*

He turned onto Washington Boulevard and stopped near the PATH train's Pavonia/Newport station. Denise climbed out of the car, looking around as Gerry walked over to the hood.

"You know what the hell you're doing?" she asked.

"I'm sure the engine is just a little overheated." He tapped the hood quickly to test if it was hot, then craned his neck around. "Do me a favor and get the—"

Denise stepped forward, holding a pair of leather work gloves in front of her.

"Uh, yeah... those. Thank you!" he said sharply, as he put them on.

"I knew this was going to happen. I'm going to kick Blue's ass!" Denise hissed.

"I thought your boyfriend, Julio, was a good mechanic! He obviously missed something!" Gerry replied.

"He's NOT my boyfriend! And he didn't even check the car, his brother did! Shaddup!" she had enough of her brother's attitude. "I'm going inside to window shop. You better not leave me!"

Denise walked across the street, heading toward the entrance to the Newport Shopping Centre.

"Always with the window shopping..." Gerry mumbled to himself.

Several minutes went by while he looked over the engine, then he felt as if someone was behind him, somehow. He turned to see a pair of thick eyeglasses looking back at him.

Gerry let out a gasp as a tall, balding, middle-aged white man said to him, "Having a bit of car trouble, huh?"

At seven foot, two inches, Gerry wasn't used to looking up at someone, but the stranger in front of him had to be nearly five inches taller. He was built like one of those American Gladiators Gerry saw on television.

"Uh, yeah, but I got it under control," Gerry replied.

"Haven't seen you around these parts. You from the city?" the man asked, as he looked Gerry up and down.

There seemed something odd about the person to Gerry. Especially the fact that he appeared out of nowhere and no one else was around but them.

"Just uh, passing through…" sweat started to appear on his brow. "Don't want no trouble."

"If it's overheated, I always find putting it in neutral, and then revving the engine a little, helps cool it down."

"I think that might work. I'll consider it." Gerry slammed down the hood and quickly walked to the driver's side of the car as the man stood back. He started the car and changed the gear, then pressed on the gas a few times.

"Sounds like it's all better!" the stranger called out.

Gerry put on a fake smile and waved. "Thanks! I'll be moving on, now!"

"Okay!"

Gerry pulled out back into the street, circled the mall, and found the parking structure behind the facility. After parking, he walked across the elevated glass hallway that led into Sears. He eventually found Denise at the food court. She noticed he was a little unnerved.

"What's wrong with you?"

"Nothing," he answered, while sitting down. "Can I have a sip of that soda?" He grabbed the cup before she could answer.

He could have been overreacting, or his paranoia could have saved his life from a hostile encounter. The stranger's friendly manner could have been harmless, but sometimes, as a black man, Gerry couldn't help being nervous.

Angie was in the study hall after her American Literature class. She wanted to get a head start on her thesis about the revolutionary period before going home. A heavyset woman caught her attention from across the room.

"Angie! Hey, I've been looking everywhere for you!" Olivia Morris said. "You've done some radio before, right?"

Olivia worked as the station manager for Queens College's local radio station, WQMC 1290.

"Hey Liv. Um, yeah, during the late 70's... early 80's. It's been a while, why?"

"An evening slot opened up. In two weeks, we'll need someone to fill in 'till the end of the year. It's just two months, think you can handle it?" she asked.

Angie shrugged. "Sure, as long as it doesn't interfere with my studies."

"Are you familiar with this type of setup? Normally I'd have some other on-air talent step in but this time of year everybody's unavailable."

"You have a producer?" Angie asked.

"Yes, real laid-back guy. He'll work the calls and promos. All you have to do is play the music with some personality, have a real good stage presence."

"Stage presence?"

"Well, you know what I mean. Radio presence, I guess. First night's on Tuesday, two weeks from now. Um... we can only pay scale."

Angie gave Olivia a look.

"Buuuuut, I can compensate you other ways. Radio giveaways, a few sponsor perks. I'll take care of you."

She sighed. "Two months, that's it."

"Thank you. It'll be fun, you'll see. It's a two-hour show at 8 pm on Tuesday and Thursday nights."

"Well, that's great because I sometimes work late on Wednesdays and classes keep me busy as it is, but I only have one 40-minute class that starts at 6:45 pm on Wednesdays and Fridays."

Olivia put her palms together in front of her and bowed slightly. "Thank you so much, Angie. I really appreciate it. I'm keeping this station's schedule together with duct tape and paper clips at this point!"

"No problem."

"Well, I'll leave you to your studies. Thanks again!"

Angie waved as Olivia walked away. She wondered if she could handle the task, but secretly felt excited to do something related to music again.

It was the end of the day, and Augustus was celebrating his victory over the investors, when Heywood knocked and stepped inside the office.

"You wanted to see me, sir?"

"Yes Learner, please take a seat." Augustus gestured.

Heywood sat down as Augustus leaned back. "There's been an emergency and the 67th Street Branch will be short an IA on Saturdays the next two months. You'll cluster over there on November 12th and 26th... then December 10th and the 24th."

"Those are both holiday weekends, sir!"

"I understand. That's why I felt obligated to tell you way in advance. If it makes you feel better, Miss Trueblood will also be doing several weekends. Perhaps you can switch with her."

"Yeah, right," Heywood sighed.

"Well, speaking of the holidays, do you have any suggestions for presentation events? I'm fresh out of ideas."

Heywood thought about Angie's idea, but it wasn't related to any of the holidays, and she still didn't submit an official proposal. "I'm drawing a blank at the moment sir, but I'll have some ideas soon."

"Very well then. We're done here."

"Yes, sir." Heywood nodded. He stood up and walked out of the office.

Zelda stepped inside, catching the door just as it was about to close behind Heywood.

"I heard you're full of good news, today," she greeted him, taking a seat in front of her corner desk.

"I had them eating out of the palm of my hand Monday!" Augustus exclaimed, with a grin.

"Indeed." Zelda adjusted her glasses and nodded.

"They haven't made the buy yet, but they're going to need more information before I can sway them to grab that land in the yards. You need to help me find out this... SIBL's proposed site the city will build it on."

"What are you planning?"

"Well, if they are going to build it out there, we'll buy the land first, and triple the price to sell it to the city."

"Wouldn't they be using your information as a form of insider trading?"

"Hmmm, that's all in the perspective of things," he replied, with a shrug.

Zelda let out a playful chuckle. "Ho, ho... you are playing with fire, here."

"Don't worry, I know what I'm doing. Just let me know if you hear any further developments."

He gave her a lingering look. She looked back and asked, "What?"

"I was waiting for you to say some obscure Shakespeare quote as a warning."

"Once the opportunity is completed, it'll come to me... don't worry." She smiled back.

"So, have you thought more about the holidays, Hon?" Tommy asked.

Sarah was in the kitchen preparing dinner, while he and Carrie were watching *Barney & Friends* on PBS. Tommy had the baby on his lap as she laughed at the characters on the television.

"Yes, I know you've been waiting for an answer, and I've been talking to mom. She's kinda leaning toward doing Thanksgiving out in Long Island and having your folks over."

Tommy sighed. "Okay, you know that's what we did last year when we announced you were a few weeks pregnant."

She turned to him from the range as he added, "We're supposed to be alternating... it's their turn."

Sarah looked into her husband's eyes. She knew he was going to do the sad puppy dog look. "Okay, let me sweeten the pot..." she always had an ace up her sleeve. "We do Thanksgiving out there in Long Island..."

Tommy smiled.

"...if *your* parents come with us out to Puerto Rico for Christmas."

The smile disappeared from his face. *Oh, holy shit.* "I... I'll see what they say."

In the five years the couple had been married, Sarah's parents have tried to do a family holiday in Acindina's hometown of Patillas, Puerto Rico. They once tried to convince them to go there for their honeymoon instead of the Poconos.

"It would be wonderful to get out of the cold city for a nice warm Christmas. Carrie's first, baby!"

All Tommy could think of was his father in swim trunks, yelling at the top of his lungs from the beach. "You might be onto something. I'll talk to mom, and she'll talk to dad about it. They'll love doing the first Thanksgiving with Carrie... that sound good, sweetie?" He playfully kissed the baby's cheek.

Sarah turned back around to finish dinner as concern came over Tommy's face.

It was a long train ride back home to The Bronx for Janelle, but she was relieved to have some free time to herself, without Simon, to figure out her next move. As she walked down the hallway to her apartment, she noticed something was in front of her door. Several trash bags tied up.

Janelle opened one of the bags and noticed it had all her clothes and belongings. Panic shook her entire body and she pulled out her house keys from her pants. The key she normally used on the bottom lock wouldn't fit. She noticed in horror that the locks had been changed.

"Mom!?" she called out, then started pounding on the door. "Mom! Mom, open the door!"

There was no response.

Janelle swallowed hard and called out weakly, "Daddy? Daddy please, don't do this…"

Inside the apartment, Leanne sat on the couch looking at the door. Chester had moved his easy chair to block the entrance and was sitting quietly while reading the paper. His daughter's cries from the other side did not faze him one bit.

After pounding on the door and screaming for over fifteen minutes, neighbors in other apartments started poking their heads out into the hallway. It was only a matter of time before someone called the police to report a disturbance.

She grabbed her trash bags and stormed out of the building. With nowhere else to go, and no idea of what to do next, Janelle walked north to a nearby park to collect her thoughts.

*I can't believe he really did this! And mom let him!*

She thought about friends or other family members she could stay with. It was a short list. With just sixty dollars in her purse, there was only one person she could turn to. After checking her watch, Janelle walked to the nearest bus stop for the Bx10 bus heading to Co-Op City.

# CHAPTER SEVEN

TANYA WAS SITTING ON THE COUCH, WATCHING TELEVISION. SHE WAS playing with some chewing gum, wrapping the wad around her finger while stretching it from her mouth. Her mother was working another double shift at the hospital, leaving her bored... and horny.

Before she could start fantasizing about Franklin, the phone rang and snapped her away from her wandering thoughts.

"'ello?"

"Wassup, Brownie?"

"Hoooooly shit, Andy! You couldn't have called at a better time!" Tanya breathed. Her nipples became engorged immediately and she fought the urge to slip her left hand in her panties.

"Oh yeah? You home alone? Wha'cha wearing right now?" his voice suddenly became deeper and that hand of hers went wandering.

"I'm wearing that white tee-shirt you gave me..." she lied. She was actually wearing a sweatshirt but began kicking off the matching sweatpants from her legs.

"What else? Imagine me sitting right there in that bedroom, girl... show me what you can do."

"Ooooooh, I'm stretching my legs nice and wide in front of you,"

Tanya teased. "My pink panties peeking underneath the shirt. No bra on so you can see my nipples poking up."

*I bet you're rubbin' that dick of yours.*

She heard him let out a low moan, confirming her suspicions, and continued, "I'm laying back, staring up at the ceiling, hips are swinging. My hand is moving down my stomach… passing my waist."

"Fuuuuuuuck," Andrew hissed over the phone.

"I'm rubbing my clit, baby… imagining it's your tongue."

All she heard from the receiver now was some quick panting. She could only guess what he was doing, but she was pretty sure he was on the edge.

"I'm going in… how many fingers? One? Two?"

"Two baby, two!" he gasped. "Say my name, tell me whose is it?"

Tanya bit her lip. "Yours baby, it's all yours…" she let out a moan. "Aaaaaandy, ugh! Aaaaaaandy, Aaaaaaandy!"

"Yeah, yeah, yeah! Fuck, baby! Give it to me, give it to me, baby!"

Tanya let out a loud gasp as she engaged in self-pleasure, thrashing repeatedly on the bed.

The couple finished their session. There was silence in the room and on the line.

"You come?" she whispered.

"Did I ever, damn," he replied. "You better clean up before your mom gets home." He let out a soft laugh.

"Thank you, Andy… I needed that release."

"Anytime, Brownie. I'm here for you."

"Don't you get any ideas. We still ain't doing nothing next Friday but having a nice dinner date to talk."

"Of course. Wouldn't expect anything other than that."

She could imagine the grin on his face after hearing the reply.

There was another moment of silence.

"Andy?"

"Yeah?"

"Just seeing if you were still there." Tanya giggled. "It's nice to hear you breathe."

"It's nice to hear you, too."

"You gonna hang up?" she asked.

"Yeah," Andrew replied. Then a moment went by. "*YOU* gonna hang up?"

They both laughed.

Tanya bit her lip and wiped a tear from her eye. She loved him so much it was scary. He wouldn't break her heart again… would he?

"Hanging up, now… for real." he announced.

"Okay."

She drifted off to sleep, not knowing if he hung up or she did.

Janelle didn't know when Sonyai would be home after working today so she waited until seven in the evening to try to contact her. She didn't want to show up at her doorstep unannounced, so she found a payphone and called her first.

"Hello?" an unknown female voice answered.

Janelle was thrown off, believing she dialed the wrong number. "Um, uh… is… there a Miss Sonyai Yi there?"

There was a moment of silence over the line, then she thought she heard someone whispering in another language.

Sonyai then came on the phone. "Hello?" She asked.

Janelle let out a sigh of relief. "Oh, Miss Yi! It's Janelle! Thank God you answered! They did it, they actually did it, Miss Yi! My parents changed the locks and kicked me out of the house! Simon is at Avery's, and I don't know what to do!" she was trying not to cry, but panic was taking over.

Sonyai cursed in Japanese, then muttered something to herself. "Where are you now?"

"I'm down the street from you on the corner of Co-Op Boulevard. I took the bus over and have been waiting for hours for you to get home."

"Stay there. I'll be there in twenty minutes."

The call ended and Janelle looked around… it was getting dark.

When Sonyai finally came to the corner, Janelle was thrown off by her appearance. She was wearing sweatpants and a hooded sweatshirt as if she were going to a boxing match at a local gym.

At the sight of the bags, she shook her head and looked down. "Unbelievable. Your mother actually let your father do this? He couldn't wait, could he? Not even a day."

"I don't know what I'm going to do. I'm on leave from the library for five weeks. The baby can't stay at Avery's, and I need time to find a place of my own."

"I'll try and help in any way I can," Sonyai said.

"Can I stay with you?" Janelle pleaded.

Sonyai looked like she had just seen a ghost. "I... I'm sorry, I... have a roommate."

Janelle's face fell as the senior clerk pulled out a wad of money from her pocket. "There's a motel on the other side of the complex, on Boston Road. Here's $200.00 for the next few days."

Janelle looked at the money in Sonyai's hand, then shook her head and held up her hand. "Oh no, I can't take that."

"I insist, and I'll pay for a cab to take you there. Come, let's go."

The pair arrived at the motel a few minutes after eight. Sonyai helped Janelle book a room until Saturday, but she didn't stay too long. Once she was alone, Janelle wondered how she could take care of Simon in such a place. The bed looked unclean, and the television barely worked. Within an hour of settling in, she started hearing loud thumping noises from the thin walls. Followed by moans and grunts of women and men.

An unbearable feeling of dread came from the pit of her stomach as Janelle sat on the floor against the side of the bed, hugging her knees in front of her.

Thursday morning, Heywood decided to take his mind off clustering during the holidays by going to his local church. He walked in a few minutes after nine o'clock in the morning, making his way to sit at a pew in a middle row.

After reaching for a bible from the slot in front of him, Heywood turned to a random page and began to read quietly. He felt better once he finished studying and made some quiet prayers, then stood up to see Father Gabriel Adams making his rounds. The priest greeted him with a smile.

"Good morning! It's nice to see you here today."

Heywood nodded back. "Good morning, Father. I needed a moment to myself. A lot's been going on lately."

"The Lord tests us in various ways… what seems to be the trouble, my son?"

"I feel slighted at work. I… I try to take some assertiveness, come up with new ideas and I keep getting shot down. What do you do when you're not being appreciated at work?"

"Job worked many labors for little recognition himself, you know."

"Times like this I ask, 'What would my father do in a situation like this?' and I think, but can't come up with anything."

"You've mentioned in the past how you seek to escape his shadow and try to find your own identity, yet look to him for guidance, still. Interesting."

"I just want a fair shot. I sense a certain bias against me, and I just want to know why?"

"The best way to prove yourself and invalidate those who doubt you is to work hard until you are vindicated. Your day will come."

"I really hope so." Heywood smiled. "I'll see you on Sunday."

"Looking forward to it."

"I'm so glad to hear Robin has been relieved from his punishment," Barbara told Zelda over the phone.

The assistant librarian was sitting at Augustus' desk in his office. As a sign of respect, she usually sat at her smaller desk that faced the right wall, but when it came to personal calls, she indulged herself.

His leather chair *was* softer than the wiry chair she had.

"He's stubborn when he believes he's right. Something *you* could relate to," Zelda replied, with a thin smile.

"He just better not get into any more trouble. My patience is wearing thin. So, to what do I owe this social call, old friend?"

"It was announced recently that a new facility is in the works."

"The Science, Industry and Business Library? You looking ahead to a new position?"

Zelda chuckled. "Oh, I could never leave 58th Street. I'll retire here! I just want to know where they're planning to build it."

"The city is exploring several locations," Barbara answered. "Only a select few are big enough for what they have in store. They're exploring The Yards, Chelsea, Murray Hill... it's definitely going to be somewhere in the 30's, east or west. Groundbreaking won't be until after the centennial, with hopes it'll be completed around 1997."

"Okay, out of curiosity, who are they looking for with the staff? I'm sure they have some candidates."

Barbara hesitated for a moment. "I almost thought they would come to me, but naturally I would politely decline. There are a few others on the shortlist. As for the senior clerk, I heard Mary Latzke at Ottendorfer is getting it."

"'Scary' Mary?" Zelda exclaimed. "Well, she has the seniority."

Barbara grunted. "She's priming her successor now, with hopes of them taking the Senior Clerk Seminar in the spring."

Zelda nodded to herself as Barbara continued. "The city is preparing to usher in the information age with this facility. We're talking personal computer rentals, televisions airing the news all day, personal spaces that can be used for meetings by the public... even a stock ticketer. It's destined to rival Penn Station."

"Indeed."

"You realize this is the beginning of the end for us."

"There you go again, Babs," Zelda scoffed.

"I'm serious! And what did I tell you about calling me—"

"Look, the World Wide Web may come along and make our jobs easier one day, but we will *always* be needed."

"Always the optimist," Barbara said. "The only consolation I have is I won't live to see us become obsolete."

"And on that note, I'll end this call and order you a bouquet of flowers."

"You do that, I'll make sure someone throws rotten fruit at your window tonight."

She hung up the phone before hearing Zelda's snort of contempt.

It was the last hour of the day Saturday and Gerry was working the returns at the circulation desk with Tommy when he asked, "How's the new car handling?"

Gerry turned back to him with a smile. "She purrs like a kitten. Took her out to Newport last week… had some fun at the mall." He didn't mention the unpleasant incident of getting it repaired and being humiliated by his sister.

"Nice. Can't tell you the last time I was out there… can't tell you the last time I had fun, either," Tommy said with a grunt.

"Wha'cha moping about now?" Gerry asked.

"First Thanksgiving with the baby is coming up. Parents from both sides are staking their claims."

"Oh, that. Yeah, well… what did you and Sarah do before?"

"We alternated. '89 we went to her parent's place, '90 was out in Long Island and my folks, etcetera, etcetera…"

"Which means this year it's *your* parents' turn, right?"

Tommy nodded.

"Hey, fair is fair."

"Right, and her parents are accepting that, but…"

"But?" Gerry asked.

"Whoever goes to the others' house hosts the next holiday. If Sarah's parents go out to Long Island for Thanksgiving, my parents come to the city for Christmas, and vice versa," Tommy explained. "Only this year… her parents want to go to Puerto Rico for Christmas."

"Wow."

"Yeah."

"Don't think your parents are the type that go to the beach or drinks Medalla Light." Gerry chuckled.

"They haven't traveled outside the United States since the 60's."

"Puerto Rico's a commonwealth. Still part of the states, man."

Tommy shrugged and worked a few checkouts. It was approaching the top of the hour when things died down again. Gerry noticed something else was eating Tommy up inside. "Anything else bothering you?"

He looked down and sighed, then nodded his head for Gerry to come closer. "You ever think about having kids?"

"Not now, but when I meet that right woman… yeah, sure."

"What if something happened and," Tommy whispered, "you had to *choose*?"

"Choose? Choose between what?"

Tommy turned his head, looking around. "What I'm telling you, stays between us, man… seriously."

"Yeah, you got it, no doubt," Gerry answered quickly.

He saw Tommy's whole demeanor change as if he was about to bare his soul. "There were complications during the birth… it was touch-and-go there… the doctor made me make a choice. Either Sarah was going to lose the baby, or she wouldn't make it and the baby would."

Gerry's eyes faltered, understanding what he was saying. "They both survived, though."

"I know." Tommy's eyes started to turn red. "I know, I know… I keep telling myself, it was God… he saved them both… but I… I told them to save Sarah. I couldn't bear to live without her." He fought back the tears. "What does that say about the baby?"

"You can't think like that," Gerry said. "Have you talked about this with Sarah?"

Tommy shook his head rapidly. "No. The doctor told me never to tell her, to take that shit to the grave." He turned to Gerry. "I had to tell someone, it was killing me. Burning a hole in my gut."

"Hey, hey…" Gerry whispered. "I'm here for you." He patted Tommy's shoulder as they both nodded.

"We'll talk about this more over drinks," Gerry said, and the two stepped apart from each other.

Alex left the branch fifteen minutes after five o'clock. There was a car parked in the street waiting for her. The driver saw the teenager walking toward her and started the car. Alex was about to pull the door handle open when a voice called out behind her.

"Nellie?" she said, and turned to see Janelle approaching, pushing a baby stroller and carrying several bags.

"Oh my God! You brought the baby?" Alex ran up to the stroller and noticed it was filled with more garbage bags.

"I left Simon with Avery for a few days," she gasped. The panic in her voice frightened Alex, taking her back to the hospital room when Janelle was in labor. "Alex, they kicked me out! Daddy kicked me out of the house! Miss Yi gave me money for a motel room, but it's full of hookers and drug addicts! I'm homeless!"

Alex didn't know what to say. She turned back and asked the driver to open the trunk.

"C'mon!" She waved for Janelle to the back of the car.

Moments later the two girls were in the backseat.

"I… I don't know what I'm going to do," Janelle whispered, looking down.

"Can't you talk to them?" Alex asked. "They probably did this to scare you. They'll let you come back after a few days…"

"It's been a few days, they're serious!" Janelle looked up. "You think I could stay with you?"

Up front, the driver turned his head slightly and raised an eyebrow.

Alex tried to think of a way to approach her parents to ask. "I don't know, Nellie. What if I give you some money so you can go to a better place?"

"I don't need money! I have money! I need a place to stay!"

It was becoming too much to handle, and Janelle started to cry.

Alex felt so guilty. There was no way she could sneak Janelle in her house without her parents knowing.

"Nellie, I know it's hard, but let me help you get to a better place—"

"Forget it! Stop the car, please? Stop the car!"

The driver found the nearest corner and hit the brakes.

"Open the trunk!" Janelle yelled and opened the door to step out.

Alex called out, "Nellie, wait!"

"Forget it! Everyone wants to help me until I actually have this baby, then I'm on my own!" she took out her belongings from the trunk and then slammed it shut.

Alex stepped out for a second, but Janelle was already walking from the corner without looking back. Suddenly a car honked its horn and she noticed they were blocking traffic. She looked back at Janelle then sighed and returned to the backseat. The car started again and pulled away from the crosswalk.

It was beginning to rain, when Augustus arrived home at seven-thirty in the evening. He took off his suit jacket and began to relax. After pouring himself a glass of brandy, he picked up his phone and dialed Dea Ximenes' number, then took a seat as it rang.

"Yes?" she answered.

"Good evening," he purred, in an octave deeper voice.

"Augustus…" she said in a coy voice. "So nice to hear from you."

"Well, I just wanted to follow up after a lovely lunch and inquire when can we expect to make the official land purchase?"

"Patience. Once we confirm the site of the proposed branch will indeed be the yards, we'll put in the bid to buy. We should easily acquire the property under the radar of anyone else."

"Excellent."

There was a pause between them, and then Dea said, "Uh, I, um… I have a rule, about getting involved with—"

"I understand completely. I wouldn't want anyone to suspect any impropriety. But someone as sophisticated as yourself, I just feel we can both benefit from a particular friendship. I have other capital ideas that you may be interested in."

She was in deep thought on the call as Augustus waited patiently for her to take the bait. He knew this approach would work. Had he been forward with his advances, she would have shut him down instantly. But being hesitant and playing coy... they both knew what they were doing.

"I suppose a mere *friendship* wouldn't hurt, provided we keep things professional," Dea conceded.

"I wouldn't have it any other way," he replied, with the smile of a shark.

"Good, as long as we understand each other. May I suggest dinner, then? Say, Saturday evening at eight?"

"Works for me. I'll see you then."

He hung up the phone and finished his drink. "Like the spider to the fly..." he whispered.

Robin was in the lobby of his building, checking the mail. The bills were getting paid, but he was still concerned about what to do when Jon's inheritance ran out. He had no clue how much he was waiting to receive anyway.

Across from him, a few people were standing in front of the trio of elevators. Robin saw his grand-aunt, Jon's sister Esmerelda Hodge, walking up to an elevator that was arriving. It had been a while since he spoke to any of his distant relatives. As his grandfather's oldest sister, she was the family matriarch who lived on the twenty-fifth floor of the high-rise apartment complex.

The door opened and Robin waved to get her attention. "Hey, Esme! Hey!"

He hurried across the lobby and called out again, "Hold the elevator! Hey!"

There was no reaction as the doors closed in front of him. Robin was certain she heard him, unless she suddenly suffered some kind of hearing loss. *Could it be possible that she just ignored him?* He thought.

*Why on earth would she do that?*

Another elevator opened up, and Robin took it to the sixteenth floor. He was walking down the hallway and noticed someone was in front of his door. She was a skinny white girl. 18-years-old with blond curly hair and wearing jeans with an oversized tee-shirt.

Robin approached slowly and squinted. "Liz?"

"Hey, Robin!" she called out. "My mother sent me up here to ask if you had two eggs for a cake."

"Um, sure, I think I still have some eggs, come on in," he said, and unlocked the door.

Elizabeth Blake and her mother Charlotte were Robin's downstairs neighbors who lived in 15D. When Robin and Jon first moved in, she would hear Robin running and jumping around the apartment and hit the ceiling complaining. The woman would still call occasionally whenever he played his music too loud. Charlotte's husband passed away when Elizabeth was nine and the two have been taking care of each other ever since.

Robin let Elizabeth in, and she gasped at the pigsty that was his apartment.

"Um, excuse the mess. I've been kinda busy lately."

"My goodness, it looks like a tornado came through here! Don't you ever clean this place?"

"Of course I do. Granddaddy raised me right, but I've just been falling behind a bit."

"Hmmm, sure..." she looked around. "You're one of the few tenants in this building that has their own washer and dryer in your apartment instead of going to the laundromat downstairs on the second floor. But look at all these clothes on the floor!"

Robin was in the kitchen. "I take my stuff to the dry cleaners and wash my underwear by hand... I don't think these machines even work. That damn dryer was so loud and the buzzer that goes off when it's done will give you a heart attack!" He found a carton that had three eggs in the refrigerator and brought it to the living room.

"Here ya go. You can keep the extra one. I won't be using them," he said, handing the carton to Elizabeth.

"You dry clean *all* your clothes?" she asked him.

"Yeah. It's just a few outfits a week, then I mix and match."

"Alright. I'm going to take this downstairs for my mother, and then we're both going to come back here and show you how to keep this place neat and *stop wasting money* on dry cleaning!"

Robin opened his mouth to protest, but Elizabeth was already out the door.

Just when he believed they weren't coming, the doorbell rang an hour later.

*Awww fuck! Maybe if I don't answer they'll go away.*

"C'mon Robin! Quit ignoring us, we're not going away!" he heard Charlotte yell.

He rolled his eyes and dragged his feet to the door. When he opened it and saw both women he started to explain, "Look, I appreciate your concern but—"

"No buts, mister!" Charlotte said, while walking inside. "When my daughter told me you were living in squalor, I finished cooking that cake and put it in the fridge because this was serious! First thing I'm going to teach you is how to do laundry!"

"C'mon! I got schoolwork!" he protested.

They both looked around. "Where? I don't see any books," Charlotte asked.

He looked at her and she cut him off again. "Nice try!"

Elizabeth grabbed a brown laundry basket and started picking up clothes, as Charlotte took Robin to the washing machine in the kitchen.

"First thing you do is turn the machine to the load size after you set the temperature." She flicked the switch to cold and turned the dial to a large load. The machine filled up with water.

"Now you separate the colors from the whites. Don't mix clothes with towels or washcloths... are you listening?" Charlotte asked.

"Yes, yes! Go on..." he waved.

She proceeded to teach Robin all the aspects of doing laundry.

"After you put the fabric softener in on the second cycle you let it finish, then put everything in the dryer. Don't overstuff it, and make sure nothing is in knots. For underwear and clothes, set it to 30 to 45 minutes, but heavier stuff like blankets or towels have to be in there longer, like an hour, hour and a half."

He nodded.

"Okay, now we're going to show you how to wash dishes..."

"Hey! I know how to do dishes. This is enough. I'll do my own laundry now, okay? No more dry cleaning. Now, you and Liz have been very helpful but it's time to go, okay?"

Robin gently pushed the ladies to his front door and opened it. "Thank you for all your help, really..."

Elizabeth walked out first, but Charlotte warned Robin as she followed her daughter. "I'll be checking on you!"

"I'm sure you will!" he said, and slammed the door. He turned and leaned back, then slid down to sit on the floor. With a long sigh, he looked up to the heavens, exasperated.

"You sent her to make sure I was doing alright, didn't you, Grand-daddy?" Robin asked.

Tanya emerged from the train station and walked in a neighborhood bodega for three small bags of Doritos. Fox and CBS both had movie features tonight and she was looking forward to watching *Sleeping with the Enemy,* rather than *Stop! Or My Mom Will Shoot.* As she approached her building, Tanya recognized Janelle waiting for her at the entrance.

"Nellie! Hey girl! How ya' doing? What's all this?" Tanya gestured to her bags surrounding her stroller.

"Hey Tee, I..." Janelle sighed and looked down. "My parents kicked me out of the house."

"Oh shit," Tanya whispered. "With the baby and everything?"

"Yeah. I've been going around town, Miss Yi gave me some money for a motel, but..." she looked up with pleading eyes. "I just need a place to stay for tonight. I'm going back to drop Simon off at Avery's for a few more days, then look for an apartment the rest of the week."

Tanya rolled her eyes. Her mother wasn't due home until eleven o'clock tonight, and she'll probably check on her then go to bed.

"Alright, but you have to be quiet. Maybe you can spend the night if my moms doesn't hear you."

She took out her house keys and unlocked the door to the lobby. "Come on in."

Once inside Tanya's apartment, Janelle took off Simon's coat and checked his diaper. Tanya took the garbage bags and the stroller to her room and hid them in a closet. When she came back to the living room, she saw Janelle eating one of her bags of chips and gave her a look.

"Sorry, I was kinda hungry."

Tanya walked over to the refrigerator and poured her a cup of Kool-Aid. They talked for a few hours, then at eight o'clock, Tanya turned on the television.

"Hey there's a new episode of *Full House* on, can we watch?" Janelle asked.

"Uh, we're watching this lame ass Stalone movie until 9 pm, then it's *Sleeping with the Enemy*." *I kinda feel like I'm in that Jennifer Jason Leigh movie, Single White Female instead!* she thought.

Janelle smiled meekly and held her palms up. "My bad."

Simon fell asleep on a blanket in Tanya's room as the girls sat in the living room. An hour into the movie at ten o'clock there was a rattling from the door of a key entering the lock.

"Shit! Mom must have got off early!" Tanya hissed. She turned the television off with the remote and waved to Janelle. "Quick! Go in my room and hide in the closet."

Janelle ran across the room to the hallway, with Tanya right behind her. The apartment door opened, and Cynthia Brown shuffled her way inside. In the bedroom, Tanya stripped and put on a T-shirt, then slipped into her bed, pulling the covers over her.

Cynthia hung up her coat and checked the mail left on the coffee table. The living room was quiet... *too quiet.*

She walked over and felt the television. When it was warm, she walked to Tanya's bedroom.

"Tanya! You ain't slick. That TV's been on in the last hour and you're not snoring... get up!"

The teenager pretended to stir and pushed up on her elbow. "Huh?" she moaned.

"What did I tell you about staying up on a school night? Do I have to—"

Cynthia stopped after hearing something that sounded like a baby fussing. Inside the closet, Janelle tried to quietly cradle Simon back to sleep.

"What was that?" Cynthia asked.

"What was what, mama?"

Simon started to wail as footsteps approached the closet and the door flew open.

"What the hell?!"

Janelle was ashamed to look up, so she put on her best smile first. "Um, hi, Mrs. Brown."

"It's *Ms.* And what are you doing in my daughter's closet with a baby, young lady?"

Tanya sat up and explained, "Mom, this is my friend from work, Janelle. She graduated and transferred to another branch. Her parents kicked her out when she had her baby. Can she stay the night, please?"

Cynthia turned to her daughter and waved her arm. "Let's talk in the living room. Now."

Tanya followed her mother. Cynthia turned and asked her daughter, "Did you really think this would work? That I wouldn't notice a baby crying in the closet?"

"I'm sorry! She had nowhere else to go!"

"Do you have her phone number? I want to talk to her parents."

"It'll do you no good, Ms. Brown," Janelle said, walking in the room dressed and carrying her bags. "They won't pick up, and even if you called them this time of night, they'd curse you out."

She started pushing the carriage toward the door. "I'm sorry I bothered you and got Tanya in trouble. I'll find another motel for the night."

Cynthia walked over to cut Janelle off. "No, you can stay the night," she said, as the two girls sighed in relief.

"You can sleep in Tanya's bed. *She'll* be sleeping on the couch."

"Hey!" Tanya cried out.

"You mean it?" Janelle asked. "Thank you, thank you so very much!"

Cynthia nodded, then reached for her purse near the coat rack. She fished out a business card and handed it to Janelle.

"What's this?" Janelle asked.

"It's the location of a woman's shelter," Cynthia replied. "Which is where you should have went to in the *first* place."

# CHAPTER EIGHT

ROBIN WAS SCHEDULED TO WORK THE LATE NIGHT, SO HE SLEPT IN FOR once, then headed to 23rd Street at Baruch College to register for classes. It felt good for him to be back on campus. He missed the beginning of the fall semester in the wake of his grandfather's death. The lines for eight-week classes were shorter, but the selection was very thin.

"All these classes are full," the registrar clerk told him.

"Look, I'm only trying to get two classes, and I gave you five different combinations!"

"Everything started back in September! And you're trying to sign up for day classes. Those go quick! Sign up for a night class."

"Night classes start at 6 pm or later. I work in the afternoon!"

"I don't know what to tell ya. Look, you got two more minutes and then I got to take the next student! You're holding up the line, here!"

"Alright, alright, um, how about HED 1917, Nutrition and Health, in this new building on 25th Street?"

The registrar opened the undergraduate bulletin to see the class Robin was referencing, then checked the computer. "You're in luck, three slots left."

"Okay! I'll take it."

"Sign here."

Robin skimmed the paperwork. "Hey! Financial aid doesn't cover the books!?"

"It's too late for the Pell book advance… a minute left!"

Robin shook his head and signed the registration papers.

"Okay, class is on Tuesdays and Thursdays from 7:45 pm till 9 pm, starting on October 25th, for eight weeks. With a break for Thanksgiving, ending on Thursday, December 15th. Happy trails!"

Robin took his registration copy and left the hall.

Lakeshia was finishing up gym class playing volleyball. It was sixth period, and lunch was next, but she decided to skip going to the cafeteria, and study in the library. She had taken to wearing baggy clothes lately to hide her thinning figure, but luckily, no one in school was noticing.

After changing in the locker room, the bell rang, and she headed out to the hallway and climbed the steps to the third floor. Coming out of the staircase, she passed someone who attempted to talk to her. A Hispanic boy who was heavyset and wearing glasses, he followed her when she ignored him.

"Um, hey, Lakeshia, I was wondering if I could borrow your notes from today's Social Studies class? I kinda fell asleep near the end."

She rolled her eyes. Miguel Franco was such a gullible student who apparently had feelings for the young page. Lakeshia had tried to let him down gently, but some guys couldn't take the hint.

"I'm pretty sure you were asleep the whole class, but sure. Meet me after school, outside the entrance, and you can make a copy."

"Um, thanks. See you then!"

The library had several students studying quietly among themselves. Lakeshia found a desk and took a seat. Mrs. Yagonitzer, the school librarian, was sitting behind a counter talking on the phone. When her head was turned, Lakeshia snuck a couple of Starbursts in her mouth. She opened her notebook and started writing some notes.

Later, after meeting Miguel, Lakeshia decided to walk across the street and up the steps past the Lincoln Center Theater and sit in the open area at Hearst Plaza, near the reflection pool. Behind her was the Library of Performing Arts. It was still early. She wasn't due at 58th Street until three o'clock and a cab would get her up there in fifteen minutes.

After a few minutes of going over her notes, she looked up and noticed someone who looked familiar hiding behind a podium. She looked down and then looked in that direction again and the person was gone now. A puzzled look came across her face.

*That almost looked like Robin's friend. What was his name, Franklin?*

She dismissed the thought as quickly as it happened.

A woman emerged from the library and walked toward the street. She had dark hair and pale skin. Lakeshia almost thought she was a model. Once she disappeared in the distance, Lakeshia packed up her books and started looking around for the nearest taxi stand. There was a line of yellow cabs near a hotel on Columbus Avenue. She headed in that direction and took one across town.

It was noon Thursday, when Janelle arrived at Wendy's, where she found her parents waiting for her, sitting at a table. Earlier that morning, Cynthia Brown reached out to Luanne and Chester, informing them of Janelle's transitional state, and pleaded on her behalf to meet them. The restaurant was just opening for lunch and was only a few blocks from where Tanya lived.

Luanne was devastated by Janelle's appearance when she saw her daughter come in, pushing the baby stroller, and carrying her garbage bags. Chester looked on, showing no emotion whatsoever, as he casually bit a french fry from the meal they ordered. When she arrived and sat down at their table, he greeted Janelle with a cold assessment.

"You look like a bag lady."

"Nice to see you, too," she replied.

Chester nodded. "Has it hit you, yet? You think you're all big and bad, going to bring a child into this world and be an independent woman? How many people have you run to asking for help? You really learn who your friends are when they're there to celebrate you having a baby, but then turn running when it comes to changing diapers."

Janelle stared back. "You wanna gloat some more? Let me know when you're finished."

Chester's right hand jumped, but he caught himself, nearly knocking over their tray. They were in a public place, surrounded by witnesses, and while he never struck his daughter before, he was ashamed that he nearly thought about it after hearing the child's tone.

"That Chinky little bitch ain't here to defend you," he hissed, "so I suggest you watch how you talk to me."

Janelle looked to her mother, who couldn't bear to look at her back. "Are you just going to sit there and let him do this?"

Chester sat quietly, humoring her attempt to pull on her mother's heartstrings. The couple had spoken several times on the subject, coming to a resolution.

"Don't you get it?" Chester interrupted. "You're talking to her as if you're still her little girl." He shook his head. "It doesn't work that way, Janelle. When you *have* a child, you should cease BEING a child!"

She had had enough and stood, then reached over and pulled Simon out of the stroller. "I want you to take *one last look* at your grand-child..." Janelle began, holding the newborn in front of them. "Because the two of you, or anyone who knows you... friends and family are *never* going to see either one of us ever again!" She held in her tears as she placed her child back down. "As far as I'm concerned... both of my parents are *dead!*"

Luanne clenched her jaw as Chester simply replied, "fine."

He then reached down himself and pulled out a manila folder from a plastic bag, slamming it down on the table. "Here is your birth certificate, immunization papers, and social security card. Once you have a permanent address, we'll forward any other mail to it once you give it to us."

He pushed the folder over to her. "Have a nice life."

Janelle looked down at the folder and picked it up. "Thank you, I'll probably need all this when I go to the women's shelter after I leave here."

She took one last look at her mother, then turned and stormed off.

After a few minutes, Chester sighed, took out another folder, and opened it.

"Okay, guess we can get this over with, too," he said.

Luanne pulled a pen out from her purse. "I'll come for my things over the weekend," she said quietly, as she signed the divorce filing papers.

He didn't reply as he added his signature and gave her a set of copies. Their deal for a mutual separation (so long as he didn't lose face in this meeting) was hard, but they both agreed it was for the best. Anticipating the outcome, Luanne found an apartment in Brooklyn weeks ago, which is where she was that morning when Janelle was looking for her.

The couple kept silent as they left the table and walked their separate ways out of the restaurant.

The women's shelter, known as Sala de Estar, was located on a side street off Lafayette Avenue, in the heart of Hunts Point. There were several community centers, churches, and a social services office nearby to help those in need of public assistance.

A line was forming around the corner of the building for first-time arrivals as Janelle approached at two-thirty in the afternoon. She made it inside to sign in at four, narrowly making the cut-off time of five o'clock. After an extensive interview and pages of paperwork, she was given a case number and a set of rules to follow. There was an orientation class tomorrow morning, but at least she had a room to sleep in with a bed and crib for Simon.

The facility had been an elementary school, decades ago, that closed due to asbestos. It was then privately sold and renovated, turning the classrooms into individual living quarters. She took the stairs to the third floor and found her assigned room. When she walked in, Janelle was thrown off when she saw two other people sitting and waiting for her.

"Oh, I'm sorry, I must have the wrong room."

"312? Yeah, this is it," one of the girls said. "There's your bunk."

"I... I thought everyone was given single rooms."

"They tell you that downstairs, but it's really three beds and two cribs. Budget cuts got us packed in like sardines."

Janelle looked around. "Are there closets?"

"Nope. I'd sleep on my stuff if I were you. After dark, a lotta people start roaming and snatching shit from under the beds." The girl nodded. "Nice shoes."

"Um, thanks. I... I'm Janelle, this is Simon," she said, putting the baby on her lap.

"I'm Candice, this here's Nadine."

The other girl gave Janelle a friendly wave and said, "Wassup!"

"Let me guess," Candice began. "Your parents kicked you out after having the baby."

"It's that obvious, huh?"

"Yeah, lots of y'all here... that, or you had your man beat you like me." She lifted her sleeve to reveal a big, dark bruise on her arm.

Janelle gasped.

"When you're settled, I'll show you around. They're very helpful here, but it can get a little crazy as well. So long as you keep to yourself, you'll be alright."

Janelle tried to relax, but anxiety was numbing her body. "Okay, thanks."

Several hours later, Simon was sleeping in the crib provided and Janelle was resting after eating dinner in the recreational area. She was finally starting to feel safe, as the lights went out at ten. A few restless people were moving around in the dark but just as Janelle fell asleep, she had a feeling that someone else was in their room.

At the foot of the bed, a stranger was holding Simon above his crib! Janelle searched the room, looking for her other roommates, then opened her mouth to speak.

"Um," she began.

The stranger turned. Her eyes were bloodshot, making her look crazed. She said nothing, but was still rocking the baby, trying to get him back to sleep.

"Please put my baby down," Janelle whispered.

"I... I heard her crying," the unstable woman said.

*"Him,"* Janelle corrected, darting her eyes around the room again, looking for help.

"She's very beautiful... I had a little girl once that looked just like her."

"Put. My baby. *Down.*" Janelle ordered with a menacing tone.

"Oh, wha'cha gonna do? I'll crush her fuckin' head with my hands—"

The knife appeared at the corner of the intruder's left eye, interrupting her threat. Candice drew her face closer and whispered in her ear, "Thought I told you, don't be wandering around here at night, Cook!"

"The baby was calling out to me..." the woman replied. "I was just... I..."

"You killed your baby months ago, Cookie, you need to get some rest." Candice pressed her knife down closer, almost breaking the skin. "Now put the baby down, or you'll be wearing an eyepatch and looking for a parrot."

The woman, now known as Cookie, slowly lowered Simon back in his crib. Candice then walked her to the door and let her go.

Janelle checked to see if Simon was okay, as Candice put her knife away and locked the door.

"What the fuck was that?" Janelle hissed.

"Cookie don't sleep, so she roams around testing the doors. She picks locks, too," Candice explained. "She drowned her infant in the bathtub when it was six weeks old. Fucking lawyers keep pushing the case claiming she insane and they keep moving her around different facilities."

"I'm reporting that bitch first thing in the morning!"

"They're getting paid good money keeping her here. As long as she don't kill nobody, they'll look the other way."

Candice went back to her bed. "Don't worry, once she gets scared off, she won't come back."

Janelle couldn't believe how nonchalant the woman was. Nadine was still asleep, not waking up from the disturbance. There was no way she could stay here much longer.

Robin walked into the Barnes and Noble college bookstore on 18th street and Fifth Avenue at five-thirty. He had brought his textbooks from the Baruch campus bookstore previously, but since he didn't have a book advance, he was on his own. The nutrition and health class required two books, *Advanced Nutrition and Human Metabolism*, and *Basic Health 101*.

The bookstore closed at seven, so he had plenty of time to browse. He wondered how bookstore employees differ from library employees, whether there was a rivalry of sorts. Like police officers and firemen. There was a woman behind a desk in the middle of the store. She looked close to his age, and wore a button-down sweater over her blouse. Her hair was tied in a ponytail, and she smiled with a full mouth of teeth as he approached.

"Welcome to Barnes and Noble," she said cheerfully.

"Why thank you. I'm looking for these two textbooks, please." He handed her a piece of paper with the titles written on it.

"I can help with that." She accepted the list and started typing on the computer. After searching for the titles, she looked up. "Okay, we have several used copies of *Basic Health 101*, but only have new copies of *Advanced Nutrition*. Follow me."

She walked from behind the desk further back into the store, Robin following behind her. They walked a long way, passing shelves throughout the huge store. After a few turns, the woman pulled out a book from a shelf.

"Here's *Advanced Nutrition*, it's $85.00."

Robin gasped, "$85.00 for a book? It's not even about computers!"

"Annnnnnnd, here's a used copy of *Basic Health 101* for $120.00."

"JESUS CHRIST! Are you kidding me? This looks like a pamphlet, it's probably no more than 30 pages!"

"Close. It's actually 45 pages, and in new condition, that book goes for $200.00. It's very popular."

All the color left Robin's face. "Uh, I really don't have $200.00 right now."

"Well, that doesn't matter, because both books cost *$205.00*, plus tax, which comes to $221.91," she said sharply.

"Okay, I'm going to level with you, I work for the New York Public Library, part-time. I tried to find these books in their collection..."

"And I bet you didn't find them, of course," she interrupted.

"No, no I didn't, and I need these two books before Tuesday, so um, can you work with me here? Library clerk to book clerk?" He smiled and played with his eyes.

"I'm not a book clerk. I'm a sales associate." The woman was no longer smiling.

Robin only had a hundred dollars on him, but luckily, he got paid tomorrow. "Alright, give me the *Advanced Nutrition* book for now. I'll be back for *Basic Health 101* on Friday."

"We only have two left, you better hope it's still here..." the associate said, putting the second book back.

"I'll take that chance," Robin replied dryly, as he accepted the textbook and walked to the cashier.

At the end of her shift Friday, Tanya hurried to her locker upstairs. She pulled out a pair of slip-on dress shoes and her book bag, then went to the staff room, locked the door, and changed. After calling a taxi to pick her up, Tanya left the branch, unseen by anyone, and climbed in. Tonight was her date with Andrew, and she was ready for anything.

*He better take me someplace nice… and I'm not giving him any… maybe.*

Instead of meeting him at the Webster Branch she took a cab and headed to Carnegie Hall. When she stepped out, Tanya looked around and then stopped, stunned. A gasp left her breathless.

Andrew stood waiting for her, this time holding a single pink daisy in his hand. She was impressed by his appearance. His normal high-top haircut was gone, settling for a low, evenly cut head of hair. With an open face, missing his rimmed eyeglasses, and wearing a dark navy-blue suit, Andrew had transformed into a stunning Prince Charming.

Tanya was taken away. "Wow," was all she could say.

"You look much more beautiful with these contacts on, Tanya." His smile beamed, as he handed her the flower.

She didn't even notice his hand in front of her, she was still lost in his dark brown eyes.

"Tanya?" Andrew said again.

She snapped out of her trance. "Oh, sorry!" And accepted the daisy, taking a quick sniff.

He caressed her cheek. "I have a wonderful evening in store."

"I can't wait," she replied, and did a double take behind them. "Are we going to a concert inside?"

"Uh no, actually we're going across the street."

Staying on 57th Street, they walked down from the corner of Seventh Avenue, heading east to the next street, then turned another corner.

The Jekyll & Hyde Club was a five-story building at 1409 Avenue of the Americas (also known as Sixth Avenue). There were banners on the outside above the entrance with gothic decorations on the stained-glass windows.

Tanya gasped in fright as they approached. "What the hell is this?"

"It's a bit early, before Halloween, but I thought this place would be something out of the ordinary for you," he replied.

*Out of the ordinary is right!* she thought.

The maître d' wore a top hat and was dressed like an undertaker. "Welcome to The Jekyll & Hyde Club, do you have a reservation?"

The couple was led inside to a small waiting room. The host made a flourish and yelled, "Cordelia! We have some visitors!"

A female's voice called out from a speaker on the wall and the lights started to flicker. Above their heads, a bed of rubber spikes protruded from the ceiling and slowly descended. Andrew pretended to be scared, while Tanya rolled her eyes. The spikes stopped a foot above them, then the lights came back on.

"Boy, she's a tough nut to crack," the maître d' muttered under his breath, then led them inside.

Jekyll & Hyde wasn't just a club where macabre presentations and entertainment were provided to a captive audience. It was also a themed restaurant with fine dining. Andrew and Tanya took an elevator to the third floor, where they were escorted to a table near the stained windows for a view of Sixth Avenue.

Despite the classier dining area, there was still a terror-themed motive in the atmosphere. The bar had spider webs and bats hanging above, and there was music playing in the background related to Halloween. Songs like "Thriller," "The Monster Mash," "I Put a Spell on You," and "Bad Moon Rising."

Tanya tried to put on a brave face and get into the spirit, but she saw all the restaurant's theatrics as corny. To her, it was equivalent to taking her to Chuck E. Cheese. They picked up their menus and skimmed the uniquely named entrees.

"Isn't this great? They just opened this past spring. This place is completely booked for Halloween weekend. I was lucky enough to get us in tonight." Andrew beamed.

She held the menu up, covering the lower half of her face. "It's great!" *Dear God, get me outta here! My coochie's dry as dust right now!*

They ordered drinks, to start the evening slow while waiting for their meals. Every once in a while, a performer would pass their table in an attempt to scare them.

Tanya contained her composure for as long as she could. "Andy, I think we're a bit... *overdressed* for this crowd," she began. "I was looking forward to something more... mature than this."

Andrew's face fell. "I'm sorry. I was just looking for something different."

She felt terrible. "Well, we can make the best of it, I guess."

"Okay then, let's talk about us," Andrew suggested.

He gave her a look that was trying to convey amorism, but she couldn't take him seriously in their surroundings.

"Move in with me," he said suddenly.

"WHAT!?" Tanya screamed.

A few people from separate tables around them turned in their direction.

"I don't mean right now!" Andrew let out a chuckle. "When you graduate in two years."

"Oh."

"It's so reassuring that the idea of living together frightens you..." he said in a sarcastic tone.

"I didn't mean to freak out like that. I just need to know you ain't gonna play me, Andy."

"I deserve that. To be honest, I really didn't want to take that promotion and leave 58th Street. Or leave you, for that matter."

"You... you didn't?"

"No. I didn't think I was ready, even though I passed the Senior Clerk Seminar. I would have gladly passed on being in charge at Webster if it wasn't for Sonyai insisting I take it."

"Really?"

"Of course." He raised an eyebrow. "Between you and me, I think she was trying to break us up."

Tanya knew Sonyai noticed that she and Andrew were close while working together, but never thought that the senior clerk would send him away on purpose. Who was *she* to stand in the way of their love?

"Okay, say that's true. How do I know it's going to work this time? I need to know if you're real."

"Well, I can tell you... or I can *show* you."

The tip of his shoe traced up her bare calf.

She straightened up as her eyes went wide. The dust had been taken over by a moment of humidity.

Angie walked in the staff room, to find Robin sitting at the kitchen table working on his first assignment.

"Hey," she greeted. "You're back in school?"

"Yeah. Just a night class, though. It was all I could sign up for since I missed the beginning of the semester. I really wanted to take more classes."

"Well, I'm sure you'll get back into the swing of things next year."

"Yeah," he replied with a sigh. "Anyway, um, something on your mind?"

Angie laughed nervously. "I'm sorry, I'm just... um, I heard you're a bit of a 'Donatello' when it comes to computers."

Robin frowned, then got the joke. "Oh! Ninja Turtles! Ha! Uh, yeah, I know a thing or two. That's actually an understatement..." he chuckled. "You know that movie *WarGames*? It was based on me."

"Yeah?" Angie couldn't resist a laugh.

"Yeah, they wanted to go with Todd Bridges at the time, but they didn't think he could carry a movie, so they went with Matthew Broderick. Test audiences, producers, and all that... so, you got some computer issues?"

"Yeah, I have no idea what's wrong. I've had it for a while. I hope it's not breaking down."

"Okay, well, I guess I can come over to your place and take a look at it. Where do you live?"

She blinked hard, not expecting him to offer help so easily. "Oh wow, you would do that?" she asked. "No offense, but I'm kinda a private person, no one from work's ever been to my house before."

"Alright, can you bring it to my apartment then? I must warn you, I live in a high rise, and my elevators sometimes don't work."

Angie grimaced. "Well, since you put it that way, and the computer *is* very big, there's no way I could move it." She nodded to him. "Can you come Sunday?"

"Sure."

"Okay, here's my number and my address..."

Robin took a piece of paper and wrote the address. "You live in Queens?" He cringed.

"Is that a problem?"

He shook his head. "No, it just brings back... *memories*." Robin thought of Shinju for a moment. "I'll be there around 2 pm."

"Thanks."

Angie sat down and unpacked her lunch, as Robin went back to his assignment.

Sonyai walked into her office at four o'clock, after doing a two-hour block at the circulation desk. She sat down and took a breath, then pulled out a stick of gum from her desk. Lately, the senior clerk was making a conscious effort to stop smoking, but chewing gum wasn't calming enough. It had been several weeks now since Janelle called her for help, and she was starting to worry.

After chewing for a few minutes, she picked up the phone and pressed for her direct line, then dialed a number.

"Van Nest Library, Brantley speaking."

"Mister Brantley, this is Sonyai Yi from 58th Street Branch. Good afternoon, sir."

"Ah, good day, Miss Yi, what can I do for you, today?"

"I'm just calling to see if you have heard from Janelle Simms. Has she stopped by to pick up her paycheck while on maternity leave?"

"Miss Simms has told me how protective you were while training her as a page. First, I must commend you. She is an efficient and valued employee, and we'll be looking forward to her return."

"Thank you," Sonyai replied.

"However, since she arranged to have her checks direct deposited, she has not been to the branch since her last day before her medical appointment. We had a nice sendoff party planned, and she's due back to return after the Thanksgiving holiday."

"I see," Sonyai replied, letting out a sigh.

"Is something wrong?" Reginald asked.

Sonyai hesitated, not wanting to reveal Janelle's personal situation, to respect her privacy. "Just wanted to know how she and the baby were doing," she lied. "I'm sure she'll stop by eventually and let the staff see her bundle of joy. He's a real looker."

"I bet! I'll drop you a line the next time I see her, and definitely give her your best."

"Thank you, sir. I know she'll make me proud. Have a good evening." She ended the call, then turned her chair and saw Ethel looking back at her.

"What's wrong with Janelle?"

"How long have you been there!?" Sonyai gasped.

"Answer my question first. Why are you checking on her?"

*I need to put a bell on her!* "Nothing is wrong, I was just wondering—"

"You don't *wonder* about anything, Yi!"

Sonyai pressed her lips together and squinted. They looked at each other and then the senior clerk finally relented. "Janelle's parents weren't exactly happy when she got pregnant."

"I bet they weren't," Ethel replied, with a snort.

"With that said, shortly after giving birth, her parents, most likely her *father*, rather... changed the locks at their home, and left her belongings outside."

"They kicked her out?!" Ethel exclaimed in surprise. "That's a little extreme!"

Sonyai nodded. "Her father was very strict." She recalled their confrontation, in which she twisted his arm after tripping him to the floor. "Janelle called me that night and I helped her find a motel, but she only stayed for a few days... and I haven't heard from her since."

Ethel took this new development in silence, slowly shaking her head.

"You must not tell anyone, Jenkins."

"Don't worry, I won't..." she dismissed. "Just tell me if you hear something."

Ethel turned and sat at her desk, matching Sonyai's concerned face.

# CHAPTER NINE

"HEY, TEE, HOW WAS YOUR DATE WITH ANDREW THIS WEEKEND?" Alex asked.

The pages were working the last hour, with very few patrons on the floor. Lakeshia was putting back some New Books nearby, as Tanya and Alex worked in the 200's.

"It was alright," she replied nonchalantly.

"*Just* alright?" Alex pressed, raising an eyebrow.

Tanya swallowed hard. "Uh, yeah…"

"You hooked up with him, didn't you?" Lakeshia asked, as she approached.

"No, NO! We had dinner at this lame-ass horror restaurant. He asked me to move in with him when I graduate, and I told him I'd think about it."

"That's it?" Alex asked, with a raised eyebrow.

"That's *it!*" Tanya emphasized. She thought back to the hotel room they shared after leaving Jekyll & Hyde. Tanya had every intention of ending the date once they left the restaurant, but Andrew mentioned that he booked a room at the Park Central Hotel and she couldn't resist spending the night, engaging in a sexual romp of legendary proportions.

"Fine. I don't believe you, but I won't press further." Lakeshia pushed her shelving cart, continuing across the room.

When they were alone Alex whispered, "Tanya... give it to me straight, girl."

The two pages walked to the reference corner and took a seat at one of the tables.

"He had hotel reservations... and he looked *so* fine!" Tanya admitted.

"Uh-huh," Alex replied flatly. "Spare me the details... so what now?"

"I'm gonna wait a few weeks, thinking of what he said... and then let him down, gently."

Alex couldn't resist a chuckle. "Bulllllshit."

They looked around to make sure no one heard them, then Alex stood up. "Tell me the rest on our break upstairs."

"Don't tell nobody. This thing didn't mean nothin,'" Tanya said quickly. "We ain't together, and I'll tell him it's over soon enough."

Alex was already turning and walking away. "Yeah, yeah, yeah..." she dismissed.

Lakeshia arrived in the 900's and started putting books back on the shelves. She noticed a patron was sitting on a stool, hunched over in a corner. The man seemed to be grunting softly to himself.

"Oh, no..." she groaned.

It was a very slow Thursday afternoon. If Robin didn't know better, the clock above the circulation desk had said it was five-twenty for the last ten minutes.

*What was it someone said about a watched pot?* he thought.

He was slowly adjusting to the thought of heading down to campus instead of going home, with it being the second day of his night class. With the last hour this dead, he was worried he might fall asleep on the train and miss his stop.

*If only there was a way to liven things up...*

Gerry was accepting returns to Robin's right. Across the floor, Angie was scanning the shelves, filling holds that were requested, while Heywood was cleaning up the periodicals. Augustus was the librarian scheduled at the information desk, but he was preoccupied in a conversation with a shapely woman in a business suit.

A patron had been waiting in front of the information desk for over five minutes, when she came over to Robin at the checkout side.

"Hello? I was wondering if you could help me. I'm looking for a book. I tried looking in the card catalogs, but they were very confusing."

He put on his biggest smile and said, "Sure, do you know the author or title?"

Robin performed a search on his terminal and was able to point to the section where she was able to find the title in question. He then checked out the book, as the woman thanked him for his help.

Augustus escorted the woman he was talking to past the security threshold and watched her leave the branch. His smile disappeared as he approached Robin at the desk.

"Walker, when it comes to issues a patron has with our cataloging system, please refer them to the information desk," Augustus scolded. "You're not qualified to resolve such matters."

Robin frowned. "Fort Washington has trained pages and clerks how to help patrons during certain situations. It's a common practice when dealing with the public... *sir.*"

Angie and Heywood returned to the information desk and exchanged glances upon hearing Robin's challenge. Augustus quickly walked behind the circulation desk. "Step inside the clerical office for a second, *young man!*" he ordered, gesturing to the doorway.

Robin obliged, as Sonyai noticed the beginning of a potential argument from her desk and turned to them, showing some concern.

"I'm sorry, you may be attending college, but did I miss the part when you acquired a master's in library sciences?! If not, stop trying to do *our* duties!" Augustus asked.

Robin scoffed. "Oh sure, make that $35,000.00 yearly salary worth something, with your $1,000.00 Armani business suit and $150.00 shoes!"

Augustus was taken aback, as Sonyai stood and approached the pair. "Okay, I think we both need to calm down, here…"

"The only reason I helped that lady is because YOU were too busy kissing that rich woman's ass as she made googly-eyes at you!"

The head librarian's eyes bulged. "How dare you!? Who the hell do you think you're talking…"

Just that moment, before things could get even more intense, Lakeshia stepped inside. "Uh, excuse me? We have a Code 57."

Groans came from Sonyai and Augustus while Robin stood confused. "A what?"

"It's a long story," Sonyai began. "Miss Seabrooke, find Iscaro."

"What's a Code 57?" Robin asked.

Augustus reached out and grabbed Robin's arm. "A pervert masturbating to the art books."

"Whaaaat!?"

Augustus had Robin by the arm as they walked across the floor to the 900's section. "Okay, mister 'Fort-Washington-trained-me!' Why don't *you* politely handle *this* situation for us?"

He gently nudged him forward and stood in place as Robin looked ahead to an isolated corner. There was a shadow of a figure, and he could hear the familiar sound of someone pleasuring themselves.

Robin slowly approached and let out an audible cough.

The person let out a frightened gasp and the sound stopped. There was an awkward moment of silence.

"I'm not a bad person," he began.

"I know. I know."

"I just have these urges, you know?"

"Hey, I completely understand, man… it's cool. But um, such behavior is really… *really* frowned upon here, sir." He took a breath. "So, I must insist… that you desist. Cool?"

"Can... can I finish first?" the man asked meekly.

"No, you *cannot,*" Robin gasped.

"Ok. Thank you for not judging me."

"Thank *you* for not finishing sir."

"You're very respectful. Has anyone ever told you that?"

Robin cleared his throat. "Uh, no, actually. You're the first."

"That's really a shame."

"Yes... Yes, it is."

The timid little man closed the book. There was a sound of a zipper zipping up, followed by silence.

"Um, can I go now?"

"Uh, yeah, you can go."

"I'm really not a bad person," he repeated.

"I... I understand. Not judging... it's cool."

"You have a nice day."

"You... you too, sir. Thank you for cooperating."

"Okay."

The patron shuffled from the corner, down an aisle of shelves to the exit turnstile, and discreetly left the branch. Augustus stepped back to the information desk as Robin emerged from the shelves himself and returned to the circulation desk. He had a frightened look on his face.

Gerry was impressed. "Wow, Walker, that was amazing! You really dealt with deviants like that back at Fort Washington?"

The clerk tilted his head and pulled the collar of his polo. "No actually, um... we had *training* when it came to dealing with unique circumstances, but th... that was my first time."

He turned toward the information desk. "Think I'll leave dealing with certain patrons to the professionals. From here on out."

Angie lived out on the border of Little Neck & Glen Oaks in Queens, near the corner of 260th Street and 75th Avenue, north of Union Turnpike. It took Robin two hours, taking two trains and a bus to get to what she gave him as her address. Living in Manhattan most of his life, he was unaware of how certain cross streets in Queens worked.

"I should have brought change for a payphone," he mumbled. "I hate Queens!"

He walked up 75th Avenue and came across a two-story apartment complex the size of a horseshoe, with a courtyard in the center. There was no gate, just foliage and small sets of steps leading to each doorway, the structure appeared to be part of a huge cul-de-sac.

*Is that an actual water well?*

Robin searched the doors looking for a house number when one door to his left opened and Angie waved her arm. He sighed in relief and walked toward her.

"I saw you from my window. You looked like a deer wandering on a baseball field!" She greeted him with a smile.

"It took forever to get out here. I thought I was going to Rhode Island at one point!"

"Don't you mean Long Island?" Angie asked.

"I meant what I said."

She closed the door behind him as he looked around. After a long wolf whistle, "and I thought my apartment was nice... I have a terrace, though."

Angie walked past him, and he noticed she was dressed differently. "You look pretty nice outside the library, yourself..." *What is going on here?* he thought.

She was wearing sweatpants and a Sergio Valente sweater with the bottom cut off, exposing her midriff. Her long black hair that usually falls past her shoulders was pulled up in a french braided ponytail.

"My computer is over here." She led him to the living room.

Robin's eyes lit up. "Oh wow, a Pack-Mate III 286!" he exclaimed.

"You *do* know your computers," Angie said, impressed.

He examined the machine, unable to keep his tongue in his mouth. "Gee-Dub's and Baruch have those slow-ass IBM PS/1 Tonka Trucks from the 80's, but this baby's fresh from the U.S.S. Enterprise."

She laughed. "Well, I spent most of my Pell grant money getting it a few years ago and it seems to be acting up."

Robin sat in front of the keyboard and turned the computer on. "What operations system are you running?"

"Windows 286," Angie replied.

"You didn't upgrade to 3.0? That's your problem." Robin reached in his book bag and pulled out six small disks. He was about to put one in the disk drive when Angie grabbed his wrist.

"Wait! What are you doing? I have all my schoolwork on this computer, and I cannot lose it!"

"Relax... the upgrade only changes the system files."

She looked at him, then nodded.

Robin proceeded to initiate the update, swapping one disk at a time. He then verified her personal files were safe. "Here you go, you know? 3.1 is out now as well. I just don't have the disks..."

"That's okay, just see if it runs better," Angie said nervously.

"Sure. I think this new system helps prevent the hard drive from overheating and improves overall memory flow."

"Uh-huh."

"Do you know what any of that means?" He asked, raising his eyebrow.

"Um, of course, I do," she replied.

Robin switched to DOS and put in another disk. "You like Tetris? I can install it for you."

"Really?" Angie smiled.

An hour later the pair were playing several computer games together, laughing and joking around.

"How are you this good in Zany Golf?" Angie asked.

"I played it all the time during computer class!" Robin yelled.

They ended their match and Robin brought the computer back to Windows. "Well, everything should be a lot smoother now." He started collecting the disks around on the desks.

"Thanks. What do I owe you?"

Robin scoffed. "What? Naaaah, this was nothing. I was expecting to break 'er open and see what was wrong from inside."

"You'd do that? A $2000.00 computer? Would you be able to put it back together?"

"With my eyes closed!" He chuckled. "When I was ten, my grandfather gave me a Commodore 64 and I took it apart. Put it back together in a weekend."

"Well, the least I can do is treat you to some pizza..." Angie offered.

"Now, you're talking! No toppings! Just plain cheese..."

"Plain cheese? What kinda Ninja Turtle *are* you?"

It was six o'clock in the evening, and after beer, two pies, along with the exchange of several stories, Robin asked, "hey, can I use your phone to call my cabbie friend? It'd take forever to get home with the bus and trains."

"Okay."

Robin staggered to her kitchen, where she kept a rotary phone mounted on the wall. "You can really hold your liquor!" he complimented.

*Who the hell keeps their damn phone in the kitchen?*

He picked up the receiver and slowly dialed the number. "Yeah, preferred customer pickup for car... car Two-Y-Sizzzzty-eight!" he hiccuped and shook his head, trying to sober up.

Ten minutes later, Robin was passed out on Angie's easy chair, when a hand shook his shoulder. He flailed his arms and was startled awake to see Angie and a tall African man in a tweed jacket, staring back at him.

"Cervantes!"

"Somebody order a ride home?" The cab driver smiled.

"You're a lightweight, Robin," Angie joked, as he began to stand up.

"Whaddya talkin' about? I'm fine... whoop!" Robin stumbled forward into the arms of his friend, who caught him at the last minute.

"I gotcha! Let's get you home."

As they walked to the door Angie asked, "You've done this before?"

"Oh yes, I owe Robin a lifetime debt," Cervantes explained.

"I saaaved hisss 'ife," Robin slurred. "It's like da 'ellaphant and da mouse… pulled a splinter out his paw…" he started giggling uncontrollably.

Angie gave the cab driver a puzzled look, to which he replied, "He's getting his fables a little mixed up. He did save me from getting carjacked, so I give him free rides once in a while."

Once Robin was loaded in the backseat Angie waved to him. "Thanks again! See you tomorrow!"

Cervantes got behind the steering wheel and started the car, Robin waved back. "See ya!" As the taxi pulled away.

"Goodness, this is the farthest I've ever picked you up from!" Cervantes said, once he was on the Union Turnpike heading back to Manhattan.

"You think she's pretty?" Robin asked, still giggling to himself.

"Huh?"

"I think she's a little old for me…" Robin started nodding off, mumbling in his sleep, "Shindy… I miss you, baby…"

"Father, watch over him," Cervantes whispered.

November had finally arrived, and it was still unseasonably warm in the city. Heywood arrived at 58th Street at nine o'clock, holding a bag of bagels he brought for the staff. He went upstairs and found Angie eating a bowl of corn soup.

"Good morning, I brought bagels. Want one?" he offered.

"Thanks, but I got some cornbread I made this morning to go with my soup," she replied.

After leaving the bag on the counter, Heywood stretched out on the couch and stared up at the ceiling.

"How was your weekend?" Angie asked.

"Kids egged my building Saturday. Such a disturbing pagan holiday Halloween is."

"You never dressed up and went trick or treating when you were a kid?"

"Nah, my parents were very strict," he replied. "Halloween was never even talked about in any way."

*That explains a lot,* Angie thought.

"How was yours?" Heywood asked.

"Great! My computer is working a lot better now."

"Oh? You were having problems?"

"It needed an update to the operations system. I had no idea…"

Heywood took a bite from his bagel, followed by a sip of coffee.

"Fortunately, Robin was able to come over and fix it for me."

Heywood suddenly started choking violently, startling her. He coughed a few times to clear his throat and gasped, "Robin!?" he coughed again and settled himself. "Oh, um, that's interesting."

She gave him a peculiar look. "He seems very good with computers, inside and out, but thankfully he didn't have to open mine. Um, is something wrong?"

"No! Nothing's wrong, um, just that, um, the coffee went down the wrong pipe, heh-heh-heh," he dismissed.

"Well, I need to get going." She stood up and washed her utensils at the sink.

"Okay, see you downstairs." Heywood waved.

Once she was gone, Heywood's eyelid started to twitch. Whether it was the coffee he was drinking or something else… was uncertain.

Even though it was only one class, Robin was pushing his body to its limits working at the branch and going down to campus. Occasionally, he would duck into one of the study halls for a quick nap, thirty minutes before class.

He entered a study hall, looking for an isolated corner where he could keep to himself, and came across a group of students sitting at a table. There were more than seven students, surrounding a drawn map with game pieces and several dice. They all looked up at him as he stood at the doorway.

"Uh, hey," he said, with a faint wave.

There was an awkward moment of silence, then Robin turned to leave.

"What's your hurry? Join us!" someone from the group called out.

Robin froze and reluctantly turned back to the group. "Um, y'all some sort of… study group?" he asked, approaching the table.

"We're playing DnD, would you like to participate in our campaign?" A female student asked.

"Campaign?"

"We're playing Dungeons and Dragons, the role-playing game," a tall, white student with red hair, announced.

He checked out the entire group, which consisted of five boys and two girls. Their fashion sense, the mixture of ethnicities, and drastic body types reminded Robin of something he would see on *The Addams Family* or *The Munsters*. Against his better judgment, he took a seat at the table.

"So great of you to join us. My name's Danijel, that's pronounced with the hard 'J' in the middle. I'm the Dungeon Master…" the tall, red-haired student greeted. "This here's Kevin, Angela, Joyce, Nik, that's with a 'K,' no 'C,' and finally, Max."

Robin nodded. *I hope they all don't say 'Hi' at once.* "I'm Robin." He waved.

"Hi, Robin!" the group said in unison.

He did a hard blink, trying not to sigh.

"Well, we're about to start our sixth campaign. All our names and characters have been set up, what would you like to be?"

"Um, a guy," Robin answered.

Angela, a short, skinny Filipino girl giggled. "No silly, a Bard, a Cleric, a Monk, a Thief, a Warrior, or Wizard."

"Oh, um… I'll be a Thief." Robin smiled. He was starting to feel a certain anticipation for the experience.

Danijel wrote some information in a small notebook with a pencil. "Alright, name?"

"Um, Robin?"

"No, no, no, the name of your character as a Thief."

He thought for several moments, then said, "Montage."

The group looked blankly at him.

"He's the main character from *Fahrenheit 451*."

"Montage... the Thief." Danijel wrote again in the notebook. "Okay, you're our second Thief next to Joyce, who is known as Alarica, Kevin is our Cleric, Delmont. We also have Angela as Warrior Saxona, Nik is a Wizard named Vinzent, Adrian and Max are twin Monks, Battista and Brentan."

Robin did his best to remember the names and characters with the faces.

"I'm a Bard who goes as Jaromir," Danijel said, and picked up a special piece of dice with 15 sides. "We need you to roll scores for your abilities... roll this six times."

Robin looked at the die in his hand, shook it, and dropped it on the table. After five more throws, they were ready to begin.

"We're playing Advanced D&D second edition circa 1989," Danijel announced.

The gameplay began, which was all imaginary. Robin was unfamiliar with what was going on, other than rolling the dice and speaking in terms that were alien to him. He had committed several faux pas, with miscues that required delays in the game to explain certain things to him. After twenty-five minutes, he had enough.

"Um, sorry..." Robin stood up. "This isn't working for me. It's too confusing."

"Give it a chance," Joyce pleaded. "You'll get the hang of it..."

He gave a dismissive wave. "Nah, I gotta go. My class starts in twenty minutes."

Before they could protest further, Robin was in the hallway, heading out of the building.

Danijel shrugged. "Well, it's a good thing I wrote everything about him in pencil!" He quietly erased thoroughly in his notebook.

After a ten-minute sprint, Robin entered the lobby of 137 East 25th Street, making a beeline for the elevators.

"Partnah, partnah, partnah!" He heard someone call to him.

Robin froze in place and turned to look behind him. A tall security guard was waving him back to the front desk.

"What?!" he barked back down the hallway.

"C'mon back here for a minute."

Robin walked back to the desk. The guard was a skinny African-American, who looked in his fifties. His salt and pepper hair straightened to the side. "Can I help you?" he asked.

"I'm attending classes here. Nutrition and Health, eighth floor."

"Sign the visitor's log," the guard instructed. "There are corporate offices in this building, as the school slowly takes over the premises. Students must sign in and out when coming in and leaving."

"I didn't see you here last week when I came to my first two classes," Robin said.

"I was on vacation. Now sign. The time is 7:35 pm." The guard handed him a pen.

Robin took out his own pen and scribbled on a space in the book. He then jogged back down the hallway to the bank of elevators.

"I'll be seeing you when you leave, and you better sign out and note the time!"

"Yeah, sure!" Robin called back, barely beating the sliding doors of the departing car.

The guard turned the book around and read the last entry. A confused look came over his face as he read, "Bugs Bunny?!"

Robin jumped out of the elevator on the eighth floor and made it to the classroom with five minutes to spare. There was no assigned seating, so he had a preference to sit in the back corner near a window that led out to an alley on the side of the building.

His teacher was a timid Greek man in his 30's, who tried to hide his thinning hair with a terrible comb-over. Once all the students arrived, the class began. At eight-thirty a radio outside started playing "Juicy," by The Notorious B.I.G., repeatedly on a loop. Most of the class was able to ignore it, but Robin was becoming annoyed.

He leaned over to the window and noticed a group of people in the alley playing dice games while smoking and drinking.

"What the hell?" Robin whispered.

"Mister Walker," the teacher called to him. "Step back from the—"

"Hey assholes! We're trying to have a night class up here! Turn that shit down!" Robin yelled.

They all looked up, and Robin quickly ducked away from the window. The music continued as the teacher finished the class. Afterward, he lingered to talk to a few other students, then went to the bathroom. When he came out of the elevator at the lobby, the security guard called out at him again. "Alright funny guy, put your real name in the book, along with the date and time!"

"What are you talking about? That *is* my real name."

"I'm not in the mood…Doc!"

Robin rolled his eyes while walking back and wrote a correct entry in the logbook. "See ya, Thursday!" he said while walking away. *"Asshole,"* he added, under his breath.

Outside the building, Robin walked south toward 23rd Street. When he approached the corner of the block, six guys stepped out from the alley that led to the side where the classroom window was located.

He stopped and recognized the same group that was listening to the radio earlier.

"Shit." He simply said.

Running wasn't an option, and he was outnumbered. It was time to grin and bear it. "Alright," he sighed, putting up his fists. "Let's do this."

Ethel came home from her latest doctor appointment to a message on her answering machine. The results from her tests were showing an improvement in her health, due to the medication and diet she was on. She went to the refrigerator for a bottle of Evian water, and with a healthy swig she pressed the button and listened to the message...

"Hey, it's me. Great news! The house passed inspection and is ready to move in. It's time girl! I hope you ready, call me back!"

Ethel dropped the bottle and gasped, "Holy shit!"

She grabbed her phone and called Ernabelle, hoping it wasn't too late in the evening.

"Yeah?"

"It's me, Ernie… you serious about the house being ready?"

"Serious as a heart attack! I'm still celebrating! The Lord has finally provided. We are officially homeowners!"

"Well alright, I gotta call my landlord then, this is great!" She hung up and dialed another number.

"Hello? Mister Aadesh? This is Ethel Jenkins from 1751 Amsterdam, is it too late to give my thirty-day notice? Yes, my house down south is finally ready… everything here is in broom-clean condition, you won't even need to paint… I can leave by December first? Thank you! I'll mail an official notice by certified mail first thing tomorrow! Good night!"

Ethel hung up the phone again and sighed. "Now all I need to do… is leave this job…"

# CHAPTER TEN

ALEX WAS WALKING UP AND DOWN THE HALLS OF NORMAN THOMAS high school Wednesday morning, handing out invitations to her birthday party, in two weeks on the 19th. Her sweet 16 will be talked about for years to come, even when she becomes a senior two years from now.

She wasn't trying to invite the entire school, even though the hall her parents rented could accommodate the entire tenth grade. Only the elite and select few, would be deemed worthy of attending. The lunchroom was the last stop, only two more people left she had to make sure would make an appearance.

The Watts brothers. Paul and his older brother Rodney, were eating together at a table when Alex walked up to them.

Paul noticed her first. "Well, hello Alex. What brings you to bless us with your appearance today?"

He was 16, with smooth caramel skin and light eyes. Rodney was 18 and a senior, getting ready for college. There were rumors about Rodney possibly being gay, but he was probably focused on getting accepted to Fordham University, which was a catholic college and very strict.

"I was wondering if I could count on you and your brother to attend my Sweet 16 in two weeks," Alex said, handing them each an envelope.

"Oh, I wouldn't miss it," he smiled. "Would you, Rod?"

She held her smile as Rodney slowly turned and accepted the envelope. "I guess. Got nothing better to do."

"Great!" she turned and walked away. When she got out of earshot, she said, "fucking asshole. If Paul weren't cute, I'd beat you with a crowbar."

Paul rarely went anywhere without Rodney tagging along, and if he was going to take her to the spring dance next year, she had to make her move now.

She exited the lunchroom and decided to spend the rest of fifth period at the school library, getting ready for math class. As soon as she entered the room, she wanted to turn around and leave quickly. There was someone there she was trying to avoid. All muscle and no brains, the class jock, Fergus Van Sloan, called out to her.

"Alex, there you are. Been waiting here, looking for you!"

"Well, you found me, Fergie. Why don't you close your eyes, I'll hide, and you can look again?"

"You're such a kidder, and it's *Fergus* not Fergie. I was waiting for you to invite me to your birthday party. I know you were saving me for last because of all the girls who want me."

"Uh, yeah, that's why…" she rolled her eyes. *This shaved ape! No way am I having him ruin my party.*

"Look, *Fergus*. I'm at the hall's capacity already, and my party's gonna be real low-key. It's not your kinda scene…" Alex began.

"Why you tryin' to play me, yo? Fine, you don't want me at your party? That's all you had to say."

"Yeah, um, okay."

"Okay, see ya." He walked past her, leaving the library, with a sinister grin.

When Robin arrived at the library at three-thirty, he still had a half-hour before starting his shift. His fight last night could have gone better. He took a beating, but so did they, leading to a draw. Luckily the security guard heard the skirmish and eventually broke it up.

After arriving at the branch, he went upstairs to the second floor. The door to the upstairs bathroom opened and Lakeshia stepped out, nearly bumping into Robin at the top of the stairs.

"Ooops," he said, catching himself. "You okay, kiddo?"

Lakeshia covered her smile upon hearing Robin's nickname he gave her. "Yep, um… just was feeling a little queasy. Been a bit under the weather lately."

They passed each other and he waved. "Okay! Hope you feel better."

He entered the staff room and pulled out a binder from his book bag. Taking a seat at the kitchen table, he opened and studied his latest notes. A few minutes later, he had a thought and stroked his chin with an audible, "Hmmm."

At four o'clock he returned downstairs and started on the checkouts side, then at five, Gerry and Tommy came out to work the last hour before the six to eight late night block. Tommy was sitting on a shelving cart, leaning against the wall on the returns side. Robin decided to hang back in a corner behind Gerry, in front of the file cabinets that held VHS tapes.

"Hey, man, what happened to you?" Gerry asked.

"Some assholes jumped me for my homework," Robin lied.

Gerry looked at him, questioning if Robin was joking or serious. He decided not to follow up, and the young clerk changed the subject anyway.

"Hey, quick question, what would you do if you suspect someone is doing something, but you don't wanna confront them, until you're sure?"

"This someone you know?"

"Yeah," Robin answered.

"Someone you care about?"

"Somewhat."

"It's not me, is it?" Gerry asked.

"Do we have a guilty conscience for some reason? And stop answering a question *with* a question!"

Gerry snorted. "Get more evidence. Don't confront them until you're sure, happy?"

"That was another question…" Robin said with a smirk, "but thanks."

"You gonna tell me what really happened to you?"

"You didn't hear me the first time?"

They exchanged odd looks, then Gerry turned back to his post, while Robin looked at Lakeshia out among the shelves and let out another, "Hmmm."

Six o'clock finally arrived, and Tommy went inside the clerical office. He came back with a pair of jackets. Gerry nodded to Robin. "Alright man, have a smooth night."

"You too!" Robin waved back.

The two clerks left the branch together, searching for a bar to get some drinks.

Heywood was sitting at the information desk, bored out of his mind, when Robin sat down at the chair next to the desk facing him.

The information assistant leaned back when Robin put his elbow on the desk and greeted him, "Hiya."

"Uhhh…"

"It's a little slow right now, so I picked this time to swing by and talk to you," Robin explained.

Heywood let out a puzzled, "Okaaaay."

"I say 'picked this time,' because I find it funny that in the eight months I've been here, me and you haven't said no more than five words to each other."

"Really?"

Robin nodded. "Yeah… why do you think that is?" He asked with a squint.

Heywood had no answer, and this conversation was awkward to him. "Have no clue," he replied with a shrug.

Robin chuckled. "We had an extensive conversation and exchanged theories on this."

"We?"

"Me and Angie. This past weekend."

Heywood's eyebrow twitched.

"Her personal computer wasn't working right, and I fixed it. I'm kinda handy that way."

"Uh-huh."

"Yeah, it was no big deal, but then we ordered some pizza and some drinks. After a while, the subject of *you* came up."

Robin waited for a response, as Heywood looked back at him.

"Do you have something against me?" Robin asked.

"No."

"You sure?"

"Yes."

"I think you do."

"Well, you're wrong."

"You sure?"

"You asked that already, and I said yes."

"Positive?"

"You're getting annoying, now…"

"Orrrrrr, was I annoying before?"

The rapid-fire exchange was extremely unnerving, as Robin tried to get under Heywood's skin.

"You weren't annoying then, but you're getting annoying *now*," Heywood replied sharply.

"Well, I wouldn't want that… I would like for us to be friends." Robin put on one of his courtesy smiles.

Heywood didn't smile back, continuing to stare.

He let the smile linger for an extra minute then stood up. "Okay, good talk."

Heywood stared blankly at Robin's back as he walked back to the circulation desk. He narrowed his gaze, then went back to his thoughts.

Robin himself wasn't convinced, sensing a certain resentment toward him for some unknown reason. He suspected that Heywood had personal feelings for Angie and learning about the time he spent with her bothered him. Or perhaps it was some other reason? Robin had enough mysteries to figure out here at the branch, but one way or another, he was going to figure Heywood Learner out.

"This looks like a decent place," Gerry said, when he walked in.

After walking around for 15 minutes, he and Tommy settled for a nearby bar at 61st Street and 3rd Avenue. They found a pair of barstools in a corner and ordered two beers. They were tired of always ending up at the Pig 'N' Whistle.

"So, we settled for Thanksgiving out in Long Island and Christmas in Patillas," Tommy said, after a few sips. "My parents said it'd be nice to get out of the city for a week during the winter. Go somewhere warm."

"Sounds great, win-win all around. Everybody's happy," Gerry congratulated.

"Yeah."

"So why does it look like you just watched Mufasa's death scene from *The Lion King*?"

"Don't tell me you didn't cry yourself from that shit, man." Tommy laughed. "But seriously... this thing with Carrie." He shook his head. "Every time I look at her face, I tell myself... I chose Sarah over her. I feel so guilty, man. It's eating me up inside."

Gerry put his hand on Tommy's shoulder. "Look, I know you wanna tell her, but if *half* of what you've told me about Sarah is true... she'll kill you."

He looked over and saw that Gerry was smiling and grinned himself.

"No one told you this would be easy man, but when you work as hard as you do, the best thing to ease your mind is to treat yourself with some sort of... recreation," Gerry said.

"Like?"

"Hell do I know? Video games? Music? What do you like to do for fun?"

Tommy had kept from everyone at 58th Street his former life of playing football in college and not being drafted to the NFL. Perhaps he could play at an amateur level?

"I like… working with my hands," he answered eventually.

"Okay, that's something…"

They had a few more beers, extending their conversation over an hour. Gerry stopped drinking twenty minutes earlier in an attempt to sober up. Tommy checked his watch and said, "I had a great time talking about this, Gerry. It really helped."

"Well, we should do this more often, man. Nothing's stopping us but ourselves."

"You're right." Tommy chucked his thumb. "I'm taking the train home. You okay to drive?"

Yeah, been drinking some water this past half-hour. I'll grab a coffee to wake me up before getting the car from the parking garage."

"Okay. Lemme walk you, just in case."

"You're the boss," Gerry joked, and let out a loud chuckle.

Gerry parked the Celica in an underground garage on Madison Avenue and 54th Street.

"Well, you seem alright to drive home. See ya' tomorrow."

Gerry climbed into the car and sat behind the wheel for a minute. He slapped himself in the face a few times and stretched his neck. In reality, he was still buzzed, but it was a quick drive to Red Hook, taking Park Avenue down to The Village and the lower level of the Manhattan Bridge. He was smart enough to drive slowly, stop at the lights, and stay off the parkways.

After pulling the baby carriage up the steps, Janelle knocked on the door and Evelyn answered. She had a look on her face as if she were expecting the young mother's arrival.

"I figured it was just a matter of time," Evelyn greeted her. "You have nowhere else to go, don't you?"

Janelle was trying not to cry. "No. I've been robbed and threatened at that woman's shelter. I haven't had a good night's rest in days."

"Mm-hmm."

"I have three weeks of maternity leave and then I'll be back to work after Thanksgiving. I'll contribute to the household the most that I can…"

Evelyn tilted her head, inviting her inside. Janelle took a seat on the couch and put Simon on her lap.

"You pay $50.00 a month for rent, due by the tenth of every month…" Evelyn started while standing in front of her in the middle of the living room. "I'll buy your diapers, formula, and other food for the baby, but *you* pay for your groceries."

Janelle nodded repeatedly. "Okay. I take it the results finally came and you're convinced he's Avery's, now?"

She replied with a simple nod. Despite being stern with her, Evelyn decided to share something. "You know, Avery doesn't know this, but I got pregnant with his older sister when I was your age."

"Really?"

Evelyn nodded. "By the time she was 20 she was falling in with the wrong type of people. Got involved with drugs." She shook her head and let out a sigh. "Found her in a crack house. Dead with a needle in her arm."

"Oh God!" Janelle gasped.

"After I had Avery, I told myself I'd never let that happen again. That's why I push him so hard, and why I'm *extremely* overprotective of him."

"I understand, ma'am."

"Good… because what I'm about to tell you, I'm only saying *once*."

Janelle straightened up and listened.

"You so much as *touch* my son again and get pregnant a second time, I will chop you up, bury the pieces of your body in seven different parks while handing out flyers saying you missing!"

Janelle took a sharp breath as a chill went down her spine.

"I'll raise that child as my own, you understand me?" Evelyn asked coldly.

"Yes," she whispered.

"Good." The mother then smiled. "The couch pulls out to a bed, keep the TV low after 9 pm. I have an old crib my sister's bringing over this afternoon." She stood up and asked, "You hungry?"

Janelle smiled nervously. "I'm starving,"

"Do you have your WIC card yet?" Evelyn asked.

"Uh, wick? What's wick?"

"Wha' the? First thing tomorrow we're going to the public assistance office! You an unwed teenage mother and don't know nothing about WIC and food stamps?! What the hell's wrong with you?!"

Janelle looked down. "I'm sorry."

Evelyn sighed. "Don't worry, baby… you gonna be alright." She nodded and turned to the kitchen. "You gonna be alright."

Augustus stepped off the private jet after it landed in Guadalajara. It always felt great to return to Jalisco and his home country of Mexico. He turned around and helped Dea walk down the steps. After meeting several times together, he was surprised when she agreed to accompany him on this trip. The pair climbed into a cab that was waiting for them.

He looked at the passing landscape and sighed. "I love it here. I wish I never had to leave."

"It is very lovely," Dea agreed. "I feel the same way about Santo Domingo, where I grew up."

Augustus turned from the window for a moment. "You're Dominican?" he asked, with a surprised look.

She smiled. "Actually, I grew up in Santo Domingo… Ecuador. A common misconception."

"Ah, yes... I didn't mean to sound shocked. I have nothing against Dominicans, it's just that—"

Dea held up a hand. "You don't need to apologize. I've heard it before. My mother is from Ecuador, but my father was born and raised in Spain."

"Fascinating. I'm so glad you decided to come with me to see my alma mater's museum dedicated to my photography."

"The pleasure... was all mine," she replied, with a smile.

The University of Guadalajara was located in the heart of the city. The cab dropped them off at the school's Center of Art, Architecture, and Design, and they were met by the faculty department head, a woman named Isis Gómez.

The trio exchanged pleasantries in Spanish, then Isis said, "We have been expecting you, Mister Chavez. Your exhibit has been a successful draw for visitors, as well as past alumni."

Isis led Augustus and Dea inside the facility. It was only three rooms, but there were over sixty photographs of all sizes displayed on all the walls. Each picture took him back to a certain time in his life.

"I remember when every single picture here was taken." He walked up to a portrait of an Australian Aborigine standing on a huge boulder, looking out across the landscape.

Augustus turned to Dea. "People always believed that Aboriginal people feared cameras and photography... but all you have to do is befriend them, and merely *ask* as a courtesy."

"Remarkable."

"I stayed among them for six months, observed all their culture, learning their way of life. Contrary to what you may believe, they're very intelligent."

He started pacing around, chest forward, proud of what was being preserved and displayed as a reflection of his career. "I've traveled the world many times, having done everything from smoking with Bob Marley to climbing Mount Kilimanjaro."

"Indeed," Isis agreed. "We hope to keep the exhibit open for at least three years, and even after that, one room will always be dedicated to your contributions."

"I really want to thank you and the university for this."

"It was our pleasure, Mister Chavez. I'll leave you to explore some more, and you can look for me when you're ready to leave."

He nodded, and Isis left Augustus and Dea to look at the pictures themselves.

"I don't mean to pry," Dea began, "but I find it amazing that a mere librarian could afford private jets and his own exhibit in a university he attended."

"Well, in the past I was much more, and merely settled for a simpler profession," he replied. "I can live comfortably with what was earned way, way back when." Augustus didn't feel like revealing too much, like his failure as an archeologist, making no big discoveries.

"I see, so was all that true?" she asked.

"What?"

"That... climbing Mount Kilimanjaro and smoking weed with Bob Marley stuff?"

"Every word of it. I'm not exactly proud of everything I did in my youth, but—"

"You don't need to do that," she said flatly.

Augustus furrowed his brow. "I don't understand. I don't need to do what?"

"To boast about what you've done."

"I'm sorry if you took that wrong. You have to understand, I achieved a lot to get this opened. The school calls it an exhibit, but I'm pretty much calling it a *museum* to what I've done. *This...*" he waved around the room, "is my legacy. And excuse me if I come across frank, but I didn't bring you down here to flaunt it."

Dea blushed, as she looked down upon hearing his speech. "I apologize, I took it the wrong—"

"You don't need to apologize," he said, mirroring her words back to her. "I've heard it all before."

She smiled at the private joke and was still looking down when Augustus walked up and lifted her face gently with his fingertip. Her eyes met his and she nearly faltered.

"What time is the flight back to New York?" Dea asked, to snap out of her trance.

"It leaves in four hours… but can be rescheduled for tomorrow."

She raised an eyebrow. "Know any good places to eat?"

Their faces inched closer. She fought her feelings, but she couldn't resist any longer as they finally shared a kiss.

"Election's tomorrow, you voting?" Gerry asked Tommy.

It was fifteen minutes past noon Monday, and the lunch rush was beginning to make the clerks a little busy.

"Yeah, Sarah's big into civic duties. Makes us go the moment the polls open. You?"

"Ah, I'll think about it. Moynihan's got the senate, Cuomo should get another term, world keeps on spinning. Nothing changes, man."

"Nice attitude." Tommy grinned. "Hey, you heading down to Barclay Street next payday, to get a free turkey?"

"You bet. I pay my union dues. I'm getting my turkey!" Gerry replied. "Wanna go together? I'm asking Robin later if he could tag along. I can give you a ride down, too."

"The kid's not full-time. Don't they check?" Tommy asked.

"Nah, every year there's always a surplus left over. I'm sure they won't care."

"Alright, you're on."

"Great, I'll make sure the three of us close that Friday."

They resumed their duties at their separate terminals.

"I don't think it's fair that I'm working these holidays, and I don't know what to do," Heywood said. Zelda was working the information desk as Heywood sat next to her. It was slow so far, so they had a moment when he could vent to her.

"The holidays are always thin, with a lot of staff traveling to visit family members out of state," Zelda explained.

"So, because I'm estranged with my family, I get to suffer?"

A male patron came up and asked Zelda a reference question, which she answered. Then, when they were alone again, she said, "if I may recall, your first two years here at 58th Street, you requested both holidays off. Which is why Augustus beat you to the punch this time."

She had him there. Heywood pouted at the memory and sighed.

Zelda knew that should have been the end of the conversation, but she felt sorry for him and offered a suggestion. "Have you asked Angie to possibly *switch* one of those holidays with you?"

"Hmmm... didn't think of that. She's been pushing this Native American presentation she wants me to pitch to Chavez. Speaking of which... how do I go about doing that? She hasn't given me anything to present to him, and he's been looking for recommendations."

"Well, he's not that complicated. A general idea of what you have in mind will be enough for him," Zelda replied.

Sonyai walked into the auditorium to find Augustus waiting for her, alone. There was something weird with him today, but she couldn't put her finger on it. He seemed more... pleasant... than usual.

"Hmph, you're here early," she greeted, approaching him.

"I know this meeting was spur of the moment, but it won't be long," Augustus said.

"Okay."

He cleared his throat. "Now that Walker's been brought back into the fray, things are back to normal, with no incidents."

"Yes, I suppose so."

"And in the spirit of keeping things pleasant between the staff, I propose we bring back the holiday gift exchange next month."

Sonyai was quiet for a moment. She then let out a sigh. "We haven't done one of those in two years... for a reason."

"Yes, I'm aware, and in light of certain individuals moving on, I think we can have one…"

"…without any incidents," Sonyai finished, arching an eyebrow.

"Exactly." Augustus smiled.

*I hate that goddamn smile,* Sonyai thought. "Okay, can't wait to see how this goes."

"Excellent." He walked past her to leave. "I knew we were on the same page, and we'll continue to be there."

He held the door open for her.

Sonyai slowly approached. *He's laying it on thick,* but smiled a fake smile as she walked through.

# CHAPTER ELEVEN

Robin, Tanya, and Lakeshia were sitting at the kitchen table in the staff room at two-thirty. Lakeshia occasionally glanced across the table to Robin, as he studied a chapter in his textbook and took notes. Tanya could sense the youngest page was eager to start a conversation with him, and after five of the longest, unbearable minutes she said, "hey, Robin, wha'cha workin' on over there?"

She put some extra volume on the question, which startled both Robin and Lakeshia, who turned to give Tanya an icy stare while Robin replied without looking up, "I just started this night class. I missed enrolling in regular classes back in September, so I had to settle for nutrition."

"Gee, that sounds… interesting," Lakeshia chimed in.

Tanya nudged her shoulder and mouthed, "You're welcome," then stuck her tongue out playfully.

"I was skeptical at first since it has nothing to do with my major, but it's been very informative." He finally looked up with a smile.

"Really? How so?" Lakeshia placed her face in her hand, giving him her full attention.

They talked for several minutes, as Tanya ignored the conversation she pushed to start, reading her copy of *The Source*.

The door opened and Alex walked in, then froze. "Oh, *you're* up here," she said to Robin, then walked around the table to the pair of sofas at the opposite side of the room. Robin greeted her with a middle finger raised in the air as she passed.

"As I was saying," Robin began, "the class really has me thinking of adjusting my meals. By eating five small meals stretched out through the day, and still exercising, I think I can tone up."

Alex snickered to herself as Tanya lowered her magazine. "What do you mean, tone up?"

He turned in her direction and explained, "I only eat two full meals a day with a few snacks in between, and drink nothing but water, orange juice, and Gatorade."

"Okay," Lakeshia said.

"I was a lot fatter in elementary school, but when I got to Gee-Dubs I started lifting weights, running, and learning martial arts, now forty percent of my body is muscle. I'm trying to get that number to forty-five, possibly fifty."

He pulled his polo shirt up over his head, revealing a chest full of curly hair and a solid stomach. Across the table, Lakeshia's eyes widened as she took in a breath, completely transfixed at the sight.

"Go ahead, take a shot," he challenged Tanya, while patting his gut. "It'll be like punching a wall."

Tanya grimaced. "That's okay."

"I'll do it!" Alex volunteered.

Robin put his shirt back on and waved her off. "No way... you'll kick me in the nuts."

She grinned. "You're right, I would. You have tiny tits by the way..."

"They're called *pecs*," Robin insisted.

"They're totally tits," she replied. "You're almost an A-cup."

"Oh yeah? Can tits do this?" he contracted his chest muscles to move up and down. "Huh? Just like Super Macho Man from Mike Tyson's Punch-Out!"

"Eww! Gross!" Alex stood up and gasped in horror, then stormed out of the room.

Robin let out a sinister chuckle then packed up his books and left a few moments later. The two girls were now alone at the table. Tanya picked up her glass of water and splashed it in Lakeshia's face.

She snapped out of her trance with a gasp. "Thank you," she whispered politely.

Angie was browsing the shelves, looking for titles to fill reserves. She had a list of books that people requested and according to the computer, they were checked in and available.

"...*The Virgin Suicides* by Eugenides... ah here it is. *The Shipping News*? Again? Wow, that one's becoming popular. Hmmm, Proulx, that's over here..."

"Excuse me, Miss?"

She turned to find an African-American gentleman approaching her.

"Are you in charge of the reserves?" he asked.

"Yes, as a matter of fact, I am."

"I was wondering if you could tell me why my hold for Octavia E. Butler's *Parable of the Sower* is taking so long."

"Well, I would have to check my computer, but I'm sure that since it's a popular book, a lot of other people have requested it, and we only have so many copies," Angie explained.

"I figured you'd say that, so *I* checked. There are over a hundred holds for *Parable of the Sower*, but only twenty-five copies are available in the entire system."

"I'd have to check that for myself, but what's your point?"

"I checked on how many other sci-fi novels you have by the likes of Arthur C. Clarke, David Webber, Star Wars, Star Trek, and Doctor Who titles and there are twice as many in the system."

Angie narrowed her gaze, knowing what he was insinuating. "Our titles are all about supply and demand. Those others you mentioned obviously have a bigger fan-base and a higher demand—"

"You only have limited copies because you don't support black authors, let alone black *female* authors who write science fiction," he interrupted.

"That is not true."

"I think it *is*."

"Look, we are not in control of the market. We go where the trends take us. There are other important factors to account for. There might be twenty-five copies available because we originally bought 30 or 40 and copies weren't returned."

"Oh, so what, we're stealing copies, now?"

"I don't mean a specific group of people. We have book thieves of all—"

"Libraries are just tools of the government to control literature and the access to certain titles to discourage minorities, admit it!"

"If there were more requests for her books, we would buy more to fill them. There is no agenda. We work independently, under *no* government's authority! Now if you'd excuse me, I have other titles to look for!" Angie stormed past him.

"Yeah, but I bet none of them are by black authors!" he yelled back.

Sonyai and Tommy were working the circulation desk, when Robin walked in the clerical office with a paper bag of sodas. He was still presenting Ethel and Gerry with refreshments every day since Ethel unnerved him with a condescending request. Robin turned the tables on Ethel, making the task into a ritual, to get back at her. Refusing to accept the drinks at first, she relented and made a note to never intimidate the young clerk ever again.

He placed a can of Diet Sprite in front of Ethel then took out two cans of regular Sprite for himself and Gerry, who piggy-backed on the ritual to upset Ethel further. Robin handed Gerry a can then put his next to Ethel's while he hung up his book bag on some shelves.

Gerry popped open his can and turned his back to read the *Daily News*.

"Hey, did the Nets beat San Antonio last night?" Robin asked.

Behind the two, Ethel grabbed a can, opened it, and took a deep chug. Gerry checked the sports section in the back of the newspaper. "Lost, 96 to 105," he replied.

"Damn!" Robin snapped his fingers.

"Local elections are tomorrow. You registered to vote?" Gerry asked.

"Didn't get the chance to vote for Clinton, so I haven't done it yet."

"These senator and governor elections are important too, Robin."

He shrugged. As the two continued their conversation, Ethel started shaking her head as her vision became blurry. Her breaths became shallow, and she felt unbalanced and disoriented.

"Since Guliani became Mayor, things aren't going to get better. Those dudes up in Albany don't care what happens here in New York…"

"That's where you're wrong," Gerry replied. "They help set aside the funds we need to keep us running. The right representative can mean the difference between getting a raise or getting your hours cut."

Ethel started waving her arms, trying to get Gerry and Robin's attention.

"Alright, I definitely plan on voting in '97. I was so pissed when Dinkins lost."

"Good. I'm holding you to it. Hey, you probably don't know this, but every year before Thanksgiving, the union gives out Butterball turkeys at their headquarters near the twin towers. Me and Tommy are going down. Wanna come with?"

"I don't eat turkey. I wouldn't even know how to cook it," Robin replied, with a shrug.

"They also give out checks for $25.00. We're taking my new car down. Tag along!"

Ethel started panting and making gurgling noises as Robin turned around and gasped, "Ethel!?"

Gerry sprang up and turned, just as Ethel began to fall forward. Robin sprang across the room, "Whoa!" He secured her shoulders and eased her on the floor. Lying on her back, Ethel started to convulse.

Gerry opened the door. "Yi! Call an ambulance! Something's wrong with Jenkins!" He then turned to Robin. "Hold her steady! Make sure she doesn't bite her tongue!"

Tommy, Augustus, and Eugene rushed inside as Robin started to panic. "Ethel! Ethel! Hold on, help is on the way! Stay still, Ethel! ETHEL!!"

Twenty minutes later, Ethel was put on a stretcher by paramedics and wheeled outside to a parked ambulance. Sonyai, Augustus, and Eugene were questioning Robin and Gerry in the clerical office.

"We were just talking!" Robin explained. "When suddenly she keeled over!"

"What, exactly, were you doing right before this happened?" Augustus asked.

"Talking!" Gerry said for the fifth time. "She was sitting in her corner, while me and Robin were minding our business on the other side of the room! Why are we getting interrogated here?"

"We told the paramedics what happened," Robin chimed in. "They said this had something to do with her having diabetes."

Eugene surveyed the room and noticed the cans on the desks. "Was she drinking one of these before it happened?"

Robin craned his head and noticed his can was open, but Ethel's Diet Sprite next to it wasn't. "Yeah."

"If she's a diabetic, wouldn't she drink the diet soda and not the regular one?" Eugene asked.

"That one's mine. She always drinks the diet."

Gerry looked himself and said, "she must have took the wrong can."

Sonyai and Augustus exchanged glances and Eugene narrowed his gaze at Robin.

The intercom line rang at Sonyai's desk, she walked over and picked up the receiver. "Yes?" She then turned to Augustus and said, "keep them outside, we'll be out there in a minute," and slammed the phone down. "S.I.U. is here!"

"Who the hell called *them*?" Augustus hissed.

"What the fuck?" Gerry yelled.

"I did," Eugene replied, and stepped forward to Robin. "We need to make sure this *was* actually an accident."

Robin's eyes went wide. "The fuck you trying to say?"

"Everyone calm down," Sonyai ordered. "Let's just cooperate with Special Investigations, answer all their questions truthfully… and sort this out later."

Everyone put on stoic faces and filed out of the office.

Heywood and Angie stared blankly as three white men stood in the middle of the branch, waiting patiently. Patrons were making feeble attempts to ignore the tension that filled the air after Ethel was removed. Two of the gentlemen wore brown three-quarter raincoats with dress shirts beneath them. The one who was in charge wore a black suit with a matching fedora and aviator sunglasses.

"They look like secret service agents," Heywood whispered.

"Who are they?" Angie asked.

"They are from the Special Investigations Unit," Zelda answered, stepping from the shelves. "Former police officers, ex-military, and criminal consultants or examiners."

"Library… cops? There's really such a thing?" Heywood asked.

"Whatever you do, keep your answers short, don't volunteer any information, and above all, say what you know for certain and draw no conclusions on your own," Zelda warned.

"Whatever you do," Augustus instructed under his breath, as he and the clerks emerged from the office, "keep your answers short, don't volunteer any information, and above all, say what you know for certain and draw no conclusions on your own."

"I've dealt with them five-oh wannabes before," Gerry replied flatly.

"Me too, on one occasion," Robin snarled.

Eugene stepped out from behind them and walked to the trio, introducing himself. "Eugene Iscaro," he said, as he extended his hand.

The man in the suit removed his glasses and completed the handshake. "Levi Kraine, Special Investigations. With me, are Harvey Applebaum and William Amend."

"I recommend questioning the staff separately, in three different locations, as per the procedure," Eugene said.

"We know the drill. I understand there's a small auditorium upstairs?"

"That is correct."

"Alright." He stepped toward the circulation desk. "Mister Augustus Chavez, you and I will talk in your office, and I will send for others to be questioned one by one."

"Understood."

"Mister... Gerrald Coltraine? ...will follow Mister Amend upstairs to the auditorium."

Levi looked around for a moment and then asked, "Where's Ms. Robin Walker?"

Robin sighed and stepped forward. "It's not Ms. It's Mister!"

The supervisor stared at Robin, then pulled out a piece of paper and scanned it for a moment. He pushed up the brim of his hat, raising an eyebrow, and asked, "Are you aware that your employee record has you listed as a woman, young man?"

"I'm aware, Elliot Ness, and *yes*, I'll get human resources on it to fix that." Robin nodded. "Yo, Detective John Kelly? Follow me to the staff room!" he said, walking to the staircase.

"It's Applebaum," the man replied, and followed close behind Robin.

"Hey, what happened to you, by the way?" Robin joked. "They wrote you off in the last episode!"

Over the next hour, the librarians and clerks were interviewed by all three representatives, who asked the same series of questions.

"Where were you, when the incident involving library clerk Jenkins occurred?"

"I was outside at the circulation desk accepting returns," Sonyai replied, when questioned.

"I was doing checkouts," Tommy explained.

"I was in the staff room," Angie told the investigator.

"I was in my office," Augustus said. "Um, is there any way we could come to an understanding about this?" he added. "I'm sure we can help each other out and minimize how serious this investigation has to be?"

"I'm not saying anything, but to say how I'm not saying anything without a union representative here to assure me that I don't HAVE to say anything…" Gerry ranted.

"I was working at the information desk, sir… yes sir, sir, yes sir I was," Heywood answered with a nervous laugh.

"I walked in," Robin began, "handed everyone a soda, and sat down. Next thing I knew, she was shaking on the floor."

Zelda sat quietly, not answering the question.

"Did you know of library clerk Jenkins' medical condition?"

"No," Angie said.

"What medical condition?" Tommy asked.

"It was no secret she was overweight," Sonyai began, "but she was a very private person."

"All I got to say is, I'm not saying…" Gerry replied.

"I had no clue," Augustus answered with a shrug, then asked, "Um, how much do you make a year?"

"Not that I know of, but I haven't been here long," Robin explained.

"Oh, no, no, no, no, no, not at all," Heywood stammered, as he shook his head repeatedly.

Zelda continued to sit without saying a word.

"Do you have any idea what *actually* happened in the clerical office at the time of the incident?"

"She seemed to have had some sort of seizure," Robin answered, dumbfounded.

"$1,000.00," Augustus offered, "for each one of you. Make a report, say nothing happened, and the money will be delivered in an envelope... no one needs to know."

"Miss Jenkins suffered an attack from what the paramedics told me, but details were very minimal," Sonyai replied.

Gerry folded his arms. "Union. Rep."

"Your guess is as good as mine," Tommy said.

"She's in the hospital. How she got there?" Angie shrugged. "I can't tell you."

Heywood just stared back, blinking.

Zelda looked back at each investigator with a smile.

"Finally, to the best of your knowledge, is there animosity between any of the employees and library clerk Jenkins?"

Each clerk, Augustus, Angie, and Heywood, universally answered, "no."

Upon being questioned by her second investigator, Harvey Applebaum, he scolded Zelda, "Miss Clein, you're being very uncooperative with us and it's unbecoming..."

Levi stepped in the room and whispered something in Applebaum's ear, then tilted his head to leave. The head investigator turned and left the room himself. Applebaum scratched his head. "Well, I guess your reputation precedes you." He waved his hand to the door for her to leave. "You have been found exempt from any further questioning."

The assistant librarian stood up and walked out of the staff room.

"Good doggie," Zelda muttered under her breath.

"We'll need to question the three library pages as well," Levi said, after the first series of questions.

"Why?" Sonyai asked. "None of them were present at the time."

"Just to cover all bases. When are they scheduled to arrive?"

"This is ridiculous. Would you like to interrogate the patrons as well?" Augustus scoffed.

The investigator stepped to Augustus and stopped an inch from his nose. "Don't. Tempt. Me." He then walked to the staircase to go upstairs. "Send the pages to the staff room when they come in. Applebaum and Amend? Make sure no one briefs them."

"I was told you wanted to speak with me?" Levi asked Robin in the auditorium.

They were still waiting for the pages to arrive. Robin had whispered to Harvey to have Levi meet him there alone.

"Yeah. Look man, I didn't want to play this card, but um..." he motioned for Levi to lean in, then whispered, "I'm The Ninth Witness."

Levi leaned back and looked at him skeptically.

"There *is* no Ninth Witness, only The Eight... *if* you're referring to what I think you're referring to."

Robin just looked back at him as Levi's eyes darted in different directions.

"Two people are walking across a bridge," Levi said suddenly. "One is the father of the other one's son. What is the relationship between the two people walking across the bridge?"

"Boyfriend and girlfriend," Robin answered, then held up three fingers.

"Okay, guess I need an updated list. When did you see *him*?"

He shook his head. "You know I can't disclose that. But I'm telling you this to show how dedicated I am to this job. The lengths they'll go to protect me. There's nothing to question in this incident."

"We'll see."

There was a knock on the door. Harvey poked his head in and said, "the pages are here."

The pages were questioned for twenty minutes, then sent to work the shelves for the rest of the afternoon. It was now after six o'clock. The branch was closed, and the entire remaining staff (except for Zelda) were waiting, as the three S.I.U. representatives conferred in private.

"Is this a good sign?" Sonyai asked Augustus.

"If Zelda has taught me anything, it's when dealing with the S.I.U... nothing goes as it's expected."

The trio exchanged nods and turned to the group. Levi cleared his throat and said, "after interviewing the employees here, we've concluded that there's a possibility that this wasn't an accident. I'm afraid a *formal* investigation will have to take place."

Robin's jaw fell as everyone reacted with shock and disappointment. Except for Alex, who couldn't stop smiling.

"A hearing will be held, with the S.I.U. presenting a case... of inappropriate behavior by Mister Walker."

"WHAT?!?!?" Robin screamed.

"Now see here," Augustus began, stepping forward. Gerry and Sonyai also voiced their objections, while Lakeshia cupped her mouth in fright.

"*With. That. Said.*" Levi said sharply. "It is our recommendation that Robin Walker be removed from duty, to prepare his defense at the hearing, while the case is presented to a panel of human resources officials." He put on his hat and sunglasses.

"This is bullshit! You're suspending me?!" Robin yelled. "I *JUST* got back!"

Levi lifted his glasses with a look. "Back?!" he asked.

Sonyai and Augustus turned and looked back at Robin with warning glances.

"Um, never mind..." he whispered.

"To compensate for the absence of two clerks, a full-time clerk from your cluster will be temporarily assigned... while a part-time clerk from the floating rotation will replace Ms. Walker, who apparently is a Mister. We'll try to get that fixed for you..." He waved for his subordinates to leave. "You all are dismissed. See you at Mid-Manhattan, Walker."

Augustus stood in their way. "I don't think this is necessary."

"I'm afraid I have to disagree," Levi replied. "If he did nothing, he has nothing to hide. Rest assured the S.I.U. will get to the bottom of it. Have a nice day."

As his men walked out the door, Levi looked back to Robin. "Mister Walker, since you're a part-time employee, and not a dues-paying member of the DC37 union, you will need outside representation to defend you... perhaps Jacoby and Myers can take your case... pro bono." A sinister laugh echoed in the library as Levi Kraine left.

Robin was still frozen in shock at the unbelievable turn of events.

Ethel woke up and looked around. She was in a hospital bed with an IV in her arm. The city outside her window was dark. There wasn't a clock in the room. Hopefully, someone would come in and check on her.

She let out a sigh of relief. *It worked.*

It was a big risk to trigger a spike in her blood sugar by drinking the regular Sprite, instead of the Diet, intentionally. It could have caused a reaction that she wouldn't recover from. But having an incident at the job, she could file paperwork to take medical leave immediately, and then follow up with her retirement.

*No one would be the wiser... I just hope no one got in trouble over this.*

Angie and Heywood left immediately after being dismissed. Lakeshia looked at Robin and asked, "Are you gonna be okay?"

He didn't know how to answer. Sonyai walked up to him. Tanya and Lakeshia looked on with concerned glances, but Alex was *still* grinning.

"Tell me you believe me," Robin pleaded to Sonyai. "That you know I would never…"

"I do," she replied. "Don't worry, there's no way…"

Robin looked past her to Eugene, who was still staring back from the information desk. "HEY!" he yelled, stepping forward. "Who the hell asked you to bring S.I.U. into this mess, Baby Huey!?"

Eugene tilted his head at the insult. "What did you say?!"

"You heard me you fat fuck!"

The security guard growled, "You wanna rethink who you're talking to with that tone…" Eugene warned. "Considering these will be your last spoken words before leaving this earth!"

"Better asswipes than you have tried!"

Robin cocked his arm back to swing at Eugene, who was prepared for a telegraphed punch, but at the last minute, Robin brought up his foot and kicked Eugene between his legs. He then followed with a hard open palm across his jaw. Augustus and Tommy grabbed Robin and pulled him back as Gerry stopped Eugene from getting up and charging back at Robin.

"You're fucking dead, kid!" Eugene roared.

"Bring your ass up to the heights, motherfucker!" Robin yelled back, waving his arm. "179th Street! 111 Wadsworth Avenue! Apartment 16D! You get me fired over this, I'm putting you in the Hudson!"

"Damnit, stop fighting!" Sonyai yelled. "What's done is done!" She pointed at Robin. "You need to leave, NOW! And think about how you're going to deal with this hearing!"

Without another word, Robin stormed off through the exit.

Alex whispered, "179th Street… Wadsworth Avenue…"

*16D…* Lakeshia thought as well, holding her chin.

The pages left a few moments after Robin's departure. Sonyai, Tommy, and Gerry went back to the clerical office to retrieve their belongings. They came out and left the branch, as Augustus and Eugene stood alone on the floor.

"You got thirty seconds to explain why the hell you didn't check with me before calling Special Investigations!"

"Before I came here, I was made aware of an incident that took place back in March…" Eugene began.

"Made aware by whom?"

"I can't say, but I know Ethel and Alex were responsible."

"Jenkins played a minimal role in the incident—"

"But it's enough to lay a foundation of animosity between the two," Eugene interrupted. "I believe Robin started this soda thing to develop a level of trust, only to switch cans on purpose to get her back."

Augustus couldn't tell if the security guard was serious. "That is so far-fetched, it reeks of a daytime soap opera!" He brought his finger up, pointing to Eugene's chest. "You were brought back here to keep the peace, not create your own 'Trial of the Century' by planting a bloody glove!"

Eugene stiffened at the comparison. "I'm leaving now. Like they said, if Robin has nothing to hide, they'll investigate, find him innocent, and let him go."

Augustus clenched his jaw. "You overstepped the line with this one. It only happens *once*, Iscaro…" He went back to his office, as Eugene headed toward the exit.

# CHAPTER TWELVE

ALEX LEFT SCHOOL AT ONE O'CLOCK IN THE AFTERNOON TUESDAY, cutting her last two periods. She also planned to call out from working at the library. With Robin suspended, she decided to take advantage and do some following of her own, now that she knew where he lived. He discovered Janelle's secrets by following her. She intended to do the same and find some dirt on him.

She exited the 1-train 181st Street station, and made her way down Saint Nicholas Avenue, toward 179th Street. The pair of high-rise apartment buildings looked daunting on the opposite sides of the street, but Robin's was one block up, on Wadsworth Avenue. Alex had no idea how she would get in, so she decided to wait at a corner across the street, to see if Robin would go anywhere.

Her so-called disguise was some baggy street clothes she bought, a baseball cap turned backwards, and sunglasses.

*I look like some reject from a Kris Kross video!* She thought, with a certain disgust.

She was so busy loathing her outfit, she almost missed Robin's exit from the building. He was heading around the corner, back toward Saint Nicholas Avenue. After giving him enough distance, Alex slowly followed him to the Fort Washington Library.

Despite living up the street, Robin hadn't been to Fort Washington since his last day back in the beginning of February. He climbed the steps from the entrance inside and turned to his right, entering through the turnstile that led to the returns side of their circulation desk. The clerk behind the terminal was an unfamiliar face, and the information desk was vacant. After weaving through the shelves for a moment, Robin came up behind a short 16-year-old wearing a red sweater and jeans.

He said something in Russian that translated loosely to, *"Your mother wears combat boots."*

Ivan Dmitrievich turned his head and smiled. "Robin Walker! Tovarish!" The page greeted him with a hug. "What are you doing here?"

"I'm just checking to see how everyone's doing, how are you?" Robin said.

"I'm fine, fine, my friend. How's life as a part-time clerk, full-time college student?" Ivan asked. "I'll find out myself in two years!"

"It's a lot of hard work, but I wouldn't trade it for anything. So, you're in charge now?" He asked.

Ivan nodded. "Yes, yes... Shinbaio moved on. He's at Inwood, I believe, and well, um..."

Robin stopped him. "Yeah, about that... is it true?"

He looked down. "I honestly didn't think Guzman would take it that far, but everyone else was going along with the gag. I thought he would eventually tell her the truth..."

"It's okay, I'm not mad... at you. But where is she now?" Robin asked.

"I don't know. Um, she left for a while, then came back, then left again. I believe she's attending school, but also works in several different branches," Ivan explained.

Robin thought about it for a moment, then nodded. "Okay, it was great seeing you again, Ivan." He smiled and left the page to resume his duties. He then turned and walked toward the circulation desk, where now two *familiar* clerks stood.

"Well, well, well... Robin Walker," Demetrius Chamberlain greeted him. "You're looking pretty healthy there... for a dead man."

The African-American clerk nudged the other clerk's shoulder and asked, "hey, you see someone over there?"

"Nah, must be a ghost... someone who died a long time ago," Tony Cedeno replied, with a grin.

"Uh-huh, very funny guys..." Robin grunted. "Who thought it'd be a good idea to tell Rose I was dead?"

"You really need to ask?" Demetrius asked.

"I just did, but you're right... I know you didn't go with it out of the goodness of your heart... What'd it cost?"

They looked at each other. "Trevor gave everyone $100.00 to go with the lie. Clerks, pages, even that IA. She left for overseas after graduation in June last year, then came back in August when you were out and started going to school."

Robin was stunned by Trevor's audacity. "But I came back and worked that weird ass split shift in September. She was gone by then, so where is she now?"

"She went to St. John's, but she's working in a clerical rotation program that sends her all over. Don't know which branch she's at now." He cocked an eyebrow. "She might be heading your way, since there's a shortage of clerks suddenly."

*How could they have found out, already!?* Robin screamed in his head.

"Rose is gonna think y'all a bunch of dicks when she learns the truth," he warned.

"Ask me if I give a shit!" The two clerks laughed, as Robin walked past and headed down the hallway leading to the back office. He approached the door, which was ajar, and knocked while announcing himself. "Knock, knock."

Fort Washington's clerical office ran deep to the back of the building and was divided by a divider made of opaque glass and wood. The ceiling was partly open, so patrons could sometimes overhear loud conversations, if they stood near the music section. On the left side was a series of desks for each of the clerks and a separate one used by the pages.

On the right side was one isolated office dedicated to Fort Washington's head librarian, Robin's mentor, Barbara Schemanske. He was surprised that Theresa Burns, Fort Washington's elderly senior clerk, was nowhere to be found. Her desk was all the way in the back of the office on the left corner.

"Nobody home," he whispered.

Robin crossed over to the right side, where the door to Barbara's office was open. He knocked on the glass and called out, "hello?"

"You really stepped into it this time, didn't you?" a gravelly voice asked.

As if she was expecting him, the head librarian sat at her desk looking back at him, her fingers interlocked and resting in front of her. Robin stepped in and closed the door. "Where is everyone?" he asked.

"It's election day. The staff has been given extended lunch breaks so they can vote."

"Oh."

"They're saying you intentionally tried to poison your co-worker with a can of soda."

"Poisoned! Oh my God! I did no such—"

"I DON'T CARE!" she bellowed. "What the hell were you thinking?!"

Robin pointed above his head, indicating there were people on the other side that probably heard her shout.

She waved her hand and said, "start explaining."

Alex entered the library she had followed Robin to. She was afraid he might see her, and the attempt of disguise she was wearing, but he wasn't anywhere to be seen. The page was impressed by the elevated shelves, accessible by a pair of steps on opposite sides, and resisted the urge to go up there for a bird's-eye view of the entire floor.

She pretended to browse the fiction section, selected a random book, and took a seat at one of the two reading nook benches underneath the huge windows at the front of the branch. From her vantage point, she could see the circulation desk, a staircase to the second floor, and the hallway leading to the back.

A page pushed a shelving cart nearby and gave her a questioning look, then continued through the arrangement of shelves. There was still no sign of Robin. He could be upstairs in the children's room… or downstairs in the reference basement. Alex decided to move down the hallway in front of the circulation desk and take the back stairwell to explore the branch reference room.

"Hey, where's Alex?" Lakeshia asked.

"She called out. Miss Yi said she was feeling sick," Tanya replied.

"Great, as if things couldn't get any *more* worse."

"Let me guess, you're worried about Robin."

Lakeshia nodded, looking out to see Gerry and Tiannah talking at the circulation desk. "He was just trying to put this thing with Sonyai and Janelle behind him, and now this happens."

"Despite him getting Janelle to transfer out there in The Bronx, I feel he didn't do anything this time around. We'll have to wait and see," Tanya said.

"Yeah."

Meanwhile, at the circulation desk, things were slowly calming down after the lunch hour rush.

"I can't believe that young boy is being accused of such an unspeakable act!" the clerk from Yorkville said. She was handling returns, while Gerry was doing checkouts.

"It's all a misunderstanding," Gerry replied. "I just didn't think S.I.U. would find evidence of whatever Robin is being accused of."

"Well, I really hope he's found innocent. Still, it is good to come help a different library during the week. I really like this cozy little branch."

"Well, we enjoy having you," Gerry said, with a smile.

"What do you plan to do, Gus?" Zelda asked.

She and Augustus were in his office.

"Nothing. Yi can handle it on her own. The less I know, the better," Augustus replied. *And besides, I got other fish to fry.*

"I was tempted to reach out to Babs. I know how Robin values his privacy, after the *previous* time I contacted her regarding his affairs."

The head librarian thought for a moment what she meant, but then put it aside to ponder another time. "We need to follow up on Jenkins' status and ensure we'll be covered."

"I haven't heard anything yet, but we have enough help coming to get us through the week."

"Good." He stood up. "I have to get the evening's film presentation ready."

"You don't really think he did this, do you?" Zelda asked.

Augustus stopped in his tracks as he pondered the question. "He's sent this branch into chaos since he arrived…" He sighed heavily. "But no. I'm certain he didn't do this. There's more to this conspiracy than what's being shown, but whatever happens, it's too early to do anything about it."

He left his office as Zelda sat alone with her thoughts.

"So that's it," Robin finished. "What do I do? I need someone there to defend me."

Barbara was rubbing her forehead. "Report to human resources at the Mid-Manhattan library tomorrow, 9 am, sharp. I know someone that can help you. If you're lucky, S.I.U. won't have a leg to stand on and they'll be laughed out of the hearing."

"And if I'm *un*lucky?"

"If it goes past the first day, you'll be terminated by Friday."

Robin gasped.

"Get a night's rest and be ready tomorrow. The S.I.U. are the most formidable opponents you'll ever face."

He turned and left, his hands shaking as he opened the door back out to the hallway. There were two sets of steps outside the back office door, one leading downstairs to the reference room, and the second that led to the staff room, which was located between floors. While lights lined the wall leading to the basement, darkness shrouded the top of the stairs where employees would enter their recreation area.

Alex was done walking around the reference area and approached the steps heading back up. She noticed another hallway lined with lockers for the staff to store their belongings, along with a shelving cart full of discarded or donated books for sale. A door opening upstairs caught her attention and she saw Robin step out of the back office.

A voice whispered out to Robin from the darkness. "I thought I smelled pussy somewhere."

From his hand shaking to the chill running down his spine, he stared up the stairs to a figure looking down at him.

"Leaving without saying goodbye? Where are your manners, Guapo?" Trevor Guzman taunted.

Robin twisted his lip in a sneer of contempt. "I thought I smelled hair mousse and Michael Jordan cologne," he replied. "What do you do? Bathe in a whole tub of it before leaving the house?"

Downstairs, Alex backed against the banister, staying out of sight and listening to their private conversation.

"Why?" Robin asked. "Why'd you do it? Why make her think I was dead? What exactly was *that* going to accomplish?"

*She thinks he's DEAD?* Alex asked herself.

Trevor laughed. "Why do I do anything? You are all pawns on my chessboard… and I'm having the time of my life playing."

He was sick of the bully's riddles and mind games. "I don't have time for this… but you and I will take care of our unfinished business one day, and then, I'm gonna kill the devil."

It was time to move on, he started heading back to the main floor when Trevor called him again, "Robin,"

He paused, as Trevor's parting words echoed in his mind. "Remember… before you dance with the devil, you must first spend a year… in hell."

"You gave us quite a scare, Miss Jenkins, but your recent tests have you back at reasonable blood sugar levels."

"Thank you doctor," Ethel said.

"I would still recommend you take it easy the next few days," he instructed.

"I plan to, sir," she said.

He nodded and left the hospital room. She was fully dressed and ready to go.

Ethel left the hospital and took a cab directly to the Mid-Manhattan library. It was three o'clock in the afternoon as she walked in the human resources department.

"I'm Ethel Jenkins, I would like to begin the paperwork for early retirement, but first, in light of what has happened this week, I'd like to take a medical leave."

It took twenty minutes of paperwork and conversations, but Ethel walked out of the building with the New York Public Library behind her. She had no personal belongings at 58th Street, and had no intention of going back to say goodbye. An emotional send-off just wasn't her style. The staff would likely be upset by her sudden departure, and only Zelda would understand, but she didn't care. She worked for the NYPL for over 30 years. She was leaving on *her terms.*

Instead of taking the train home, she decided to treat herself to a shopping trip up Fifth Avenue.

Alex waited ten minutes to go by after eavesdropping on Robin's conversation. This Trevor Guzman was the same person she heard about who had a history with Robin when he was a page. She needed to meet him. When she got to the top of the steps, back on the main floor, the voice came out of the darkness again. "Well, well, who is this?"

She gasped and looked up. "I... I'm looking for Trevor Guzman," she whispered.

"And why would someone following Robin be looking for him?" Trevor asked.

Alex chose her words carefully. "I know... about The Game."

Trevor's laugh chilled her to the bone. "Oh really? Run off, little girl. What you know and may have heard, you could never understand."

"Aren't you curious to know why I'm following Robin secretly?" she asked.

*The enemy of my enemy is my friend.*

"Okay... let's see what you know, and what you can *learn*. Go to the Young Adult books section and find yourself a seat." His voice gave her a chill as it echoed in the stairway.

Alex looked to see if there was movement from the shadows, then walked to the main floor. It was almost five o'clock now, and Robin wasn't anywhere in the branch. She walked down an aisle of shelves to the back of the library, past several reading tables, and found the Young Adult books in front of another pair of reading nook benches. She took a seat in front of the opaque windows that led to the building's back alley. A shadow appeared and moved alongside her profile.

"T... Trevor Guzman?" Alex asked.

He didn't answer.

"I know about you, Robin... and Rosana Comanos."

He still didn't answer.

"Okay, Robin took my best friend's position at our branch. She had to transfer because of him... and I'm looking to make him pay!" she yelled.

"Ah..." Trevor finally replied through the glass. "And what better way than to hurt someone than to ally yourself with their enemy? Interesting..."

"Will you help me?" Alex asked.

"I will..."

She smiled.

"... in time," he finished.

"Huh? Wait! What about now?" she asked.

Once again, there was no answer, the shadow was gone. "Shit!" Alex hissed.

Sonyai was sitting at her desk, when a call to her direct line rang.

"Sonyai Yi, 58th Street Branch," she answered.

She listened carefully, and was physically shaken by the news from the caller.

"I... I understand," she said, in a solemn tone. "An unfortunate turn of events, but we will take appropriate steps... thank you for informing me. Goodbye."

She hung up the phone and swallowed hard. "Jenkins," she sighed.

After composing herself, the senior clerk made several calls. Apparently, Ethel Jenkins would not be returning to 58th Street.

Heywood and Angie were drinking at the Pig 'N' Whistle. Last week she started filling in at her college's radio show, and they were taking a break discussing her first week.

"I was hesitant at first, but I'm feeling this college radio show gig," Angie said.

"Hey, that's great, could be something to put on the resume," Heywood said.

"Yeah, I guess, but I'm trying not to get gassed up. I know this is only for two months."

"Hey, extracurriculars are always a plus."

Angie drained her beer and ordered another. "So, spooky stuff with this S.I.U. stuff, eh? I never thought there would actually be... library cops!"

"Neither did I, glad I was nowhere near there when it happened," Heywood agreed.

"Cheers to that!" She held up her bottle.

They clinked their bottles and resumed drinking quietly.

Heywood then quickly asked, "Um, could you switch a Saturday with me?"

"Huh?" Angie grunted.

"The 26th?" He asked.

She shook her head. "No, not Thanksgiving... but I can do Christmas."

"Really?!" He gasped.

"Sure. It's no big deal, I'm not doing anything."

"Dear God, thank you! I'm buying you a Christmas gift!"

Angie scoffed. "Stop it, you don't have to. I know working the holidays suck. I don't mind."

"I'll let Augustus know first thing tomorrow!" He stood up, paid his tab, and ran to the exit.

"So that's it?!" Angie screamed back at him. "You're done for the night?"

When he didn't answer, she shook her head and resumed drinking alone.

Augustus walked up to the library entrance as Tommy waited outside. With Sonyai and Gerry attending the hearing this morning, along with Robin, the branch needed a lot of help this week.

"Thanks for letting me in. I believe we have help coming at 10 am," Tommy said.

"Least this happened on a Tuesday. Wednesday's the halfway point of the week. We have the late night tonight, but it'll be dead during the day," Augustus said, entering the key in the lock. Once they were inside and he locked the door again, the librarian asked, "you sure you can handle this?"

"Yes... I think," Tommy answered, unsure of himself.

"That's the spirit, you got this!" Augustus slapped Tommy hard on his back and proceeded to walk to his office.

"Right," Tommy sighed. "Okay, let's see. Open the safe and set up the cash register, check in all the items we got overnight... you got this!" he repeated.

Doing the returned books from other branches was normally a two-man job, but he managed to get it done himself.

Ten o'clock finally came and Tommy let in Tiannah and Lucas Avery. Lucas greeted Tommy with a hefty handshake. "How's it going, man!"

"I'm hanging in there. Glad you can come by and help," Tommy greeted.

"Happy to do it! Feels good to get some experience in other branches, and I hear 58th Street is a *lively* little branch."

Tommy chuckled. "Don't know about all that. We're just a tiny, regular library. No drama here."

Lucas chuckled back. "Well, I hear otherwise." He punched him playfully in the shoulder and walked inside the clerical office.

Tommy noticed Tiannah was browsing the magazines, minding her own business. He approached her across the floor. Despite it being November, she was wearing a bright, floral-print, long sleeved dress. Even though Tommy was married, he had to admit she was very beautiful.

"So glad you could make it on such short notice," Tommy said.

"Clustering is such a thrill! I wouldn't miss it for anything!" she replied with enthusiasm. "You have so many magazines that we don't have at Yorkville." She turned to Tommy and smiled a bright smile. Her energy was infectious. People just felt happy in the presence of the woman. She was definitely a kindred spirit.

"Thank you. We try to get everything for all the different types of readers."

"I think that's awesome. Despite your reputation, I really think this is a marvelous branch."

"Our... reputation? Um, what have you heard?" Tommy asked.

"Oh, um, nothing, just rumors. You know how branches talk. It's nothing to be concerned with."

"Uh, right! Well, thanks again, make yourself at home!" Tommy said.

"Thank you!"

Tommy walked back to the circulation desk, once again wondering what things had been said... and by whom?

Sonyai and Gerry arrived at the Mid-Manhattan Library at eight o'clock Wednesday morning. Both were wearing no-nonsense type business suits. After signing in, they took the elevator to the third floor. Robin was waiting in the hallway when they stepped off.

After looking at them he said, "Holy shit! What is this, the Iran-Contra hearings? Why are you so dressed up?"

"When you were here for your job interview, how did you dress?" Sonyai asked.

"I interviewed with Miss Burns at Fort Washington. I didn't have to come down here."

Robin wasn't wearing a suit, but he did have on slacks, a dress shirt with a vest over it, and a suit jacket.

"You should have worn a tie," Gerry suggested. "Who wears a dress shirt without a tie?"

"And why are *you* dressed up? You only decide to step out of the 70's when my ass is on the line?"

Gerry frowned and the elevator opened again. Barbara Schemanske stepped out next to a tall, white man with combed-out straight hair. A few strands came down the middle of his forehead. He was carrying a briefcase and wearing a pinstripe suit. The five individuals exchanged glances at each other.

"I'm glad you didn't wear a tie, you needed to look comfortable, with nothing to hide," Barbara told Robin.

He turned to Gerry with a smug look.

"I don't believe we've had the pleasure," Sonyai said to Barbara. "I'm Sonyai Yi, senior clerk of the 58th Street Branch Library."

Barbara turned from Robin to Sonyai and stared for a long thirty seconds. "It is nice to finally meet you... face to face."

They didn't shake hands.

Robin sensing tension in the air asked, "Who is this?" Referring to Schemanske's companion.

The man extended his hand to him. "Blackjack Molloy, public barrister, and solicitor, how ya' doing this morning?"

Robin shook his hand and asked, "your first name's really 'Blackjack'?"

"Mom was a compulsive gambler," he replied, with a wide smile.

"You look like a used car salesman... no offense."

"None taken, so look here, junior..."

Robin cocked an eyebrow at being called 'junior.'

"You need all the help you can get, from what Miss Schemanske tells me. So... don't say anything until I tell you to. Keep your cool, and things will be just fine."

Robin let out an awkward chuckle. "Fair enough. Now *you* look here, Joe Isuzu, call me junior one more time, and you'll be wheeling into the next courtroom like Ironside, we understand each other?"

"Walker!" Barbara barked.

Sonyai and Gerry exchanged worried looks.

He darted his eyes toward Barbara, then back to Blackjack and waved his arm. "I believe room 315 is *this* way."

The group walked down to the hearing room.

# CHAPTER THIRTEEN

"With Yi and Coltraine down at human resources for Walker's hearing, you took care of things here in the morning pretty well," Augustus told Tommy.

"Thank you, sir. Hopefully they'll be back in the afternoon once the hearing is done," Tommy replied.

"Well, yes. I believe the hearing may go on for a few days, so keep up the great work."

*A few days!?* Tommy screamed in his head.

"Coltraine is scheduled for the late night, and I only have Miss Yi for one hour after 1 pm on the schedule. We have Tiannah from Yorkville, Lucas Avery and a part-timer from 67th Street, um Jasmine, uh, I can't remember the last name now, but we're covered."

"Very good." Augustus nodded. "I know it looks bad, but we're going to get through this."

"Yes, sir."

"How's things at home with the baby?" the head librarian asked, changing the subject.

Tommy put on a fake smile. "Doing great."

"Good!" Augustus patted Tommy on the shoulder and walked back to his office.

Tommy rubbed his shoulder. *Okay, he's gonna stop with the slapping me!* Then walked back to the circulation desk and turned on the terminals.

"You're putting on a brave front, Tommy..." Zelda began, as she worked on the New Books display several feet away from the clerk. "...But I can tell you're nervous about all this. Or is it something else?"

"It's not Robin or this thing with S.I.U... I just... hope Ethel's alright."

Zelda had a theory, but she refused to share it... with anyone.

"We'll hear from her, soon... I hope."

The pair continued to work their separate duties quietly.

Room 315 was the size of a football stadium as far as Robin was concerned. Three long tables formed a triangle, each with five chairs. On the left of the room was Levi Kraine and his two investigators, while Robin and his supporters sat behind a table on the right. The opposite side of both tables was a third, with five empty chairs. It was five minutes before ten o'clock.

Levi stood and looked over the opposing table. "Mister Walker, you can save yourself a lot of time and embarrassment if you would like to give us a statement now. We might show you leniency and make this all go away with just a reprimand on your record."

Robin rolled his eyes as Blackjack stood up beside him. "Not interested, you got nothing, and we're going to be out of here before lunch."

Levi grinned. "Okay. May the best man win." He sat back down and waited.

Blackjack nodded and sat down as well.

"You think you should have come back with something there?" Robin whispered. "Get the last word in?"

"It's all about picking your battles. Watch and learn."

The door to the office opened and the panel from human resources, composed of three men and two women, took their seats at the final table.

"I'm Casey Hawkins, in the administrative hearing against one Ms. Robin Walker..."

Robin lowered his face into his palm.

"...we will hear the evidence presented by the Special Investigations Unit. Let us begin."

Blackjack stood up. "If it would please the panel, I move to conclude this hearing before it even begins on the grounds of lack of evidence."

Levi flinched at the statement.

"In order to conclude for said grounds, we would need to determine such lack of evidence by *listening* to the evidence first."

Blackjack sat down and whispered, "it was worth a shot."

Robin fought the urge to look at his defense counsel questioningly.

"We will now hear opening statements," Casey announced.

Levi stood up and addressed the panel. "Good morning, ladies and gentlemen. The evidence we will present today through testimony and questioning will prove a pattern of misappropriate behavior on behalf of the defendant, a *Mister* Robin Walker. A young man who was recruited to the New York Public Library from an *urban* neighborhood in an effort of charity.

With a questionable reputation in school, Walker was approached by someone who had a tendency to collect troubled youths for wards to mentor. Probably to make up for their inability to have children, in the likes of that Batman superhero, Bruce Wayne. But the problem with bringing some of these miscreants in, is that some of them have a problem following the rules.

Robin Walker has had a problem with authority in the past, he was only a page for a little over a year before being promoted to a part-time clerk and moving on to another library... to be someone else's problem. He lacks the discipline that's required to be a productive employee of the New York Public Library and should be removed from his position."

Levi sat back down and adjusted his suit jacket with a satisfied smirk.

"Quite an opening statement, Investigator Kraine. We will now hear the opening statement from the defense."

Blackjack rose. "Before I begin, I would like to state for the record that Mister Walker has *no* intention of answering questions or testifying in his defense."

Robin's eyes bulged in shock. As Gerry and Sonyai fidgeted uncomfortably. Barbara was a body of stone, despite the jabs at her character. Levi stood to object as Blackjack continued, "it is the contention of the defense that if the evidence presented is solid enough to make a case, let the decision be judged on that and that *alone*."

"It isn't unusual not to testify in your defense, but we must still ask," Casey warned. "Are you sure about this course of action?"

Blackjack turned to Robin and nodded. He, in turn, stood up. "Yes," he answered, then sat back down.

"I object!" Levi yelled. "Mister Walker is accountable for his actions and needs to be questioned…"

"He answered all the questions during the investigation that was done at the branch. That should be sufficient enough." Blackjack interrupted.

"The defense has a point. Mister Walker has the right not to testify. We will proceed with Special Investigations' findings, and if necessary, questioning and hearing testimony from the two clerks involved in the related incident. Mister Coltraine and Miss Yi."

"Thank you." Blackjack nodded. "I will now deliver *my* opening statement."

Robin couldn't help noticing the cold stares he was getting from Sonyai and Gerry.

For two hours the S.I.U. presented their case, mostly using background information about Ethel and her medical condition, along with the unlikelihood of her picking up the incorrect can. The panel then adjourned for the day with testimony from Gerry scheduled for tomorrow.

When Robin and his party stepped out, Blackjack said, "you did good in there."

Sonyai was the first to turn and voice her concerns. "I hope you know what you're doing."

"Yes, yes I do. I'll prep you two tomorrow. Everything they put out there today was filler, and without Robin to question, they can't establish any rationale as to why he would even do anything to Ethel. Hopefully, you two won't give them a reason to."

"They're going to ask how this all got started, going back to whatever the hell happened between him and Alex back in March!" Gerry exclaimed.

"You weren't there, so you have nothing to say about that." Blackjack then looked at Sonyai. "And you?"

"I won't say anything about it," she replied.

"Even if they ask?"

"Even if they ask."

"So, you're willing to lie as you're being questioned by these people?"

"Yes," Sonyai answered sharply.

"Cold as ice, I love it," Blackjack replied with a smile. "See you tomorrow!" He waved while leaving.

"You know why he did that, right?" Barbara asked Robin.

They were riding the 7-train to Times Square, which was a stop away.

"If I'm up there, they can ask about other incidents from the past," Robin answered with a nod. "This guy's smart, just a bit theatrical." He turned to her and asked, "where'd you find him?"

"The Yellow Pages."

Robin didn't know if she was joking or not.

"This can go either way. Two on the panel I know personally. They'll vote in our favor."

"Aren't they not supposed to show bias?"

She smiled a devilish grin.

"Well, we'll see how tomorrow goes."

After transferring to the A-train heading uptown, Robin asked, "um, what's the deal with you and Sonyai? I couldn't help noticing y'all looked like Krystle Carrington and Alexis Colby, without the shoulder pads."

Barbara didn't reply. Robin looked on, expecting an answer.

They were approaching 175th Street and the George Washington Bus Terminal when Barbara said, "I won't be able to attend tomorrow morning, but I'll be there Friday to hear their decision."

Robin shrugged, "okay, you've been there for emotional support..."

"And I provided your defense," she grunted.

"I'm thankful, I'm thankful!" Robin exclaimed with his hands up.

The train stopped. A beggar came down the train asking for money, Barbara stood up and walked past him to the platform, with Robin following behind.

"Gerry, before you testify, you need to know something," Sonyai began.

It was the second day of the hearing. Sonyai was dressed in a more relaxed, conservative dress, and Gerry himself wore a pair of casual slacks and a buttoned-up shirt.

"You must think of the branch when answering certain questions, especially to the origin of the ritual. We cannot bring 58th Street under more scrutiny."

"What are you saying?" Gerry asked.

"You know what I'm saying. You must lie and say that Robin didn't start bringing in sodas to spite Miss Jenkins."

"I don't see the harm in admitting that—"

"I *do*," Sonyai emphasized.

Gerry looked around. "This might put a strain on an already difficult relationship between the two of us. We've been on pins and needles since our fallout after my birthday celebration."

"You have to think about the bigger picture. This can open the door for more investigations by the S.I.U. If we can sweep this under the rug as an isolated incident, we'll be free and clear. Please think about this when you're up there testifying."

She turned and walked down the hallway as Gerry blew an audible sigh from his mouth, then slowly followed her.

"Please state your full name for the record," Levi said, beginning the hearing.

"Gerrald Clarence Coltraine, that's C-O-L-T-R-A-I-N-E, unlike the jazz musician," Gerry answered.

"Mister Coltraine, how many branches of the NYPL have you worked in?" Levi asked.

"Four, unless you count the times I clustered."

"And how long did you know library clerk, Ethel Jenkins?"

"Three years," he answered.

"How would you describe your relationship with Ethel Jenkins?" Levi asked.

Gerry shrugged. "We've butted heads a few times, but both of us are mature enough to work peacefully."

"So long as neither one steps on the other's toes, right?" Levi suggested with a smile.

"Right," Gerry replied, feeling relaxed.

"So, let's talk about Monday afternoon. You and Miss Jenkins were alone in the clerical office, then young Mister Walker came in."

"That's correct."

"Now... he's got a bag of cans, three to be exact. Why?"

Gerry frowned. "I don't understand your question."

"Why is Robin bringing cans of soda for himself, you and Miss Jenkins?"

"You'll have to ask him."

"Unfortunately, I cannot, so I'm asking you," Levi replied sharply.

Gerry snuck a glance to Sonyai then looked out to no one in particular. "I guess he's just being... nice."

Robin frowned, then whispered something to Blackjack.

"Aww, that *is* very nice of him, isn't it? But what I don't understand is... why?"

Gerry chuckled. "Again, you would have to ask him."

"But I'm asking *you*," Levi pressed.

There was a minute of silence as the investigator stared down Gerry. Gerry stared back, unflinching.

"Are we just going to watch these two do 'The Chicken or The Egg?'" Blackjack asked.

Levi pointed to the ceiling, not turning his back. "I'll get right to the point, when you were questioned on the day of the incident, it was implied that Robin Walker brought in cans of soda for you and Miss Jenkins every day."

"That's right."

"Would you like to explain how that arrangement happened, please?"

Gerry swallowed hard, looked at Sonyai again, then replied, "I don't know how it started, that's between him and Miss Jenkins."

Robin cocked his head and frowned again.

"You don't know how it got started?" Levi asked.

"No... no, I don't."

Robin stood up and yelled, "you lying sonofabitch!"

Blackjack pulled on his arm, trying to control the outburst as Gerry shifted in the chair.

"Mister Walker, control yourself!" Casey warned.

Robin then turned to Sonyai. "Did you put him up to this?!?"

"It... it's close to lunch time," Blackjack called out. "The defense would like to call a recess."

"It's 11:15 am!" Levi cried out.

Robin was about to go on a tirade, but Blackjack used both hands to cover his mouth and restrain him. Gerry kept his composure, sitting uncomfortably.

"Well, I don't know about you, but I'm famished, I think we can adjourn for a... half an hour?" Blackjack asked with a light laugh.

Casey sighed. "Fine. Half-hour lunch, everybody. Be back at a quarter to noon."

The panel filed out, while Levi stepped out of the room himself. When it was just Sonyai and Gerry in the room, along with Robin and Blackjack, the lawyer took both hands and grabbed Robin's collar. "Whattaya doing? Having a damn outburst like that. Do you WANT to get fired?"

Robin ignored the question and looked past Blackjack to Sonyai. "Why did you tell him to lie? What difference would it have made?"

"I don't have to explain anything! You should listen to your advocate! He's trying to—" Sonyai began.

"I don't care! This is my life on the line! You two should be HELPING me, what the hell?" Robin screamed.

"Alright, calm down! We'll clean this up, but from now on... no more bullshit! Do what I say, and don't say anything until I tell you to! Got it?! I'm all you've got, so listen... to... me!"

Robin saw a different side of this Blackjack Malloy now, and he didn't like it. But he needed his help. "Fine!" He answered. Then he looked at Sonyai and back over at Gerry. "You two, I'll deal with later!" He then stormed out of the room.

At noon, Rosanna took her lunch break and went to McDonald's a few blocks down from Lincoln Center, on the corner of 56th Street and Eighth Avenue. She walked up to the counter and ordered a number six, which was two cheeseburgers, fries, and a soda. Once she received her order, she went to a booth and took a seat.

Franklin sat a few seats from her, coming in ten minutes before. He wasn't in disguise this time, but was uncharacteristically dressed down more than usual, and still kept his face hidden with a baseball cap tilted down. He originally didn't plan to engage in a conversation, but after weeks of following her, it was time.

Standing up from the table, Franklin slowly approached Rosanna. He was nervous, but remained calm. A foot away from her, at the last minute, he changed directions when Rosanna waved at a co-worker and called him over. Another male came over and sat on the other side of the booth. Franklin didn't look back as he headed to the exit.

He sighed to himself. *Another time, I guess.*

At twelve-fifteen, back at Mid-Manhattan, Levi stood up. "For our final witness, we call Sonyai Yi, 58th Street's senior clerk."

Sonyai stood up and took a seat next to the panel to testify.

"State your name for the record," Levi ordered.

"Sonyai Yi, that's S-O-N-Y-A-I," Sonyai said.

"Miss Yi, can it be said that 58th Street has changed radically since Robin Walker started at the branch?"

"It can take some time. Starting at a new position is challenging, even for the best of us," she answered.

*A neutral answer if I've ever heard one.* Robin thought.

"Hmmm. A security guard was hired recently, but until now, you didn't need one for over a year. What changed?" Levi asked.

"Okay, I'm not going to sugarcoat it, there was an incident in March, between Mister Walker and one of the pages. She was the aggressor of the two and she was disciplined. The matter was settled. Since then, Robin has been a welcomed member of the 58th Street Branch, with no further incidents."

Robin's eyebrows almost hit the ceiling as he noticed she didn't mention he was removed from clerical duties for three months.

"Except this incident in question!" Levi pointed out, sharply.

"I wouldn't count this, because this entire investigation is frivolous," Sonyai said coldly.

"Move it along, Mister Levi, and get to another line of questioning," Casey ordered.

"Fine, let's talk about Robin and these sodas. Why was he bringing them to Mister Coltraine and Miss Jenkins?"

"I don't know. As far as I was concerned, it was just a nice thing to do," Sonyai answered.

"You don't think he had any ulterior motive?" Levi asked quickly.

"Not to my knowledge."

Levi shook his head. "I don't know WHY you are sitting here, defending this person, who you KNOW is responsible for poisoning Ethel Jenkins. Admit it!"

"You're grasping at straws, young man. This case is as real as dragons were thousands of years ago."

Levi sighed.

Casey sighed, too. "Do you have any more questions for this witness?"

Levi growled. "No, I suppose not."

"We will hear closing statements and come to a decision tomorrow morning. We are adjourned," Casey said.

"That was great. We got this in the bag," Blackjack said, after everyone cleared out.

"It was looking touch and go there, 'specially with you bringing up what happened in March."

"Like I said, I wasn't going to sugarcoat it," Sonyai replied.

"I dunno, I kinda sensed a little sugar in that explanation." Blackjack grinned.

"I did too," Gerry said.

"Yeah, me too," Robin agreed.

Sonyai gave each of them a look, then Blackjack said, "Anyway, closing arguments tomorrow. Stay sharp, come in on time, and we'll be out before lunch." He put on his coat. "We're almost done, guys!" He walked out of the room, holding two fingers up for a peace sign.

Robin left on his own, as Gerry and Sonyai walked around and found a bar nearby.

"You as confident as this lawyer that Robin's getting off?" Gerry asked. He ordered a beer and Sonyai ordered a Brass Monkey. The bartender didn't have any Rum, so she settled for a Screwdriver.

"I wasn't at first, then I realized S.I.U. actually has no case," she said, then took a swig of her drink. "This is all a waste of time."

"I agree," Gerry said. "All this makes no sense. But I see what you mean about the branch's reputation, now."

"Yes. We have to protect the branch, above all things. Let me share something with you." She lowered her voice so only Gerry could hear. "Augustus has enemies everywhere, and they are of his own creation. He is his own worst enemy, and if he isn't stopped, the branch... will be compromised."

"Oh, yeah?" Gerry asked.

"Walker izzn't da problem." Sonyai was starting to slur her speech. "Augustus... will bring destruction... to the library. So, it's up to us to stop 'im."

"Well, I got your back. We may have our issues, but you know I'm loyal to you and the library clerks."

"We need that solidarity, Coltraine. I don't know how long this... thing with Augustus is going to last, but he's going to try and take advantage sometime soon, and we have to make sure... he does not get his way!"

"Okay, easy there, Tiger. You're getting a little bit carried away." He caught her from stumbling over.

"Sorry," Sonyai said.

"You're a lightweight with your liquor," he observed.

"I'm fine. It's just the damn Rum offsets the Vodka on a Brass Monkey. A damn Screwdriver gets you drunk... quicker." She stumbled again. "Okay, maaaaybe I indulged too much, lemme get some water, please."

She took a moment to gather herself while he ordered some water.

They took several minutes to drink in silence.

"You okay, now?" Gerry asked.

"I'll tell you once the room stops spinning," Sonyai said.

Ten minutes later, they left the bar, Sonyai was feeling much better. "Remember what I said, Coltraine…"

"I'll remember, Yi," he told her.

She wanted to tell him that outside the library he could call her 'Sonyai,' but at least he didn't call her ma'am. Instead, she just nodded and said, "see you tomorrow."

"See you!" He waved as she walked down to the 7-train station for Times Square. When she was out of sight, he grinned to himself, never seeing Sonyai drunk before.

At 58th Street, the afternoon was winding down, with Alex and Tanya working the shelves. Alex was distracted, occasionally looking at the circulation desk, where Lucas Avery was currently working checkouts.

"Looks like you got a little crush on that clerk from 67th Street," Tanya said.

"Huh? Oh, um, no, not at all! I was just looking in that direction," she said.

"Riiiiiight," Tanya said, with a smile.

"Alright, you got me. I may have a little crush on him, but it's nothing like you and Andrew!" she said quickly.

*Yeah, it's more like Lakeshia and Robin!* "I mean, he is cute, just not *my* type."

"Well, good! I don't need the competition," Alex said with some confidence. "And besides, you may have fooled Lakeshia with that story that nothing happened, but *I* know you better."

"Do you?" Tanya asked, with a cocked eyebrow. "We did nothing but talk. After finding out about him moving on, we both agreed to slow things down a bit and wait until I graduate. That's all."

"Slowing down doesn't sound like you, Tee."

"Well, maybe I'm taking Janelle's advice to heart, instead of you. Because I do not plan on having no babies ANYTIME soon!"

"Hmph, that's true," Alex said.

Heywood was working the final hour of the day. Thursdays always felt long due to the early opening of the library at ten. It almost looked like it was going to be a regular day, ending on a mundane note, until a patron got too close to John Paul Jones, and he had a reaction. Eugene was quick to shield the person from the behemoth, but the security guard and the homeless vagrant collided violently.

The two pushed each other and a shouting match started. Very few people understood John Paul Jones, since he spoke in nonsensical phrases and slurred words. Heywood was almost afraid he would have to assist with the altercation, but Eugene managed to eject the patron out of the library with his belongings.

It was five-thirty and Eugene approached the information desk and sighed. "That guy always starts something right before closing."

Heywood shrugged. "To be fair, that woman ignored the obvious warning signs and got too close to him... not that I'm blaming her," he quickly added, when the guard gave him a look.

"You're actually saying it was her fault?"

"No, I'm not saying that... hey, if it was up to me, homeless people wouldn't even be allowed in here. But with all these bleeding-heart liberals around, I guess I've gotten a bit cynical."

Eugene looked at him silently for over a minute, then pointed and said, "you lucky you're a great drinking buddy... politics aside."

Heywood smiled nervously as the security guard took the seat facing him. He then whispered to Eugene, "you really think Robin poisoned Ethel?"

They both looked around, checking if anyone was listening to them, then Eugene said, "I'll be honest with you... I'm 50/50 with that. But I had to sound confident enough for S.I.U. to make their move. I got a call from them saying they were looking for some dirt on this kid."

"But why?"

He shrugged. "I dunno. He's got some enemies in high places."

"But he's a kid. Who gives a shit enough to take out a... a part-time clerk who's focused on college rather than his position here? What do *they* know about him that we don't?"

"What does it matter? Something tells me you wouldn't mind seeing him get kicked out yourself."

Heywood gave a casual shake of his head side-to-side. "Well yes, that's true, but I believe there's more to this than we know. Someone once told me, '*if someone's out to get someone else, they must be doing it for a reason.*'"

"So, you think they're out to get Robin because... he's part of some... conspiracy?" Eugene asked, with a raised eyebrow.

Heywood just stared back at him.

Eugene chuckled. "Man, whatever you're smoking, pass that shit to me." He stood up and left Heywood to his thoughts.

He may not have any evidence yet, but Heywood was certain someone was pulling the strings on whatever was going on here.

Lakeshia was off Thursday, and she was so worried about Robin she couldn't bring herself to eat her dinner that evening. Just picking at her food.

Her mother showed some concern. "Honey, you haven't been eating much lately. What's wrong?"

"I'm just worried," she replied. "A situation at work, that's all..."

"It wouldn't happen to be a situation involving a certain person, would it?" Jennifer Seabrooke asked.

Lakeshia didn't answer.

"Wanna talk about it?"

She pushed her plate back. "May I be excused, please?"

"We will still talk about this when you're ready, you hear me? Between your father doing a double shift, your little brother visiting your aunt, and your older brother working at the radio station, we girls need to stick together."

"I will, I promise," Lakeshia said.

"Go on."

Lakeshia left the table and went to her room. Jennifer sat and looked around the empty table. She hoped everyone would be back sitting, eating, and sharing conversations for Thanksgiving.

Meanwhile, in her bedroom, Lakeshia pulled out the Knicks shirt Robin gave her at the basketball game. She had never washed it, still believing a trace of his scent remained.

"I can't lose you, Robin..." she whispered. She wouldn't admit it to anyone, but she was genuinely scared that Robin would lose his job and she would never see him again.

# CHAPTER FOURTEEN

BARBARA STOOD ALONE IN THE HALLWAY AT SEVEN O'CLOCK FRIDAY
morning, when the elevator opened and Sonyai stepped out. They
exchanged glances, as Sonyai stepped forward and stopped in front
of her.

"The only thing that you absolutely have to know..." Barbara
began.

"...is the location of the library," Sonyai finished. "Albert
Einstein."

There was a look of approval between the two of them. Sonyai then
said, "when Robin quoted the credo, I was very proud. To hear those
words that were spoken by him, taught to him... from a younger gener-
ation, I knew... that someone close to *him* was still out there."

Barbara nodded. "He... spoke highly of you, very highly as a
matter of fact. Of all the others he inspired and mentored... he considered you to be his best student."

Sonyai nodded and wiped a tear from her cheek. "I didn't realize
who you were until I saw you," she whispered. "He spoke of you
fondly... despite never mentioning your name."

"Our relationship was... estranged. We *were* married, but I refused
to take his name after developing a reputation on my own. Intimacy...

wasn't my strong suit." Barbara took a breath and sighed. "I pushed him into the arms of another woman."

Sonyai shook her head. "It may have been an emotional dependency, but he *never* broke his vows!"

"I have reason to believe otherwise," Barbara replied coldly.

"In… his final hours, he regretted not making peace with you."

"Sentiment is a sign of weakness. After what he had done, there was no way I would let him have the last word." Barbara took a step forward. "I really hope you continue to pass on what he taught you. That way his legacy lives forever. As a husband, he may have faltered, but as a human being, an educator, a humanitarian… his contributions are tenfold."

Sonyai nodded. "I plan to honor him for the rest of my life."

Their connection to the individual who Sonyai knew as The Man in White, but Barbara knew as Oliver Prince would be one to bond the two adversaries. Opposite sides of the same coin, the yin and the yang. After today, Sonyai wondered if they would ever cross paths again.

Gerry was glad to be back at the branch. With Sonyai supporting Robin at the hearing, the morning was pretty lax. He came in at ten o'clock, so he could close with Tiannah. Tommy and Lucas arrived at nine. It was a quarter after ten and all four of them were in the clerical office. Gerry was telling Tommy about his conversation with Sonyai yesterday.

"I have never seen Sonyai drunk. It actually humanizes her," Gerry said.

"So now you don't think she's a stick in the mud?"

"Not when she's drunk!" Gerry replied, with a laugh.

Tommy laughed along with him, but then Gerry got serious. "She is *super* convinced Augustus is going to destroy the branch one day."

"Well, isn't she right? He's done some risky things for the sake of just doing them," Tommy said.

"Hey, her hands are no cleaner than his, and as loyal as I am.

They're both the same side of a coin that's on a continuous flip, never to hit heads or tails."

"That's pretty deep," Tommy praised.

"Hey, I have my moments. So, how about you? How'd it feel, coming here all by yourself with just some clusters for help?"

"Kinda scary, but I pulled through. Augustus tried to instill some spirit with a pep talk and all that."

"He did okay," Lucas said, coming up and playfully punching Tommy on the shoulder. "It's been fun coming down here from 67th Street. Ms. Gray's been a hard-ass on the clerks lately. Y'all are so laid back and cool here."

Gerry chuckled. "We're not as laid back as you would believe." He left the pair to talk among themselves and walked across the room where Tiannah was quietly reading.

"Hi," he greeted with a smile.

She looked up and smiled herself. "Hello, how have you been?"

"I have been well."

Lucas and Tommy stole glances at the two on the other side of the room, then with a gesture, they both left the room.

Lucas whispered to Tommy, "you think they got something going on there?"

Tommy shrugged. "Your guess is as good as mine."

They both grinned at each other and then went to their separate terminals to turn them on.

"Well, it's judgment day for Robin. If we're lucky, they'll find him guilty, and we'll be rid of him," Augustus said.

Zelda and the head librarian were adjusting the New Books section that was in front of the branch.

"You really think he tried to do something to Ethel?" Zelda asked.

"Not that it matters what I *think*, it's just that he's been nothing but trouble since he came here. If he's found guilty, he can easily be replaced with someone who *actually* follows the rules around here."

"Hmph, I assure you they would be the first to do so," Zelda replied.

"Hey, I follow the rules… but I bend them ever so slightly, as well." Augustus grinned.

"Well, despite Robin's current predicament, you and Sonyai have been working very well together, and I commend you on it."

"It hasn't been easy. I've been avoiding conflicts by letting her win them," he grunted. "She's been walking all over me like a doormat."

"The two of you haven't had any opposing opinions on policies so far," she replied.

"No, but it's only a matter of time. I do have one last ace up my sleeve. I've been buttering her up with hopes she'll play ball once I play it. Which is why I'm bringing back the holiday gift exchange, once all this blows through."

Zelda stopped in place and looked at him. "Gus, we stopped doing that after the incident with Ethel two years ago."

Augustus nodded. "I remember, but something tells me she won't be here, let alone participate in the festivities. This gesture may finally bring Sonyai around to seeing things *my* way."

"…being aware Necessity doth front the universe with an invincible gesture," Zelda warned.

"Shakespeare?"

"Elizabeth Barrett Browning," she replied.

Augustus chuckled. "Ah, great to have you back with your quotes."

"Mister Levi, we will now hear your closing statement," Casey began.

Levi stood up and adjusted his tie. He looked at the wall to his left, not to stare at his audience or Robin.

"First and foremost, I would like to point out the defendant's refusal to testify is an obvious sign of guilt. Combined with what we have presented, it is clearly a case of animosity at the workplace. When a young man of questionable upbringing, taken out of his element… transferring into a fish-out-of-water situation and being welcomed with cold arms. In an attempt to make friends, he starts a daily routine, all while planning on getting revenge, biding his time, before he strikes!

You all saw his outburst yesterday. This type of behavior cannot be from one who works for the New York Public Library! We are expected, by the people we serve, to provide a positive customer service experience. Robin Walker is incapable of providing this and should be terminated immediately.

Thank you."

Levi sat back down.

"We will now hear from the defense," Casey said.

Blackjack patted Robin on his shoulder, as Sonyai and Barbara looked on with no emotion. He stood up and faced the five individuals who held Robin's fate in their hands.

"Okay, I can sum up the S.I.U.'s case in one word… 'Imagination.' It's all made up! In reality, Ethel Jenkins picked up the wrong soda can, which sent her blood sugar level through the roof, and resulted in her having a diabetic episode. That's it. An unfortunate accident. This whole… drawn-out conspiracy about two clerks not getting along, starting a ritual, switching the cans… is all a product of an overactive imagination.

They have presented no physical evidence and the testimony heard was completely unrelated to what happened. No one has confirmed Mister Walker started the ritual for any particular reason, other than to be nice. Finally, I'd like to add, if this was actually a serious case of poisoning, he would be in handcuffs, and I would be defending him in a courtroom!

But it's not. There's only one decision to make here… to find Robin Walker *innocent.*

Thank you."

Blackjack sat back down, as Robin nodded.

Casey stood up and announced, "we will break for lunch and reconvene afterward with our decision."

The panel filed out of the room, then Robin left with Sonyai, Barbara, and Blackjack.

Levi stayed in the room, waiting patiently for the decision.

"Well?" Robin asked in the hallway.

"As I said before, it can go either way," Barbara whispered.

"I believe there will be a positive outcome in this hearing," Sonyai added.

Robin turned to Blackjack. "You're not saying anything."

"I never predict a verdict. It's bad luck."

"If I may ask then, what's your record when it comes to cases you've argued?"

He smiled. "183-0."

"Bullshit!" Robin spat.

"Walker!" Barbara hissed.

He snapped his head back to her and looked down, blushing. "Ahem... very interesting. Um, I think I'll walk down to the vending machine for something."

He left the trio standing outside the hall for a moment. Twenty-five minutes passed when they were called back to the room.

The five representatives walked back in. Their faces were hard to read, and Robin braced himself for the worst. He thought about holding Sonyai and Barbara's hands but changed his mind.

"We have reviewed all the evidence and listened to the presented testimony," Casey began.

Robin took a breath and held it.

"We were very divided in our discussions, and after a vote of three-to-two..."

Levi leaned forward in anticipation.

"...it is the final decision of this panel, that the evidence presented is inconclusive to make a determination of inappropriate behavior on behalf of library clerk Robin Walker."

Robin exhaled, closed his eyes, and swallowed hard. Blackjack nodded once solemnly in relief, celebrating the victory. Sonyai patted Robin's shoulder.

Levi fell back and sagged his shoulders against the chair.

"This decision is absolute, final, and not up for debate or appeal. The investigation is now closed. Statements, evidence, and testimony will be sealed and archived, not to be used in any future proceedings.

The S.I.U. is thanked for its service, albeit a bit overzealous. And *Mister* Robin Walker? We will make the correction to your name on your employee record, and hope you continue to be a productive member of the New York Public Library... with no future incidents similar to this matter. We are adjourned."

Blackjack, Sonyai, Barbara, and Robin exited the room. The panel did the same, but Levi just sat, accepting the defeat with disbelief.

"'Inconclusive?' That doesn't mean 'innocent,' right?" Robin asked, once they stepped out to the hallway.

"No, but it doesn't mean 'guilty' either," Blackjack replied.

"I'd like to believe that they didn't think you were responsible, Walker," Sonyai said.

"I beg to differ," Barbara began. "They believed in some impropriety, but S.I.U.'s case was faulty. You got *lucky* Walker, as I also said before." She turned to leave. "If you'll excuse me."

Sonyai hurried behind her as Blackjack pulled out a business card and handed it to Robin. "Take my card. Something tells me you're going to need my services again. Been fun defending you. See ya!"

Robin took the card and watched the lawyer walk away. The card had his name and phone number, but no address, and a picture of two playing cards. The king of spades next to the ace of spades.

"Blackjack indeed," Robin said.

"Hey, you could have been a little easier on him," Sonyai said to Barbara, after catching up with her.

She raised an eyebrow and turned to Sonyai. "If you had *any* idea... when he first started at Fort Washington, Robin was a challenge, but I molded him. Because I was hard on him, he became the efficient, dedicated, hard-driven employee you saw when he walked in your branch! And what did *you* do? Look at what's become of him, now! This incident would have *never* had happened on my watch!"

Sonyai was appalled by the speech, her mouth hanging open in shock.

"All because of a teenager with lack of judgment or birth control! You say that you take care of your own, that Robin is family, as was the page that you lost. Obviously, that is not the case."

Sonyai was enraged now. "How dare you!?" She turned and stormed away.

"You did everything you could to save *her!*" Barbara yelled at her back. "But the fact that *I* had to step in and provide assistance in his defense tells me that you haven't fully accepted him into your flock!"

Sonyai stopped and turned, but this time the librarian turned and started walking. "He's still an outsider to you, Yi, and will continue to be one."

The senior clerk looked down the hallway, burning a hole in the back of Barbara's head. She didn't know which was worse, the fact that Barbara was possibly right, or the fact she called her out on it. Sonyai planned to prove her wrong, one way or another.

Robin and Sonyai returned to 58th Street at five-fifteen in the afternoon. "Not guilty!" He cheered.

Gerry punched Tommy playfully on the arm, as Lakeshia jumped up and clapped from the shelves. Augustus stood up and coughed. "Let's keep the celebration to a minimum please!"

Robin gave Eugene an icy look as the security guard stood next to Augustus and then nodded. "Sorry, sir. Just a little enthusiastic to still be employed at the best damn job in the world."

"High five!" Gerry said, holding his hand up.

"You're not off the hook, yet!" Robin snapped, then turned away from Gerry to Sonyai. "I'll see you Monday. Um... thanks for believing in me."

"You're welcome, I hope we can put this behind us and start with a clean slate."

"I'd like that. Have a great weekend."

She smiled and nodded. "You too."

Robin waved to Tommy and Lakeshia, then left. Sonyai walked to Augustus and Eugene at the information desk.

"Well?" Augustus asked.

"Not that it matters now, but Walker oversold the decision a little bit," Sonyai explained.

"Meaning?" Eugene asked.

"S.I.U.'s case wasn't strong enough for them to make a decision either way."

"Inconclusive?" Augustus asked, with raised eyebrows.

The senior clerk nodded. "Everything is now sealed and archived, never to be mentioned again."

"Okay, fine… where are we on Jenkins's condition?"

"She's on medical leave," Sonyai answered, based on what was told to her in confidence, it would be unlikely that she would return. "We'll continue to receive help from other branches for the rest of the year."

She turned to Eugene. "I don't know if you heard me, but I told Robin we would start things fresh Monday, which means no animosity from you, do I make myself clear?"

"As long as he doesn't sucker punch me again, we'll be just fine," Eugene said.

"Good. Now, it's been a long day and I have to be back here tomorrow…"

She turned and left the branch. Eugene stared hard, disappointed by the decision, but proceeded on his rounds.

Levi walked back into the Special Investigations Department at six-thirty and slammed the door to his office. He couldn't believe his case fell apart. It should have been a slam-dunk.

He turned on the intercom. "Hold all my calls, nothing gets through."

The department secretary replied, "yes, Mister Kraine."

The verdict played over and over in his head. *Three-to-two, Three-to-two... Who was that tiebreaker?*

The panel was supposed to be random and impartial. If someone got to them, and he could prove it...

He suddenly hit the intercom again. "Are the personnel files computerized yet?"

"Yes, sir, Mister Kraine," the secretary replied.

"Excellent."

The NYPL was in the process of modernizing their files, creating a database that most ranking officials could access on a computer.

He turned his on and started typing for a search, starting with Robin's name. He found the file, where there was the usual information, but Levi knew there was a space put aside for confidential information that only certain individuals knew about. He typed for further information and hit a roadblock.

"Icarus? What the hell is Project Icarus?" He asked no one in particular.

He typed in a master password, but access was denied.

Apparently, something was going on with Robin Walker that was above his pay grade.

*He did say he was The Ninth Witness, could it be some secret project to protect those who have seen...*

His door suddenly flew open, and he looked up to see Eugene walking in his office.

"What the hell? I said no visitors. How did you get in?" Levi asked.

"Shaddup! You made a fool of me! You told me this would work!"

"Extenuating circumstances."

"Don't bullshit me! What the fuck went wrong?!" Eugene demanded.

"He refused to take the stand. That pretty much destroyed my case! I couldn't... *question* him!" Levi explained.

"So, what now?"

"You go back to the branch and await further instructions."

"Fuck that! Your calls go unanswered. I don't know you, and any favors for the S.I.U. are rescinded!" He turned and opened the door.

"Fine!" Levi yelled back. "You're just a washed-up nightclub bouncer with mob connections. You weren't even a *real* cop!"

The door was halfway open and Eugene was already gone. Levi turned away and stared at the wall in silence for a few moments.

"Tsk, tsk, tsk…" a female voice replied. "Such hostility."

Levi let out a sigh. "I must have moved," he began, "because people are coming and going in *my* office like it's Grand Central Station across the street!"

"Well, I'm more discreet. I can't let anyone see me here," Alex said, stepping out of the shadows and slowly closing the door.

Levi turned his chair around to face her. "Tell your father it didn't work. We'll get him another way."

Alex nodded. "My father's not used to failure. Expect to hear a mouthful."

"Hey, I told him this wouldn't be easy. I agreed to do this because I thought we had a case… don't worry, we'll get him."

"You better, because if he has to get his hands dirty, and do it himself, you lose *everything*. Think about that and try to sleep tonight." She opened the door and turned to leave, closing the door behind her.

"What makes you think I actually sleep?" Levi said. He looked at the screen and read, "Project Icarus…" He whispered again, "who the fuck *is* this guy?"

It was Saturday, and it had been a hell of a week. Which was why Heywood was happy to be working at the 67th Street Branch today. He approached the library at eight o'clock. 67th Street was located in the heart of Lenox Hill, on the east side between First and Second Avenue. It was surrounded by several hospitals and medical schools.

He rang the doorbell and waited. The door opened slowly, and Head Librarian Beverly Onyskow stood behind it with a warm smile. "Ah, Mister Learner, you're here nice and early."

She stood aside to let him in. "Yeah, I'm an early riser."

They climbed the steps to the main floor. "Well, feel free to browse around. The schedule for the day will be up shortly."

"Okay."

The interior of the two-story branch was similar to most libraries, with the circulation desk in the opposite end, next to the staircase to the second floor, while the information desk was located in the center of the room. Heywood wandered around, checking the shelves. A door opened at the middle of the staircase leading up to the second floor and a sheepish white guy with baggy clothes stepped down.

"Hi, I'm Heywood, an IA from 58th Street."

"Larry, Larry Ritter, pleased to meet ya." He extended his hand and Heywood shook it.

"Never seen you here before," Larry said.

"I've clustered a few times here before, just not on your Saturdays, I guess," Heywood replied.

"Yeah, I guess so."

"Well, I'll see ya around." Heywood waved.

"Yeah, see ya."

Larry walked past him. Heywood looked back and mused, "nice guy."

The daily schedule was posted, and Heywood had two separate hours at two and four and no time upstairs in the children's section. It was an easy afternoon.

After three, the information assistant took a break in the staff room. Awaiting inside was Larry, reading a magazine.

"Hey again. Busy enough for ya?"

"Heh, sure... hey, can I ask you a personal question, real quick?" Larry asked.

"Sure, I guess," Heywood replied.

"Is it true what happened at your library?"

"Wha... what have you heard?" he asked, shifting his gaze.

"I heard this guy nearly killed someone over there with a soda can. The details are sketchy, but that's the story."

"What!? Where did you hear something like that?!" Heywood gasped.

"Rumors everyone's talking about it!"

"Oh my God, no! Nothing like that happened. No matter who told you that, don't believe it."

"Okay, sorry I mentioned it, just thought I'd ask. I'm really sorry."

There was a couple of minutes of silence, then Heywood asked, "can I ask *you* a personal question, now?"

"Uh, sure," Larry said.

"How often do you worship?"

He smiled. "Every day."

"I thought so. I don't know how I do it, but I can always sense a fellow Catholic."

"I had a feeling about you, too," Larry said. "Hey, I know this is kinda forward, but Tuesdays I attend a social club near Alphabet City. I think you'll like it."

"Well, since I live down there, how could I not?" Heywood replied.

"Awesome, I'll give you the address!"

The day moved on, and at five o'clock, Heywood was walking toward the exit with Larry. "I had a great time here, see you Tuesday?"

"Sure!" Larry opened the door, letting Heywood out.

# CHAPTER FIFTEEN

AFTER THE REALITY OF ELECTION DAY'S STUNNING RESULTS FINALLY set in stone, the city started preparing for Thanksgiving. Augustus was in his office reading the newspaper.

"I can't believe Pataki pulled this upset off!" he said.

"I'm sure voter turnout had something to do with it," Zelda said, sitting at her desk.

"Well, you know we got some serious budget cuts coming our way now."

"Yes, but I'm sure they'll be *after* the centennial celebration next year, then the hammer will come down," Zelda agreed.

"We were due for a renovation. That'll likely get pushed, and our new operating system. This puts a monkey wrench in everything we had planned the next two years."

"We will make do with what we can. Quit complaining, Gus."

The head librarian scoffed. "Fine, change of subject... you have any plans for next week?"

"Not really, you?"

"No, neither do I. These investors are eating out of my hand, and philanthropic whales throw their money around to the less fortunate this time of year."

"Yes, the library must take a back seat to those starving and misfortunate individuals around Thanksgiving and Christmas..." Zelda quipped.

"I know you're being sarcastic, but these things do have certain periods of the year where they hit their highs and lows."

"I suppose."

"Don't worry, they get more charitable again after taxes are paid in April." He stood up, leaving the newspaper at his desk. "Maybe I *should* have..." he mused, as he approached the exit.

"What was that?" Zelda asked.

"I was just thinking, maybe I should have endorsed Pataki independently. I mean, no one could have predicted the election, but it would have been nice to hedge our bets a bit."

"Well, what's done is done."

"Yes, you're right, but it's never too late to change someone's mind," Augustus said, and walked out the door.

Robin walked inside the clerical office, where Sonyai was waiting for him. "Ah, Walker, glad you're early. There's a change in plans for you working this Saturday. We're sending you to cluster at the Webster Branch instead of working here."

"Cool! It'd be my first time going over there."

"Yes, now, I want you on your best behavior, Walker." She raised a finger. "The senior clerk there is a former pupil of mine."

"The one who," he cleared his throat, "had an inappropriate relationship with one of the pages here?"

"Yes, that is correct. Your discretion on that subject would be appreciated."

"Okay. Hopefully, he won't even be there, and I won't have the *pleasure* of being disgusted by him."

She tilted her head and cocked an eyebrow. "Actually, he *will* be there, so I stress again Walker, be on your *best behavior*."

Robin sighed and pouted.

"If I hear you so much as sneezed loud..." the senior clerk threatened.

"You don't have to finish that sentence." He held his hands up in front of him. "I got it."

She gave a curt nod, confident she got her point across, and then turned to her desk. Robin thought, *I wonder... which page was it?*

Alex was among the shelves, looking for Lakeshia and Tanya. When she found them, apprehension took hold of her as she approached her two co-workers.

"Hey, guys," she began, as they turned to her.

"I know you've probably heard about my birthday party this Saturday..."

"Well, we would be dumb to ignore the whispers. You've been going on and on about it..." Lakeshia said.

"...and I'm sure you would have invited us if we weren't working this weekend," Tanya finished.

Alex put on a nervous smile. "Yeah, so I was thinking, maybe the three of us do something Friday instead."

"Oh," Lakeshia said. "What did you have in mind?"

Alex's nervous smile turned into a mischievous grin. "How about going to see *Interview with The Vampire*?"

"Are you kiddin'?" Tanya asked. "None of us are 18, and could you imagine the nightmares Lakeshia would have? Actually, that *would* be fun... we're in."

"Hey! I could handle it, can't be any scarier than *Bram Stroker's Dracula*."

"Awesome! It'll have to be a place independent. That way they don't care," Alex said.

"The RKO on 181st Street has been working well for me." Tanya smiled, remembering her date with Franklin up there.

"Hmmm, they might still card up there, but I remember going to

The Nova on 147th Street to see *The Firm*, which was lame, by the way... we can see it there."

"Alright, bet!" Tanya turned to Lakeshia. "Bring your teddy bear, little one."

Lakeshia stuck her tongue out and resumed working her shelves.

"So, I'm clustering to Webster for the first time this weekend," Robin said.

Tommy and he were working the circulation desk, Robin working the checkouts while Tommy accepted returns.

"Oof, Andrew is such an apple polisher."

"A what?"

"A brown-noser? A suck-up?"

"Oh, a kiss-ass," Robin said.

"There ya go!" Tommy pointed at him.

*White people and their terms...* Robin rolled his eyes. "So, I heard this guy was under Sonyai's wing. Lot of room under there, with all the mother henning she does."

"Hey, she's just molding and shaping those to be like her when they move on. Nothing wrong with that."

"You plan to follow in her footsteps, too?"

Tommy thought about it for a few minutes, as Robin tended to a patron.

"I'm not ready..." Tommy finally answered. "Sonyai was talking about getting me in the Senior Clerk Seminar next year, but... I don't wanna let her down."

Robin shrugged. "That's reasonable."

"What about you?" Tommy asked.

"What about me?"

"Wouldn't you like to be a senior clerk someday?"

"I would do the exact same thing when someone else asked me that, but I don't want to draw any attention to myself... let me just say, no, no, no, and hell no, to that idea. I'm not the leadership type, and I don't plan on staying here too long."

"Oh, that's right, you're going to one day go to Microsoft and take over the world."

Robin made a face at the sarcasm. "Be skeptical all you want. It will happen. Until it does, my time here will do just nicely. But tell me about this... apple polisher? You said? What's he like?"

"Your typical do-gooder, straight-arrow, chip-on-the-block, over-achiever, you know... like you, but not getting into trouble so much."

"Oh please, if he was half the man I am, he'd be at 96th Street running the entire region!" Robin scoffed.

"Right. Like I said, just like you, but not getting into trouble..."

"Well, I'm sure he's not THAT squeaky clean..."

"Meaning?"

"You tell me, I heard he had a thing with one of the pages..." Robin asked.

"That's news to me."

"Oh, c'mon! Your head can't be that much in the sand. You've heard something!"

"Hey, when you have hair that looks this good, you miss a lotta things," Tommy said, with a snap of his neck.

"Damn if that ain't true," Robin agreed. "I guess ignorance *is* bliss."

Gerry was doing the last hour with Sonyai, so he was taking a break in the staff room and found Zelda there as well.

"I've been looking for you," he greeted.

"Oh?" she asked.

"Yeah." He took a seat at the table to face her. "I figured you would be the only one who could tell me what *really* happened to Ethel."

Gerry noticed how her demeanor changed. "I have nothing to tell," she dismissed.

"C'mon, it's been weeks, they cleared the kid of any wrongdoing, what's it gonna hurt?"

Zelda didn't budge.

"Look, I know the two of you were friends, but I was the closest thing, next to you, she called a friend, too."

She stared at him, and he gave back a goading look. She sighed and gave in. "Alright. She was diagnosed with diabetes. Insisting that it was borderline, Ethel refused to believe it until her doctor put the fear of God in her."

"I figured. She never met a honey bun she didn't like," Gerry said.

Zelda nodded. "Yes, but what you didn't know is that she and her sisters were fixing up a place down south."

Gerry's eyebrows shot up upon hearing that. "Really?"

"She didn't think they would get it done so soon... so she needed a reason to go on leave, *then* retire at the end of the year."

Zelda let that statement hang as Gerry slowly put two and two together. "Wait a minute, you're saying that Ethel drank the wrong soda... on purpose?"

"Gerry, you can't—"

"I won't say anything, I won't say anything... but damn, she took a serious risk."

"Yes, she did," Zelda agreed.

"Still, that's Ethel... she wouldn't want some sappy goodbye send-off, with gifts and a card. She would have played it off, told Sonyai and no one else, then at the last minute say, *'So long, I ain't coming back Monday,'* then walk off into the sunset." Gerry chuckled.

"Yes, that's exactly what would have happened. Sonyai didn't know, though. No one did. I've come to this based on knowing her diagnosis, secretly."

"We have people coming in to provide coverage until December, and we'll get someone new first thing next year," Gerry said. "It's the end of an era."

"And the start of a new one. We're going to need consistency if we're going to get through what's in store for us next."

"I agree. The question is, how long Sonyai and Augustus are going to keep being nice to each other?"

"*That's* something not even *I* know," Zelda said.

Wednesday evening, Angie was once again hosting her local college radio show. After several weeks, she was feeling more comfortable behind the microphone, playing music and reading news blurbs.

"It's a little past nine o'clock and you're here with me for the next hour as we discuss what's going on with the world today and play some tunes. The phone lines are open, so give us a call. In the meantime, here's the Lemonheads with "It's a Shame About Ray"."

She let the song play and took some pre-air calls. All her projects and papers were done, so doing the show wasn't interfering with her studies. Although, she still hadn't put together a proposal for Heywood about her exhibit idea yet.

After the song ended, she let the tape play of some playful banter and the first series of calls recorded earlier. There would be some paid commercials to run after that and her sign-off at the end of the hour, followed by some more music.

She almost made it look too easy... and fun!

When the start of the commercial break began, she started recording her next segment. "Okay, I have a few more songs to play before I'm out of here! I wanna thank our callers this past hour, as well as our listeners out there. You can catch me on here from 8 pm to 10 pm on Tuesdays and Thursdays 'til the end of the year. Once again, you're listening to WQMC 1290 college radio. I'm your host, Angie With The Attitude. Thank you for listening. Here's the latest from Toad the Wet Sprocket, called "Fall Down"."

Angie did the recording in one take. On the other side of the booth, her producer and soundboard operator, Butch, gave her a thumbs up. Once they were off the air, he stood up and opened the door to the studio.

"Nice work. You got a knack for this! The music you're playing ain't too bad, either."

She leaned back and gestured with her hands. "It's like riding a bike. I guess you never forget it."

The next hour's radio personality came in and Angie gathered her belongings. "Well, I'll leave you to the next guy. Same time tomorrow?"

"You got it, take it easy." Butch waved and returned to the engineering room as Angie left through the opposite studio door.

Heywood walked up to the address Larry gave him. The place was within walking distance from his apartment, and it was a nice night for a stroll. There was a sign on the window that said, *Knights of Columbia*. He knocked on the door and it sprang open. A burly, clean-shaven white man gave Heywood the once-over and said, "yeah?"

"Uh, I think I may have the wrong place," he replied, and started backing up.

Larry suddenly appeared at the doorway. "Heywood! So glad you could make it, c'mon in! He's with me." Larry waved him back as Heywood slowly walked through the doorway.

"Sorry about Hugo over there. He's mostly for appearances. We have water here, if you're thirsty, among other drinks. Feel free to walk around, introduce yourself to the others. There are two floors. We'll have an open discussion in about fifteen minutes, then read from the bible, and end the night with a prayer."

"Sounds great," Heywood said. He looked around and started to mingle.

There were close to sixty people divided on the two floors of the building. Several table games were being played and a bar was serving wine. The atmosphere was very low-key and friendly.

Heywood noticed a woman standing by herself. He was hesitant to approach her, but after ten minutes and a glass of water, he gathered the courage.

She had shoulder-length hair, blue eyes, and was wearing a gray zipped up sweater over a yellow tee-shirt.

"Hi," she said.

"Hi, I'm Heywood."

"Pleased to meet you, I'm Tina," she replied with a smile.

"This is a nice setup here, clean, wholesome fun," Heywood said.

"I know. It's so rare to find something like this in the city," Tina replied.

"Yeah, yes, it is. So um, are you here... alone?"

"I... might be, but I'm not here to make friends. I represent Jews for Jesus. Spreading the word for those who would listen."

"Oh! That sounds... interesting," Heywood said.

"Thank you, if you're interested, I could tell you more."

"I'm... gonna work the room a little bit more, but I'm not saying 'no,'" he said, putting on his best smile.

"Sure. It was nice meeting you."

"Pretty sure we'll bump into each other again," he said in parting.

She moved to another person, introducing herself again as Heywood took a sip of his water. He was unfamiliar with whatever she was affiliated with but kept her in mind in case he saw her again.

After ten minutes, they broke into groups for independent discussions, then came back together and sang a few hymns. The evening ended and a few people exchanged numbers while asking when the next meeting was.

"Thanks for coming," Larry said, when Heywood was leaving.

"I had fun, think I'll come back at the next one."

"Glad to hear it!" Larry said, as Heywood walked back out to the sidewalk.

The Nova movie theater was showing *Interview with The Vampire* at seven o'clock Friday night. The trio barely made it on time, and surprisingly, had no problems getting in. This was the second week since the film's release so there was still a crowd of people in the audience. Despite all this, they got good seats, but missed the trailers because they were getting concessions.

Tanya paid for the tickets, despite Alex offering, both declined since she was the birthday girl in question. Lakeshia was frightened several times, and cried once, but made it through the film. Alex felt that Brad Pitt complained too much and was just moody to be a vampire but loved Kirsten Dunst's Claudia character. Tanya felt the movie was too long, with a few good parts sprinkled in.

After the movie, the girls walked to the McDonald's two blocks down on 145th Street and Broadway.

"Okay, you paid for the movie, I'm paying for our food," Alex said.

"Think again! I'll pay, you're still the birthday girl!" Lakeshia said.

Alex rolled her eyes. "Okay, I'll take a number one with a Pepsi."

Tanya asked Lakeshia to order a number three with a Sprite and looked for a booth. Alex joined Tanya while Lakeshia waited in line.

"So, what did you think of the movie?" Alex asked.

"It was alright, I just expected more action," Tanya replied. "I gotta give it to Tom Cruise, though."

"He was in like 40% of the movie!" Alex exclaimed.

Lakeshia came with two trays and just some fries for herself.

"What's with you? You barely ate popcorn and now you're just having some fries?" Tanya asked.

"Mind yours! I eat what I eat!" Lakeshia replied.

"I'll give you your props, Leelee. You were a trooper for most of the movie, but I saw you get misty-eyed when Claudia died."

"Misty-eyed? She was bawling!" Tanya said.

"Shut up!" Lakeshia cried out. "It was a moving scene."

"I could have gone without the nudity though," Alex said, and nodded to Lakeshia. "This the first time you've seen someone naked in a movie, Leelee?"

"No, I've seen *Splash*, when I was younger," Lakeshia said, as she ate a french fry.

"Well, now that we've discussed the movie, time for your present!" Tanya said, as Lakeshia drummed up a fanfare.

"Aw, c'mon, y'all didn't have to—" Alex said.

"Yeah, yeah, yeah. Spare us, your majesty, you've been watching this bag I was carrying all night," Tanya said, with a grin.

Alex accepted the wrapped box with a smile and tore it open, then her smile disappeared. "What the heck is this?"

She pulled out the first edition copy of *The Vampire Lestat* and cringed.

"It's the next part. Hopefully they'll make that one into a movie too!" Lakeshia cheered.

Alex put on a fake smile. "Thanks!" and quickly put the book back in the box.

They finished their meals and headed back outside. "Well, this was fun…" Alex said.

"Yeah, we should do this more often," Tanya agreed.

"If we ever agree on a movie, again!" Lakeshia said.

"That's true," Alex said. "Good night, see y'all Monday." She crossed the street where a car was waiting for her.

"Happy birthday, enjoy your party tomorrow!" Tanya waved, and then turned to Lakeshia, "You okay to walk home?"

"I actually live nearby so I'm good," Lakeshia said. "I don't think my parents would have let me go anywhere else with y'all. I have to be home by 10 pm."

"Geez," Tanya sighed, noticing it was nine-thirty. "Good night, Leelee." She turned and entered the 145th Street 1-train station.

"Good night, Tee!" Lakeshia said, and then walked back up the street.

The Webster Branch Library was one of the oldest in the city. It was originally known as the Webster Free Library, named after Charles B. Webster, who donated the branch's building at its first location on East 76th Street. The current location of the library was constructed on 78th Street and York Avenue as one of the Carnegie Libraries, funded by donations from Andrew Carnegie.

Robin was inside, waiting in the main floor after arriving at noon. The head librarian, a soft-spoken Hindu-American named Satwinder Singh, had let him in. He had a mullet ending with dark, curly hair in the back with a thick mustache. The branch wasn't due to open until one o'clock, and it was up to Andrew to show the clerk around the facility.

"Mister Walker!" A voice behind him greeted.

Robin turned around and saw Andrew Friedman approach him, with his hand extended. "You were scheduled to arrive at 1 pm. You're pretty early."

He gave the hand a hearty handshake. "Just looking to make a good first impression," and emphasized his grip, testing the senior clerk's strength.

The handshake went longer than a minute, then they broke it off, looking back at each other.

"Uh, lemme show you around," Andrew said.

"Lead the way," Robin replied, with a nod.

Robin followed him to the clerical office. There he found the desk schedule hanging on the bulletin board. Andrew formally introduced Robin to Charlie Finn and Carol Sora, full-time clerks, and mentioned that part-time clerks, Ira Haim and Henrietta Gastone, would be joining them shortly.

Andrew then asked Robin to follow him upstairs to the children's room.

"Hey, is that him?" Charlie asked Carol.

"I think so… I thought he'd be taller. They said he was intimidating," Carol replied.

"How is he still here, if he actually did what he did?" Charlie asked.

"Hey, he was found not guilty, maybe he didn't do it," Carol said.

Andrew took Robin upstairs to the second floor, where they had a dedicated children's section. Robin was having flashbacks to his time at Fort Washington, working their area where they had small shelves and unkept books.

"Um, I don't have a shift up here, do I?" He asked Andrew.

"Nah, you're downstairs for the two o'clock hour, then the four o'clock hour, that's it," Andrew replied.

He gave a quiet sigh and thought, *thank you, Jesus!*

Andrew tilted his head. "C'mon, last stop is the break room."

"Alrighty," Robin said, with a smile.

Andrew and Robin walked down to the main floor and to the back where there were two areas, the clerical office and a break room. In the break room, Andrew turned on the light.

"You can leave your coat in any of these lockers. No one will mess with them."

"Uh, I'll leave my coat where I can keep my eyes on it, thank you," Robin replied, with a nervous laugh.

He was still leery of leaving his coat unattended after a childhood incident left him emotionally scarred.

"That's... a bit unorthodox, but I suppose you can leave it in the office," Andrew said, with a nod. "Is there also a story behind your glove?" he said, pointing to his left hand.

"Um, there is... I had an accident and was burned, severely."

"How severe?"

Robin pulled the glove off and showed him. Andrew raised an eyebrow, but kept his stoic demeanor. *Does anything unnerve this guy?* he thought.

"Yes, I guess that would be hard to explain to our patrons," Andrew replied dryly.

Robin put on the glove again. "Guess that's it, then, yes?"

"Yes. You can go back out on the floor and look around until ten minutes to one, then report to the clerical office for a light briefing."

*Oooh, a light briefing!* "Um, sure," Robin said, and exited the room.

Back at 58th Street, Saturday afternoon was very quiet, perhaps too quiet. Augustus was sitting at the information desk, when a patron came up and requested *The New York Daily News* classified section.

The branch carried several copies, because of people marking up, or even keeping certain pages, when finding a specific ad they might qualify for.

After searching inside the desk, Augustus looked back up and said, "I'm sorry, all our copies are out at this moment."

"This is unacceptable! I've asked every 30 minutes and each time someone else has it!" the patron yelled.

"I apologize for the inconvenience, sir. Please, keep your voice down…"

He ignored the head librarian and looked around, then pointed at a stranger. "You! You have the classified section?"

"No."

"You? You? How about you?" The patron continued asking around.

"Sir, you're making a scene—"

"I don't care! Someone here is hogging the damn classifieds and I'm going to find out who!"

Another patron stood up. "Hey man, just calm down…"

"Don't you tell me to calm down! I've been out of a job for three weeks now! Who's gonna pay my rent? You?"

"Hell no, I ain't paying your rent!"

Their voices were carrying, and more people were watching, including Gerry at the circulation desk, with a smirk on his face.

The man looking for the classifieds lunged at the other man, and they started fighting. A woman screamed, as the two people tussled in the reference corner.

Eugene stood up from his chair and yelled, "hey!" then ran across the room.

The two men were still fighting as Eugene got between them, trying to break them apart. Augustus then stepped forward to help.

"That's it! Outta here, both of you, now!" Eugene barked.

"He started with me, man!"

"All I wanted was the classifieds!" the other one said.

"Now you're both out of here. We don't condone fighting in the library! Period!"

"Hey, let me go!" Eugene led the less aggressive one to the door as

Augustus dragged the other patron. Then suddenly he reached into his pocket. Augustus saw the move and immediately let him go. "Eugene! He's got a weapon!"

The security guard turned around and sucker-punched the man, who dropped a knife before falling to the floor.

"Goddamn!" Eugene yelled. "He did NOT have a glass jaw. Good call there, Augustus."

"Comes with the territory," Augustus said, kicking the knife away.

"Hey, obviously, dude got some mental issues," the other patron said.

"Yeah, and you're lucky he didn't use that knife on you." Eugene chucked his thumb. "Get going!"

"Whatever." The man walked out of the library peacefully.

"So, what now?" Eugene asked.

"Check if he's okay, then drag him down the street." Augustus took a handkerchief out of his pocket and carefully picked up the knife by the handle. "I'll see to it the police get this."

"Just a regular Saturday afternoon at 58th Street, eh Chavez?" Gerry said.

Augustus was not amused.

# CHAPTER SIXTEEN

ALEX'S BIRTHDAY CELEBRATION WAS STARTING SLOW. SHE WAS wearing a new pant suit, since she rarely wore dresses, and it was already a half-hour after two o'clock, with no one in sight yet.

"Where *is* everyone?" she hissed. "Albany!"

A door opened, and an African-American man, whose name was actually Abernathy came out and answered, "yes, Miss Stevens?"

"Has anyone called saying they're coming late?" Alex asked.

"No, Miss Stevens."

"Are all the highways in the area running smoothly?"

He thought about it. "To the best of my knowledge, Miss Stevens."

All her guests' RSVP'd. They all knew the party started at two o'clock and ended at four. This hall cost her a lot of money to rent. Naturally, her parents weren't scheduled to come until the last half hour when everything was winding down. This was a public humiliation!

"Do me a favor? Check the entrance for me, please?" Alex asked.

"Of course, Miss Stevens." The gentleman opened the door again and disappeared.

She started pacing back and forth. Then minutes went by, and the door opened again. She turned to find Abernathy walking back in, holding a gift.

"This was waiting outside the entrance for you, Miss Stevens," he announced.

She took the wrapped package and put it on the table. There was a card that simply said *For Alex, with love.* With some hesitation, she opened the box and found a note. She narrowed her eyes and read the note aloud.

*"There once was a girl named Alex,*
*who threw a party that no one decided to attend.*
*She was so spiteful and callous,*
*that her so-called friends never spoke to her again."*

Alex tore the box up in a furious rage, this was a complete nightmare. "Oh my God!" she screamed.

"Call my parents, tell them not to come!" she ordered. "Make something up. The hall was booked. Tell 'em we had to cancel. I'll just have cake and ice cream at home and eat the deposit. Tell NO ONE of this!"

He nodded. "Yes, Miss Stevens."

She sighed. "After that, bring the car around."

"Of course, Miss Stevens," Abernathy replied, and stepped back outside from the hall.

When she was certain he was gone, Alex tried, but failed, to hold back the tears. She sobbed quietly, alone in the hall.

Robin was doing his second, and last, hour of the day at three-thirty. The branch was pretty lively for a Saturday, with a handful of dedicated patrons. One of the clerks was a white guy in his early 30's. He had been eye-balling Robin all day, for some reason. He felt stares from most of the staff today, which he chalked up to being here the first time, but now it was time to get some answers.

"Uh, Charles, was it?" Robin began.

"Charlie," he corrected.

"Oh, my bad, uh, um… Charlie, man… um, why are you giving me looks, man? What's up?"

"Oh, um, sorry about that, it's just that, um… you got a reputation, man."

"What do you mean?" Robin asked.

"I mean, I don't have the whole story—"

"Well, allow me to fill any blanks," he replied quickly.

"Okay, is it true you crushed a soda can in one of your co-worker's head?" Charlie asked.

Robin waited for a second, to see if the clerk was serious, then said, "what? Where did you hear that?"

Charlie thought about it before he answered, then looked around and whispered, "I hate to break it to ya, but people have been gossiping about this incident with you, man."

"What incident?" Robin asked.

"Look, I don't know when it happened, I don't know all the details. All I *do* know, is you had something to do with someone involving a soda can. That's all I know."

"When did you hear this? Who the hell told you?" Robin said, getting agitated.

"I just heard it, people talk… they, they've nicknamed you…"

"What?" Robin asked.

"They've nicknamed you... The Soda Can Killer."

Robin gasped. "Are you kiddin' me?"

"Well, is it true?" Charlie asked.

"No, it ain't true!" Robin yelled.

He noticed he was getting loud and apologized.

"None of it?" Charlie asked again.

"No, what the hell?" Robin asked, then stepped away from him, returning to his post. His eyes were darting anxiously in all directions.

Upstairs outside the staff room at 58th Street, Tanya walked up to Lakeshia as they put their coats on, preparing to leave at the end of the day.

"Leelee?"

She turned to her. "Yeah?"

"I didn't wanna say anything, but I've been noticing something with you, and I just wanted to ask… are you okay?"

She frowned. "Uh, yeah, why?"

"I just want you to know, you can talk to me about anything," Tanya said with concern.

"Girl, what are you talking about?"

"Alright, I'm just gonna come out and say it. You getting skeletal on me, girl. You need to eat something before you fall out!"

"I'm fine! Okay? I eat, I'm not throwing up—"

"You were skinny before, but now this is something else," Tanya pleaded. "I'm just looking out for you."

"Well, thank you for your concern, but I'm fine." Lakeshia stepped past Tanya and headed downstairs to leave.

It was a dull gray evening as Heywood walked into the bookstore. He was meeting Larry here, as the two were becoming very friendly as of late. Heywood found Larry near the entrance inside.

"Hey, man," he greeted.

"Hey, how's it going?" Larry asked.

"Same old, same old," Heywood said, with a grin.

"I hear that!"

They started browsing some shelves when Larry asked, "so, how long have you been an IA?"

"Little over three years. Started at Aguilar back in late 1990, then transferred to 58th Street. Why?"

"I did some research on you, hope you don't mind, and I couldn't help but notice… you already have your master's in library science, but you're still an IA?"

"It's kinda complicated. I technically do have my Masters, but I earned it at a school that's not officially recognized by the American Library Association. Which is also why I haven't been promoted to a librarian yet."

"That... is fascinating, I've never heard of anything like this," Larry said, as they found a couple of chairs and sat for a break.

"While it's a difficult thing, I'm patient, and believe I'll make a rank in time. It's not like I'm strapped for cash or anything," Heywood said, with a chuckle.

"Well, that's great to hear, but I'll tell ya, man... some days, I feel like an overpaid babysitter, ya know?"

"Heh, do I ever. We got this behemoth at the branch who starts up against the patrons all the time, and we can't do anything!"

"Yeah, the rights of the public, and all that crap!" Larry agreed, shaking his head. "Things should be better."

"They should, and they will... so long as we're here to fight the good fight!" Heywood said.

"Hear, hear! Hey, you ever think about... being in charge?"

"All. The. Time." Heywood held up his hand. "Not that I have anything against the current administration. I just believe that things would be a whole lot better if I was in charge."

"Go-getters like you have that drive. They have a vision," Larry encouraged.

"Yes we do, yes we do!"

"But you wait, you bide your time, and you wait for that opportunity, man."

"Yes!"

"I knew we saw eye-to-eye!"

"So, what do you have planned?" Heywood asked.

Larry made a hesitant sound. "All in good time, my friend. I just wanted to make sure we were on the same page."

"Hey, I'm with you. I'm on board if you got a plan to change things... I want in," Heywood said.

They got up and started browsing again. Larry kept the conversation to a minimum the rest of the time they spent together. Heywood was curious as to what Larry's plans were, and how serious he was.

Augustus walked into the coffee shop and took a seat at a booth. "Thank you for seeing me," he began.

Donald Langston sat on the other side of the booth and was enjoying a BLT. He was more relaxed in a black and white striped buckled back waistcoat and jeans.

"We're making the buy for the land tomorrow," Donald started. "Once it's successful, we will then proceed with your plan to have it under a shell corporation and take comfort in our anonymity."

Augustus nodded.

"After that, the city will buy the land from us at triple the cost and we'll split the profits equally."

"Excellent."

Donald took another bite from his sandwich, then wiped his mouth and said, "but I don't have to tell you that if this deal goes wrong and we take the hit, well I won't mince words... I'll fucking kill you myself."

A chill went down Augustus' spine, but he replied, "I assure you nothing will go wrong."

"Good, because you're in the big leagues now. Big money, big risks... the sharks will smell blood in the water and eat you up."

"If you're trying to scare me—"

"I don't scare, I make promises. I didn't get to where I'm at just to have some *spic* tear it all down."

Augustus stared at Donald as he finished his meal. They looked at each other quietly for a moment then Augustus said coldly, "money is green, no matter who holds it. Truth be told, I could buy your shitty investment group and freeze you out in a heartbeat! You think you're above me and been brought down to my level? Ha! Please, it's actually *me* who's slumming it, working with the likes of you! So, take your concerns over the S.E.C. and bullshit threats if this goes south, and shove them up your ass!"

The waiter came to their booth and without taking a breath Augustus looked at him and said, "I'll have a cup of coffee, please. Black, with two sugars."

The waiter left and the two were staring at each other again. Donald actually smiled. "Well, here's to making more money."

He pulled out a twenty-dollar bill and left it on the table, then stood up and walked out of the coffee shop.

Augustus' coffee came, he sat and sipped it slowly. The busboy approached the booth to collect the plate and utensils Donald left. Augustus noticed the young man was Hispanic and asked him, "how much was his bill?"

The busboy whispered something to the waiter passing by and then replied, "$18.57."

Augustus pulled out a fifty-dollar bill and swapped out the twenty. The busboy smiled as Augustus stood, nodded to him, and left.

Monday morning Sonyai called Andrew and asked how Robin behaved himself.

"He's an odd individual, I'll give you that," Andrew began, "but he carried himself very well. No incidents to report, ma'am."

She rolled her eyes at him calling her 'ma'am,' but let it slide. "Very good, Andrew. I'm trying to give this young man a second chance to redeem himself. I honestly believe deep down he's a good kid, who is just a victim of circumstance."

"He does seem a bit high strung, but he's fast when it comes to checking out stuff and keeps quiet when it's downtime. Whatever he's been through, hopefully it's passed."

"I hope so too, Andrew. This weekend was a test and I believe after a rough start, he's finally coming along. Talk to you again soon. Goodbye."

Sonyai hung up the phone just as Tommy walked in. She waved as he said, "good morning."

"Good morning, how was your weekend?"

"It was okay. Ready for Thanksgiving this week?" Sonyai asked.

"Uh, yeah, can't wait."

"You're going through hell, aren't you?"

"It shows, doesn't it?" Tommy asked.

She nodded. "Be strong, concentrate on the positive. This is your child's very first holiday celebration."

"It's not like she's going to remember anything."

"That's the point, Thomas. It's up to you and the rest of your family to record and preserve as much as you can, so you can show her years from now."

"I'm stuck in the middle of two different families. My parents and my in-laws are—"

"That happens to all families," Sonyai interrupted. "Look at me for example. Yes, I embrace most of my father's Japanese aspects, but I take after my Scottish mother as well."

"Really?" Tommy asked.

"Yes, I follow soccer, which I secretly still call 'football.' Go Aberdeen! I also like rugby and eat various Scottish delicacies. And despite all these things, most still believe I'm just Japanese, but even other Japanese people don't believe I'm Japanese enough for their standards. It's a double-edged sword."

Tommy nodded. "I get it now."

"Have your daughter embrace both her cultures. She'll thank you when she's older, even if it drives you crazy," she smiled.

"Thank you, Miss Yi. I feel a lot better now."

"Glad I could help." She walked out of the office to turn on the terminals at the circulation desk.

Students were off the entire week for Thanksgiving, so Alex had time to do some investigating. It was so awkward Saturday afternoon to explain things to her parents, but she was ready for some answers. She took the train downtown to 28th Street and found Paul and Rodney Watts doing charity work at a local shelter.

Naturally, this scenario required some tact, but Alex was beyond that point. "Paul! What the hell?!" she screamed.

Paul turned and approached Alex to speak with her privately, "Alex, I can explain…"

"Good, because I'm about to punch your lights out!"

"Easy! It was Fergus's idea. He wanted to flex on you to see if everyone would actually do it, and it worked. I honestly thought he was joking!"

*Fergus! I knew it was that sonofabitch!* "You have any idea how humiliated I was?!" Alex asked.

"I'm SO sorry, Alex. I really am."

"What did Fergus say for you and everyone else not to come?"

"I… I can't say."

He took a step back as she advanced on him. "Look, you can take it out on me all you want, but I'm not telling you what he did."

"You're not worth the effort! I don't know what I saw in you!"

She turned away. Now that she knew who was responsible, she just needed to find him.

The first hour after the branch opened went well. There was little activity among the patrons, since everyone was getting ready for the holidays. It was quite peaceful.

Sonyai was still getting used to Ethel not being around. She was still receiving help from various branches until her replacement could be found. At one o'clock she walked into her office to find Robin waiting for her.

"We need to talk!" He slammed the door closed.

"Wha… what's wrong? What is going on? Why are you upset?" Sonyai asked.

"It got out. Everyone in the entire cluster has heard multiple stories... I've become an urban legend!" Robin exclaimed.

"What are you talking about?"

"The incident with Ethel! All the details are scattered, leaving everyone to draw their own conclusions!" He took a breath, trying to relax. "Everyone is spreading rumors... they're calling me *The Soda Can Killer!*"

Sonyai couldn't believe what she was hearing. "Wh... what?"

"They think I tried to KILL Ethel with a soda can, some are saying I crushed the can in her head, some think I sliced her head open. The stories are completely absurd, and they won't stop!" Robin explained.

Sonyai was quiet for a moment, as her mouth slowly shaped into a smirk. "Um, really? That's terrible."

"I know, we have to do something, these rumors spread like wildfire, and I..." he stopped and turned toward her. "What are you... are you... are you *laughing?*"

"No! NO!" She shook her head as the smirk grew. She couldn't fight it, and her face started turning red.

"You're lying! You can't hold it in. You're dying to laugh at this, and it's NOT funny!" Robin pointed at her with his finger.

She couldn't contain herself anymore and exploded in a fit of hysterical laughter.

"Oh my God! Unbelievable!"

He stormed out, leaving Sonyai cracking up alone in her office. *I should have told her I had sex with her niece,* he thought.

Zelda was off Monday afternoon, so she made the trip up to Washington Heights and met with Barbara in the George Washington Bus Terminal.

"You keep asking for these meetings, someone's going to think we're going together," Barbara said bluntly.

"Like you ever cared what someone else thought of you."

Barbara nodded to herself, accepting that Zelda was right, then asked, "so, why are we here then?"

Zelda let out a sigh. "Robin's little indiscretion has leaked out and it's running away like wildfire."

"This is news to me, and I don't take lightly to surprises."

"No kidding," Zelda said sarcastically. "It probably hasn't made its way up here yet, but it will."

Barbara shook her head. "So how bad are we talking?"

"Well," she stifled a chuckle. "They're calling him… 'The Soda Can Killer.'"

Barbara closed and rubbed her eyes. "I'm sorry, what?"

"You heard me. I'm not going to repeat it, I'll crack up laughing. But details are all over the place. People are just throwing in their own details. It's a real elephant game situation."

"Well, you know what? I'm not doing anything. Let him deal with this. He needs to grow."

"You really want to go that route with this situation?"

"I just finished paying $2,000.00 to that attorney who saved his skin. He will deal with this on his own and use it as a life lesson."

"Okay, so much for the head's up… you have to admit, it's kinda funny, though."

She started walking to the pair of escalators that lead to Broadway. "Yeah, I'm sure Robin's laughing his ass off."

Tuesday at two o'clock Sonyai was upstairs in the staff room, enjoying a rare, quiet meal to herself. She was still worried about Janelle and planned to visit her at Avery Boone's home, where she heard she was living there temporarily. The door opened suddenly, and Zelda walked in.

The assistant librarian took her lunch out from the refrigerator and took a seat at the table. "You're here pretty late for lunch," she told Sonyai.

"I did a two-hour block at twelve," Sonyai explained.

"Ah."

A few minutes went by as they ate their meals in silence, then Sonyai said, "I hear Chavez has been asking questions about SIBL."

Zelda pondered the harm in letting her know about his land deal. She wasn't the type to sabotage some real estate scheme that may or may not make him some serious money. "He's looking to buy the proposed site and resell it to the city for a markup."

The senior clerk scoffed. "Is that all? And here I was hoping he was planning for bigger and better aspirations, possibly running things over there."

Zelda giggled, actually giggled. "Oh heavens. Augustus would never leave 58th Street..."

Sonyai registered an annoyed look at Zelda finding her suggestion so humorous. "Indeed. Well, based on what I've heard, the branch will be on the far end of 34th Street..."

"Yes, the yards, I believe," Zelda replied, and took a sip of her tea. After a minute she said, "you know, the two of you have been remarkable together these past months. Isn't it a good thing when both supervisors get along for once?"

Sonyai, once again, wasn't amused by Zelda's pandering, but twisted her mouth in a sarcastic smirk. "Yes, I believe the *last* time that happened was when Natasha Santiago and Oliver Prince were here," she said, referring to Augustus' predecessor and her mentor, who was also known as The Man in White.

Zelda stopped eating and gave Sonyai a distasteful look. "And they say we Jews know how to hold a grudge. You wouldn't happen to have a distant relative from Israel, would you? A grand-aunt or uncle—"

"I hold it against him because that is *not* the way you advance in the system! He underhandedly stole this branch and patted himself on the back on how clever he was, to blackmail someone for having an innocent friendship!"

"Did it ever occur to you that perhaps it wasn't so innocent? That Nat and Oliver were actually involved in an improper relationship?"

Sonyai scoffed. "There was no proof! They were seen eating together at a restaurant, big deal!"

"*Several* restaurants, and there were the trips they took together."

"Those were ALA conferences!"

"It doesn't matter, Sonyai. Even though Oliver was estranged from his wife, he was still a married man!"

"Yes, and what about that? I finally met Barbara Schemanske, for the first time. For *any*one to survive a marriage with that…"

Zelda raised a pointed finger to Sonyai. "She is a close, personal friend, Sonyai… watch what you say…"

The conversation had become extremely intense. The senior clerk held her tongue, for fear of saying something that would bring out the worst in the assistant librarian.

Zelda sighed. "Look, I get it. You have the utmost respect for your mentor, but he was still a man."

"And men… always cheat, right?" Sonyai asked.

She took another sip of her tea. "You said it, not me."

"Spoken like a spiteful old spinster." Sonyai stood up, gathered her belongings, and walked out the door.

"*Mekhasheyfe,*" Zelda whispered.

# CHAPTER SEVENTEEN

ROBIN WAS JUST SITTING DOWN FOR DINNER WHEN HIS DOORBELL RANG. He approached the door questioningly, and called out, "Who?!" then opened the door to find his cousin Pepsi standing in the hallway.

"Hey, cousin! What's up?"

"My mother wants to see you." Pepsi waved his arm. "Let's go."

"Oh, I've been summoned?" Robin asked with a tone. "If she wants to talk to me, have her call, or bring her ass downstairs herself!"

"Don't be like that, c'mon."

"Fine, let me get my keys. Hold on."

They took the elevator down to the lobby, then up to the twenty-third floor where Esme lived.

Her apartment was on a different line of letters, and was only a one-bedroom, with no balcony. The view was on the opposite side of the building, so she was facing the first building on Saint Nicholas Avenue and the expressway that was built underneath the four high-rise apartments.

Robin was let in by Pepsi and found his Great Aunt sitting on the couch in the living room.

Esme had her brother's light complexion. Her hair was completely white and done up like Oprah, and she was wearing an open black and white business suit over a blouse. She sat quietly, waiting for Robin to acknowledge her. When Robin stood quietly looking back at her she let the disrespect slide and cleared her throat.

"I suppose you're wondering why I asked you here," she began.

He had nothing to say so he continued to look at her.

She scrunched up her face. "Whatsamatter, cat got your tongue?"

"I'm waiting for you to get to your point."

Esme raised an eyebrow at his disrespectful tone and decided to, once again, let it slide. "Well then, let me *get* to that point… we would like you to join us here, for Thanksgiving dinner, Thursday."

Now it was Robin's turn to raise his eyebrow at the invitation. "Wow, that's kind of you…"

Esme gave him a thin smile until he finished.

"…but I respectfully decline."

"I beg your pardon?"

"This…" he let out a sigh. "This is the first time we've spoken in six months. You… *any* of you… haven't so much as checked on me to see how I'm doing. I'm only seven flights down from you and we haven't even shared an elevator together!"

Esme's smile turned to a scowl.

"Yeah, I saw you purposely avoiding stepping in one with me that time. You've pretty much shunned me since Jon died, and now you wanna extend the olive branch?" He shook his head. "I don't think so."

"I'd watch that tone, young man…"

Pepsi stepped in between them, holding his hand up. "Be careful what you're doing here," he warned.

"I know exactly what I'm doing here. You've made it clear where I stand in this family back at the funeral, so I refuse to sit at the kiddie's table while all the grown-ups talk about me behind my back!"

He raised his finger and pointed. "I see you… whispering to everybody. Talking about some God-awful event granddaddy did in the past! You snobs look down at us, as if our ancestors weren't out there in the fields picking cotton! It's people like you, who agree with Donald Trump about what he said about those kids in Central Park! Who thinks OJ actually had something to do with the death of his ex-wife!

It's Uncle Toms like *you* who think Yusef Hawkins had no business being in Bensonhurst!"

Esme stood up. "You've got some fucking nerve!" she spat.

Pepsi stepped back, a concerned look on his face.

"I offer my hand to you, and you just smack it away! We've tried to treat you nice, but you're just a spiteful little piece of shit! My brother took pity on you for what he did to your mother! He begged me to watch over you, to hold no grudges..."

Robin tilted his head but stood quietly as she continued. "But if he didn't, he wouldn't give an upstart like you a pot to piss in or a window to throw it out of!"

The outburst made her short of breath, and she coughed for a few seconds, then gave Robin the coldest death stare. "I may not have that many years left, but I will spend the rest of them making sure *no one* in our family acknowledges your existence! Get the hell out of my sight!"

Robin turned around and headed for the door.

"My only regret is that your mother never finds out what a deplorable human being you are!" she gasped.

Robin opened the door, stepped out, and looked back at her. "Trust me! She already knows!"

He slammed the door behind him.

A limousine picked up Augustus from the branch at five o'clock and dropped him off at the financial district. He walked a few blocks to Pearl Street and arrived at the Rex New York Cigar Club. After climbing the steps to the second floor, an escort walked him to a private room where Cleopheous Baker was sitting, smoking a Montecristo.

He took a seat opposite of Cleopheous and picked an Arturo Fuente to smoke. Augustus then ordered a glass of tequila and waited until they were alone, taking several puffs.

"You have any plans for Thanksgiving?" Cleopheous asked.

"Not really? You?"

"I'm heading up to Scarsdale to have dinner with Estelle's family. It's been ten years since her passing, but they still reach out on the holidays, so I don't feel alone."

Augustus nodded. "That's nice of them."

Cleopheous snorted. "Heh, not really. They're all a bunch of assholes. Not a cultured bone in their bodies."

They both chuckled and blew smoke in the air quietly. Then Augustus's drink arrived.

After a few minutes, Cleopheous sighed. "A real shame about D'amato. We have hard times ahead of us, my friend. A Republican mayor, and now a Republican governor... the first thing they're going to do is slash the budget."

"Agreed." Augustus nodded.

"We had several renovations planned..."

"And that new operating system."

"Oh, that's still happening. The money's been set aside, so they can't touch that."

They took another moment. Cleopheous blew some more smoke as Augustus finished his drink.

"I've been thinking..." Augustus began, "if we acknowledge Pataki's victory and contribute a charitable donation to their administration... after the fact, late as it may be, we could save face."

Cleopheous put out his cigar and leaned forward. "What good would *that* do?"

"We had our chance to get ahead of this. I was approached by one of their people, just like you said, and despite the union endorsing D'amato, Pataki wanted minorities on his side. We can talk to the community leaders and convince them that this new governor still has their best interest at heart."

The regional head librarian brought a hand to his chin in deep thought. "It could soften the blow... you willing to do the legwork?"

"So long as you help with the donation," Augustus replied quickly.

"Heh, I knew there was a catch..." Cleopheous tilted his head. "You know, he could keep the money and still cut our budget."

"If he does, the community will start looking for his next opponent in four years and back them. He barely won *this* election. If he wants to be re-elected, he'll need to make more friends."

Augustus finished his cigar, extinguishing it in a glass ashtray.

Cleopheous gave an approving nod. "You sure know how to make some good out of a bad situation."

"In this business, you have to."

After the branch closed, Tommy, Robin, and Gerry walked to the garage where Gerry's car was parked.

"Nice wheels," Robin complimented.

"Thanks," Gerry said.

Robin climbed in the back seat, while Tommy rode shotgun.

The ride to the financial district was quiet, which annoyed Robin for some reason.

"Y'all so quiet, what gives?" he asked.

"Just tired from work, that's all," Gerry replied.

"I can't speak for Gerry, but I'm nervous about this first Thanksgiving with the baby," Tommy replied.

"I… don't think the kid's gonna notice, Tommy. What's to be nervous about?"

"You don't have my in-laws or even *my* parents to know why I'm nervous, so you wouldn't understand," Tommy said.

"That might be true, but trust me, I got family issues myself, man," Robin said.

Tommy didn't pry, and they drove in silence again for a few minutes, then Robin asked Gerry, "what about you, man? Wha'cha got planned for the holiday?"

"I don't particularly celebrate the event when Native-American's got run over for their land and livelihood. It's just another day to me. But my sister goes and has dinner with my folks."

"Oh, you're one of *those* types, huh? Yeesh."

"Doesn't mean I have problems taking a turkey as a token of solidarity in the workforce. It's the least they could do."

"Doesn't the union show their appreciation in other ways?" Robin asked.

Gerry and Tommy exchanged glances and then laughed in unison.

They finally arrive near the twin towers, where Gerry parked the car in *another* garage for two hours.

"Hey man, you ever try *looking* for a parking space instead of wasting money on 24-hour garages?" Robin asked.

"You don't drive, so you have no idea how hard it is to look for parking," Gerry replied.

They walked across Murray Street from North End Avenue. Once they made it to West Street, they turned and arrived at the DC37 head-quarters. The turkey handout was always in the parking lot on the side of the building.

The trio arrived at the waiting area and found a long line filling up the entire lot.

"Oh, hell no! No turkey is worth waiting through this!" Robin screamed.

"They're real quick. It'll be an hour, tops," Gerry said. "Why'd you think I paid for two hours at the garage?"

"I'd thought you were going for drinks afterward!"

"Well, yeah… we are!" Tommy joked with a grin.

"Look, I thought this would be nice and quick, but I ain't waiting here for an hour." Robin started walking back to the exit.

Gerry quickly grabbed his arm. Robin tensed up and turned his head, his eyes wide at his audacity. "Tell you what, I'll give you a ride home if you stay with us."

He looked at the grip and snorted, pulling away. "You were going to do that *anyway*, but fine! I'll wait."

True to Gerry's word, the line moved pretty quickly. Within forty-five minutes, they approached a table with a parked truck that was opened from the back.

"Uh-oh," Tommy said.

"What's wrong?" Gerry asked.

"They're asking people to sign a book."

"So?" Robin asked.

"Um," Gerry began. "We kinda didn't tell you… only full-time staff are union members, and it looks like they're checking employee names and asking them to sign for their turkey."

"So, you mean, I'm waiting here… for nothing?" Robin asked.

"Relax, we'll think of something," Gerry said.

As the line moved up and they got closer, something interesting happened. A man at the table called out, "we're starting to issue out checks now, since the turkeys are almost gone! If you haven't received a turkey yet, we apologize and wish you a Happy Thanksgiving!"

"What?!" Gerry screamed. "Hey, I want my turkey I was promised!"

Tommy approached the table first.

"Sign your name in the book," a man instructed him.

Tommy took a pen at the table and wrote in the book.

A woman next to the man wrote a check for twenty-five dollars and handed it to Tommy, without looking up the name.

He accepted the check and moved aside.

Robin was next, looking very nervous.

"Sign your name in the book."

He obliged, signing the book quickly.

The woman looked at him. "You look pretty young for a full-time employee," and looked at his signature.

"Uh," Robin balked.

Gerry called out behind him. "You got no more turkeys on that truck?! I want my turkey, not some damn check!"

"Hey, calm down, now, calm down! If you want one that bad, we can get one, just calm down!" the man told him. "C'mon, let's speed this up! We only have around 30 more people to go!" he told the woman.

She looked at Robin again and signed the check, handing it to him.

Robin took the check and quickly stepped away from the table, looking for Tommy.

Gerry stepped up and pointed to the truck. "You better have a turkey in there!"

The man turned and someone from the truck handed over a twenty-pound turkey. The man handed the bird to Gerry and said, "Happy Thanksgiving. Sign the book already!"

"Watch that attitude, man!" Gerry took a pen and signed his name in the book.

"Next time come earlier. Not everyone is promised a turkey!"

"Yes, they are. It's in our contract! Y'all better be prepared next year or else!" Gerry stormed off without a chance to hear the man's reply.

Tommy and Robin were back outside the parking lot on the other side when Gerry found them.

"Whoa, that was close!" Robin gasped. "All this for a damn check? I'm never doing this again! I want my ride back uptown!"

"Well, I don't know about you guys, but I'm going to a bar for a while, and then home to my wife." Tommy took off in the opposite direction, hoping to find a good drink.

"Well, give my regards to Broadway! I think it's two blocks in that direction!" Robin yelled.

Gerry nodded to him. "C'mon man, this bird's gotta be back in a freezer before it goes bad."

Robin followed behind him as they walked back to the garage.

Sonyai was resting at home Wednesday morning when her phone rang.

"Hello?" she answered.

The caller started speaking Japanese then she said, "speak English, Bunji, your dialect is ancient. You sound like a kung-fu movie."

"You're so American, sister. It's a miracle you even recognize our language," Bunji Yi said.

She rolled her eyes. "How is business?"

"Business… is well." She could practically hear Bunji's smile over the phone.

"Right. The less I know, the better."

"Indeed. And how are you, dear sister?" Bunji asked.

"I am fine. I miss you dearly, of course. I don't suppose you could tear away from your business and come to New York for once? I've come out there to see you."

"Aww, I do miss you too, sister. Perhaps I can move some things around early next year. I'll let you know."

"Happy to hear it, how is Shinju?"

"Difficult, as usual. I really believe she misses New York. She keeps whining about it, among other things."

*I bet,* she thought. "It can be difficult to raise a teenager that is becoming a woman. I hope she comes to understand that you only have her best interest at heart."

"She knows I do. She has such little time left before her obligation arrives."

Sonyai's stomach turned. "Yes…" she said dryly.

"I know you do not approve of such things. The old ways are lost to you, but an order must be maintained."

*He's trying to start a fight. Don't engage him.*

"Well, I have to go. I'm doing the late night, working from noon to 8 pm."

"Of course. It was great talking to you, we must do this more," Bunji said.

"We would if you would call more often."

"There you go again, blaming everything on me. Take care, sister." He hung up the phone.

She shook her head. "Such a *kuso-tama.*"

After asking several students, Alex found out Fergus Van Sloan lived in Central Park West. She took the M10 bus, and got off near the Museum of Natural History. She approached the building doorman inside the lobby.

"Hi, I'd like to talk to Fergus Van Sloan, please?"

"Is he—"

"He's NOT expecting me, but all you have to do is give him a call and he'll come down."

"Uh, yeah, I'm not going to do that. The people who live here pay me a shitload of money for their privacy."

They exchanged glances for a minute, then Alex pulled out a hundred-dollar bill. "$100.00."

He picked up the phone and dialed. "Yeah, someone to see you... It's a girl... uh, yeah, that's about right... okay." He hung up the phone and took the bill. "Apparently, he *was* expecting you. Ten minutes, wait outside."

"It's freaking cold out there!" Alex whined.

"There's no loitering in the lobby."

She squinted. "You are such an asshole."

"Yep, but I'm nice and toasty in here." He pointed to the door. "Outside!"

Fergus kept her waiting for fifteen minutes before stepping outside. "Wow, look who it is, somebody who just celebrated her 16th birthday, all alone."

"I can't believe you did this, Fergie! And for what? As Paul said, to flex?"

"It's Fergus! You needed to be cut down a peg, Alex. You're obviously too full of yourself, now take your lumps and move on. Maybe now you'll be more respectful, and people will actually like you!"

She shook her head. "Nothing was wrong with me, and you're going to pay for this."

Fergus smiled. "Heh, bring it on."

She walked off, determined to make his life miserable, only she had no clue where to start.

Gerry came home and changed his clothes. He then opened the refrigerator to check on the turkey he brought home and took it out.

He arrived at the Brooklyn Community Church on Saint Edwards Street and donated the turkey he was so adamant about receiving from the DC37 union. Gerry felt it was his civic duty to give to those less fortunate than him.

There were families and homeless people lined up to receive boxes of food and servings of a hot meal.

He was greeted by the reverend Gregory McMillian, who accepted the frozen bird.

"It's not much, but it's—"

"It's perfect, son. Thank you so much for your donation," Gregory interrupted.

Gerry looked around. "Y'all are really busy tonight. Um, need any help?"

"Sure! Head over to the sign-up table and they'll get you started." The reverend pointed behind him.

Gerry put on his biggest smile and headed toward the table. After he gave his name and contact information, Gerry was assigned to a post, helping people all night. He went back home in the early hours of the morning and slept most of the Thanksgiving holiday.

# CHAPTER EIGHTEEN

IT WAS FOUR O'CLOCK ON THANKSGIVING MORNING WHEN FRANKLIN'S mother, Bridget, walked in the kitchen to start cooking the turkey. She had been up since midnight, working her last flight to LaGuardia airport, which landed at two. She took off her uniform and changed into some comfortable clothes. Her blond hair was cut in a pixie cut and she stood at an average five-foot-ten. Bridget took care of herself, and being an airline stewardess, she was known to turn some heads. She would never cheat on her husband, though, and she had a hard time convincing *him* of that.

The entire family was in the apartment, for the first time in over a year. Her eldest son Leonard was sleeping on the sofa, while LaSandra and Franklin were in separate beds in one bedroom. Her husband was still sleeping silently in the other bedroom.

The turkey was defrosted and ready to be stuffed, it was six when she put it in the oven, and she heard her husband walk into the bathroom to wash up. Bridget took a break with a cold glass of milk as Supa entered the living room.

"Hey," he greeted.

"Good morning, you're up early," Bridget replied.

"Got a few things to check up on first thing. I'll be back by 10."

"The building can survive you taking Thanksgiving morning off."

"I don't recall telling you how to point out the exits on a plane, do I?"

She pouted at their tense exchange. It was obvious he still objected to her occupation choice.

"Hmph, you'd think that after three years, you would finally accept me working... how do you think our son is going to college? With your money?"

"We are NOT going over that again. You could have picked anything else that would have kept you home! But you chose to 'fly the unfriendly skies' nearly 45 weeks in the year!"

There was a groan from the couch as Leonard started to stir. "Ugh, could you guys not? It's Thanksgiving. At least make an effort to be cordial to each other..."

The eldest son was a tall, stocky young man, who started college a couple of years late. He was twenty-two years old and only in his second-year term at New York University. At six-foot-ten and nearly two hundred and seventy pounds, it was a shame he didn't know how to play football, which his father reminded him of every day of his life. Unlike his younger brother, Leonard wore his red hair straight and long with curtain bangs. He flipped his hair and looked at his parents, squaring off at each other.

Supa looked at his son, then his wife of twenty-five years, and sighed. "I gotta get dressed." He turned to walk back to the bedroom.

Bridget nodded to Leonard. "How are your grades?" she asked.

"You got twenty minutes for an explanation?"

"Better you tell me now, instead of later, surrounded by your siblings."

"I'll take that chance." Leonard grinned.

She smiled back and took another sip of her milk.

Tommy, Sarah, and little Carrie were driving out to Long Island, with Sarah's parents following behind. It was a few minutes after eleven and they were due at Tommy's parent's house at noon.

"We're making good time, hon…" Tommy said. "Your father could keep up though. I'm afraid of losing him."

"He's not used to driving fast, you're going over 80!" Sarah yelled.

"It's the flow of traffic. Once you're clear of the city, you can open 'er up a little bit."

"What is with this kid? He's driving like it's the Indianapolis 500!" Lorenzo complained to Acindina.

"Well, you could be following closer. What are you afraid of? Step on the gas!"

A car sped by them and the driver called out, "Sunday driver!"

Lorenzo cursed back in Spanish. "Fucking maniacs!" he shouted in English.

The pair finally arrived at their exit, and Lorenzo was able to catch up to Tommy as he took the side street through Ronkonkoma and arrived at his parent's complex. There was a special parking lot across the street for visitors. Sarah got out of the car and took out Carrie's stroller from the trunk, as Tommy unlocked the baby from her car seat in the back.

Lorenzo came out of his car first and ran around the other side to let Acindina out. She was carrying a pot roast they brought to contribute to the dinner. He looked around. "We are definitely not among our people here," he whispered to Acindina.

"Just behave," she told her husband. "Don't embarrass us and we'll be fine."

He rolled his eyes as they walked over to see Sarah put Carrie in the stroller.

They walked across the street and entered the lobby. Each of them had to sign their name in a visitor's log and they found Maureen and Jarlath Carmichael waiting for them outside their unit in Building 12.

"Happy Thanksgiving!" Maureen greeted.

Jarlath shook hands with Lorenzo and hugged Sarah, while Tommy gave his mother a peck on the cheek.

"We brought a little something," Acindina said, lifting the container.

"Oh good! I'll set it on the table inside. Come on in!" Maureen said.

She opened the door and moved aside, letting everyone in.

At noon Sonyai took a cab from The Bronx to 145th Street and Saint Nicholas Avenue. She walked up to the familiar brownstone building and pressed a button on the intercom. After being buzzed up, Sonyai climbed the steps to the second floor and saw Janelle waiting for her at the door. They exchanged smiles and Janelle gave her a spirited embrace.

"You're looking a whole lot better than the last time I saw you."

Janelle took her coat as she walked in and put it on a hook that was behind the door.

Evelyn was setting the table while Avery was sitting on the couch holding Simon on his lap. There was some pregame coverage of the NFL on television.

Sonyai made a beeline for the baby in his father's arms and scooped the infant away from him.

"And it's so nice to see *you* again, too!"

Simon was wearing a blue onesie and Janelle couldn't believe her eyes as Sonyai started babbling incoherent baby talk to him while smiling. It was a side of the supervisor Janelle had never seen.

After three minutes Sonyai noticed that everyone in the room was staring at her. She blushed and handed the baby back to Avery. "Ahem… it's, um, something about babies that can make even the most solemn of people break character… sometimes."

"I see," Evelyn said with a smile. "Dinner will be ready in ten minutes."

When all the food was done, they all sat around the kitchen table and joined hands.

"Miss Yi, since you're the guest, may you bless the food before we eat?" Evelyn asked.

She blushed again. "I'm afraid... I'm not quite sure how..."

"Just speak from your heart and the words will come."

They all bowed their heads as she began. "Uh, bless us... O Lord, ah, we are forever thankful... to, um, receive this food... ma-may it nourish our bodies... A-amen?"

"Amen," Evelyn, Avery, and Janelle repeated.

Sonyai smiled nervously, as Evelyn said, "that was very good, Miss Yi."

"Th-thank you."

The conversation was light and fun as Janelle shared how she was looking forward to returning to work at Van Nest. Sonyai gave Janelle an update of what's happened at 58th Street (without mentioning Robin, of course) glossing over the exact details, but mentioning that Jenkins has retired.

Evelyn brought out a camera and everyone posed for several pictures as a group, then separately with Simon.

Sonyai was completely infatuated with the child and part of her was devastated when she noticed how late it was. She didn't want to overstay her welcome.

"I had a great time. You may have lost your parents, but you and Avery are going to take great care of that baby together."

"Thank you, Miss Yi. You're welcome to join us for Christmas if you're not doing anything."

She thought about it and nodded. "I might take you up on that... and I think you can call me Sonyai, now. I'm no longer your supervisor."

"That may be true, but you'll always be Miss Yi to me," Janelle replied.

They hugged again and Sonyai left the apartment. She walked several blocks before she found herself sobbing again.

Franklin approached the living room with the cordless phone in his hand. He saw his sister watching the highlights of the Macy's Thanksgiving Day parade from that morning and put the phone back on the cradle.

"Um, I think we can get ready to eat," he began. "I don't think Robin's coming. He hasn't answered his phone."

"Oh dear, I was hoping he'd stop by," Bridget said. "I know this is his first Thanksgiving alone. He's always welcome to join us."

Supa took a seat at the head of the table. "The boy will deal with his emotions his own way. Sometimes being alone is the answer, and we need to respect that."

LaSandra turned off the television and took a seat at the table, along with Franklin and Leonard. Bridget brought out the turkey and placed it in the middle of the table, which had plenty of other food for a feast.

"Carl, would you say grace?"

Bridget was the only person Supa allowed to use his first name. Not his children, his employees, or even strangers meeting him for the first time.

Everyone bowed their heads as Supa blessed the food. "Bless us, O Lord, and the food we are about to receive from Thy bounty, through Christ our Lord, Amen."

"Amen," the rest of the family repeated, then started eating.

After several minutes of eating in peace, Supa asked, "LaSandra, how's your aunt doing in Maspeth?"

Franklin's younger sister was sent to live with Supa's sister when Bridget began working for the airline. Bridget wasn't exactly on board with the decision at first, but LaSandra understood that she needed the guidance of a woman, and her father didn't have the patience. She had been enjoying the experience, even attending Martin Luther High School.

"Aunt Mathilda's fine. We've been having so much fun, and my grades have been good, as you can see." She handed Supa her latest report card.

Franklin and Leonard exchanged glances, secretly resenting their do-gooder sister.

LaSandra's red hair was crimped and loose at shoulder length. She just turned fifteen a few months ago and was slowly discovering boys at school. Not a heartbreaker like Franklin, but puberty was approaching, and the plain Jane may turn into a beautiful swan someday.

Both parents nodded with approval. "Very good, LaSandra," Bridget said, then turned to Leonard. "And how about you, now... since you were so eager to talk about your grades this morning."

"Ah, don't you want to know what Franklin's doing with his life first?"

Franklin gave his older brother a dirty look as he threw him under the bus.

"Yes, let's talk about what his plans are, since he's no longer working in a women's clothing store anymore..." Supa said with a harsh tone.

"Now, now, I'm sure whatever he has in store for his life, we'll be here for him," Bridget said.

*Says the woman who's barely home watching over him,* Supa thought.

"Well..." Franklin began, "I've been thinking of applying to Bronx Community College."

Supa dropped his fork.

Bridget froze in mid-chew. She didn't even blink.

After two minutes of silence, Franklin said, "okaaaaaay, did I say something wrong?"

Supa cleared his throat. "Son, as much as I'd like that idea of you continuing your education, I have to state the obvious... we can only afford to send one child to college."

"Well, maybe with some grants and loans..." Leonard started.

"We're a two-income family that makes over $40,000 a year. You're not going to qualify for any financial aid, honey," Bridget said frankly.

"Well, all I can do is try, *thank you* for having so much faith in me.

May I be excused?" Franklin said as he stood and left the table. He was gone, and in his room, before they said anything.

Leonard let out a sigh. "Well, it's going to be hard to top that."

The Carmichael and Gonzales families were surrounding the table, having various conversations. Baby Carrie was in a highchair at the head of the table playing with her small serving of mashed potatoes.

Sarah grabbed Tommy's arm to get his attention. "This is great. I'm so glad it worked out."

"Yeah, I dunno why we were so worried."

"Yeah, me neither. Thank you for all this, baby."

"No problem, honey. We're a team, and the team always works it out," he said, with a peck on her cheek.

Jarlath and Lorenzo were talking about how the Giants were looking good and their chances of making it to the Super Bowl. The two eventually got up from the table to watch the Green Bay vs. Dallas game on television.

Maureen and Acindina started clearing the table, and washing the dishes in the kitchen, as they talked about various recipes and Maureen's paintings.

The happy couple remained seated at the table and watched their daughter. Tommy, once again, flashed back to the hospital. Watching Carrie alone in a crib next to Sarah dead, with a sheet over her face, then the two of them holding Sarah's stomach and looking somber.

"What's wrong?" Sarah asked, snapping him out of it.

"Oh! Nothing. Just drifted off…" he smiled nervously.

"Yeah, I'm getting sleepy myself, I'm so full." She went to the highchair and picked up the baby. "I'm taking Carrie to the bedroom to check her diaper, then maybe take a nap."

He nodded. "Okay."

Sarah walked to the bedroom, Lorenzo also got up and went to the bathroom. While his father was alone, Tommy walked over to him.

"Hey dad, let me ask you something real quick."

"Sure Son, what's happening?" Jarlath asked.

"I remember you telling me before, how you keep your marriage strong..." Tommy began.

"No secrets! Yeah, best advice anyone can give you, son."

"Well, I got a problem. Don't freak out or anything, it's nothing serious." He held his hands out in front of him. "I've been holding this inside, and it's eating me up, Dad."

Jarlath looked over his shoulder and around the room, nobody was paying them attention. "What happened?" he whispered.

Tommy let out a sigh and explained the choice that was put before him during Sarah's delivery. When he finished the story, his father nodded, his face unfazed.

"That's tough, Tommy... I have to agree with the doctor. You can't tell her."

"But you just said—"

"I know what I said, but some things you just can't blurt out! When it comes to your wife and your child, you know she will always sacrifice herself in a heartbeat. The fact you beat the odds and chose her over the baby? You tell her, and she will *never* forgive you!"

"Dad," he whined.

"Dammit. I'm sorry you told me, now I gotta keep this from your mother! I'm going back to the game!" he said, waving his hand dismissively.

Jarlath muttered to himself and turned back to the television.

At six o'clock, Franklin and Leonard were out of the apartment at places unknown while LaSandra watched *Home Alone* on NBC. Supa and Bridget were sitting on the couch behind her.

"Carl, we really should support Franklin if he really wants to go to college," Bridget said, leaning on his chest.

He rolled his eyes. "I don't know, Bridget... we're barely on top of Leonard's tuition..."

"Hear me out. Suppose he does get some help, somehow. I know student loans just pile up the debt, but you know he can pay them back if he gets a better job," Bridget said.

"You really think he can do it?"

"I think he can, and who are we to limit what he can or can't do?" she asked.

"Hmmm, I'll see… Now, what do you wanna do about Lenny?"

"I kinda figured his grades took a slide when he didn't want to talk this morning, but he still got all B's this semester," Bridget said.

"That's not good enough," Supa grunted. "He needs to apply himself and do better."

"And he will, with our *encouraging* support rather than being hard on him. These aren't workhorses that you whip to make them pull more. You have to treat your children like human beings, Carl."

"I'm just hard on him because my father was hard on me. He didn't want me to mop floors and take out garbage all my life, so I applied myself, moved up the ranks, and here I am. Now if he wasn't hard on me, I never would have made anything of myself."

"Well, I'm not doing this stewardess thing forever. I only wanted to help Leonard while he was in school. With Franklin trying to attend school too, we need to come up with something. What if LaSandra wants to attend college as well?" Bridget asked.

"We'll cross that bridge when we get there. I'm just living one day at a time," Supa said, with a sigh.

She sighed back, "yeah, I am too," and patted her husband on his chest.

Angie nearly jumped out of her skin at the sound of erratic knocking on her door. She grabbed a hunting knife and slowly opened the curtain, looking out the window to her doorstep. She gasped, "what the?!" and threw the knife behind her across the room, then opened the door. "Robin!?"

"Heeeeey! Sorry to drop in unannounced!" Robin yelled. "May I come in?"

Angie looked past him nervously. "I *would* say no, but my neighbors may call the cops." She pulled him inside.

Robin stumbled in the living room as she closed the door behind him. "I... kinda had a falling out with what was left of my granddaddy's relatives... so I went to the movies instead. Saw *Star Trek: Generations*... a great movie, by the way."

"Then came all the way out here?"

Robin turned to her with bloodshot eyes. "I didn't have nowhere else to go." He dropped to his knees and started sobbing.

"They *KILLED* Captain Kirk! Can you believe that? Oh my God!!!"

"Okay, you're drunk, and overly emotional at the moment," Angie said.

"He was in the nexus, for over nearly eighty years! Stuck in time! Then this Doctor Soran guy... tries to go back to the nexus and..." he scoffed. "It's all a crazy story. You just have to see it!"

"I will, I will. Now, let's step over to the couch and sleep this off..." Angie escorted Robin across the room.

"Nah, nah, nah, we gotta catch you up! C'mon now, you got somethin' in here to get you tipsy. If not, I'll go get some!"

"No, no, no... we can drink, just promise me you'll sit down, and we can talk... quietly," Angie insisted.

"I... I can do that!" Robin yelled and took a seat on the couch.

Several minutes later, they were both drinking beers and Angie was feeling more spirited.

"Yanno," Angie began, "Disney's coming out with a Pocahontas movie next year, and I don't think it's going to be historically accurate." She shook her bottle for effect.

"No?" Robin asked.

"Not at all, and I can't wait to see how they butcher it up!"

"That's a shame. You Native-Americans deserved better. You're such a, such a... a really great type of people, ya knowwhatimsayin'?"

"I understand exactly what you're saying."

"There's not enough of you guys and gals out there on TV, music, and films. That needs to change."

"Yes!" Angie took another chug of her beer, then her eyes started to water.

"Those people respect their families, respect their culture. You never hear anything bad happening with Native-Americans…"

"Wha?" Angie asked, straining her ear.

"I said, YOU NEVER HEAR about anyone bad when it comes to you people."

Angie didn't say anything, but tears were streaming down her cheeks. Robin looked on in silence, puzzled by what just happened.

"Uh," was all he could bring himself to say. "Angie?"

"My stepbrother tried to rape me," she whispered.

"Um, what was that?" he asked.

"I said my stepbrother tried to rape me. When we were teenagers."

"Oh." *What a major buzzkill!* "Um…"

"I never told anybody before now." She began to sob.

Robin just sat there, unsure of what to do.

"You mind if you hold me while I go to sleep, please?"

"Um, sure," Robin replied.

She stood up and curled up like a kitten on his lap, quietly sobbing. He held her, not knowing what was going on, but immediately sobered up at the shocking confession. Reality started setting in, as he wondered what made her blurt out such a painful childhood memory. Robin wondered if it was suppressed all this time.

# CHAPTER NINETEEN

THE DAY AFTER THANKSGIVING WAS ALWAYS CALM. SOME PEOPLE HAD the extra day off, in which they would engage in a food coma in front of the television watching a marathon of shows. Library pages weren't so lucky. Sonyai asked all three girls to earn some overtime, working a full seven and a half hours (with a lunch break, of course) to do some weeding.

Tommy was at the circulation desk behind a terminal, checking the books each of the pages brought up to him. Reviewing each item's statistics to see if they would stay in the collection or pulled. This was the process on slow days, usually at the beginning of the year, the first day of summer, and today, of course.

Sonyai came out of the office. "How are we doing here?"

Tommy turned his head. "The girls are doing alright. We're up to the K's in fiction. We've eliminated over 50 books so far. They'll go on the Book Sale cart, and hopefully sell for a pretty penny."

Sonyai nodded. "Any of these best-sellers from three years back?"

He smiled, knowing the procedure. "Nope. I know those don't get discarded, no matter the stats."

"Very good, Thomas. Carry on," Sonyai said.

Returning to the clerical office, Sonyai noticed Gerry was stamping date due cards. It felt so weird to see someone, other than Robin, doing the menial task after so many months. She cleared her throat to get his attention. He stopped and looked up at her.

"The Wreathing of the Lions ceremony is next Friday. Chavez arranged for himself, me, one clerk, one page, and one of the IA's to attend." She handed him a sheet of paper. "This quiz will determine who gets picked."

Gerry took the page and looked at the questions. "You know I'm the last person he would want to see come to this." He then gave a wide smile. "I hope I win."

Sonyai grinned as she returned to her desk.

Outside among the shelves, the pages were going through the fiction section.

"So how was your Thanksgiving?" Lakeshia asked. "We just had a regular dinner ourselves."

"We went back up to Yonkers to my grandparent's house. They had a nice spread and grandpa watched football with my cousins," Tanya said.

Lakeshia nodded, then turned and asked, "Alex?"

"It was alright. I just don't wanna talk about it right now," she replied.

"Fair enough." Lakeshia could sense that Alex was still mad about her birthday party, so she didn't pry.

The girls continued weeding books in silence, then Lakeshia let out a sigh. "I miss Nellie. I hope she's doing alright." She smiled. "Remember when she challenged us to that contest to see who the best page was?"

"Oh yeah! I remember that last year, you were just starting here at the beginning of the summer, after that weird chick didn't work out. What was her name?" Tanya asked.

Alex stepped forward. "Ginette something-or-whatever. She had a screw loose. Was only here for three months before Sonyai let her go."

"She talked back to Miss Yi way too much," Tanya added. "Just because she was tall. She refused to take orders from someone shorter than her."

"As for that contest, Nellie narrowly beat me in the shelving competition. I'm pretty sure I'd win now between the three of us."

"Oh yeah? How'd 'bout we settle this on Saturday and see for sure?" Tanya asked.

"You got yourself a bet, Tee," Alex said with a smile.

Robin was avoiding Angie after that emotional moment they had yesterday. He had only a few hours of sleep, arriving home at four o'clock in the morning. During his break at four-thirty, he went up to the auditorium instead of the staff room to eat his lunch. Unfortunately, Angie thought the same thing.

*Shit!* he thought. "Wow, um… great minds think alike," Robin said, with a light laugh.

"I guess we do," Angie replied. "Um, we need to talk."

He stepped inside and closed the door behind him. "Yeah, I guess we do."

"First off, I'm so sorry I dropped that bomb on you. I was drunk and just blurted it out."

"Hey, as far as I'm concerned, it's in the vault. No one will ever hear it from me. I'll take it to the grave."

"Heh, okay Seinfeld, thank you for that."

Robin smiled at the joke, feeling more at ease with the information assistant.

"Um, I was wondering if you could clear something up for me," Angie began.

"Uh, sure."

"I… I, um, this is embarrassing, but um, I don't… remember… changing into my sleeping attire and climbing into bed."

"Well, um… I carried you upstairs, and um, dressed you."

"You WHAT?"

"I was blindfolded the entire time! I didn't see anything!"

"Are you serious?"

"I swear to God," Robin said, raising his right hand.

"Well… that was very nice of you."

"Yeah, um, so if that's all… I'll be…"

"You don't have to go because of me. If you want the room, we can just sit here quietly."

"Um… I, uh, sure…" he started nodding his head. "Why not? Heh," and took a seat.

They both sat. Neither said a word, in one of the most uncomfortable moments of either of their lives.

Sonyai extended the overtime to the pages until Saturday, so at eleven o'clock the girls gathered in the mysteries section of the branch for the first of their challenges.

"Okay, I've misplaced ten books on this shelf," Tanya began. "The page with the quickest time wins. Leelee, you go first, then Alex will set the shelf up for me, then I'll do it again for her."

Lakeshia did some stretches then said, "okay, ready."

Alex held up her digital watch, which was in timer mode. "And… GO!"

The youngest page furiously attacked the five shelves against the wall. She found the first book within ten seconds, then finished with a time of three minutes and twelve seconds.

"Piece of cake!" she cheered.

Tanya and Alex exchanged glances and held in their giggles, letting the page have her moment.

"Okay, I'm next. Alex, mix up ten books again. I'll be on the opposite side of the room." Tanya began to walk away from their location, then came back when Alex was done.

"Alright Tee, show us how it's *really* done," Alex said, looking over to Lakeshia with a grin.

Lakeshia gave her back a stink face.

"Ready... GO!"

Tanya worked the shelves and finished with a time of two minutes and forty-five seconds.

She folded her arms in front of her, with her chin held high as Lakeshia said dryly, "okay, obviously I have more to learn."

"Don't feel bad, Leelee... it's all in the wrist."

"It's my turn. Take my watch. I'll be back when you're ready." Alex handed Lakeshia her watch and walked around the floor while Tanya misplaced ten more books again. When she returned, Alex took in a breath as Lakeshia held up the watch.

"Ready... GO!"

Alex worked the shelves and finished in a minute and fifty-six seconds, but she was out of breath. "You did 11 books! What the heck, Tanya?" Alex gasped.

"I did ten!"

She pointed to the "M" section, "MacFarlane comes *before* McConnely, Tee."

Tanya looked where Alex was pointing then said, "oh, well you know those weird "Mac and Mc" names confuse me... anyway, you won by a landslide. Let's move on to the next challenge."

Alex looked annoyed as they walked over to one of the reading tables, where there were stacks of books waiting for them. It was eleven forty when the doorbell rang. Tommy came out and walked to the door, where Robin was waiting. He was due at twelve, so while Tommy went back inside the clerical office, Robin noticed the pages were doing something and decided to observe.

"Y'all having a contest?"

The girls all turned around to see Robin looking back at them with a grin on his face.

Alex stepped forward. "As a matter of fact we are!" she snarled. "We're looking to see which of us is the best."

"Oh really? With challenges like these?" he asked. "I could do them in my sleep. Why don't I take on the winner next week and see what y'all *really* made of?"

Alex snorted with contempt. "I bet my next paycheck to yours, I can beat you in whatever contests you wanna do."

Robin shook his head. "I don't bet money... but I'll school you for kicks!"

Lakeshia and Tanya looked at each other as Alex explained their latest challenge. "Well, we were doing the second contest before *someone* interrupted us. This is called 'How Heavy?' We each make wagers on how many books we can carry from the reading tables across the floor to the New Books section in the front of the branch. I can do 30 books, easy."

"I'll see your 30, Alex... and raise you 35 books myself," Tanya challenged. Then looked over to Lakesha. "Leelee?"

The page was pretty intimidated by this challenge and decided to go with a safe bet. "Um, I... I can do 20."

Alex nodded. "Alright, the bets are set. I'll go first, you guys pick 15 books each."

Tanya had a smile on her face as she went to the fiction section to pick some books. Big, heavy books. Lakeshia just randomly selected 15 ordinary books. Some paperback, some hardcover. Tanya emerged from the shelves with heavier selections.

"Hey, that's not fair!" Alex exclaimed.

Robin chuckled, familiar with such tactics himself.

"I got *War & Peace, The Brothers Karamazov, Les Miserables, Lord of the Rings,* a special unabridged version of *The Stand,* and my favorite, *Insomnia.* Those alone and the rest should make this interesting."

Alex couldn't believe Tanya and squinted. "You know I'm going to use these same books when it's your turn."

"Yeah, I know, but *I* can handle them," Tanya replied, bringing up her arms and flexing her muscles.

"There's your 30, Alex, let's go," Robin said, sitting on a shelving cart, leaning against the wall.

Alex almost responded, but ignored him instead, and placed the books in two stacks, then took a deep breath. The stacks came up to her chin as she started to lift. Her knees buckled as she started to move. It was a slow pace, but in an enormous show of strength, she made it across the room.

Robin was impressed but didn't show it.

"Okay Leelee, you're next, You actually make it, you still lose points for only doing 20," Tanya said.

"I'm only carrying what I can. I'm not trying to kill myself!"

Lakeshia took her 20 books and easily completed the challenge, walking across the room pretty quickly.

Alex set up Tanya's books, using the same heavy ones Tanya had her carry, plus more. She stepped forward to the pile and rearranged them a bit, then started to lift. Tanya started with a great effort, but halfway, in the middle of the library, she started straining.

Robin grinned. "Uh-oh, I think you bit off more than you could chew, Tanya."

She took another step and her hands started to slip. Tanya finally relented, and the books fell, crashing down on the floor. "Damn it!" she cried.

Robin started laughing as he clapped his hands. "This is great! What's next?"

Lakeshia and Alex stepped forward to help Tanya pick up the books. "The last challenge will be at the end of the day," Alex announced, then turned to look back at Robin. "Show's over! Best believe I'll be seeing *you* next week!"

Rather than reply with a witty comeback, Robin sat up from the shelving cart and walked into the clerical office.

Larry Ritter was unsure about meeting Heywood at a bar, since he didn't drink, but he decided to go anyway. It was a comfortable stroll down from 67th Street, and he walked in a few minutes after four o'clock. He looked around and couldn't see Heywood anywhere. Was he early? A hand suddenly waved out from the back and caught his attention. Larry spotted Heywood in the back of the room and walked toward him.

"I usually sit at the bar, but I got us a table since you wanted to talk about something privately," Heywood greeted.

They shook hands and Larry took a seat at the opposite side of the table.

"Uh, thanks. I had a *quieter* place in mind, however."

"We'll be fine," Heywood dismissed with a wave. "You could talk about nuclear launch codes in here and no one would blink."

"I actually believe that," Larry said with a smile.

Heywood ordered a beer while Larry settled for a Sprite. When the waitress left to fill their orders, both men relaxed a bit.

"So, what's on your mind, man?" Heywood asked.

"We've been talking, exchanging ideas, and we're definitely on the same page, so I feel I can trust you."

"Okaaaaay. Why do I feel like you're about to ask me to invest in something?"

"Nah, it's nothing like that. I'm talking about this new SIBL branch. I've been hearing things, and I just don't like it, man."

Heywood heard nothing of the proposed new library, Augustus had been holding the details close to his chest.

"Sybil?" he laughed. "What are you talking about?"

"S-I-B-L. It might as well stand for Spanish, Indians, and Blacks Library… a facility for the advancement of minorities."

Heywood was taken back. "Woah, man… what's that all about?"

Larry held up his palm. "Hear me out… I don't have anything against these people, but when the city starts bending over backward to give extra help, it tips the scales to an unfair advantage. You know what I'm saying?"

Their orders arrived. Heywood immediately sipped his beer, still shocked by Larry's comments. Larry felt the cold reception to his opinion and decided to change the subject. "I'm sorry. I'm sometimes too passionate about my beliefs. I understand others may not share the same thoughts…"

He trailed off and Heywood gave him a playful slap across his arm. "No big deal. Um… let's go play some darts."

Larry smiled. "Heh, alright."

They stood up and took their coats to the corner of the bar where there were several tables for pool and air hockey, as well as three dartboards on the wall. They started a game, and after a few minutes Larry whispered, "hey man, I didn't wanna scare you back there."

"No problem. We all got our opinions. I didn't even know about this SIBL thing."

"Must be nice to not worry about such things... I bet you sleep like a baby at night."

"I wouldn't say all THAT now," Heywood said, with a grunt.

"Oh, what's troubling you, then?"

"Nothing major..."

"But there is something, eh?" Larry asked.

Heywood didn't reply, focusing on the game.

After a few minutes, Larry moved on as well... but he didn't forget.

It was Tuesday afternoon, at five o'clock, when both supervisors approached the circulation desk to announce the results. Robin was working with Ira Haim, a part-time clerk from the Webster branch, who was clustering for the week. Zelda sat at the information desk, while Angie and Heywood stood near the returns side.

"We have our winners," Augustus announced. "Heywood, you were the only IA who answered all the questions correctly. I'm sorry Angie, you had one wrong question."

Angie shrugged. "Hey, I tried." She wasn't really interested in attending.

"All three clerks and two pages got the questions right," Sonyai said. "I'm very proud of you all for knowing *most* of your history of the library. Our two page finalists are... Tanya and Lakeshia!"

Alex rolled her eyes and sighed. "It was that Schomburg Center question, wasn't it?"

Sonyai smiled. "It's okay, Alex, there's always next year. So, after a random selection of our two finalists, our first winner is… Lakeshia!"

Lakeshia did a quiet cheer in celebration as Tanya congratulated her.

"Now for the clerks… we did another random pick and I'm happy to say that…" Sonyai began.

*Please be Robin, please be Robin, please be Robin…* Lakeshia pleaded in her thoughts.

"Our last attendant will be… Thomas!"

Lakeshia's eyes showed her disappointment, but she put on a brave face.

"Awww, thanks, but I didn't wanna go," Tommy nodded to Gerry. "You can go, Gerry."

Gerry thought about it for a moment, then said, "nah, I don't wanna go, let Robin go!" then looked at Sonyai with a grin.

Sonyai grunted with annoyance at the two full-time clerks. "I guess you'll be joining us, Walker." She looked toward Lakeshia, who showed no emotion to the change, but was secretly ecstatic by the development.

"Well, that's our party," Augustus said. "We leave at four o'clock Friday. It's expected to last a couple of hours. Plan for a great time." He smiled and walked back to the information desk.

Sonyai, Gerry and Tommy went back inside the clerical office. Right before the door closed, Sonyai gave Gerry an icy stare.

Ethel's apartment was bare as she swept the last bit of dust from the floor. This was it. She was finally ready to leave the city behind, for better or worse. It would be an adjustment, but she was ready. All her belongings had been sent down to the house this past Sunday, and on this last day of November, she was leaving her apartment. The landlord would come and inspect the apartment tomorrow morning and instructed her to leave her keys on the counter in the kitchen, where he could find them.

Instead of flying down as she did before, Ethel decided to take the train, so she could relax and arrive in downtown Atlanta by tomorrow evening. Her letter to Zelda, (along with a check post-dated for January first next year.) would be mailed tonight on her way to Penn Station, everything was set. She decided to leave the broom and dustpan in the apartment for the landlord and took one last look around.

When she was satisfied, Ethel turned off the lights, closed and locked all the windows, left the keys on the counter, and walked out of the apartment. The door locked behind her and she walked down the hallway. Out on the street, Ethel walked to the nearest mailbox on the corner and slipped the letter in. She waved her arms and eventually got a cab. "Take me to Penn Station, I'm getting the hell outta this city!" she said triumphantly.

"Yes, ma'am," the cabbie replied, and took off.

Derrick Seabrooke drove his car down the West Side Highway. It was a few minutes after midnight, and he was due for an interview in the wee hours of the morning at The Quad recording studio. The assignment was passed down to him after the original guy got sick. He grabbed his recording equipment and credentials so fast he didn't even hear WHO he was actually interviewing. All that he knew was to be there at twelve-thirty in the morning and have it back at Hot97 the following day.

Turning off the highway and hitting the side streets, he made it to Seventh Avenue with ten minutes to spare. Derrick found a parking spot on the corner of 47th Street, a block away from the building, and stepped out. He made a few steps away from his car and suddenly heard gunshots. They were extremely loud.

"What the fuck!?" he screamed, ducking for cover behind a mailbox.

Up the street, in front of the entrance to The Quad, two men ran out, followed by a third. They ran together as a group and turned a corner. A police siren was heard from a distance. Derrick came out of hiding and ran to the entrance. He saw three people laying in the lobby.

"Holy shit!" Derrick gasped. He almost stepped in the building to check if they were still alive, but flashing lights from the distance caught his eye, and he immediately ran from the scene. He left his car, made it to the Rockefeller Center station, and took the D-train home.

If anyone asked Derrick, he would tell them he didn't make it down there in time, and take whatever punishment awaited him. For all he knew, he had just witnessed the assassination of Tupac Shakur!

Fifth Avenue was blocked off from 39th Street to 44th Street as the town car parked in a garage on Sixth Avenue. Augustus splurged for the rental car as he, Sonyai, Heywood, Robin, and Lakeshia stepped out.

"It's a block walk from here. Everyone stay together," Augustus said.

The group made their way to The Main Library and found a great place near the front of the crowd. Mayor Rudolph Guliani was expected to address the crowd in twenty minutes. Lakeshia was annoyed that Sonyai made Robin stand furthest from her, at the supervisor's left side, while she was on the right side of Augustus, with Heywood in the middle.

"Are we expected to stand here for a while?" Robin asked.

"They'll be some entertainment to warm up the crowd, be patient," Augustus said, annoyed.

Sonyai sensed Robin's restlessness and decided to finally share something with him.

"Walker, do you know what a betrothal is?" Sonyai whispered.

"No," Robin replied, puzzled by the question.

"Various customs around the world, India, The Middle East, Asia, even parts of Africa participate in arranged marriages. Sometimes it is of convenience, to unite families of industry, or to bring peace to a feud." She took a breath and rolled on the balls of her feet.

"Interesting… why are you telling me this?"

"My brother's… occupation requires his firstborn daughter to be married, on or before her 21st birthday."

Robin was surprised by this information. He raised his thumb and forefinger to his chin. "Wow, so *that's* why she wanted to leave…"

Sonyai raised her eyebrows. "Excuse me?"

"Before you discovered us, she asked me if I was willing to go with her to Hong Kong. She obviously doesn't want to go through with it."

He noticed that she was disturbed by what he just told her. "It is not her decision to make. This arrangement was made before she was even born. She cannot run away from it."

"She's going to try, trust me," he said with certainty.

The senior clerk nodded. "If you truly love her, Walker, you will leave her be. If she doesn't go through with the betrothal, the consequences would be dire."

"Can't you at least tell me where she is?" he pleaded. "For closure. She has three years of her own life left to live."

Sonyai pressed her lips together, but after seeing his pleading eyes she sighed. "Very well. She's in Seattle with her father. He has enrolled her in a local university there."

Robin's heart fluttered with the news. He contained his composure in the face of Sonyai's harsh glance. "I warn you, my brother is not as reasonable as I am."

"You call yourself reasonable?!" he gasped.

Her harsh glance turned into a dark scowl.

Robin backed up with his open palms in front of him. "Sorry, sorry. Thank you."

She nodded, and after a few minutes of silence she tilted her chin. "You know… you don't *have* to resign now, you know."

"Huh?" he replied, confused.

A thin smile came across her face. "Remember your promise? You said that you would quit if I told you where she was."

Robin relaxed, with a smirk to himself at the memory of himself on his knees in tears. "If you don't want me to leave, why did you tell me?"

The mayor finally arrived and walked to the podium to address the crowd and the rest of the city.

"Because I'm confident you will do the right thing," Sonyai said.

# CHAPTER TWENTY

ANDREW FRIEDMAN ALWAYS CAME IN EARLY ON THE FIRST SATURDAY of each month at Webster. But the senior clerk was spooked when he heard someone tapping on the glass of the entrance at seven-thirty in the morning. He slowly approached the door and unlocked it when he saw Tanya waiting for him. She was wearing a long, conspicuous trench coat and sunglasses.

"Well, *this* is a surprise!" he exclaimed.

"C'mon, let me in, it's freezing out here!" she complained.

He moved aside and she quickly stepped in.

As Andrew locked the door again, he said, "it's been quite a while since our date. I was beginning to think you didn't want to see me again."

They walked further inside and Tanya looked over her shoulder. "I dunno what gave you that idea. I just needed some time to think, that's all. You dropped a bomb on a girl."

"Don't lie, Brownie. I can tell you were less than impressed with that scene, *despite* what transpired afterward."

They both chuckled at the private joke, as she remembered the night at the Park Central Hotel.

"So, with that said… about my proposal, what's your answer?"

She turned and looked at him. "Direct, aren't you?" She thought about this for weeks. What it would mean between them, and the commitment.

He looked at her, and felt her hesitation, then braced himself for the worst. "It's written all over your face, Brownie. You're not ready."

She sighed and looked down. "You mad?"

"Of course not! I understand you wanna be out there and experience other… people. But I'll tell you right now, I'm not giving up on us. I'm willing to wait 'til you come around."

*Oh, bullshit!* Tanya thought. "What if another white girl gives you the time of day?"

Andrew held up his palms. "I deserve that. I slipped. That was a mistake, and if it was the one that made you walk away, I'll regret it for the rest of my life… but I'd rather spend that time making it up to you… if you let me."

*Fuck, he's good! And he knows he's that good. Hang in there, just give him your answer and walk out!*

She lifted her chin and looked back at him again. "I guess we'll see down the line, but for now, we both need this break."

He nodded. "Fair enough. I hope you find your happiness, whether with me or with someone else."

"Good." She untied the belt and opened her coat, which revealed that she wore nothing underneath, but a pair of panties with a sprig of mistletoe attached. "Now, how about one last holiday kiss?"

Andrew took off his glasses slowly, a toothy smile came across his face. "Someone's definitely on the naughty list."

Sonyai let Robin inside the library at ten o'clock, and, against her better judgment, allowed Alex and Robin have their contest. Tanya was off, and Lakeshia wasn't due to come in until two o'clock in the afternoon. Alex came in early, of her own accord, with the intent to teach Robin a lesson. She was originally scheduled to start at noon.

Robin took off his coat, putting it up on a shelf above his desk, and stepped out of the office. "It's a pity your fellow pages won't see you lose. I don't want you making excuses because they weren't here."

"That's why *I'm* here, to be a fair and impartial judge to this ridiculous pissing contest between you two," Sonyai said.

Robin ignored the snide remark and looked at Alex. "We do two challenges. One of yours, and then one challenge of my choosing."

"Alright. Whatever you can cook up, I can handle with no problem. I choose the shelving challenge. Ten books, shelved correctly on a five-shelf bookcase. Best time wins."

"Sonyai sets up the shelves. I don't trust you," Robin replied, waving his finger.

Alex nodded. "Fair enough. No peeking."

"Agreed."

They both looked to Sonyai, who rolled her eyes and walked to the fiction section, while Robin and Alex stared at each other.

Twenty minutes later Sonyai came back to the middle of the floor. "Okay, will you be doing this one at a time or what?"

"I'll be a gentleman, ladies first," Robin said, with a wave of his hand.

Alex approached the "D' bookcase in the fiction section and did a few stretches. "Whenever you're ready, Miss Yi."

Sonyai held up a stopwatch. "Ready... begin!"

Once again, Alex attacked the shelves, finding one, then two books, and finished with a time of two minutes and ten seconds.

"Ha!" Alex cheered. "Beat that!"

Robin just shrugged. "Wow, that was... pretty fast," and smirked.

He approached the "F" bookcase and simply cracked his knuckles. "Okay, let's get this over with."

Sonyai reset the stopwatch. "Okay... begin!"

Robin worked furiously, then yelled, "Time!"

Sonyai stopped the watch at three minutes even. Alex cracked up in a hysterical laugh. "You call that fast? Oh, *please*!"

Robin strutted away from the bookshelf. "Judge, check our work."

Sonyai stepped forward and did a thorough examination of both sections. After ten minutes, she came back and announced, "Robin, you found all ten misplaced books. Alex, you missed two."

"What!? No way!" she screamed.

Robin put on a smug grin and took a bow.

"I was still faster!"

"Speed means nothing without accuracy. Time for *my* challenge," he said, and walked over to the circulation desk.

"Fine!" Alex spat.

Robin started piling books on the checkout side, lots of books. Sonyai observed and noticed they were from the discarded books.

"What's the deal? You challenging me to checkout all these books, to see how fast I am?" Alex asked.

"Nope. These are discards. Put them in a cardboard box and tie it up. Quickest time wins."

"We don't do that!"

Robin looked over to Sonyai, who pressed her lips together and sighed. "It *is* a required task pages are expected to do, SO LONG as the boxes are 30 pounds or less."

"This is unfair! You got enough books to pack for yourself?"

"As a matter of fact, I do. You discarded a *lot* of books when you did the weeding last week."

"You planned this all along, didn't you?" Sonyai asked.

He shrugged. "It may have crossed my mind," Robin replied, and fluttered his eyes innocently.

Sonyai looked at Alex. "You can do it. Tie the box tight, like wrapping a present."

"Start the clock," Robin said to Sonyai, with a playful smile.

Alex grabbed a flat cardboard box that was provided and prepared for the task.

"Ready… go!" Sonyai started the stopwatch.

Alex unfolded the box and tucked in the flaps to make a sealed bottom, then turned it over and started filling the box with discarded books. When the box was full, she folded the flaps close and grabbed the twine. This is where the page struggled. Tying the twine around the entire box proved very difficult. Sonyai looked on, ashamed that she never taught her pages the procedure involving this task. Alex finally finished her attempt, with a tightly tied box of discards, and stepped back.

Sonyai stopped the stopwatch. "Sixteen minutes, thirty seconds," she announced dryly.

"Wow..." Robin stepped forward to examine her handiwork. The box was loosely tied, and he was certain if he pulled it a certain way the knot would unwind, but he didn't tempt fate. "...astonishing craftsmanship," he chuckled.

"Okay, Walker, you've made your point," Sonyai said.

"No, no, no, no, no, no... I believe it's my turn, it's only fair." He went back in the office and brought his books to the returns side. "I'd move your box, but I have a feeling, if I so much as breathe hard on it, it might come undone."

Robin chuckled again and grabbed a flat cardboard box. "Whenever you're ready, ma'am..."

Sonyai sighed. "On your mark, get set... go!"

Robin had the box filled in three minutes, then took the end of the twine and made a loop. He proceeded to tie the box tightly and efficiently, several times over, and finished in five minutes.

"That's time," he said triumphantly. "Don't feel bad. After all, I'm a clerk. I've done this in my sleep for two years. Kinda perfected it. You still got time to get better..."

Alex lunged at him, but Sonyai pulled her arm. "I don't *need* time. I'm better than you and I can prove it! I wanna rematch, you smug sonofabitch!"

"No rematch! This is it between you two!" Sonyai yelled.

"Yeah, right. You'll get a rematch when you've earned it. Just be a gracious loser." Robin turned and headed for the door upstairs.

Once he was gone, Alex looked back at Sonyai. "I know I'm better than him!"

"And you will prove it... in time. Getting angry solves nothing," the senior clerk said. "Learn from this and focus. You will get there."

She sighed as Sonyai put her hand on her shoulder. "Come on. I'll teach you how to tie a Parcel Knot, which is what Robin did. It's real simple."

Sonyai and Alex walked around the circulation desk to her box. Sonyai pulled at the twine and instantly unraveled it. Then slowly explained how to start the loop.

Zelda had a list of possible hires to replace Ethel. She prepared the list since Ethel told her she intended to leave at the end of the year. Her early departure put a monkey-wrench in Zelda's plans, but the assistant librarian knew how to adapt. There was a waiting list, as well as a transfer list of clerks looking for current openings. Naturally, the person selected would have to be approved by the senior clerk of the branch, but Zelda was putting together a list that would be presented to Sonyai with the delusion that the final selection was her call, but nothing happened in 58th Street, unless Zelda arranged for it to happen.

The transfer list was quickly eliminated. The branch didn't need someone established looking for a stepping-stone to move up the ranks. *We need someone new,* she thought, as she skimmed through the list of pages who have finished high school at various locations. With Robin attending college, she also wanted someone fully committed to the job, so she weeded out those that were planning to continue their education. When Zelda was finished, she had ten women picked to be the next possible full-time clerk.

She picked up the phone and called human resources, in order to set her selections aside temporarily, until the beginning of next year.

"New York Public Library human resources department, how may I direct your call?"

"Miss Abigail Swanson, please. Tell her it's Zelda Clein from 58th Street Branch."

"One moment please," the secretary said.

The call was put on hold, then rang again after being re-routed.

"Yes?" A woman's voice answered.

"Abby? It's Zelda."

"Hmmm, I was wondering when you'd call... got yourself a real hornet's nest at that tiny little branch of yours."

"Who you telling?" she chuckled.

"So, I assume you're calling to line up some candidates to replace Ethel Jenkins, am I right?" Abigail asked.

"Nothing gets past you."

"And nothing will, but as much as I'd like to be accommodating, you got yourself a problem."

Zelda scrunched her face. "Pardon me?"

"We got the estimated budget for next year, and it doesn't look promising. There's going to be a shift in funds, and libraries are getting the short stick."

"Bullshit!" Zelda spat.

"I'm afraid so. Augustus will get the official word in a week or two, but since it's just us girls here, I have to tell you that all you can afford... is a *second* part-time clerk."

"We have three full-time clerks as it is! There's no way we can function six days a week with such a skeleton crew!"

"Good thing, because you won't have to function for six days anymore."

"Oh no, oh no, no, no... you can't be serious. We *just* started back to being open for six days four years ago."

"Well, the newly elected governor plans to change all that, it's two years in the making but he's looking to fast track things."

"Oy vey." Zelda lowered her head into her palm, then snapped her head back up. "Alright, there's still at least five people I can see for a... part-time position." She choked at the end of the sentence, then listed the names.

Abigail took down the names and told her, "we've gone through this before, Zelda. It gets hard, but we'll survive."

"Yeah, you can say that, because you're only 50!" Zelda hung up the phone and shook her head.

She couldn't believe what she was just told. Everything was so good, and now the dark times were coming back. She contemplated telling Augustus, but he would know soon enough, and there's no telling what desperate things he'd do to compensate for these future shortcomings.

Augustus summoned the entire staff inside the clerical office at five o'clock for a quick announcement. Zelda was working the information desk, while Lucas Avery, once again clustering from 67th Street, covered the circulation desk outside the closed door.

"I'm glad you could all meet here," The head librarian began. "This will only be a moment."

Everyone listened attentively.

"We've experienced a lot these past few months. Departures that have been unexpected, and tensions have been at an all-time high."

There was complete silence in the room as everyone intentionally kept blank stares.

"So, um… for the first time in several years, Miss Yi and I have agreed… in the spirit of the holidays… to bring back the office gift exchange!"

Robin sucked in a breath, as a frightened look came over his face, but nobody else reacted.

Sonyai pulled out a plastic bowl from her desk. "The price limit is $25.00," she explained. "Those who wish to participate can write their name on a piece of paper and throw it in the bowl. We'll then pick names and exchange gifts at the office holiday party on December 20th."

Lakeshia tugged at Tanya's shirt and whispered, "if you get Robin's name, switch with me."

Tanya rolled her eyes.

"No offense, but I'll pass," Robin called out.

Lakeshia let out a disappointed whimper.

"Well, moving on… I'm sure the rest of you will be willing to participate," Augustus said, with a chuckle.

"With Walker not participating, we might have an odd number. Perhaps Eugene will even things out," Sonyai suggested, writing the security guard's name on a separate scrap of paper. Lakeshia turned to Robin and attempted to encourage him to reconsider with a glance, but he didn't budge.

With all the pieces of paper in the bowl, names were drawn one by one.

"Alright, dismissed," Augustus said, with a smile.

Robin and Tommy went back out to join Lucas, while Sonyai and Gerry left for the evening.

Heywood stepped out and found Angie searching the shelves to fill any open reserves. "Hey, you didn't want to do the Christmas gift exchange?" he asked.

"I have exemption. We respect other people's traditions, and may participate out of the spirit of friendship, but our people, as a whole, don't celebrate Christmas."

"Oh. Well, this was a nice surprise. I don't usually buy gifts for Christmas... it would have been nice to get *you* something, instead of..." he looked down and unraveled his piece of paper, reading the name. "Uhhhgggghaaaah!" he growled.

The three pages walked down separate aisles of shelves and regrouped in the back of the floor.

"Hey Leelee, I thought you didn't celebrate holidays," Alex said, with a puzzled look. "With you being... you know..."

Lakeshia had recently confided that her family was practicing Jehovah's Witnesses. A secret known only among the trio.

"I know. *We* don't do holidays, but we can participate with others outside our household for school or work," the page explained.

"So... who'd y'all get?" Tanya asked.

"I got Miss Yi!" Alex squeaked.

"I got... Miss Clein?" Lakeshia scrunched her face.

"I... can't say!" Tanya said, after checking hers.

"What? Why not?" Alex asked.

Tanya shifted her eyes left and right.

"Oh boy," Lakeshia sighed. "She got one of us."

"I'm not saying nothing!" Tanya hissed.

At the circulation desk, Tommy asked Robin, "so, why you going all 'scrooge' on this gift thing? Suffered some childhood Christmas trauma when you were eight? Found out the truth about Santa Claus the wrong way?"

"You mean like when you found him sliding a candy cane in your wife?" Robin replied.

Tommy shook his head. "Just when I think you're getting better, you go back to 'Dick Mode.'"

"Look, I don't do Christmas, okay? I never did. Even when my grandfather was alive. Can you imagine this first one *without* him?"

"I understand, but what's the harm?"

Robin didn't answer. After what he went through on Thanksgiving, Christmas wasn't looking any better.

Augustus stepped off the crosstown bus, in front of his building, at five-thirty. He didn't go inside, though, and waited for nearly ten minutes until a limousine pulled up, and Dea stepped out of it.

She greeted him with a peck on his cheek. "You didn't have to send a car for me," she said with a smile. "I could have easily taken a cab from the office."

"I know, I just like my friends to travel in style," he replied, with a smile. "Call it a perk... and besides, you still haven't told me where you live."

Dea tilted her head. "I can't help it if I'm a bit old-fashioned. I like to keep a little mystery in our... friendship."

As close as they were getting to know each other, the couple agreed not to acknowledge their "official" relationship status yet. That didn't stop Augustus from what he was about to do.

"Okay, you can tell the driver where he can drop you off after you leave here. I won't pry… I just wanted to give you an early Christmas gift, as my way of saying thank you."

He pulled out a felt box from his left pocket, and she gasped.

"Th-this better not be what I think it is…" she said quickly.

Augustus chuckled at her reaction. "I'm not on one knee, so you can relax… for now," he added with a wink.

She sighed in relief, reached out for the box, and opened it. There was a pair of diamond earrings inside. The disappearing sunlight of the dusk bounced around as they glittered.

"Oh, I can't. This is simply too much," Dea said, closing the box and handing it back to him.

"It's yours. No strings, no backsies!" Augustus joked with his hands up, and then took a step back. "Wear them with your best outfit. Merry Christmas!" He slowly began walking to the entrance of his building as she looked at him in awe. Once he was at the door, he gave her one last wave and turned to go inside.

Dea sighed and opened the box again. They *did* look nice. She turned and walked back to the limousine. The driver opened the door for her, and she climbed in and closed it behind her.

"What am I going to do with you, Augustus Chavez?" she asked, shaking her head.

It was the end of the day. Gerry closed the cash register, as Robin turned off his terminal. He noticed Lakeshia picking up a few books that were left on the table in the reference area. It was time. It wasn't going to be an easy conversation, but it had to be done. He came from around the circulation desk and walked up behind the page. She sensed him approaching and turned with a smile.

"Lakeshia," Robin started, using her regular name to bring emphasis to the question, "do you have an eating disorder?"

She was caught off-guard by the question. With a series of stammers she answered, "Wh-what? No!"

Robin pressed on. "Your nails are brittle, you have dry hair, and I caught you coming out of the bathroom after throwing up."

"I was sick! Yes, I threw up because I ate something, but it doesn't mean—"

"Since we're both off, I want to take you to see someone Saturday." His face softened. "Please, will you come with me?"

As angry as she was, she melted as she looked into his dark brown eyes. "Oh... alright."

"Good, I'll pick you up at your place. Don't back out on me."

He walked back to the circulation desk, leaving her looking back at him with a worried glance.

It was noon, and Gerry was clustering at Yorkville this Thursday afternoon. He was working the circulation desk with the part-time clerk named Curtis.

"Things are kinda slow on Thursdays," Curtis said.

Gerry was writing in his notebook, not falling for the clerk's attempt to make conversation. It didn't stop the young clerk from trying several times.

"Um, it's a wonder that... that guy Robin Walker is still working at that branch of yours... after I heard what happened down there."

Gerry finally stopped writing. "Whatever you heard, I'm pretty sure it's far from the truth, and I'll leave it at that."

"Heh. Y'all trying to keep it under wraps." Then, he walked up to Gerry and whispered, "but everyone's talking about... *The Soda-Can Killer*..."

"The WHAT!?" Gerry exclaimed.

From the information desk, Erin Aniyah looked up in the direction of the circulation desk and shushed the clerks.

"What the hell are you talking about?" Gerry hissed.

"You tell me. Is it true that he accidentally sliced off Ethel Jenkins's scarf from her scalp?" Curtis asked.

"What? Bullshit! Where is this coming from?"

"Man, I heard from someone who heard from somebody else who heard from someone over at S.I.U., that Robin cold took this soda can and accidentally sliced her forehead on some scalping Indian-type shit!"

"Who did you hear this from?" Gerry asked again.

"People, man."

"Anyone specific?"

"No. It's all rumors and shit, but somewhere there's always some truth…"

"Not in this case. Nothing happened. Spread that around, instead of all these crazy stories that clearly make no sense."

Gerry turned away from the part-timer, as his mind started to race. Who could be spreading these lies, if everything about the hearing was supposed to be sealed?

Tommy entered the A&S Mall at six o'clock in the evening. The place was busy with Christmas shoppers looking for gifts, which was also why he was there. Tommy picked Eugene's name out from the bowl and had no clue what to buy him.

He went to JC Penney first, and checked the first two floors for something nice, but nothing jumped out at him. He didn't know the security guard's favorite sports teams, what kind of music he liked, or any television shows he watched.

*He WAS happy when the Rangers won the Stanley Cup back in June.*

Tommy checked the directory and then went to the third floor where men's sportswear was located. He found the section, but the hockey gear was nowhere to be seen. There was a woman nearby restocking socks and checking footwear. He waved to get her attention.

"Do you work here, Miss?"

The woman looked up at Tommy's tall and muscular frame then put on her friendliest smile, "Yes, yes I do... I get off in two hours as well, if you're interested."

He let out a small chuckle and ran his left hand through his hair slowly enough for her to see the ring on his finger. "Uh, thanks, but I was wondering if you had any hockey jerseys, specifically the Rangers?"

"Well, the new season just started, but football and basketball have taken over most of the sports section. We might have some Rangers gear in that far corner on the left." She pointed in the direction and let out an awkward giggle.

"Thank you, ma'am." Tommy flashed a smile and headed in the direction she pointed out.

She let out a sigh. "Anytime." *Why are all the good ones taken?*

The hockey jerseys were in a small corner among the Giants and Knicks, but Tommy found a Mark Messier jersey in a 4X that would fit Eugene, discounted at $26.99.

*It's a bit over the limit but I'm sure no one will mind.* He walked to the nearest cashier and paid extra for store gift-wrapping. After browsing a few other stores, Tommy went to the basement where the food court was and helped himself to a pepperoni slice and a coke from Sbarro's.

It was nearly eight o'clock when he rode the train back to Queens. He hoped Sarah didn't cook him dinner, but if she did, he could always store it for leftovers.

Angie was recording a segment for the radio show, and when she finished, Olivia Morris tapped the glass of the studio to get her attention. She put on some commercials and stepped out of the booth.

"Hey, what's up?"

"I stayed here late to show you our ratings. They're really going up since you took over. You have a knack for this," Olivia said, showing her a clipboard.

"So, I've been told," Angie replied with a smile, while bouncing on her toes.

"People are tuning in, and they are loving you!"

"Really?" Angie beamed.

"Yeah. I know we said till the end of the year, but between you and me, they're ready to offer you this gig a whole lot longer. Like, 'until further notice,' type status."

She cocked an eyebrow. "You're kiddin' me!"

"We're also having a hard time getting someone permanent at the moment. Two previous radio personalities have rejected our offers."

She snickered. "You're not offering enough, I take it?"

Olivia made a face. "Just think about it." She turned and walked out the other door from the control room.

Alex walked in the library at two-thirty Friday and Sonyai caught her attention as she passed the circulation desk.

"Alex?"

"Yes, Miss Yi?"

"This came for you in the interoffice mail," the senior clerk said, handing her an interoffice envelope.

Alex gave her a puzzled look and accepted the envelope.

As she walked upstairs to the staff room with a puzzled face, *Who would send mail to me?* Alex checked if anyone was inside and when she knew she was alone, she unlooped the envelope. There was a note inside which she quietly read:

*I checked you out,*

*You have resources that can prove useful, but discretion is best exercised if it's revenge you seek. Patience is a virtue, and the true hunter slowly stalks their prey before they strike. In the meantime, I offer you a gift. A small tidbit of information that will guarantee you some entertainment. Use it wisely, then wait for further instructions. I'll be in touch.*

There was no signature, but she knew exactly who it was from, when she read the rest of the note. Alex smiled. She was in, and with Trevor Guzman's help, she was going to make Robin Walker wish he was never born.

# CHAPTER TWENTY-ONE

Lakeshia met Robin in front of her building at ten o'clock on Saturday. They took a cab back up to Washington Heights and got out at 181st Street between Wadsworth and Broadway. She followed Robin inside a building and walked up a steep staircase to an office on the second floor.

He knocked on the door and then walked in, "Leelee? I want you to meet Carmen Hernandez, Carmen? This is Lakeshia Seabrooke."

"Hello." Lakeshia waved.

Carmen nodded as they sat down, and touched her fingertips. "Robin tells me you have a problem I'm familiar with."

Lakeshia looked down and said nothing. Robin gave Carmen a nod and she opened up a folder that was on her desk.

"I'd like you to look at the following pictures for a moment," she said, and pushed the folder forward.

After a moment, Lakeshia looked up and reached for the folder. Inside there were pictures of various models. They were very beautiful, but thin, nearly skeletal.

"I know what you're gonna say. '...*But I have it under control. It's not a big deal,*'" Robin said.

"Those girls…" Carmen began, "were barely 100 pounds, some were even 90. Do you know where they are now?"

Lakeshia shook her head.

"Dead."

Lakeshia's eyes went wide, and she looked at Robin, who simply nodded. "My sister was close friends with each of those models. They ran in the same circles. The same thing almost happened to Raven, but Carmen helped her before it was too late."

"You think you have it under control, but just looking at you I can see that you don't. If you don't get help, your teeth will fall out and one day, you'll collapse from—"

"Okay, okay, okay…" she interrupted. "What do I need to do?"

Carmen took out a business card. "I'm going to give you a number to a nutritionist, who will see you twice a week… for free. This person usually charges $30.00 a session, so don't waste their time if you're not serious about getting help."

She nodded. Robin put his hand on her shoulder as Carmen continued.

"They'll go over several meal plans to start you off, and once you're at the average weight, you can then go at your leisure. I want to stress this to you. They will NOT make you fat. The object is to get you eating healthy, and not starving yourself, okay?"

She started to cry. "I'm sorry…"

"Hey, hey, hey… you did nothing wrong, okay?" Carmen stood up and handed her a box of tissues.

"You have nothing to be ashamed of," Robin said. "I'm just glad you're getting help."

"You'd be surprised how many girls deal with this," Carmen began. "The modeling industry, specifically, sets this standard of beauty that is SO hard for some to deal with."

"I… I feel so ashamed, it's so embarrassing," Lakeshia whimpered.

"There's a distinct look out there among the fashion world that's slowly becoming popular. It's called, "Heroin Chic." Women are getting so skinny, they look like they're strung out. It's making girls your age that idolize them become so thin at an alarming rate."

It was a bold move, but Carmen bent down and hugged Lakeshia. "You're going to be okay."

Lakeshia looked over to Robin, who nodded.

After several minutes, the pair left the building, and Robin once again assured her, "it's going to be okay, kiddo."

"Thank you. I really appreciate it."

"I know you don't like riding the subway, but I'll walk you back home if you want," he offered.

She smiled. "I'd like that very much."

"And look, this is your personal struggle. If you don't want anyone else to know, not even your parents, this will stay between us. Okay?"

"Okay."

"Let's go," he said, and they started walking to Saint Nicholas Avenue, where the 1-train station was located.

Gerry traveled to The Bronx and arrived at the Soundview Branch Library. He parked his car on Taylor Avenue, behind the building, before walking into the first library he worked in as a page.

"My goodness, the place ain't changed a bit," he said.

The person he came to see was behind the circulation desk, a pudgy man of average height, wearing jeans and a sweater.

Gerry walked up and said, "how ya doin', LaMarque?"

"Gerry, my man, it's been a while!" LaMarque Thompson greeted his friend quietly.

LaMarque and Gerry were both pages during his last year of high school back in 1980. It was Gerry's second year working for the NYPL, and LaMarque's first. Gerry enlisted in the marines when he graduated, and after six years he resumed working for the library, at age twenty-four. LaMarque transferred to several branches as a full-time clerk before coming back to Soundview.

"What brings you by?" LaMarque asked.

"What is it that Brother Malcolm taught us is power? Knowledge," Gerry replied.

"Can't have enough of that. Speak on it."

Gerry nodded. "You know of all that goes around here within the system."

"That would be an understatement," LaMarque replied.

"Okay, what do you know about "The Soda-Can-Killer"?"

"Ah, the latest urban legend, Mr. Robin Walker himself. Works downtown at your 58th Street Branch and was at Fort Washington before that. He had a reputation before all this happened. Now it's just more to pile on."

"What the hell are they saying, and where are they getting it from?"

"The whispers came from S.I.U. themselves. After Levi Kraine lost the case, everyone wanted to know what happened. Despite all the details supposedly under lock and key in the archives, it got out and spread like wildfire."

LaMarque took a moment to check out books from a patron, then continued when there was no one around. "The information, though, was taken with a grain of salt. It all got murky, and the tall tale took a life of itself."

"So, what's that tall tale?" Gerry asked.

"Robin used a soda can to cause bodily harm against Ethel Jenkins and got away with it. What exactly he did, how he did it, and why he got away with it, is a mystery. Some say he tripped and sliced her head with it, others say he crushed the can on her head. Like I said, details are sketchy, but the legend is born."

"This is crazy. Why would anyone be talking like this, spreading all these lies?"

"Why does anything happen? It's juicy gossip in a boring work environment. No one cares what's actually *true,* so they're going to make it bigger than it actually is, until the next juicy gossip."

"When I first heard this, I thought it was crazy. Now that it's going around, it's just going to get worse for this kid."

"Possibly. Wanna tell me what *really* happened that day?"

"What makes you think I know?" Gerry asked.

LaMarque smiled.

"Well, my lips are sealed. Who else is here today?"

"A couple of familiar faces. Come on back and let me show you around."

Gerry walked to the back of the desk and the clerk knocked on the door to the clerical office.

Sarah was playing with Carrie in the living room, coaching her to talk.

"Can you say 'Mama'? Come on... 'Ma-Ma?'"

The baby replied with nonsensical gibberish.

"No... 'Ma-Ma.' You can do it baby girl, c'mon..."

The phone rang and she stood up, picked up the baby, and walked over to answer it. "Hello?"

"Hey," Acindina greeted.

"Hey, Ma, what's up?"

"Against my better judgment, I contacted my sister."

Sarah let out a gasp. "Tia Ada? Will she see me?"

"She agreed to do a... whatchamacallit? Tarot reading? But only after the Spring Equinox next year. Apparently, witches take the winter off, la puta!"

"Mama! How can you say that about your own sister?"

"That woman is *crazy*, mija! You can't believe anything she says!"

"Let me be the judge of that. When is the Spring... whatever she said?"

"Equinox. It's the 20th or 21st of March, I think."

Sarah sighed. "Geez, that's so far away from now."

"Well, hopefully by then, you'll forget all about this."

"No way. I'll never forget what happened, and I need answers on what to do."

"If you want answers, there are other ways, but I'm not getting into that with you, now. I was just calling to let you know. Take care."

"Thank you, Mama, 'bye," Sarah said, as she hung up the phone.

Carrie fussed and said more gibberish, Sarah looked down and said, "yes, baby... both of them *are* crazy, I know," and walked back to the living room.

It was officially thirteen days until Christmas, and everyone could feel the festive spirit in the air. The unusually mild weather took a break today, as the temperature finally dipped below freezing for the first time since winter started. Zelda was working the last hour at the information desk, and just finished helping a patron find a copy of *The Gift* by Danielle Steel.

As she returned to the desk in the middle of the branch, a man was waiting for her. He was a tall, middle-aged man, wearing a heavy winter coat and gloves. Despite being bundled up, he was uncharacteristically pale.

"May I help you?" Zelda greeted him, after sitting down.

"Yes, I'm looking for several books, and I was wondering if you could help me. I'm used to academic libraries, and I can't make heads or tails of your cataloging system."

"Well, I can help you. What are the books you're looking for?"

"I have a list here." He pulled out a piece of paper and handed it to the assistant librarian.

After studying the list Zelda said, "Microbiology?"

"Yes. The call number system we use in universities has an alphanumeric entry. We're unfamiliar with the Dewey Decimal system you guys still use."

"University?" she asked. "I guess these books weren't found on campus."

"Ah, um, unfortunately no, they weren't. I'm using these for a presentation to show my students next week."

"Interesting. Well after checking our system, I can tell you, two of these books are right here in our branch. Follow me."

The pair walked toward the 500's.

"You know, I read something interesting recently…"

"Oh yeah?" Zelda replied.

"Yeah, apparently… December 10th was Melvil Dewey's birthday, so they deemed that Dewey Decimal Day. It's a nice honor, eh?"

Zelda grunted. "I suppose," she said dryly.

"Oh? You don't think the creator of the Dewey Decimal system deserves some recognition? You, a librarian?"

They stopped suddenly and Zelda looked at the man. "Sir, his classification system notwithstanding, Melvil Dewey was a sexist pig, and an anti-semite. He felt that women should only serve men *on their knees*. So no, I don't wish to recognize Mister Dewey, despite my occupation."

She accented her speech with a curt nod and resumed walking. The man slowly followed behind, stunned by the new information he learned.

Tuesday evening, Heywood and Eugene walked into the Pig 'N' Whistle. They rubbed their hands a bit to warm up, as Eugene said, "first round's on me!"

"Cool, I got the next round," Heywood answered.

Several rounds later the two were buzzed and having a random conversation at the bar.

"So… who you get for the gift exchange?" Eugene asked, after a series of laughs.

Heywood sobered up quickly at the subject. "Damn, why'd you bring THAT up? I'm going to need another beer," and signaled the bartender, who brought another bottle and popped it open. Heywood accepted the bottle and took a swig.

"Before I tell ya, who'd you get?" Heywood asked.

"I got Lakeshia. Bought her a nice Christmas teddy bear."

"You got your gift already? I still don't know what I'm going to get…" he stopped and hiccuped. "Augustus."

"Oh wow, you got him?" Eugene let out a belly-aching laugh. "That's hilarious."

"Yeah, yeah, yeah… I got a week to find something… what would *you* get him?"

"I wouldn't even try. I'd switch the name with someone else." Eugene let out another giggle.

"Well shit, I can't do that now. Damn it, why couldn't Angie participate, so I could have bought her something?" Heywood noticed Eugene wasn't listening anymore. He was dozing off on his crossed arms.

Heywood thought about waking him up, but then decided to let him sleep. It had been a long Monday. Five minutes went by and suddenly, Eugene shot straight up on his own. "Shit!" he yelled.

The security guard looked around and shook his head.

"Welcome back. Me and the bartender were about to solve Final Jeopardy without you," Heywood joked.

Eugene chuckled. "Sorry about that. It's been a long day."

"Yeah, I know."

"Think I'll sober up a bit with some coffee." Eugene signaled and ordered a cup. "Black and no sugars."

After two cups of coffee, Heywood found Eugene more sensible to talk to again. "Hey, let me ask you a phil... philosophical question," Heywood asked, with a bit of slurred speech.

"Shoot."

"You think that all people... are good?"

"Shit, that's really deep," Eugene said, with a nod. "Yeah, I like to think they are, but I could be a bit naive."

"I only ask, because I've been talking to this guy. He might be planning something, I just don't know what."

"Well, how serious do you think he is?"

"I... I don't know."

Eugene took a chug of his third cup of coffee. "Well, until he makes a move, you can't go on assumption alone. Keep a sharp eye, but don't jump the gun."

"Alright, thanks for the advice," Heywood said, followed with a swig of his own.

Tanya was working Saturday, so she had Wednesday off. She couldn't believe her luck that she picked Alex's name from the bowl. She wanted to get her something special, since Alex gave her a fresh pair of sneakers for her birthday back in May. Alex *was* hard to shop for, though. As evidence showed when she reacted funny to that book idea Lakeshia suggested for her birthday. Tanya remembered how Alex didn't want to talk about what happened that weekend with her party. She wondered if something went wrong.

Tanya put her thoughts aside for a moment, as she arrived at 125th Street and Malcolm X Boulevard, at four o'clock. She walked east to Park Avenue, browsing several stores in the heart of Harlem, then turned around and headed west toward Amsterdam Avenue. She checked music stores, electronics, several clothing boutiques. Nothing was jumping out at her.

Then she came across a street vendor on the sidewalk, who was selling African paintings. They looked very professionally done. The vendor was a short, dark woman, wearing sweatpants with a long coat, and an African headscarf on her head.

"Hey, these are dope, who drew them?" Tanya asked.

"Thank you, I *painted* them," the woman corrected, with a slight accent.

"Oh, I'm sorry… um, how much for… this one?" she asked, pointing to a picture of a country landscape.

"$80.00."

"Woah."

"Hey, if you cannot appreciate art when you see it, I suggest you go to a museum, where you can look at it for free."

"Okay, I get what you're trying to say, but I'm just trying to find a nice gift for my friend."

The woman thought about it. "Well, in that case…" she pointed to another painting, with blended colors in a unique pattern. "I can part with this piece for $20.00."

Tanya made a face. "I don't even know what that is. How about that one, with the two babies, for… $30.00?"

The vendor narrowed her gaze, then said, "$40.00, and it's yours…" After sensing Tanya's hesitation she added, "…and I'll even gift wrap it for you."

*It's over our limit, but who cares?* "Alright, you got a deal."

Tanya fished two twenties out of her pocket as the woman picked the painting and placed it on her gift-wrapping table. The vendor smiled at the sale she made, considering she bought these paintings for five dollars apiece from the Salvation Army resale store.

*Teenagers are so gullible. They'll believe anything.*

Alex had the luck of the draw. She pulled Sonyai's name for the gift exchange, and she wanted to give her something special. Thursday after work, Abernathy drove Alex down Fifth Avenue and stopped at 37th Street. She got out of the car and told him to meet her at the same spot in a half-hour, then watched him take off into traffic.

The streets were busy with tourists and shoppers taking in the sights. Alex took a moment to look at the Lord & Taylor Christmas display, then made her way to a fragrance store on 39th Street and Madison Avenue. When she walked in, several of the customers registered questionable looks. Not used to a black teenager shopping in the store. She ignored them and made her way to the back where the owner was writing something in a notebook.

When the man ignored her, she cleared her throat extra loudly. "I'm here to pick up something."

The gentleman looked up and arched his left eyebrow. "Oh really?" he asked skeptically.

Alex felt the eyes of everyone in the store on her now. She couldn't resist giving the owner a smirk as she revealed her name. "Yes. The name is Stevens... Alexandra Stevens."

The man recognized the name given to him by Alex's father, but naturally questioned who was standing before him. "Ah, um, do... do you have some... identification, miss?"

"Madam," she corrected him.

"I beg your pardon. Do you have some identification, *madam*?"

Alex reveled in the man's attitude change, once he knew who he was dealing with. "Why, yes, of course I do," she replied, and handed over her state identification card.

After a lengthy examination, the man gave Alex back her ID and went to a shelf to retrieve a small bottle. He brought it back and placed it in a gift bag. "The Japanese Cherry Blossom fragrance you requested... madam. Um, thank you for your patronage. We hope to see you again."

She picked up the gift bag. "Well, improve your customer service and you just might. Have a good evening."

Alex turned to see all the customers involved in their own conversations and looking away as she walked out of the store.

*Yeah, that's right, bitches.*

# CHAPTER TWENTY-TWO

Angie was heading to the study hall, to work on her latest paper about 19th Century Literature, when she bumped into Olivia.

"Hey, have you thought more about the position?" she asked.

"I have, and while I'm very flattered, I think I'm going to pass."

She didn't hide her disappointment. "Really? Why?"

"It's just too much of a commitment. I have a lot on my plate now, as it is. I'm sorry."

"If it's a money thing…"

"No, it's not that." Angie scoffed. "I just really don't have the time…"

"Well, alright. If you change your mind, you know where to find me. Thank you for filling in until the end of the year. You might have found your calling in broadcasting."

"I'm a jack-of-all-trades, but my heart belongs to the library." Angie smiled.

"I see. Well, our loss is their gain. It was nice of you to help us for as long as you have. Take care, Angie."

Angie nodded, as Olivia walked past her.

It was the last day of classes for the term, and Robin was sure he was going to pass his class. He walked in the 25th Street building and noticed the security guard was away from his desk. Without signing the logbook, he headed quickly toward the elevators and made it inside, just before the guard came back to his desk.

"Hey! Hey you! I saw you! Sign the damn book when you leave! You know the drill!"

Robin smiled to himself in the elevator. He admitted it was juvenile to ignore the guard's request, and he was just doing his job, but the idea of routinely signing his name in a log was against his principles and he enjoyed every time he outsmarted the guy.

The class didn't help much toward his curriculum. It wasn't required, but he didn't want to waste time skipping another term. He planned to resume attending college full-time next year, during the day. Robin also noticed how standoffish the students were in evening classes. It was extremely hard to make friends. He missed Walt, Kim, Gillian, even Jarvis and Mouse.

The final was Tuesday, and on this last day of classes the professor was giving out the results and revealing final grades overall. Robin got an A- on the final and passed the class overall with a 90%. Halfway through the class, the teacher let everyone leave early, and opened the floor to any discussions the students had. Robin took the cue to leave instantly and headed back toward the elevators.

When he was back in the lobby, Robin made a sprint to the exit. The security guard ran from behind the desk and jumped him from behind. The two tussled on the floor as Robin fought to get free.

"Has anyone ever told you that you take this job a *little* too seriously!?" he yelled.

The guard nearly put him in a chokehold, but Robin slipped out and brought his knee up into his breadbasket. He fell to his knees and Robin pushed off the man, running through the door. The youngster ran two blocks south to 23rd Street before finally stopping to catch his breath. Hopefully, that would be the last time he had to go inside that building.

"Whatta maroon." he muttered, with a tired breath.

The holiday party was tomorrow, and Heywood still didn't know what to get for Augustus. Buying a present for a supervisor, especially after getting back in his good graces, could be very tricky. Should he try to play on the head librarian's funny side with a gag gift, or something serious?

Heywood decided to try his luck inside Sharper Image. The store was known to be a favorite for Augustus. There were a lot of gadgets in the store that caught his eye, but he wasn't looking for himself, he was looking for a thoughtful gift.

A sales representative in a suit approached from behind. "May I help you?"

Heywood jumped slightly and said, "um, yeah. I'm looking for a gift for my boss."

"Ah, yes… the workplace Christmas Party, heh, heh, heh… tons of fun, are they male or female?"

"Huh?"

"Your boss? Male or female?"

"Oh, um, male."

"Okay, tell me about him. Tell me about your job."

*Geez, this guy's really going for the sale,* Heywood thought. "Um, we work in a library. He's Mexican, he likes photography… he's… bald…"

"Well, we have several cameras here…"

Heywood held up his hand. "Uh, we have a $25.00 limit. I need something simple."

"$25.00!? Yeah, you're not gonna find your gift here." The man walked away, mumbling to himself, "whatta cheapskate."

Heywood took the hint and walked out. "Thanks a lot, pal!" he yelled over his shoulder.

Back outside, Heywood saw the other stores on the block were closing, and he was getting desperate. He rolled his eyes. "Fuck this," he whispered, then walked over to a newsstand and found a gift certificate.

Christmas was officially five days away, and today after the branch closed, the staff would be having the library's holiday party. Robin could care less. With his classes done, all he was thinking about was next year's term, and resuming classes during the day. Once all this holiday nonsense was behind him, he was looking forward to rebounding in 1995.

The young clerk managed to get through his day, working the circulation desk with Angela Pinkson from Yorkville, for two separate hours. Six o'clock was finally here. He was looking forward to going home and sleeping late, as he was scheduled to work the late night tomorrow evening.

After closing up the cash register and turning off his terminal, Robin was putting on his coat in the clerical office, when Sonyai and Augustus appeared at the doorway.

"And where exactly are *you* going?" Sonyai asked.

"There's a party going on upstairs, Walker," Augustus announced.

"Uh, I didn't do your little gift exchange so, I think I'll just take off. There are some Who's in Whoville that need their Christmas Trees… repaired."

He excused himself as he sidestepped in between them, heading to the exit.

"I'd reconsider if I were you," Augustus warned.

Robin stopped in his tracks and looked over his shoulder. "And if I refuse?" he asked, with a cocked eyebrow.

"Then there *might* be an unfortunate misplacement of your paycheck next Friday," Sonyai said in a light tone.

Robin turned slowly.

"Tis' the season…" Sonyai said, with a rare smile.

"Ho, ho, ho," Augustus added, also smiling.

Robin wasn't smiling as he narrowed his gaze. "30 minutes…" he growled through his teeth. "I'm not singing, I'm not dancing," then took off his coat, "and I want one drink."

"You're only 18," Augustus replied.

"And I want one drink!" he repeated.

"Aw, goddamn it, fine!"

Robin sighed, and followed Augustus and Sonyai upstairs to the auditorium, where everyone was eating and drinking while engaging in conversation. Augustus handed Robin a champagne flute. "Here you are, try to be merry." Robin pointed to his face and put on a fake, insincere smile. Augustus turned away, resisting the urge to strangle him.

Sonyai walked across the room to talk to Alex and Tanya, as Lakeshia was talking to Angie about something. Fifteen minutes went by, several more conversations continued, and the atmosphere gradually felt more festive.

"Okay, time for the gift exchange!" Zelda exclaimed. She pulled out a wrapped present from her bag and walked over to Tommy. "I drew your name, Tommy. Merry Christmas!"

The rest of the staff began exchanging gifts. Sonyai handed Heywood his gift as the pleasantries began.

Robin, in true grinch form, found a chair in the corner and sipped his champagne. *Is this Prosecco?*

Lakeshia gave Zelda her gift, then turned back to see Robin. She approached him and smiled. "I know you didn't want to participate, but I wanted to thank you for helping me with that... you know, issue I had."

He nodded. "I'm just glad you're eating normally and getting over your self-consciousness." He then cringed. "Don't tell me you brought me something anyway..."

"No, no... I knew that would just make you upset... but I *did* buy you a card. Merry Christmas, Robin."

He sighed and put on a fake smile. "You couldn't help yourself, could you? Thank you, Leelee," and accepted the envelope.

She then took a seat next to him. "So... why don't you like Christmas?"

Robin closed his eyes, fighting the urge to sigh again. "It's a long story," then looked at her attentive face, goading him on. "And I guess I'm going to tell it to you."

Across the room, Sonyai noticed Lakeshia sitting next to Robin, but said nothing.

"I was in the third grade," Robin began, "and the class did a gift exchange before the Christmas break. It was a class of 30, so there would be 15 even pairs and we all drew names…"

"Okay." Lakeshia nodded.

"When it was time to do the exchange, a few days before we went on vacation, everyone gathered in the classroom. But the student that had my name got sick with the measles. So, all those kids were opening gifts and being happy…" Robin swallowed hard, his voice cracked as he said the next part. "And I'm there all by myself, waiting for mine. Waiting, waiting, and waiting… nine-years-old, watching everyone get a gift but me. I… I started crying, then the homeroom teacher saw me and started panicking. She sent me home early but gave me something, as sort of a consolation gift."

Lakeshia didn't know what to say. "Wow, what a sad story." She was on the verge of tears herself. "Um, what was the gift?"

Robin took a sip and smiled. He even snickered a little. "It was a huge, inflatable purple crayon."

Lakeshia looked puzzled, and Robin looked back at her. "That's why I don't like Christmas gift exchanges."

"Well, I can promise you, that'll *never* happen with us here," Lakeshia said, patting his knee.

"I'd like to believe that Leelee… I really would." He finished his drink and stood up. "Think I'll sneak another drink while no one's looking."

He walked from the corner to the table, while Sonyai approached. Lakeshia was still sitting in the corner. The child looked up to her supervisor staring back at her and said, "we were just talking, Miss Yi."

"Indeed," she grunted.

Robin noticed the staff were very relaxed after opening their gifts, and there was more drinking and eating involved. Gerry, Heywood, and Tommy were drinking stronger stuff than the champagne he was given, and Augustus was passing around a plate of rum cake that he made. Zelda and Sonyai were the only ones (besides the pages of course) that were drinking very lightly.

It was seven o'clock, finally, and Robin was ready to leave. Luckily, the party was winding down, and the rest of the staff were ready as well.

"Well, it's been fun." Gerry waved. "But I'm taking off."

He giggled to himself and staggered to the door, Robin noticed, and quickly stepped in front of him. "Woah, woah, woah…" Robin held his hand up. "Why don't you share a cab with me tonight? I'll call my friend Cerva—"

"Nah, I'm good. I'll shake it off with some coffee before I get to my car. I'll be alright."

Gerry tried to move past him, but Robin grabbed his arm. "I insist. You're in no condition to drive… seriously man, c'mon."

"Hey, Gerry's good, man…" Tommy interrupted. "His car is in a garage a few blocks from here."

"Yeah, don't be such a worrywart, Robin," Heywood chimed in.

Robin insisted, and chased after Gerry when he pulled away, heading downstairs.

The rest of the staff sobered up, showing concern. Sonyai started after them as she heard Robin yelling outside the auditorium.

Gerry once again pulled off Robin as he grabbed his arm, then the young clerk ran in front of him, blocking his path to the exit turnstile. Everybody followed them, pouring out of the staircase door.

"Alright look! No more bullshit, I'm not fucking around! You're not leaving until a cab comes, you hear me?!" Robin yelled.

Gerry pushed Robin back and said, "muthafuckah, I'd like to see you try and stop—"

Robin caught Gerry with a right cross out of nowhere. There were gasps from around the floor as Robin brought his hands together and brought them down on Gerry's back, making him fall to his knees.

Sonyai raised her hand to object, but Robin continued his assault on Gerry, raining down several blows, then continued with a headbutt and finishing with several punches across his face.

Gerry collapsed on the floor, blood pouring out of his nose. The staff was frozen in shock over what transpired in just seven minutes. Robin composed himself, and calmly walked over to the phone behind the circulation desk. He picked up the receiver and dialed. A trickle of blood started dripping between his eyes.

"Uh, yeah, is car 2Y68 driving tonight? Could you send him to 127 East 58th Street? That's between Park and Lexington... yeah, the library. Customer 338... ten minutes? Okay, thanks."

He hung up the phone and wiped his forehead, then noticed everyone was still looking at him, so he felt inclined to say something.

"I'll... um, I'll take him to the hospital, I... might need some medical attention myself," he began. "Other than that, I think... yeah, I think the party's over... it... it might be... a good time to... call it a night, yeah?" he nodded repeatedly.

Gerry was moaning to himself, as the rest of the staff took that moment to disperse. Eugene just rolled his eyes and gave Augustus a hard look before leaving. Zelda, Angie, and Heywood quietly grabbed their coats from the information desk and proceeded to the exit as well. Tommy and the pages also walked out. He followed the girls, making sure they left safely.

Cervantes arrived and with help from Augustus, the cabbie escorted Gerry to the back seat behind the driver side, with Robin sitting across from Gerry behind the passenger seat. No one said a word. The cab then took off to the nearest hospital as Sonyai and Augustus cleaned up the library floor, before locking up for the night.

Sonyai half expected Gerry to call out Wednesday, so she was surprised when he walked in the office at ten o'clock that morning.

"You okay?" she asked.

He simply nodded and took a seat at his desk.

She leaned on the desk, nearly eye-level with him. "You *would* have sobered up before driving home, right?"

"Of course," he mumbled, his jaw still stinging from the haymaker.

"You could have just said that. I don't understand why you were so belligerent—"

"I wasn't in my right mind at the time. That's all I'm going to say."

"Well, Robin's doing the late night. He's expected at 4 pm, and he'll be at the desk that first hour with Mister Avery."

"I'll be fine when I see him. Don't worry about any retaliation."

Sonyai chuckled. "Oh, I know you won't. You know better. I'll deal with Robin, myself."

Gerry sighed and thought carefully, before saying his next sentence. "I know you want to punish him but go easy…" he wanted to say more but didn't want to talk, and just let his sentiment sink in with the supervisor.

The pages were on holiday break from school, so they all came in nearly an hour before they started their shift and hung out in the staff room. Lakeshia was reading an issue of Vibe, while Alex and Tanya were playing Go Fish at the kitchen table.

"Do you have any threes?" Alex asked.

"Go fish," Tanya replied.

Alex took a card as Tanya said, "helluva party last night."

"It certainly came to a crashing end…" Alex replied.

"To be honest, if Gerry was going to drive home, I'm glad Robin stepped in and beat the shit outta him."

Lakeshia wanted to chime in but kept reading quietly.

"While there was a chance of Gerry having an accident, Robin was way outta line."

"Oh, please, Lexi, you're just pissed at him because of Nellie. I honestly think if he didn't take her spot here, you and him would actually get along."

"You wish!" Alex scoffed. "Never say that again!" She shuddered at the thought.

"Anyway, I'm sure Miss Yi's gonna bring the hammer down on him again. Maybe he'll end up stamping cards for another three months."

"Well, we'll see… you still playing or what?"

"Oh yeah, um, you got any nines?" Tanya asked.

Alex rolled her eyes and slid over a card.

Rosanna Comanos decided to walk from the A-train station at Columbus Circle to Lincoln Center and appreciate the sights of the neighborhood before transferring to her next temporary clerical position in the system. She loved moving around from branch to branch, not knowing where she would end up next. It was the only reason she stayed on as a clerk after graduating from high school as a page. Rosanna refused to accept a stable part-time position for fear of getting bored and other personal reasons.

Franklin was once again following her from a distance. This time he had on a wig and sunglasses, in an unrecognizable disguise. He kept gathering the nerve to approach her, and time after time again something would happen, and he would chicken out. It took him all this time to find out where she was, and it was time to reveal himself and let her know how he felt.

Back when they were both pages at Fort Washington, they were good friends. She looked up to him because he excelled at all the duties presented to them at the time. Franklin shelved all the books in the quickest times and was pretty much the unofficial leader of the four of them during that time. When he resigned, and Rosanna graduated, he lost touch with her for two years. Despite everything else that he's been dealing with, he believed it was fate that he found her again. Now, it was time to see if they would have a future together.

Rosanna arrived at the library finally and was greeted by several clerks she had known for six months now. Next year, she would start at a new assignment at another branch that was short-staffed. For now, she was in the process of saying her goodbyes to everyone in the clerical office. The senior clerk of the branch was a Hispanic woman named Felicidad Modesta.

"Well Ms. Comanos, it's been a pleasure having you here in the middle of our shortage," Felicidad began. "You have been nothing but exemplary in offering your assistance."

Rosanna bowed modestly. "Thank you, Miss Modesta. It's been an honor to serve."

"As a token of our gratitude, we would like to present you with this cake, and wish you the best in your next assignment."

She smiled at the sight of the yellow cake on the desk that was frosted with vanilla icing. "Thank you."

"Now, we need to get back to work, people," Felicidad ordered.

Rosanna wasn't due on checkouts until the top of the hour, so she helped herself to a slice of cake.

Franklin waited until things died down during her first hour and was now ready. He removed his wig and straightened his clothes. With a few random books in his hand, he slowly walked up to the circulation desk and prepared what he was going to say. Pretending to randomly bump into her at this branch after months of secretly watching her.

He was halfway there when a patron walked up to her side of the desk. There was a huge, foldable shopping cart behind him. The gentleman was short with thinning hair, and wore a brown tweed suit.

"Good afternoon, I would like to donate these records and books to your wonderful institution, please."

Rosanna looked past him to gauge the massive collection that was in the cart. She put on a modest smile. "Wow, um, thank you sir. We usually don't accept donations, without assessing their value and evaluating if it's worth the effort to add said items to our collection. Perhaps—"

"That's no problem at all, I assure you," the elderly man interrupted. "The library would be honored to accept these items. My recently departed wife was a supporter of the arts, and it was her final wish to have her collection shared with the public. This was one of her favorite branches you see, where—"

Rosanna gestured with her hands. "Okay, okay, I understand sir…" she craned her head, looking around the room for someone, then sighed. "Um, let's take these inside and um, get them itemized. I can give you a receipt for the donation."

Rosanna came around and gave the other clerk a look. "Um, cover for me, will ya?"

The clerk secretly laughed at her discomfort and nodded as she pulled the cart and disappeared into the back office.

*What the fuck?* Franklin thought.

He brought the books up to the line at the circulation desk, hoping she would eventually come back. After ten minutes, it was obvious she would be busy for a while. Another clerk eventually emerged from the office to help with the returns.

"Are you ready to check out those books, sir?"

Franklin stammered when he realized he was next in line. "Uh, you know what? I'm sorry, I've forgotten my library card." He let out an awkward chuckle. "Sorry… um, you can take these and put them back on the shelves."

He left the books and went through the threshold, crestfallen that he missed another opportunity.

# CHAPTER TWENTY-THREE

Robin walked inside the branch at three o'clock. He was scheduled for the late night and didn't start until four but knew there would be a *discussion* before he started. There was a bandage on his forehead which would always be a reminder not to headbutt someone ever again.

Sonyai saw Robin first and stepped out from the clerical office. Augustus also emerged from his office after Zelda called him from the information desk. Tommy and Charlie Finn from Webster were working the desk and stood quietly as the tension built. Robin didn't need to be a mind reader to know a conversation was coming, so he proceeded behind the circulation desk and walked past Sonyai inside the office.

Once Augustus and Sonyai followed Robin inside, Sonyai closed the door behind her. Robin reached into his book bag as Sonyai said, "we need to talk."

"Yeah, we do," Robin replied quickly, "but first I'd like to tell you a story."

He pulled out a manila folder, opened it, and held up a picture that shocked Sonyai and Augustus to their core.

"*This* is an accident photo of one Diedre Nicole Anderson..."

Robin began. The picture was a gruesome sight of a teenage girl in the passenger seat of a car that was involved in a crash. Her body was twisted, and her head was turned at an angle that likely made death instant. Both Augustus and Sonyai were no strangers to macabre scenes in their lives, but they were still visibly disturbed.

"...born April 16th, 1975," Robin continued. "Killed June 24th, 1993. 18-years-old. Due to complications she suffered, while being in an incubator after she was born, Diedre's brain development was delayed, and it made her mentally challenged."

Robin took a breath and swallowed hard. A tear streaked down his cheek.

"Despite her learning disabilities and her mental capacity of someone four or five years younger, Diedre was a math genius! She was amazing with numbers, and passed all her special education classes, graduated from George Washington High School, then got accepted to Rutgers University."

His hand started to shake as it held the picture up in front of him.

"But she never made it to college and study to become an accountant, you wanna know *why?!*"

Robin noticed he had just yelled but didn't care as he tried to maintain his composure.

"Because she broke up with her boyfriend of four years... and took an early ride after the graduation breakfast. While driving with her classmate and his parents... at 10:27 am, a man named David Suarez, who was going home after working the third shift, *and* early morning drinking, lost control of his car while taking an exit on the FDR."

Augustus looked down as Sonyai gasped.

"Suarez plowed into Diedre's side of the car at over 70 miles per hour, causing both cars to slam into the ramp divider and tumble several times before landing upside down on the southbound side of the parkway."

Robin reached into the folder and pulled out a second picture. It was more graphic than the first.

"She was the only one in both cars... who *didn't* die instantly. Suarez's head was crushed in the windshield. The mother, who was driving in Diedre's car, was ejected. The father and his son? Diedre's classmate, who offered the ride uptown because he hated her boyfriend? They were both crushed by the roof of the car when it came down... look at it... LOOK AT THE PICTURE, DAMN YOU!"

The supervisors snapped back at attention.

"Someone should have taken David Suarez's keys that morning. Someone should have driven him home. *SOMEONE* should have beaten the shit out of David Suarez before he got behind the wheel of his car! So... when Gerry was so adamant about driving home last night... let me ask you, were *you* going to stop him... *Gus!?*"

Augustus clenched his fist as Robin turned to Sonyai and asked, "were you? Was Tommy? Heywood? Or how about our resident super-cop, Eugene, eh? When he's not busy trying to figure out what *really* happened to Ethel, would *he* have stopped Gerry from possibly killing someone? HUH?! Didn't think so."

Augustus had heard enough. "Okay. Your heart was in the right place, and yes, Gerry wasn't taking 'no' for an answer. But we are civilized people... we do *not* settle matters with violence..."

Robin opened his mouth to reply.

"I'M SPEAKING NOW! YOU LISTEN!" Augustus barked.

Sonyai jumped at the outburst. Robin closed his mouth and stared back at him.

"You engaged in a fistfight in front of *my* branch. You *choked* a page with your bare hand until she nearly passed out and then later slammed her through a table."

Sonyai raised her eyebrows at the head librarian's implied ownership of the library.

"Now you've beaten someone in the name of some *noble* cause while playing the 'dead girlfriend' card as an excuse for your actions? I don't *fucking think so!*"

Robin's eyes grew wide.

"You're suspended. *For real* this time. Two weeks."

"That's not for you—" Sonyai stepped forward and objected.

"*I'm* taking precedence here!" Augustus interrupted. "You finish this week, you come back next Friday for your paycheck, then you don't come back until January 9th!"

He took a step closer to Robin, towering over him. "And when you come back... you don't put your hands on *anyone* else in or around this branch, do I make myself *clear*?"

Robin looked up at him. To disrespect his memory of Diedre... he fantasized grabbing him by the suit jacket and headbutting his chin. "Yes. Sir," he finally replied.

Augustus turned around and left the office without another word. The door slammed shut and Robin put the pictures back in the folder. Sonyai thought carefully before she attempted to speak. "Robin..." she began, speaking his first name.

"I don't think I can do this, anymore," he said flatly.

"Please don't say that..." she pleaded.

"He talks about fighting in front of *his* branch? I didn't start that fight... I didn't spread a message of *hate,* over shelves of books that are supposed to contain knowledge." He traced a finger down the scar on his face. "I slammed someone through a table after *they* broke a hot coffee pot on my face. And now, I prevent someone, who could have easily killed someone, along with himself..." his voice cracked as he trailed off.

The image of Diedre in the car, and then on a medical examiner's table at the hospital. He didn't hold back the tears this time. "After Diedre... Shinju... and losing my grandfather!" he sobbed.

"You made a valid point," Sonyai began. "Your intentions *were* good, but your methods..." she shook her head. "Your methods are excessive, young man! You're a sledgehammer on a 1-inch nail."

She reached out and lifted his head by the chin. "You need to step back from the edge, Robin... before you go over."

Robin wiped his face as his whole body shook in anger. "Edge... EDGE?! I've been treated as an outcast for no reason whatsoever. What's left of my family has forsaken me! I am *not* over the edge. I am floating blind and aimlessly in the abyss! The edge has been long gone, and all I am now is an angry black man being oppressed by society!"

He stood up as Sonyai backed away from him.

"No matter what I do, no matter what I say... it'll NEVER be enough." He reached down and grabbed his book bag. "Whether you want to believe it or not, I saved someone's life last night by stopping Gerry from driving drunk... nothing you or Augustus say will convince me otherwise!"

Lakeshia took a break at three-forty-five and went upstairs to look for Robin. When she didn't find him in the staff room, the young page found him sitting alone in the auditorium, listening to his walkman. The rows of chairs were lined up in two sections on opposite sides of the room, setting up for a movie presentation later on at six o'clock.

"Robin?" she called out from the door.

She wasn't sure if he heard her, as he sat motionless in the room, so she slowly approached him and waved to get his attention.

He turned and gave her a half-hearted wave back, then turned back to stare at the front of the room.

Lakeshia took a seat next to him and they both sat in silence. She was about to say something, but Robin spoke first.

"Man, I wish that piano was still here, instead of being in storage."

"It is a shame... what are you listening to now?"

He didn't reply, so after a minute, Lakeshia reached out and pulled his headphones off, putting them on herself and listening.

"Jazz?" she said, with a confused look on her face. She had expected something totally different.

Robin nodded.

"Nice. Unexpected... but a nice song." She then gave the headphones back to him.

"It's Kenny G's album, *Breathless*... it was given to me at the beginning of my senior year. That was my favorite song on the tape." Robin rested the headphones around his neck.

"What's the name of it?"

He stopped the tape. "It's titled, "Alone"."

The pair shared another minute of silence, as they exchanged glances.

Lakeshia looked down, slightly embarrassed. "If you don't wanna talk or anything, I can leave…"

"Leelee, there will never be a time where I *don't* wish to talk to you," he smiled. "And I mean that."

"Wanna talk about yesterday then?"

"Sure, what the hell…" he replied with a smirk, then thought for a moment. "Remember what I told you about my high school girlfriend?"

She nodded. "You said she went to college in New Jersey, after the two of you broke up."

Robin nodded back. "Yeah… I lied. Her name was Diedre… and she was killed in a car accident caused by a drunk driver."

Lakeshia gasped. "Oh, Robin, I'm so sorry."

"That's why I couldn't let Gerry get behind the wheel last night. He didn't budge so I did what I had to do… and I'd do it again if I had to." he added seriously.

"I… I'm glad you stopped him." *Not the way I would do it, though.*

"I know you feel I overreacted, and maybe I did, but I was ready to leave at 6 pm. Sonyai and Augustus insisted I attend that damn party. They should have just let me go home. What happened is on them… but *I* get suspended for two goddamn weeks."

His head sunk into his chest as Lakeshia just patted him on the shoulder, then stood up and left the room.

Robin began his first hour at the circulation desk. Gerry came back from outside and froze. The hospital patched him up pretty good, but his lip was still swollen. The two locked eyes as Robin walked out from behind the desk to the middle of the branch. He leaned forward and extended his arms. "One punch," he invited. "I won't punch back, so take your shot… make it count."

Gerry just stared at him.

Inside the clerical office, Lakeshia held her breath. Out among the shelves, Alex watched with anticipation.

"Go 'head, man. Do it."

Eugene looked across the floor to Augustus, who gave a hand signal to hold steadfast.

Sonyai stood behind the circulation desk emotionless, bracing for the worst.

Everyone else around them looked on, staff and patrons alike. No one moved, a scene frozen in time... for a very long minute.

"You did the right thing," Gerry said, finally.

Robin dropped his arms and tilted his head.

"I have a problem, and no one's confronted me about it before."

Before he could react, Gerry reached out and pulled Robin in for a hug. It was the second time Robin has been in an uncomfortable embrace with Gerry. He closed his eyes, letting his mind leave his body temporarily until the moment passed.

Lakeshia let out a sigh, as Sonyai looked on and smiled privately. Alex was disappointed and resumed shelving some books.

Gerry let him go and took a step back. "I'm planning on getting help."

Robin thought about saying something, but Gerry walked past him and headed upstairs to the staff room.

Augustus stood up from the desk and walked over to Robin. "And *that's* why we are civilized people," he whispered.

Robin turned and gave him a hard stare.

"Think about that, while you're on suspension." He turned and walked back to the desk.

That day, Robin made a personal vow to himself. One way or another, he would make Augustus eat his words.

Two hours later, Eugene walked into Augustus' office as he was cleaning up his desk, preparing to leave. He looked up at the security guard's face and knew immediately this conversation was going to be difficult.

"Gerry may have forgiven Robin, but this still doesn't sit well with me," Eugene began.

"I've handled it. He's suspended for two weeks. By next year he'll learn his lesson, and if he puts his hands on anyone else—"

"That's not good enough!" Eugene interrupted. "I'm sick of you making excuses for this kid. You brought me back because of him. I demand the authority to do something about it!"

"And I would have granted it... if you didn't overstep your bounds involving the S.I.U. in his previous incident. But you just HAD to go over my head, didn't you?"

Eugene balked at the question, as Augustus put on his coat.

"Okay, I fucked up before, I'll admit that, but the longer he stays here, the more trouble he's gonna get into. You know I'm right."

"You might be, but I've taken care of it for now, and that's that."

Augustus came around from his desk and stared down at Eugene. "Now get back to work."

"This ain't over," the security guard promised, then turned around and left the office.

Tommy and Sarah were packing for their trip. He packed very light, expecting warm weather and a lot of time swimming at the pool or relaxing at the beach. Sarah, on the other hand, had enough luggage to stay in Puerto Rico for a month.

"Did you pack a swimsuit?" Tommy asked, with a playful grin.

Sarah turned and looked at him. "I have to lose the baby weight, before I wear something skimpy again."

"Aww, c'mon, you look great no matter—"

"I won't hear another word. End of discussion. Now where's our suntan lotion?" She started searching the room.

Tommy closed his suitcase and placed it near the door, then turned to look at Sarah. "Um, Sarah? You got a sec?"

She noticed he actually used her first name and immediately became concerned. "Yeah, what's wrong?"

This was it. He went through this conversation several times in his head, and his anxiety was going through the roof. It was time she knew.

"I got something I have to tell you, but—"

Carrie started crying from her playpen in the living room. Sarah hurried out past him. "She probably needs her diaper changed. Hold on."

He made an exasperated look and followed her.

Sarah picked up the fussy child and grabbed a nearby box of pampers. As she began changing Carrie, she looked up and asked Tommy, "what was it you wanted to tell me?"

Tommy shook his head. "Nothing... it can wait, don't worry about it."

Denise heard a knock on her door and was surprised when she answered and saw Gerry standing in front of her house.

"Well, this is a nice surprise, what's up?"

"Hey," he stepped in. "Um, I know we talked about sharing the car..."

"Oh, no you don't! I put money into that car, it's just as much mine as yours—"

"Well now it's all yours," Gerry interrupted, holding up the keys.

"What?" she gasped, then made a skeptical face. "What's this all about? You do something to the car? Or did you find out it was stolen?! Why you dumping it on me?"

"Let's just say, someone opened my eyes and I realized I have a drinking and driving problem. I'll be taking public transportation for now."

Denise looked back at her brother. She could see this was a hard decision to make. "You sure about this?"

He nodded. "Since it's yours completely, I'll be asking for *my* $1,500.00 back that I paid."

"I don't have that kind of money!"

"You don't have to give it all to me now. I'll take monthly payments."

She thought about it, then said, "I'll give you $200.00 dollars a month, for six months."

"That's only $1,200.00!" Gerry gasped.

"We've shared the car for six weeks. Depreciated value."

Gerry mumbled something under his breath, then brought his palm down his face. "Fine."

She took the keys, and they shook hands.

"You miss ONE payment and I'll be taking you to court!" Gerry threatened, then handed her the bill of sale.

"We still going half on the insurance?"

"Hell no!" he yelled. "I canceled my insurance this morning. You put it on your own policy." He turned to the door and opened it. "See-ya!"

Denise shook her head as he slammed the door closed. "You truly are a piece of—"

Tanya came home and checked the mailbox in the lobby and found a letter addressed to her with no return address. The envelope had a certain scent on it of a familiar cologne. She quickly opened and read the letter:

*"Hey Brownie, as far as goodbyes go, our last goodbye was mind-blowing. I'm respecting your choice, but if you ever want to hook up, no strings attached, I'm only a phone call and hotel room away. We belong together and I'll be holding that candle, lighting that dark tunnel that will lead you back to me. Merry Christmas and have a happy new year, Andrew."*

The letter was sprayed and the smell of it brought her back to when she was in his arms. She ached for him, but it was time to move on.

The best thing to do was to tear up his phone number and quit him cold turkey. Whether or not she would actually do that, remained to be seen.

Robin only had one hour left. Leaving at five o'clock was rare, since he usually closed the branch. He entered the staff room and found Lakeshia sitting on the couch, eating a snack.

"Glad to see you eating more. How are those sessions going?" Robin asked, taking a seat at the table.

She wiped her mouth and smiled. "They're going well, thank you for asking. I'm becoming more comfortable with my body."

He smiled and nodded. "That's good. You're filling out a little bit, already... chubby," he added playfully.

"Hey! That's not nice! Mister Soda Can Killer!" she taunted.

Robin stood up and grabbed a pillow from the second couch. "Oh my God! Who told you about that name?" and threw the pillow at her. She giggled and threw it back, then Robin walked up to her and pretended to smother her. "I got'cha, Soda Can Killer! How about Couch Pillow Killer instead? Huh? How about that?"

They tussled playfully, pushing the pillow back and forth between them, then stopped and slowly locked eyes. Robin looked down as she looked up at him, they both began to lean their faces together, but then Robin snapped his head back, coming to his senses.

"WHOA! Um, I think I need to go..." he scooted back from the couch, looking down embarrassingly.

Meanwhile, Lakeshia sat up and stammered, "Uh, yeah... I... I..."

Before she could finish her sentence, Robin was already out the door.

Friday night, Sonyai was working the last hour of the day with Gerry, when Jessica Coons walked in the branch. She stopped when she saw Sonyai behind the desk, with a shocked look on her face.

"I didn't think you'd be here," she said softly. "I wanted to drop this off on your desk, to find Monday morning."

She held up a small bag that had a present inside.

"Secret Santa indeed," Sonyai whispered. She looked across the desk and saw that Gerry was helping a patron fill out an application for a library card. When she turned back, Jessica was nowhere to be seen, but the bag was sitting on the circulation desk. The regional senior clerk was gone, as quickly as she came.

Sonyai looked around the floor, then smiled. She respected the privacy of their friendship so much and she didn't want to embarrass her. Sonyai quickly took the bag to her office and left it on her chair to open Monday. As she prepared to walk back out to the circulation desk, she stopped and looked back at the gift.

*I suppose I can treat myself to an early peek.*

The senior clerk closed the door, went back to grab her present, and sat down. With a rare childlike grin, she pulled out the wrapped present from the shopping bag and tore it open. There was a white box inside. Sonyai opened the box and pulled out a bonsai tree. She always wanted one of her own but was afraid of the commitment to take care of it.

"Damn you, Red..." she whispered, and smiled.

There was also a card in the box. Sonyai pulled it out and read, "Merry Christmas, Freckles."

In all their years of knowing each other, they never exchanged gifts. Sonyai had no idea what made her friend start now, but next year she planned to one-up her in generosity.

# CHAPTER TWENTY-FOUR

"Well, here we are at the end of another year," Augustus said with a tired sigh.

It was Christmas Eve, Saturday morning. He and Sonyai were meeting in the staff room, probably for the last time before the new year.

"Yes... this was a memorable one, that's for sure," Sonyai replied. "We made it, though, receiving help from clustering clerks... but sooner or later we are going to need a new full-time hire."

"Yes, about that. I'm afraid budget constraints will require us to hire another part-timer instead." He reached over to a folder that was placed on the table. "Which brings me to my proposal."

Sonyai tilted her head as the head librarian pushed the folder in front of her. She opened it and gasped at the employee photo of Janelle Simms and her library performance record.

"In exchange for your cooperation," he began, "I can arrange for Miss Simms to return as a part-timer... back to your flock. She'll lose her benefits, of course, but she has no need for them, *now*." Augustus added with a tone.

"What do you mean... *'My cooperation'*?" Sonyai asked, looking up and narrowing her eyes.

"We've been on opposite sides for far too long. These past few months of us working together have been encouraging. I'd like to believe the new year approaching can bring a new era for 58th Street... where you and I have no more secrets or hidden agendas." He put on a fake smile and opened his palms up. "I'm putting all my cards on the table."

Sonyai studied the file again, Janelle was earning high praise since returning from maternity leave. The senior clerk at Van Nest had put in a commendation for excellent customer service, stating she has promise to be considered for the senior clerk seminar within the next two years.

*She's doing so well...*

"The two of us, Yi... running this branch and bringing it to its full potential!" Augustus shook his fist with excitement.

Sonyai looked up again. "Are you willing to operate under an honest guideline of ethics?" she asked frankly. "No manipulation? No favoritism? Treating everyone as equals?"

Augustus strained to keep his smile. "Well, heh, heh, heh... not everyone *is* equal, Yi. You can understand that, right? We have wealthy benefactors who are very, very generous..."

She frowned. "Chavez..."

"You will get her back, Yi... and maybe when fiscal year '96 starts we can even hire a fourth page. I'm throwing you a bone here, in exchange for a little leeway."

Sonyai looked across the table at the smiling librarian for over a minute. Seeing through his deception, she slammed the folder closed. "No," she replied flatly. "You're asking me to get in your pocket."

She slid the folder back to him and stood up. "Your corruption will lead this branch down a dark path, and it's my job to prevent that from happening."

Augustus looked back at Sonyai, as his smile turned into a twisted scowl.

"For the good of the branch," she whispered, then walked past him to the door.

Augustus pounded both his fists, then turned and stood. "The people ARE the branch, Yi!" he called out to her, she was already out the door, walking down stairs to the main floor. "They are the ones who sustain the libraries and ask for little in return!" His bellows echoed from the second floor, unheard by the senior clerk. "You will see this my way, or you will be taken OUT of my way! You hear me, Yi?! You will NOT stop me! I am in charge here, I run the show! I WILL NOT BE STOPPED!"

The ravings of a madman, falling on deaf ears. Sonyai stepped out of the branch and fought the urge to light up a cigarette. She looked out at the street, holding back her tears. *I'm sorry, Janelle... I'm so sorry.*

She wished she could bring her back, but the price was too high, and she refused to be bought.

Augustus stormed into his office and slammed the door behind him. There was a figure sitting at Zelda's corner desk who didn't flinch at the sound.

"She didn't take the deal, Zee! I guess we're going to do this the hard..." He turned and stopped. "How did you get in here!? Who the hell are you!?"

The visitor stood and stepped out of the shadows. "Someone who needs *no* introduction," Barbara Schemanske answered.

"You!" Augustus gasped.

"You've been living quite an interesting life, to say the least, Augustus Caesar Chavez," Barbara began.

Augustus stiffened upon hearing his full name.

"I have followed your career very closely. As a matter of fact, *I* was responsible for your recently opened 'museum' at your former university."

Augustus narrowed his eyes as she continued.

"Your campaigns since taking over 58th Street have been very ambitious. You definitely have your eyes on the prize. But it has given you tunnel vision."

"You might have a reputation that is well earned, but you don't scare me, madam," Augustus hissed.

"Those who don't fear me are either brave, or a fool. Which one are you?"

"State your business," the head librarian spat.

"He doesn't know I'm here, obviously... but I'd like to talk about Robin Walker."

"Ah, yes..."

"I would like to ask... what kind of head librarian would allow nearly all his staff members to gang up on a transferred employee and welcome them with nothing but bias, animosity, and a blatant disregard for morals?"

Augustus scoffed. "Okay, first off, I don't have to explain myself to *anybody*. Second, that upstart of yours has a serious anger problem. And you trying to rationalize his behavior really says something about *your* morals."

He walked to the door and opened it. "I think you should leave."

Barbara tilted her head. "Very well. But before I go, I'd like to warn you that upper management would be extremely disappointed to hear about alcohol beverages, and laced food like rum cake, being served at a holiday celebration where branch employees *drive* home."

"Surely, such behavior would be frowned upon, *if* word happens to find its way to certain individuals..."

Barbara walked past Augustus, his hand squeezing the doorknob. "Feliz año nuevo, Señior Chavez," she said in parting.

It was Carrie's first Christmas morning and Santa had been very rewarding. After several phone calls from family members, Tommy and Sarah finally had a few hours to themselves to rest, before getting ready to meet their parents at the airport at four o'clock for their six-thirty flight. Carrie was laying on her back in the middle of the living room playing with her Baby Born doll.

"She really likes her new toy, baby. Great choice," Tommy said with a smile, on his sofa chair.

Sarah took what might have been the 100th picture with her fourth disposable camera. She had at least eight more packed in her luggage for when they landed in Puerto Rico.

Carrie suddenly started rocking from side to side, as Sarah lowered her camera. "Oh!" she gasped. "I think she's turning over! You can do it, baby, c'mon!"

Tommy looked on as Carrie slowly rocked and then successfully rolled over for the first time. Sarah cheered and started clapping at the milestone.

Tommy couldn't take it anymore, he started sobbing uncontrollably.

"Honey, wh... what's wrong? Whatsamatter?" Sarah asked.

"I... I gotta tell you something. Promise you won't get mad..."

She just looked on without saying anything.

"Wh... when you were in labor... the doctor asked me to make a choice... they couldn't ask you... I had to make the decision."

"What are you talking about? What decision?" Sarah asked.

"There was a chance... that either you or the baby wouldn't make it... so I told them to save you because I couldn't imagine raising Carrie alone... I'm so sorry, baby... she's just so beautiful... and I told them to save you instead! I'm so sorry!"

Sarah was speechless.

"Baby, say something..."

She started shaking, furious with rage... "Get. Out," she whispered.

"Huh?!"

"Get. The fuck. OUT! Get out of this house!"

"Wait, please, let's—"

"Tommy, I will hit my face till it bleeds and call the cops on you, if you don't get out. Now!" Sarah screamed.

"Where am I supposed to go?!"

"I don't care! Just get the fuck outta this house. NOW!"

Tommy grabbed a gym bag and some clothes and was gone in five minutes.

Sarah rang the doorbell to her parent's apartment. She tried to put on a brave face but couldn't hide how angry she was still feeling. The door opened and Acindina greeted her daughter. "You're here early, the flight doesn't leave for five hours…" She stopped, when she saw only Sarah and the baby carriage. "Wh-where's Tommy?"

"I don't want to talk about it. We're going to Puerto Rico by ourselves," Sarah said quickly, as she walked in.

Lorenzo called out from the bedroom, "is that Sarah? Why is she so early? We got like four hours!"

Acindina just closed the door behind her.

Lorenzo adjusted his shirt as he stepped out of the hallway to the living room. "Tommy brought the car? I thought you were taking a cab—"

"Tommy's not going, and neither are his parents. We're going by ourselves," Sarah said.

Acindina and Lorenzo exchanged glances, then Acindina asked, "what happened?"

"I said I don't want to talk about it," Sarah hissed.

"Well *I* do, and we have at least three hours, so talk!"

"Look, whatever it is, we bought non-refundable tickets, so we *have* to take this flight," Lorenzo said.

"And we will, only Tommy and his parents are not going. That's all." Sarah stormed off to the bathroom and closed the door.

Acindina walked to the bathroom door and yelled, "you're not 13 anymore so that hiding-in-the-bathroom trick doesn't work, young lady! When you come out of there, we're going to discuss this! Coño!"

She walked back to the living room and sighed. "Why is it that holidays are always the time of year couples get into arguments?"

Lorenzo shrugged. "Are you kidding? That's like asking, 'why is the sky blue?'."

Gerry barely heard the knock on his door Monday morning as the celebrations for the first principle began. He flung it open to find Tommy outside, holding a gym bag and looking down. Gerry froze and said, "Tommy?"

"I told Sarah," he said, still looking down. "She kicked me out of the house and took the baby to Puerto Rico."

"Shit," was all Gerry could say.

Tommy finally looked up and made a face. "What the hell are you wearing?"

Gerry opened his mouth to answer, but his father cut him off. "Ah, the Gods have answered our prayers, sending us a friendly stranger in our call for unity, Harambee! Come in, come in, for the celebration is just beginning!"

Gerry explained to Tommy, "we, uh, celebrate Kwanzaa at my house, uh, come on in."

Tommy walked in, to see Gerry's parents and his sister wearing kente cloth and dashikis, with the women wearing headwraps.

"Woah," Tommy whispered.

"Happy Kwanzaa, Tommy!" Denise cheered.

"Um, thank you," he said with a half-hearted smile, then looked back at Gerry who closed the door behind him. "Can I um, use your phone?"

"Sure, it's in my bedroom, down the hall," then drew in closer and whispered, "I know you're a little freaked out by all this, man... I'm sorry." He then stepped back and patted Tommy on his shoulder. "Our stranger friend needs to use the telephone."

Everyone cheered as Tommy gingerly walked through the living room and down the hallway to Gerry's bedroom, where there was a phone on his nightstand. He took a breath and picked up the receiver. It was hard to believe this was happening. After dialing a number Tommy heard his father pick up the phone.

"Hello?"

"Hey, Dad."

"There you are, Tommy, what happened? We didn't hear anything from you guys about the trip, what happened?"

He let out a sigh. "I... I told her, Dad..."

"Oh, Son," Jarlath whispered, "what happened?"

"She kicked me out of the house. Took the baby with her parents down to Puerto Rico."

"Well... it's a good thing we didn't go without you. That would've been awkward."

Tommy knew his father was trying to make light of the situation, but this wasn't the time for jokes.

"Just trying to make ya laugh, son."

"I know, Dad."

"Are you staying at a hotel?"

"I'm at a friend's house. I need to stay in the city so I can still go to work."

"Okay... I know she's mad, but she just needs time to cool off. It's not the end of the world."

"It kinda feels like it, Dad... I've never seen her this—"

"In 35 years of marriage, Son," Jarlath interrupted, "I can tell ya, you'll always see a new side of your wife when you fuck up. But she loves you, and she'll forgive you... eventually."

Tommy fought back the tears and nodded. "Thanks, Dad."

"You're welcome, I'll think of something to tell your mother, so she doesn't panic. And if you need any money, don't hesitate to ask."

"Um, thanks, I should be okay on that end. We have separate bank accounts." *Thank goodness,* he thought.

"Okay. Stay strong, Tommy. It'll be alright." He hung up the phone.

Tommy put the receiver back on the phone and just sat. His father told him it wasn't the end of the world, but for him... it might as well have been.

Robin heard a knock on his door, and he slowly walked over and checked the peephole. He rolled his eyes and opened the door to see the man known as 'Synclair with a Y.' The mysterious figure who contacted Robin right after his grandfather passed away.

"Mister Walker," he greeted.

"Now, you see? That's better. Instead of you sneaking in my house, standing by the window waiting for me to shoot you. Knocking on the door works a whole lot better."

The man instinctively felt his right arm, recalling their first meeting. "Yes, well... it's time. Miss Hernandez would like to meet you."

"Alright. I was just there a couple of weeks ago. She could have killed two birds with one stone."

"I'm pretty sure things were still not ready back then, but they are *now*."

Robin's patience was wearing thin with the stranger. "Right. I'll get my coat."

Twenty minutes later, the pair walked into Carmen's office, who greeted them with a smile.

"So, how was your Christmas, Robin?" she asked.

"It sucked," he replied flatly, taking a seat in front of her desk.

Synclair stepped forward. "I believe this concludes my obligation to Jon."

Carmen pulled out a small envelope from her desk and handed it to the gentleman. "Thank you for your services, Synclair. Go in peace."

After placing the envelope in the pocket of his jacket lining, he turned to Robin. "It's been interesting to have known you, young man. If you live a good life, we should never meet again."

Robin was puzzled by the parting words. He opened his mouth to reply, but Synclair was already walking to the door. It closed behind him, and Robin just looked back at Carmen.

"Something tells me I'll be seeing him again."

Carmen ignored the remark and got straight to business. "Robin, I need to reiterate how responsible you need to be with this money..."

He twitched the corner of his mouth in annoyance but continued to listen.

"Deposit this check into your bank account, while I close your grandfather's and transfer the remaining balance."

"I… um, don't have a bank account," Robin mumbled.

"What?!" she exclaimed.

"I've been meaning to get around to it…"

"Goddamnit! Of all the irresponsible—"

"Hey, calm down! Alright? I can go up to the branch on Broadway next to McDonald's and open an account in like, two seconds."

"That's something you should have done months ago, Robin," she said with some annoyance.

"Um, so… you want me to go… like now?"

"Apple bank closes at 4 pm, *and* my time is priceless."

He nodded and left the office.

An hour later, Robin came back and gave Carmen the information she needed from his new savings account.

"Why didn't you get a checking account as well?" she asked. "Do you know how to write checks?"

"I sorta do, but I didn't think it was necessary."

She let out an exasperated sigh and just shook her head.

"Look, I really think you're making too much of this over Granddaddy leaving me a few thousand dollars…"

"Robin, Jon left you exactly $56,350.27."

Robin's eyes jumped out of his sockets as his entire body shook. "Holy shit, what?!" he gasped.

"He originally had around $5,000.00 in his savings, until April 24th, when he hit a bet on a horse and won a little over $50,000.00," Carmen explained.

"Wait, what? The 24th?" *That was the day of the Knicks game with Lakeshia!* "I didn't know he was still gambling. He told me he quit."

"I know. He told me the same thing, but it was something about this horse, I dunno. Anyway, I'll transfer the balance to your account, and I'll be watching it like a hawk! If I suspect you're blowing through it, I will step in and put it in a trust."

Robin was flabbergasted. All he was expecting at most was $10,000.00, but $56,000.00 and some change? "Hey, I'll be fine, but I should be good to spend a few hundred here or there, right?"

"Within reason. Anything over, say… $800.00, should be cleared by me for the first 12 months. Once I can trust you, feel free to spend it however you want."

"And he left *nothing* for mom or Aunt Regina?" He asked before, but considering the amount of money, he had to be certain.

"No, it's all yours," she said with a shrug.

"Okay. Wow, I guess that's it, then. Um, thank you, Carmen. This was definitely a shock to my system."

"I understand, and like I said before, you represent the good Jon tried to accomplish at the end of his life, to make up for his past atrocities."

Robin wished she would elaborate, but he decided not to pry. He stood up again and walked out without saying another word.

After splitting a pizza pie with some beers, Robin and Franklin finally started cleaning out Jon's room. The task was hard for him, but Robin knew it had to be done. He was keeping Jon's bed, but everything else, including furniture, was going to various charities.

"What the heck are these?" Franklin asked, holding up some old pamphlets.

They were going through most of Jon's personal belongings he had on several shelves hung up in the bedroom.

"Those are his old racing forms, you know. OTB? He used to hang with his friends as they did bets over at the bus terminal."

Robin opened the drawer from Jon's dresser that was going to goodwill Wednesday, among the sorted socks he came across his grandfather's wallet. He cut up the credit cards and placed his driver's license in an envelope. There were a few pictures of several family members, including himself, his mother, his aunt, and two cousins.

There was no money in the wallet, but Robin found something else that caught his attention. He pulled out a betting slip for a horse race.

Franklin noticed Robin staring at the piece of paper. "What's that?" he asked with a nod.

"Carmen mentioned granddaddy winning some last-minute money on a horse... this must be the winning ticket."

"So, he kept it, so what?" Franklin asked.

"The name... the name of the horse." He looked up. "Reggie and Ronnie."

His friend looked back at him with a blank stare.

"Regina and Veronica... the names of his daughters."

The horse that paid five hundred to one odds that fateful day haunted Jon Walker. What he believed was providence, reminding him of Robin's aunt Regina, and his mother, Veronica Walker, who everyone called 'Ronnie,' won him a serious windfall that helped secure Robin's future.

Robin took a moment to process this shocking turn of events, then resumed emptying the dresser of the rest of Jon's clothes.

"Um, so how much did he leave you?" Franklin asked, sensing some tension.

"Just a few grand," he lied. "He had a lot set aside for the funeral and taking care of me these past few months. Once the lease ends in three years, I'll probably move. After next year, I probably won't be able to afford to stay here."

"Well, maybe you can sell some of these things and get a few more bucks."

Robin turned to the closet, but then stared back at Franklin, who shrugged. "Um, maybe not."

"All his clothes are going to Wadsworth Baptist. It's what grand-daddy would have wanted."

The clothes that didn't fit Robin were packed in several cardboard boxes. There were magazines and newspapers he was taking over to the Fort Washington Library to see if they could be archived. Any electronic devices that didn't work, Robin promised to Franklin, in hopes his friend could repair or salvage them for parts.

"Have you heard from, um..."

"I haven't heard from anybody," Robin began. "I'm sure super-models take breaks for the holidays themselves," he said, in reference to his sister.

He had reached out to his mother several times before Jon's death, but still hadn't heard anything back from her or his sister.

While reaching his arm around an overhead shelf in the closet, Robin felt his hand brush against something.

"Hey, what was that?" he gasped.

Franklin grunted, "Huh?"

Robin stretched further, standing on his toes. "There's a step ladder in the hallway. Get it for me, will ya?"

A few minutes later, Robin found a small, carved wooden box, tucked away in the corner of the closet's top-shelf. He held it in his hand and examined it.

"What's in it?" Franklin asked.

"I don't know," Robin replied. He pressed the button on the latch, which flipped up, and the box unlocked. Inside was a small pin on top of a folded piece of paper.

"Is this... a medal?" Robin whispered.

He showed it to Franklin, who took it and held it up to the light. After unfolding the note inside the box, Robin read it quietly.

The pin was white, with gold lettering around a red cross in the middle.

"It's Latin," Franklin said. "It means, *For One's Country.*"

After finishing the note, Robin lowered his hand and looked up. "According to this, a nurse gave it to granddaddy during the war... with the assurance that he'd come back to England and bring it back to her. She said it was her way of wishing the soldiers luck. There's a postcard in here, with an address. I remember him telling me about going to London. This must be what he meant."

"Wow," Franklin said. "What are you going to do?" he asked, handing him back the pin.

Robin accepted it back. "I... don't know."

Hours later, Robin was in the living room, standing in front of the window thinking. Franklin went back home with a few trinkets, and

Jon's bedroom was now bare. The boxes and bags of donated items would be picked up in a few days.

It had been an emotional couple of weeks. The holiday party, learning about Shinju, the inheritance, and now this pin and Jon's promise. Classes at Baruch start again in mid-January, and Robin had a decision to make. Should he travel to Seattle and find Shinju? Spend what time left she had before her arranged marriage? Or keep his grandfather's promise and travel to London?

*There will be a time...*

Robin remembered Jon's words on his deathbed.

*...when you believe that you are alone. When you don't know what to do.*

He believed he was at the crossroads Jon had told him about... searching for guidance and the will to go on.

*Your eyes... they will not see anything... your ears will not hear a sound.*

"Seattle... or England?" he mused, staring out the window.

*But it will be as if I'm standing right beside you...*

A book suddenly fell on the floor from the bookshelf. It startled Robin from his thoughts with a loud bang. He turned from the window and saw what the book was.

*...and the path will present itself.*

A smile came across his face as the answer came to him. There was a travel agency on 179th Street and Broadway, a few stores down from Tony's Pizza. Robin put on his coat, grabbed his keys, and left the apartment to make arrangements.

A few moments after leaving, the phone rang in his apartment. The answering machine clicked on with the recorded greeting.

"You've reached the Walker residence, we're unable to answer the phone right now, but leave a message at the beep and we'll get back to you."

The message ended with a beep and a voice came over the machine, "Robin... this is your mother..."

The snow was falling lightly outside Friday evening. Most of the staff who weren't working Saturday were bundled up and filing out, saying their goodbyes until after the holiday. Robin stood behind the circulation desk after swinging by to pick up his paycheck. His hands rested on the desk as he surveyed the library floor.

He was still amused by the revelation of his inheritance and couldn't help thinking about what to do next. It was possible he could live off the money for a little while. Invest in stocks, let it grow and mature, or travel the world to find himself, which is what his grandfather would have wanted.

Lakeshia approached Robin from behind. "Hey, Robin."

He greeted her with a smile. "Hey, how's it going, Leelee?"

Her smile beamed back as she gazed at him.

"You wanna hear a secret, kiddo?" he suddenly asked, looking around.

Her eyes got big as saucers. "Sure!"

Robin took a breath and smiled. "I just inherited $56,000.00."

The pair shared a minute of silence to let the statement sink in. "Wow," Lakeshia said finally. "With that kind of money, you could... leave the library."

A flash of concern registered from the young page as she whimpered with that last thought. Robin turned to her, acknowledging the same notion.

"*That's* something to think about."

After everything he endured, since arriving in February, this could be God's way of giving him a clean slate. A weird smile grew across his face, as he noticed Lakeshia was still staring at him.

"I'm gonna be going out of town for a few weeks," he began. "You have a happy new year, Leelee... see you next year."

Robin stepped from behind the desk and headed to the exit turnstile. He stopped at the security threshold, turned, and looked at her still standing in place. "Or not. Hmmm..."

He was undecided on his decision, leaving everything up in the air until he returned from his trip. And with that, Robin Walker walked out of the 58th Street Branch Library, possibly for the last time.

Lakeshia thought about the possibility of never seeing Robin again, that he would leave an impression on her that would last a lifetime, in which she contemplated what *could* have been. She was positive that they had a future together, and it would only be a matter of time before it would come to pass... he wasn't done with her, yet.

"Happy new year, Robin Walker," she whispered. "I'll see *you* in 1995."

THE END
Call Numbers will continue in Book 4
Love In The Stacks: Wild Hearts, Run Free

# ABOUT THE AUTHOR

Syntell Smith was born and raised in Washington Heights, Upper Manhattan in New York City. He began writing while blogging his hectic everyday life experiences in 2004. After gaining an audience with a following of dedicated readers, he studied scripts and plays and got into screenwriting. Syntell has written three books in his *Call Numbers* series. He loves comic books, video games, and watching reruns of Law and Order. Syntell is active on Twitter, Facebook, & Tumblr and currently lives in Detroit.

# ALSO BY SYNTELL SMITH

Call Numbers: The Not So Quiet Life Of Librarians

Book Endings - A Call Numbers novel: Loss, Pain, and Revelations

CPSIA information can be obtained
at www.ICGtesting.com
Printed in the USA
BVHW052151100223
658310BV00014B/71/J